God's Highlander

E. V. Thompson was born in London. He spent nine years in the Navy before joining the Bristol police force where he was a founder member of the 'vice squad'. Later he became an investigator with the BOAC, worked with the Hong Kong Police Narcotics Bureau and was Chief Security Officer of Rhodesia's Department of Civil Aviation.

Over 200 of his stories were published in what was then Rhodesia, and he returned to England committed to becoming a full time writer. While pursuing this goal he supplemented his income with a variety of jobs, from sweeping floors in a clay-works to working as a hotel detective in London. He then moved to Bodmin Moor, his explorations of which were to provide the powerful background for *Chase the Wind*, published in 1977, a book that won him the Best Historical Novelist Award. Its success has been followed by many other historical novels, including the acclaimed saga of the Retallick family and the popular Jagos of Cornwall series.

E. V. Thompson continues to live in Cornwall although he no longer occupies a nineteenth-century miner's cottage on Bodmin Moor. He now shares a charming house overlooking the sea near Mevagissey with his wife, two young children and a wide variety of family pets.

E. V. Thompson

GOD'S HIGHLANDER

PAN BOOKS
in association with Macmillan

First published 1989 by Macmillan London Limited
This edition published 1990 by Pan Books Ltd,
Cavaye Place, London SW10 9PG
in association with Macmillan London Limited

9 8 7 6 5 4 3 2 1

© E. V. Thompson 1989

ISBN 0 330 30892 0

Printed and bound in Great Britain by
Richard Clay Ltd, Bungay, Suffolk

Ill fares the land, to hastening ills a prey,
Where wealth accumulates and men decay:
Princes and lords may flourish or may fade;
A breath can make them, as a breath has made;
But a bold peasantry, their country's pride,
When once destroyed, can never be supplied.

OLIVER GOLDSMITH, 'The Deserted Village'

CHAPTER ONE

THE TINY steam-powered launch sliced through the deep green waters of Loch Eil. In its wake an expanding herringbone pattern gathered strength, only to die when it touched the loch shore, no more than a quarter of a mile on either hand. From the vessel's tall thin funnel a plume of black smoke rose high into the air before changing form and becoming one with the clear mountain air. To the north and the south, steep-sided mountains took the coughing of the steamer's engine and tossed the sound back again, sending long-necked cormorants beating a retreat across the surface of the narrow loch. High above the water a lone gliding eagle wheeled away to seek an afternoon meal in quieter glens.

The long ridges of the mountains still wore mantles of white, but on the wooded lower slopes the snow was melting fast, tumbling down the mountainsides in a skein of streams, rivulets and waterfalls to the loch, more than two thousand feet below.

On the fish-stained deck of the steam-launch a young man stood with legs braced wide against the movement of the vessel. Dressed in a sober black suit, he sucked in lungfuls of the heady cool Highlands air. The Reverend Wyatt Jamieson had been treated to a surfeit of mountains and lochs during the uncomfortable three-day voyage from Glasgow, but he was enjoying every moment. For him this was a triumphant return to the land of his birth.

An aborted career in the Army had been followed by studies at university in Edinburgh. Now, after two years working as an assistant minister in a Glasgow slum, he was returning, at the age of twenty-eight, to the Highlands of Scotland, where he belonged.

A change in the rhythm of the steam-powered engine broke

into Wyatt's thoughts as the launch changed direction, heading towards a small lop-sided landing-stage no more than half a mile ahead.

Scattered haphazardly about the flimsy landing-stage were a number of low-built single-storey houses. Some were of stone, others of mud and mortar. All had thatched roofs. This was the village of Eskaig, where Wyatt was to be the new resident minister for the Church of Scotland. The heart of a parish that included many square miles of Highland territory.

The people who inhabited this lonely place were of a breed unlike any other in the land. They were 'Highlanders'. Fiercely proud of their heritage and independence, they had been rendered tragically vulnerable by that very independence in this the fifth year of the reign of the young Queen Victoria.

Donald McKay, coxswain, engineer, sole owner and crew member of the little steam-launch, removed a rough-briar pipe from his mouth and used it to point ahead to Eskaig.

'It would seem you're expected.'

The sunlight slanting down over the mountains was reflected from the surface of the loch, and Wyatt raised a hand to shield his eyes against the glare. At the water's edge a small crowd of people was gathering, brought from their homes by the sound of the boat's engine.

'I wasn't expecting a welcoming party. . . .'

'Don't hold your breath waiting for welcoming words, Minister. You're here to take the place of Preacher Gunn. He was in Eskaig for forty years and might have lasted a full half-century had he not been hounded to death by the landlord's factor.'

Donald McKay's quiet voice and gentle west-coast accent could do nothing to soften the harshness of his words. Shifting his gaze to Wyatt, he added: 'Leastways, that's what's being said – and you're here as the landlord's man.'

'Is there any truth in it?'

'Enough.'

Some of Wyatt's pleasurable anticipation seeped away. He wondered why he had been told nothing of the situation in Eskaig when he had visited the Moderator's office in Edinburgh. Although it was not really surprising. The Highlands might as well be on another planet as far as churchmen in Scotland's capital were con-

2

cerned. Few of the men responsible for the spiritual needs of the Highland communities had ever set foot here.

Wyatt was aware, too, that he *was* the landlord's man – presented to the living by Lord Kilmalie himself. Wyatt had a special reason for accepting a post as preacher of Eskaig and was convinced he could serve the community well. Perhaps he should have paused to consider whether or not they would *want* him to serve them.

By the time the steam-launch eased its way slowly alongside the ageing jetty the waiting crowd had grown to around sixty, and Wyatt looked in vain for a smile of welcome. The faces of the men were set in grim dour lines. The expressions on the faces of the women were more animated – but only because they were less inclined to disguise their displeasure.

When the launch bumped against the jetty the structure groaned alarmingly. Unconcerned, Donald McKay took a turn around a bollard with a mooring-rope. When he was satisfied the boat was secure McKay heaved Wyatt's weighty leather chest ashore.

'I wish you good luck, Minister, but I fear it's more than wishes you'll be needing here in Eskaig.'

Clutching a bulging canvas bag, Wyatt was following his chest ashore when a small dried-up man stepped from the crowd. Grey-haired and elderly, the man wore a suit of dark best serge similar to Wyatt's. More coarsely woven than the one worn by the minister, many years of assiduous brushing had removed the last vestige of nap from the material.

'Don't cast off yet, Boatman. You'll no doubt be taking the pastor away with you again when I'm through talking.'

'Oh? And will you be paying me his fare, Angus Cameron? I've been given money to bring the minister as far as Eskaig – and not a single mile farther.'

'You can beg his fare from the man who sent him to Eskaig unasked: Lord Kilmalie.'

The spokesman's words provoked a growing murmur of assent from the men and women standing on the loch-bank behind him.

'Since I'm the subject of your discussion, perhaps I might say something on my own behalf. . . .' Wyatt set his bag down beside the chest and confronted the hostile Eskaig spokesman.

'My name's Wyatt Jamieson, and I've come here as your new

minister. I know I'll never be able to take the place of Preacher Gunn, but I'll do my best – if you'll give me the opportunity.'

Angus Cameron was taken by surprise by Wyatt's words and he cast an uncertain glance over his shoulder at his fellow-villagers before speaking again.

'We've nothing personal against you, Minister, you understand, but the people of Eskaig will choose their own preacher. We'll not have one foisted upon us by a landlord who's never set foot within a hundred miles of Loch Eil for twenty years.'

'Lord Kilmalie's not an absentee landlord who cares nothing for his tenants. He's a sick man, unable to travel. He's forced to leave his affairs in the hands of his factor. . . .'

A howl of derision interrupted Wyatt's words, and a woman's voice rose above the rest, shrill and excited: 'We want no city man here. We need a pastor who speaks our own tongue. Tell him, Angus.'

'Don't waste your breath. In a few more years there'll be no one left in the Highlands. He'll be preaching to an Englishman's sheep.'

This voice was a woman's, too, but the words were spoken in Gaelic, the predominant language of the Highlands.

Looking beyond the villagers, Wyatt glimpsed a tall dark-haired girl standing in the midst of a small group a few paces apart from the others. Barefoot, she carried a plaid shawl about her shoulders. The men with her wore soft grey bonnets and had shepherd's plaids wrapped about their bodies.

'I'm no city man,' Wyatt replied in Gaelic that was as fluent as that used by the mountain woman. 'I was born in *Eilean an Fhraoich* – in the Isles. My father was the preacher there until he was dispossessed, along with his people. He brought them along this very road to take a boat to Canada from Fort William. He would have gone with them, had the Lord not taken him first. He's buried right here, in Eskaig. As for the preaching, I was proud to wear a shepherd's plaid as a boy, and I know from experience there are worse congregations than a flock of sheep.'

Wyatt's reply brought a fleeting smile to more than one tense face. Pressing home his temporary advantage, he asked: 'Will someone show me to the minister's manse? I'd like to be well settled in before dark.'

'You'll not be settling in Eskaig, Minister. Go back to where you came from. As I've told you, we'll not accept a landlord's man here.'

'I'm the *Lord's* man, Mr Cameron. Appointed to preach *His* word – not those of any landowner. If you won't show me the way and help with my things, I'll need to manage as best I can by myself.'

With a swift movement that revealed unexpected strength, Wyatt swung the laden chest to his shoulder and held it in place with one hand. Tucking the bag beneath his other arm, he accepted his stout walking-stick from the boatman.

'Thank you for your company on the voyage, Donald. You can go now. I'll be all right.'

Unlooping the mooring-rope from the bollard, Donald McKay removed the pipe from his mouth and raised it in salute. 'Ay, Minister. I do believe you will.'

As the engine beat out its noisy rhythm once more, Donald McKay allowed the vessel to drift clear of the jetty before engaging forward gear. Executing a wide turn, he steered the boat away from Eskaig without a backward glance.

The villagers of Eskaig were numerous enough to block the road from the jetty completely, but whether or not they intended to bar Wyatt's way was never put to the test.

A number of hard-ridden horses were heading towards Eskaig along the rough road that followed the shoreline. As the riders drew closer Wyatt could see that all except one wore the red tunic of a yeomanry regiment. There was an officer with the militiamen, but it soon became apparent who was giving the orders.

As the part-time soldiers neared the villagers they began to draw in their mounts – but not the civilian who rode with them. He drove his horse on into the crowd, scattering villagers on either hand before hauling the animal to a sliding halt in front of Wyatt.

'Where the hell do you think you've been? I've just ridden to Fort William and back seeking you.'

It was an English accent, and the man's voice was no more gentle than his riding. 'Were you not given my message before leaving Edinburgh?'

The rider made no attempt to dismount, and his horse danced nervously in front of Wyatt, bothered by the crowd about him.

'I was given a great many messages before sailing from *Glasgow*. I don't recall one from you among them.'

Wyatt did not need an introduction to know the man sitting on the horse was the factor in charge of Lord Kilmalie's Highland estates. It explained the man's arrogance. John Garrett's position made him the most powerful man in the district.

'I sent word you were to come no farther than Fort William. I said I'd bring you from there in order to avoid a confrontation with this rabble. What's that damned lieutenant doing? MacGregor, drive these people off the road and send them about their business.'

The militiamen sat their horses uncertainly at the edge of the crowd. Now, at a less than wholehearted order from their youthful commanding officer, they kneed their horses forward, driving the villagers before them.

Only the small group of plaid-wearing Highlanders held their ground. There were some nine or ten of them, and they stood to one side of the uneven roadway, watching the proceedings with a detached interest.

Pointing in their direction, John Garrett called: 'Get rid of *them*, too. Make sure they move off with the others.'

A number of militiamen wheeled their horses about to obey his instruction, but one of the grey-bonneted Highlanders, a large man with a red beard tinged with grey, stepped forward. He addressed John Garrett in halting English.

'We've come down to speak to you, Factor. There are rumours we're to be cleared from our lands—'

John Garrett cut the older man's words short. 'Rumours are for old women, Eneas Ross. When there's a need for you to know anything *I'll* tell you. Until then be sure your rent's paid on time. Move them on, Lieutenant.'

The factor signalled impatiently, and the militiamen drove their horses forward, but Eneas Ross stood firm. He was still looking towards John Garrett when one of the horses cannoned into him, knocking him to the ground.

There was an angry murmur of protest from the small group of Highlanders, and two of the younger men stepped forward quickly. Wyatt thought he saw the glint of metal in the hand of one of them – and some of the militiamen saw it, too. Without waiting for an order, half a dozen of the part-time soldiers drew sabres from their scabbards.

Hurriedly dropping his chest and bag to the ground, Wyatt step-

6

ped forward to place himself between militiamen and Highlanders.

'There's no need for steel.' He addressed his words to the militia lieutenant, at the same time using his stick to arrest the downward movement of the sabre-blade.

'Attend to your own business, Minister. Leave me to attend to mine.' The lieutenant's eyes were on the Highlanders as he spoke.

'Before becoming a minister I was a captain in the Seventy-Second Regiment – a *regular* officer. I could no doubt teach you a thing or two about fighting – and I'm telling you this isn't the time.'

The lieutenant shifted his gaze to the preacher, and now there was a part-time soldier's respect for a professional in his eyes. Wyatt had mentioned one of Scotland's finest Highland regiments and, as a captain, Wyatt outranked the lieutenant.

Taking advantage of the situation he had created, Wyatt called softly to the Highlanders in their own language: 'Go. Quickly now, before there's blood spilled.'

The two younger men helped Eneas Ross to his feet, but he shook them off and stooped to pick up the plaid which had fallen to the ground. After looking briefly in Wyatt's direction he turned and walked away, the younger men falling respectfully into step behind him.

As the three men joined the others, Wyatt caught another brief glimpse of the dark-haired girl, her face flushed with anger. Then the Highlanders began to walk away, and Wyatt lowered his stick, greatly relieved.

John Garrett was less pleased.'You should have kept out of things and allowed the militia to deal with them,' he said angrily to Wyatt.'It's high time they were taught a lesson.'

'I've come here as their minister and will need their acceptance before I can be inducted. It won't be given if half of them are cut down by militiamen within minutes of my arrival.'

John Garrett sat his horse and looked at Wyatt thoughtfully for some moments. Then he shrugged. 'The people of Eskaig will have little say in your induction. You've been appointed by Lord Kilmalie, and that's an end to the matter. Anyway, the rabble you saved are from the mountains. I doubt if they've ever seen the inside of a church, or spoken to a minister before. They're parasites. The sooner they're driven off good sheep-grazing land the better it will be for everyone.'

'Missionaries sent out by the Church are tramping thousands of miles through the jungles of Africa to bring God to the heathens, Mr Garrett. Are you saying I should abandon my own people because there are a few miles of Highlands between them and my kirk?'

'*I* didn't appoint you as their minister. What you do here is between you and Lord Kilmalie. Just don't get in my way, that's all.'

The factor jerked his horse about. A lad of about ten was hurrying along the bank of the loch, away from the village. John Garrett called out to him: 'You there . . . boy. Come here. Help the minister to carry his things to the manse.'

For a moment the boy hesitated, and it seemed he might refuse. A woman's voice called from the crowd of retreating villagers and, sulkily, the boy came to where Wyatt stood beside the mounted factor.

John Garrett scowled down at the boy. 'If I ever have occasion to call you again, you'll come running, you understand? What's your name?'

'Ewan Munro . . . sir.'

The scowl had not completely disappeared when the factor returned his attention to Wyatt.

'You're expected at my house for dinner tonight. You'll find it about three miles along the road, this side of Corpach. My wife and daughter consider it their duty to wring the last drop of information from anyone foolish enough to leave the city for the Highlands. If you've another suit in your luggage, I suggest you wear it. That one stinks of the fish Donald McKay carried in his boat on the last trip.'

CHAPTER TWO

WYATT COULD NOT draw a single word from Ewan Munro during the half-mile walk from the jetty to the minister's manse. It was evident the boy was poor. His ragged clothing, bare feet and skinny limbs bore witness to this, but he refused to be drawn on the subject of his family. Even when asked a direct question the boy would only grunt ambiguously.

Wyatt's bag and trunk were deposited unceremoniously on the doorstep of the single-storey whitewashed cottage, and Ewan Munro walked away, still without speaking. His manner was untypical of the respect usually shown by the Scots to their church-men. Wyatt would have a hard time gaining the respect of these people, but the rules governing the Church of Scotland were clear: a minister had to be approved by the community he was to serve before he could be inducted into their parish.

He did not doubt they *would* eventually accept his induction as their new preacher, albeit with some reluctance. Only a very brave or a very foolhardy man would openly defy Lord Kilmalie and refuse to accept the landlord's nominee. Nevertheless, Wyatt would need the support of his congregation if he was to make a success of his appointment.

The manse was a comfortable little house, kept neat and tidy. There was food in the cupboard, too, although Wyatt doubted whether such thoughtfulness had emanated from the villagers.

Wyatt spent a little time exploring the house and then made his way to the church. *His* 'kirk'.

Situated close to the manse, the stone-built church was probably the largest building in Eskaig. As an acknowledgement of its status

9

it possessed a slate roof, the only one in the village. The inside of the building was whitewash-clean and starkly simple. As he stood in the pulpit and looked around him, Wyatt tried to imagine what it would be like to preach a sermon to a packed church.

After spending a while enjoying such self-indulgence, Wyatt descended the five wooden steps from the pulpit and for some minutes remained on his knees in front of the altar with its simple wooden cross before going outside to the churchyard. Here in a quiet corner he eventually found what he was looking for. It was a simple stone headstone on which was inscribed: 'Reverend Donald Jamieson. Died serving his fellow men, 19 September 1836.'

Looking down at the grave, memories of his childhood flooded back to Wyatt. Childhood days on the Isle of Lewis – his *Eilean an Fhraoich*, or 'Island of Heather' – but here the *happy* memories came to an end.

In common with many other landlords, the proprietor of Lewis had tasted London life – and the simple pleasure of living among the Highlands and Islands of Scotland palled against all the capital had to offer.

Unfortunately, London society life required money. The landlord's first step was to raise the rents of the tenants. They were doubled ... trebled ... and doubled again. Then the discovery was made that larger profits could be made by clearing tenants from their holdings and grazing sheep on the hills and in the glens of the islands. Soon flocks of the bleating woolly creatures were being driven north in their thousands and tens of thousands. Tiny cloven hoofs ground the proud traditions of the clansmen into the soft turf on which they had so often spilled their blood when fighting their laird's battles.

Turned out of their homes and dispossessed of rented lands, the Highlanders were resettled on rocky shores useless for sheep-grazing. When they complained the Highlanders were told they must learn to earn a living from the sea. Disillusioned and bewildered by all that was happening about them, many set sail for new lands. Others – and they were becoming fewer with every passing year – clung tenaciously to the only way of life they had ever known. Defying landlords, sheep and all that nature itself sent against them, they fought to retain their identity.

On the Isle of Lewis, Wyatt's father exhausted himself fighting for justice for his people, but his efforts were in vain. He left with the last of his parishioners and trod the long road from the Isles. A weary and defeated man, he dropped dead outside the village of Eskaig. His death was attributed to 'natural causes', but those who were closest to him knew he died of a broken heart.

While all this was happening, Wyatt had been gaining renown as a fearless soldier in the Kaffir Wars in Natal, in far-off South Africa. Landing in Africa as a sergeant, Wyatt saved the life of his commanding officer in action and succeeded in beating off an attack by warring Zulus. For this feat he was commissioned as a lieutenant on the field of battle. Twelve months later, by now a captain, but broken in health, he was in a ship heading for Scotland. What had promised to be a brilliant career was brought to an end by a recurring fever which struck down great numbers of the British soldiers in Natal.

The officer whose life had been saved by Wyatt died of the same fever. He was the heir of Lord Kilmalie, landlord of Eskaig. The Scots peer never forgot the man who had saved his son's life, albeit for only a brief period. It was Lord Kilmalie who helped Wyatt through university, and when the living of Eskaig became vacant there was only one minister the titled landlord would have there.

Wyatt was still engrossed in memories of the past when he set off to keep his dinner engagement with the factor and his family later that evening. He was no more than half a mile from Eskaig when the train of his thoughts was broken by the sound of shouting from the undergrowth, close to the loch's edge. Moments later a barefoot boy broke from the tangle of gorse and heather. It was Ewan Munro.

The boy was carrying a fair-sized salmon in his hands and when he saw Wyatt an expression of alarm came to his face. Then he turned and fled, vanishing into the foliage on the other side of the road as quickly as he had appeared.

'Hey! Wait a minute. . . .' Wyatt ran to where the boy had disappeared and called again. He could hear the crashing of undergrowth ahead of him along a narrow overgrown glen that appeared to follow the course of a stream, deep into the mountains, away from the loch.

Acting on an impulse, Wyatt followed the path of the boy for perhaps ten minutes. When he stopped he could no longer hear sounds of the boy's flight. He continued the chase until he came up against a barrier of almost impenetrable thorn-bushes and was forced to admit defeat. Ewan Munro had given him the slip.

The shouting near the water's edge had moved off towards Eskaig by now. Whoever was searching for the ragged young boy was not aware he had made good his escape to the mountains.

Thoughtfully, Wyatt made his way back to the road. Seeing Ewan Munro had perturbed him. He was not concerned that the boy had so obviously poached a salmon from the loch – he looked as though he had need of it – but where was the boy going? Were there others not far away as badly off as himself?

Wyatt mulled over the questions until he saw the houses of Corpach in the distance. Almost immediately he came upon the house occupied by Lord Kilmalie's factor.

If the house had been built with the intention of impressing those who saw it with the importance of its occupier, it was an undoubted success. Built of stone, it was a rounded turret-like structure, standing a slim four storeys high. Tall pines flanked a long driveway and also marked the boundaries of the house and its extensive gardens.

The inside of the house fulfilled all the promise of its exterior. Shown in by a servant, Wyatt was met in the hallway by the two Garrett women.

The factor's wife, Charlotte, was a small, thin, grey woman with such an air of tiredness about her that Wyatt wondered whether she was not in fact ill. She greeted Wyatt unenthusiastically, her hand as limp as her expression. Then she introduced the preacher to her daughter.

Evangeline Garrett was everything her mother failed to be. Not tall, the factor's daughter was well rounded in a way that had been considered highly fashionable only twenty years before. She also chattered incessantly, and Wyatt quickly learned that John Garrett had not exaggerated his daughter's interest in the latest news from Edinburgh and Glasgow.

The factor did not appear to be in the house, and in answer to Wyatt's question Evangeline said: 'Someone came to the house to say there were poachers somewhere along the loch. Father went out to help catch them. . . . But, tell me, what are people talking about in Edinburgh? Is there anything new happening there? And the clothes. . . . What are the women wearing?'

Wyatt smiled. 'My visit to Edinburgh was brief. I stayed at Lord Kilmalie's house for only two nights and spent the days in the office of the Moderator. The women who came there wore bonnets and cloaks, as far as I noticed. As for Glasgow, the parish where I worked contains the worst slums in Scotland. Clothes worn there have been handed down by so many generations it's impossible to tell if they were *ever* fashionable.'

Evangeline found his reply disappointing, but some interest returned when her mother's questioning brought out the fact that the newly arrived Eskaig minister had served with the Army in the Kaffir Wars in Africa.

Wyatt was in the middle of relating some of his experiences in Africa when a loud voice was heard calling from the hall. Charlotte Garrett started as though caught out in some misdemeanour and hurried from the room. Moments later John Garrett strode in. He made no apologies for not being at home to greet his invited guest. Indeed, his opening words contained an implied criticism.

'I expected to meet you on the road. I've been nigh to Eskaig chasing poachers. They're becoming so brazen we'll have them stealing fish from the garden pond if we don't put a stop to them.'

Wyatt remembered the scared and ragged boy he had seen on the road. 'Perhaps they're hungry.'

'Hungry?' The factor dismissed the suggestion scornfully. 'They're *lazy*. Too damned lazy to work for a living. *They're* the reason Lord Kilmalie's estate isn't providing him with the return it should. The Highlands won't begin to pay their way until we get rid of tenants and cottars and bring in sheep.'

Wyatt bit back an angry retort based on his own experiences. He did not want to begin his ministry in Eskaig by falling out with the factor.

He was saved from having to make a reply when Evangeline handed a well-filled glass of whisky to her father.

'Drink this and forget about your old work for one evening. I'm fed up with hearing about poachers and sheep and Highland clearances. Wyatt's the first person to come to Eskaig from a city for *months*. I want to hear of the things that are happening in the *real* world. Where people talk about parties and the theatre and can go visiting dressed respectably because they know they won't arrive wet, bedraggled and covered in mud.'

If John Garrett noticed his daughter's use of the minister's first name, he made no comment, and his manner softened as he looked at her.

'I doubt if a preacher has an eye for fashions – and the Scots aren't the best-dressed women in the world, not even in Edinburgh.'

'Oh, I don't know. I expect Wyatt met quite a few fashionable ladies while he was staying with Lord Kilmalie – as his guest.'

It was apparent from the very casualness of her manner that Evangeline knew well the effect the information would have on her factor father. She was not disappointed.

John Garrett lowered his whisky-glass and stared at Wyatt. 'You stayed at Lord Kilmalie's house? As a guest?'

The appointment of a minister to a living was a comparatively minor matter. Most preachers were selected without the landowner ever seeing them. His appointment would be dealt with by those paid to administer the landlord's estates. For a titled landowner to entertain a minister in his own home was almost unheard of!

Before Wyatt could reply, Evangeline added more fuel to the speculative fire she had lit in the mind of her father.

'Wyatt was in the Army with Lord Kilmalie's son – the one who died. He was an officer, too – a captain.'

John Garrett made a rapid reassessment of the man standing before him. Only *gentlemen* became officers in the Queen's army. Wyatt Jamieson might be no more than a minister in the Church of Scotland now, but there was more to his background than was usual – *and* he had the ear of Lord Kilmalie.

The factor was a very important man in this remote Highland community but he, too, was an employee. He and the Edinburgh-based landowner did not always agree on the methods needed to keep the Highland estate profitable – especially when it involved the forcible eviction of peasant tenants. Managing the Eskaig estate was easier when Lord Kilmalie was kept in the dark about such activities. John Garrett wanted things to remain that way.

'Well! You've led an interesting life, Minister. Small wonder Evangeline seems delighted with your company. She seldom meets anyone who can talk of anything other than sheep, fishing or poaching. Your coming here will be good for her. You'll find her good company; she's a bright girl. A *clever* girl, though I say so myself. But your glass is empty. Evangeline, give the minister another whisky while I go off and find your mother. It's time we ate.'

Evangeline poured Wyatt another generous drink, and as he took it from her he thought he heard the sound of voices raised in argument somewhere towards the rear of the house. The factor's daughter immediately suggested that Wyatt should come with her to see the garden she had designed. It was dusk outside, and it would soon be impossible to see anything, but Wyatt concurred. It was clear she was trying to keep him from hearing the argument between her parents.

As they reached the front door John Garrett bellowed angrily. Then there came the sound of running feet as Charlotte Garrett ran across the stone-flagged hall and fled upstairs, her face turned from Evangeline and their guest.

'Come, before it's too dark to see.' Evangeline Garrett put a hand on Wyatt's arm.

'But . . . your mother . . . ?'

'She'll be all right. As right as she's ever going to be, stuck up here in the Highlands. She was brought up in a city, surrounded by people. She can't cope with what she calls the "emptiness" of Scotland. It unnerves her.'

'Hardly the qualities one expects to find in the wife of a Highland factor, surely?'

'That's what Father's always telling her.' Evangeline shrugged. 'You and he are right, I suppose, but I understand how she feels. I get like it myself sometimes. It's almost as though we've lost the rest of the world – the *real* world, that is. I would never be surprised if one day we set off to return to Edinburgh, only to learn it had gone and the whole world was as empty as here.'

Wyatt smiled at the thought. 'Edinburgh was very much in evidence a week ago. But how can you pine for what man has made when God offers you such beauty as this?'

They were in the garden now, and Wyatt made an expansive gesture. It included Loch Eil, the dusk-shadowed woods and mountains that surrounded it, and the high snow-wrapped bulk of Ben Nevis to the south-west. 'You'll never see anything more beautiful.'

'Perhaps that's the trouble.' Evangeline's gaze followed the sweep of his arm. 'It's all *too* beautiful. Too perfect to be real. I find it unnerving.'

Her words took Wyatt by surprise. He had been born and bred amidst such scenery and had never questioned its perfection. Yet he recalled the reaction of soldiers belonging to non-Highland regiments when they first marched through the Drakensberg Mountains in Natal. Until they had been there for a day or two they were completely overawed by their surroundings, their own insignificance magnified by the lofty grandeur of nature. It seemed the Highlands affected strangers in the same manner.

Then Wyatt was being shown the results of Evangeline's 'gardening'. It appeared to be no more than indistinct clumps of frost-attacked foliage collapsed against the chill damp earth, but he uttered insincere sounds of appreciation. Fortunately, it was already too dark for Evangeline to expect him to differentiate between the various species of woebegone plants.

Wyatt was saved from further hypocrisy by John Garrett, who came to the door and informed them in stentorian tones that a meal was sitting on the table awaiting their presence.

Dinner was a somewhat subdued affair during which Wyatt was required to repeat the story of his adult life for the benefit of the factor. Evangeline prompted him to fill in many more details, while Charlotte Garrett maintained an unnatural silence, creating a strained atmosphere around the table.

John Garrett drank heavily throughout the meal, becoming increasingly belligerent. He began to describe in detail how he would put an end to the 'idle uselessness of the Highland peasantry', by raising their rents to a point where they would be forced to abandon their tiny homesteads.

'Lord Kilmalie should leave me to do whatever's necessary,' declared the factor loudly, his face red and perspiring. 'I'm not taken in by their cringing and whining. I'd have 'em out in no time. Had it been done years ago, the estate would be showing a handsome profit now.'

'Not too many years ago the men you're talking about were holding the line at Waterloo, in regiments raised by their landlords,' declared Wyatt firmly. 'They didn't march off to war in order to make a profit.'

John Garrett snorted scornfully. 'You sound just like *them*,

Preacher. All such rubbish is in the past. Anything owed to them has been long paid. No man's entitled to be a millstone around the neck of a landowner just because his grandfather or great-grandfather fought in a war. I doubt if there's a man left about here who's been within a mile of a battlefield.'

Wyatt felt very strongly about landowners and factors who cleared people from the land for no other reason than to increase profits, but he knew it was useless reminding the factor that Waterloo had been fought only twenty-seven years before. A man did not have to be ancient to have fought in the army of the Duke of Wellington – and local regiments had been in the thick of that battle. John Garrett would not have accepted such enlightenment, even had he been sober.

Instead, Wyatt downed his drink, and as the fiery liquid burned a path down his throat he said: 'It's time I was leaving. I want to be up and about early tomorrow.'

As Evangeline pouted her disappointment, John Garrett eyed Wyatt suspiciously. 'Don't start getting any half-baked ideas about the rights of the men of Eskaig, Minister. You tend to their *spiritual* needs; that's what Lord Kilmalie pays *you* for. He pays *me* to see to everything else. Remember it and we'll get along famously. It's *them* and *us* up here – and you'll find you need me far more than I need you.'

Suddenly, John Garrett relaxed. 'But I don't need to be telling you this, do I? After all, we're both Lord Kilmalie's men.'

CHAPTER THREE

DURING THE NEXT FEW DAYS Wyatt thought often of the factor's parting words. John Garrett was the second man to tell him he was 'a landlord's man'. It disconcerted Wyatt greatly. He had come to Eskaig as a preacher. A man of God with a duty to serve the people.

Certainly, John Garrett had been right about one thing. Wyatt *could* be inducted against the will of the people and in defiance of church law. A number of recent rulings in the civil courts had confirmed this. The man who had caused a church to be built – in practice the landlord – was deemed to possess the sole authority to appoint a minister to that living. Yet only a fool would deliberately go against the wishes of a Highland community if it was his intention to live and work in their midst.

Wyatt wanted to follow the age-old traditions of the Church of Scotland and have his induction endorsed by the people of Eskaig. His parishioners.

Between settling in at the manse and preparing for his first Sunday in Eskaig, Wyatt spent much time walking about the village and also visiting the small communities scattered around the edges of the seven-mile-long loch. Everywhere he was given a reception that was polite, but as icily cold as the waters of the burns tumbling from the snow-capped mountains. His questions were invariably answered with a terse 'Don't know'. He did not learn the names of the church elders until, in a cupboard inside the church, he discovered a book containing details of church meetings. Even then, not a single villager would raise an arm to point the way to the homes of the men named in the book.

Worse was to come. Believing that his Sunday sermon could be a way of bringing the Highland congregation and their preacher closer together, Wyatt spent many night hours at his desk, working by candle-light. A powerful yet conciliatory sermon was completed in the early hours of the Sabbath — Wyatt's first as minister of Eskaig.

Sitting back in his chair, Wyatt stretched and rubbed tired eyes. No more could be done now. His future among the Highlanders would be decided in the small Eskaig church later that morning, when sunlight had chased away the shadows lurking inside the manse and warmed the recesses of his tired and over-imaginative mind.

The day began with a threat of rain, but the mountains held back the cloud. By ten o'clock, when Wyatt closed the gate of the manse garden behind him and set off for the church, the risk of rain had receded and the sun was breaking through. It would be a good day for those members of the congregation who needed to walk miles to church across the springy Highland turf.

At half-past ten, thirty minutes before the service was due to begin, Wyatt stationed himself at the doorway of the church. He waited with some trepidation to welcome worshippers to his first service.

By eleven-thirty Wyatt conceded that no one intended to come to morning service in the parish church. It was a bitter disappointment. He had returned to the Highlands with such high hopes, determined to dedicate his life to the community which had buried his father. It seemed they were not prepared to give him such an opportunity.

Wyatt had returned inside the church when an old woman, dressed in clothes that no stretch of the imagination could consider to be 'Sunday best', entered quietly through the doorway. She was hardly a congregation, but by now Wyatt was ready to clutch at the most unlikely of straws.

'Have you come for the service? Here . . . let me guide you to a pew, right here at the front. I promise you a sermon as stirring as though I were delivering it to a thousand of the Lord's most devout followers. . . .'

The old woman shook his hand free of her arm. She looked about the church with obvious disapproval, and her pursed lips put Wyatt in mind of the mouth of a drawstring pouch.

'No use you talking to me. Not unless you can work more miracles than the good Lord himself – and it doesn't seem you're strong on miracles, Minister.' She put a finger to one of her ears. 'I'm deaf. Haven't heard a word these ten years.'

'What ... are ... you ... doing ... here?'

Wyatt spoke in the exaggerated manner adopted by those unused to speaking to the deaf, carefully enunciating each word.

'Eh? Can't hear you. I'm deaf, I tell you. Factor pays me sixpence a week to clean out the church after Sunday services. I do the same for the manse once a week for another sixpence. I'll shop for you, too, given money in advance. I like to come in here and sit at the back on a Sunday, so I can make a start as soon as the service is over.' The old woman looked pointedly about her. 'This will be an easy day's money.' Looking up into Wyatt's face, she added: 'Neither of us is going to die of hard work here today, Minister.'

She was still cackling merrily when she passed Evangeline Garrett on the path that went through the small churchyard.

Entering the church, Evangeline acknowledged Wyatt with a nod before looking about her. She frowned. 'I thought you'd be taking a service this morning. Or is it over already? I rode here hoping to be in time to hear your first sermon.'

'You and that old woman are the only ones to have set foot inside the kirk this morning – and she only came here to clean up.' Wyatt hoped the disappointment he felt could not be detected in his voice.

'Oh, Wyatt, I'm so sorry! I really am. Everyone is being absolutely horrid to you.' Evangeline laid her hand on his arm in a spontaneous gesture of sympathy. 'Please don't be too upset. I'll tell my father. He'll make them come to church—'

'No!' The word sounded unduly loud and harsh inside the empty church. 'I'm sorry. . . . Look, I know you mean well, but this is a problem I must solve in my own way if I'm to succeed as minister here.'

'Yes, of course. . . .' Evangeline removed her hand from his arm and brushed an imaginary speck of dust from his sleeve. 'You'll be holding an afternoon service?'

Because many Highland parishioners needed to travel long distances in order to reach their church and return home before dark, an afternoon service took the place of the evening one.

'It hardly seems worthwhile. . . .'

'Nonsense! We're not early risers on a Sunday,' she explained apologetically, 'but the whole family always attends church in the afternoon. So do our servants. You'll have a better congregation then, I promise you.'

'In that case the service will go ahead as usual.'

Evangeline gave Wyatt a warm smile. 'Good! Can I persuade you to come home and have lunch with us?'

Wyatt shook his head. 'Not on a Sunday. This is the day I devote to my church.' He did not add that if he were ever to gain the confidence of the people of Eskaig he needed to steer a course that kept the factor at arm's length as far as possible.

'Then, I'll see you this afternoon – but, I warn you, I'll expect you to return to the house for dinner afterwards.'

There were twenty-three men, women and children in church for the afternoon service. It was far fewer than Wyatt would have wished, and he was aware all were drawn from the families of those who worked in the Garrett household. But it was enough to make the service worthwhile, and Wyatt ensured the small congregation was given a service to remember. He preached a sermon that promised 'fire and brimstone' for those who did not follow the path of the Lord. The wide eyes of the children told him it had been a powerful sermon, at least.

Evangeline was almost as awed as the children when she met him outside the church afterwards. 'That was a *wonderful* sermon, Wyatt,' she enthused. 'The people of Eskaig don't know what they've missed. They *will* come to your church, you'll see. When they do they'll realise they have a better preacher than Minister Gunn ever was.'

Charlotte Garrett echoed her daughter's sentiments, adding: 'It *was* a fine sermon. I'll look forward to Sundays with much more pleasure now you are here.'

Out here in the daylight Charlotte Garrett was paler and more gaunt than she had appeared in her own home. There was a brittle intensity about her that Wyatt found disconcerting. He was a Doctor of Divinity but, for Charlotte Garrett's sake, he wished he was also a Doctor of Medicine.

John Garrett was less impressed with Wyatt's preaching skills.

Shrugging a heavy cape about his shoulders, he looked up at the dark grey clouds lowering over the mountain-tops. 'There's a deal of rain up there, Minister. Don't be too long in making ready. You'll find our pony and trap by the gate.'

It was a tight squeeze in the light two-wheeled carriage, and the lochside track had not yet been repaired after suffering the ravages of winter, yet Evangeline did not mind the discomfort. Seated next to Wyatt, she occasionally clutched his arm in order to maintain her balance. When this happened she would smile up at him happily while her father cursed the state of the road.

They had travelled for about a mile when Wyatt suddenly cried: 'Stop!' It was such an urgent cry that the factor hauled on the reins, bringing the pony to a restless halt.

'What is it?' the factor demanded.

'There's a young lad over there in the bushes. I want to have a word with him.'

Wyatt had glimpsed Ewan Munro to one side of the track. The boy had darted for the cover of a clump of straggly gorse just before the pony and trap passed by, but before he disappeared from view Wyatt had spotted a bloody rag wrapped about Ewan Munro's bare leg.

John Garrett erupted in anger. 'I'm damned if I'm going to risk a soaking while you talk to some urchin. Get back in the trap.'

There was some justification for the factor's concern about the weather. Heavy black cloud was beginning to roll down the mountainside towards the loch, and specks of rain were carried on the wind. But Wyatt was already out of the trap.

'I'll not be a few minutes. . . .' Wyatt had seen the boy scrambling towards an area of broken rocks, higher up the slope.

John Garrett flicked the reins over the pony's back angrily. 'Then, you'll need to *walk* to the house.'

A moment later pony and trap were clattering off along the track. As the two women occupants looked back at Wyatt he saw distress on the pale face of Charlotte Garrett, while Evangeline's expression was one of increasing anger.

Wyatt did not pause to wonder whether the anger was directed at himself or at her father. He began scrambling up the mountainside to where he had last seen the ragged boy. Ewan Munro was in need of help, and this was more important to him than missing a meal with the Garrett family.

When Wyatt reached the spot where he had last seen the boy there was no one in sight, but a few hundred yards away was the narrow glen where the boy had eluded Wyatt on their previous meeting.

Wyatt followed the glen, heading towards the increasingly loud sound of a fast-running mountain stream somewhere ahead. Soon he was enveloped in the grey mist of the clouds, and up here there was both rain and a hint of snow in the wind. Wyatt had almost decided to abandon his search when he heard a sound from the mist somewhere below him. It was a boy crying.

Painfully forcing his way through the undergrowth, Wyatt headed towards the sound, which by now had become a low inter-mittent snuffling. Quite suddenly Wyatt cleared the undergrowth – and almost tripped over the boy.

Ewan Munro was seated by the side of a rapid-flowing stream, splashing handfuls of water on his leg. Startled by Wyatt's sudden appearance, he tried to scramble away along the stone-strewn stream-bank, but Wyatt was quicker. He caught the boy before he was more than an arm's length away.

Ewan Munro fought desperately for his freedom for some moments. Suddenly he cried out in pain, and his struggles ceased as his face contorted in agony.

Releasing his grip, Wyatt had no need to ask the young boy what was wrong. As Ewan Munro straightened his injured leg Wyatt saw it was far worse than he had realised. Beneath the knee the leg was bloody, swollen and discoloured. It was also dirty as a result of their recent struggle.

'How did you do this?' Escape and pursuit were forgotten as Wyatt kneeled beside the boy and examined the injured limb.

Receiving no reply, Wyatt repeated the question in Gaelic, although he was aware the boy understood English.

'I was shot . . . by the factor's men.' Ewan Munro's reply was in Gaelic.

'When?' Wyatt's question was tinged with disbelief. He was aware that the factor held the Highlanders in low esteem, but he could not believe any man would order the shooting of a boy.

'The day you last chased me. When I had the salmon.'

Wyatt's lips tightened to a grim thin line as he completed his examination of the wounded leg. The boy had been wounded by scattershot from a sportsman's gun at close range, and the leg had not been properly treated. It was hardly surprising the wound was showing signs of infection.

'The first thing we need to do is get this cleaned up so we can see how bad it is.'

Making no attempt to escape now, Ewan Munro followed Wyatt back to the stream. He sat on the stony bank, trying hard not to cry out when Wyatt began cleaning the wound.

As he worked, Wyatt questioned the boy. He learned Ewan Munro lived with his family 'a wee walk away'. The vague information was accompanied by a wave of the arm indicating only that it was farther along the glen.

When the blood and dirt on Ewan's leg had been washed away the puffiness of infected tissue became more apparent. Wyatt suspected a number of pieces of lead shot were still lodged beneath the skin. If the leg was to get better, all the shot would have to come out.

'You should see a doctor. There's some work needs to be done on this leg.'

Ewan Munro looked at Wyatt with all the scorn a ten-year-old could muster. 'The doctor's all the way to Corpach. Like yourself, he's the landlord's man. It's the factor's shot I'm carrying. If I go to him, he'll have me in the lock-up without so much as looking at my leg. No doubt you'll try to do the same – but you've got to get me to Corpach first.'

There it was again. The assumption that Wyatt was 'the landlord's man'. But this was neither the time nor the place to put the young poacher right.

'Can you walk well enough to take me to your father?'

'What do you want with him? It's me who's been taking the laird's salmon, not my pa.'

'I don't care who's been taking what, or from where. You need to have shot removed from your leg. If we can't trust a doctor, then *I'll* need to do it, and I have neither knife nor fire here. Will you take me to your home, or would you rather come down to the manse, in Eskaig?'

Ewan Munro looked at Wyatt uncertainly. He had no intention of accompanying the minister anywhere near the village. Turning away abruptly, he limped off into the mist, leading Wyatt further into the mountains.

In spite of Ewan's wounded leg, Wyatt was hard put to keep up with him. They had been walking for at least half a mile when Wyatt smelled wood-smoke in the damp air. A few minutes later they reached a small clearing in the heart of the thick undergrowth that choked much of the glen floor.

Here the Munro family had their 'home'. It was no more than a lean-to shelter composed of grass, tree-branches and turfs, supported by two growing saplings. Beneath the scant cover provided by the structure a man lay on his side beneath a single threadbare blanket, his face turned away from the opening. The remains of another blanket lay on the damp ground beside him. On this, two very young girls were playing. Despite the chill and wet weather one was as naked as the day she was born, no more than a year before.

Three more girls were squatting beside a low-burning fire. They were watching as a woman Wyatt presumed to be their mother turned a wooden spit on which a hare was impaled, above the flames.

The woman was so startled when she looked up to see Wyatt emerging from the undergrowth behind her son that she dropped the hare, and it fell in the fire.

One of the small girls pounced on the meat immediately. Lifting it carefully to safety, she replaced the spit in the forks of two sticks driven in the ground on either side of the fire.

'It's all right, Mother.' Wyatt used the term in a bid to put the woman at ease, but in spite of her large family she could have been no older than himself. 'I've brought Ewan home. He has a bad wound on his leg. It needs to be treated right away. I'll do it, if you wish, but I'll need a sharp knife. Would you have one?'

'Who's that? Elsa . . . who's that out there with you?' The voice was that of a querulous old man, yet Wyatt found it hard to believe an old man had sired the Munro brood.

'It's all right, Pa. . . .' At the first sound of the man's voice Ewan Munro had moved to the lean-to shelter. He leaned low over the blanket-covered figure to reassure him. 'It's the new preacher from Eskaig.'

'Preacher? I don't need no preacher. Give me another day or two to get back on my feet and we'll be on our way again. . . .'

The declaration ended breathlessly, as though the speaker had over-exerted himself. Wyatt moved closer to the lean-to.

'I've brought your son home. He has a piece or two of lead in his leg. It's not serious, but they need to come out quickly. I need a sharp knife.'

The sick man struggled to sit up in bed, but even as Wyatt stooped to help him he fell back again.

'I'm sorry. I didn't realise you were such a sick man.'

Ewan Munro's father rolled his head from side to side impatiently. 'I'm a mite weak, that's all. I'll be as right as summer tomorrow. I always am. Elsa, give the preacher my knife.'

Elsa Munro hesitated for a moment, as though reluctant to obey her husband's breathless instruction. Then she brushed past Wyatt and from the lower end of the lean-to pulled out a bag made from faded tartan cloth. Again she hesitated, looking at Wyatt before plunging her hand inside the bag. Lifting out a dirk that had no place in the possession of a ragged and homeless Highland family, she handed the weapon to Wyatt. Housed in a scabbard of shiny black leather heavily ornamented with gilt, the knife's handle was designed in the shape of an inverted thistle and carved from highly polished ebony. Inspecting the knife more closely, Wyatt saw a silver '72' worked into the base of the handle, close to the hilt.

Wyatt looked up quickly and caught the expression of apprehension on the face of Elsa Munro. 'This is the dirk of an officer in the Seventy-Second Regiment. How did *you* come by it?'

'It isn't stolen, I swear.' Elsa Munro was close to tears. 'Lachlan's never stolen a thing in his life —' less it was a salmon or a hare to feed his family.'

'She's right, Preacher. But it's not usual for a churchman to have such a knowledge of military weapons. The dirk was given to me by a lieutenant in the Seventy-Second. I was his batman.'

Wyatt leaned low over the sick man. Lachlan Munro was unshaven, and his face was pinched and gaunt as a result of the fever that racked his body — but it was a face Wyatt had seen before. Long ago, and far away.

'And you served him well, *Sergeant* Munro — the regiment, too. But what on earth is a brave man like you doing out here on the mountains with no roof over your head?'

This time nothing could prevent Lachlan Munro from struggling to a sitting position. As Wyatt kneeled down in order to support him, the man looked hard at the preacher and his face lit up with sheer delight.

'Captain Jamieson. Well, I'm damned – begging your pardon, Captain.'

'You'll not be damned if I have anything to do with it, Sergeant. But what are you doing *here*?'

Lachlan Munro sagged back against the supporting arm, and Wyatt gently lowered the sick man to the ground.

'You've asked a good question, Captain – sorry, *Minister*. But it's small wonder I never recognised you as a preacher. You was a hero to all of us. . . .'

'It's *your* story I want to hear, Lachlan. You were going to tell me what's happened to you.'

'I caught the fever in Africa, Captain, same as you. More than half the regiment went down with it. I was shipped home. Must have been eighteen months after you. When I got back I discovered the factor had turned my family from the house. Sheep were grazing over what Garrett's men had left standing. Took me three months to learn where Elsa, Ewan and the others had gone. I found 'em all right, but they'd have been better off without me. Twice I've managed to get work, but each time the fever's come back and laid me up again. No one wants to employ a man who's lying abed ill as often as he's working.'

Wyatt was well acquainted with the African fever. It was the reason he had been invalided out of the Army. He, too, still suffered recurrences that would strike him down for days at a time.

'How do you live?'

'Best way I can, Captain. Sometimes a nice salmon will jump from the loch and land at my feet. Hares have been known to drop dead when I look at 'em too. You know how it is. If they don't . . . well, a man can't sit back and watch his family starve.' Lachlan Munro turned his head, and his eyes found his son. 'When I'm laid low Ewan needs to be the provider. He's a good boy. A man couldn't ask for a finer son. We'd have all starved for certain, had it not been for Ewan.'

Talk of the boy reminded Wyatt of what he had to do. When he told Lachlan Munro, the sick ex-soldier closed his eyes as though in sudden pain. Then he nodded. 'Do what you have to, Captain. He won't make a whimper, I promise you. He's a brave lad. He'll make a good soldier one day. It's all he thinks about. Ewan, come here, boy.'

When Ewan came to stand beside his father, Lachlan Munro said: 'The captain here was in my regiment, in Africa. He was a sergeant once, but he was so brave they made him an officer. I've told him *you're* brave, too. He'll no doubt hurt you with what needs to be done, but I've said you'll not cry. Am I right?'

The expression on Ewan Munro's suddenly pale face was an uncertain and apprehensive mixture of fear and pride. He nodded his head.

'Good boy! Give me your hand now. While the captain's about his business I'll tell you what the Seventy-Second did in Africa, and why they made him an officer. . . .'

Prising the lead pellets from Ewan Munro's leg took longer than Wyatt would have wished. Yet, apart from a whimper when the crude operation began and another when Wyatt needed to dig deep in the flesh of the thin leg for the last pellet, Ewan never made a sound. From somewhere behind him Wyatt could hear Elsa Munro crying softly, and one of the girls wept with her. Wyatt never looked round. Working as swiftly as he could, he hardly noticed the perspiration and drizzle running down his face.

When Wyatt eventually straightened up, his back and arms ached from the sheer tension of the operation he had just performed. 'There, it's all done.'

Lachlan Munro was cradling his son in his arms and he blinked to clear his eyes. 'He's fainted, Captain. It's not that he's a coward. He's only a wee lad. . . .'

'I've known grown men scream with less cause. He's a brave boy.' As he spoke, Wyatt was ripping up his clean linen kerchief to make a flimsy bandage. 'You can be proud of him. But what's to be done about you – *all* of you?'

'Don't you concern yourself with us, Captain. We'll be all right when I'm up and about again. Just give us a day or two, that's all.'

Wyatt looked about the makeshift camp. The abject poverty of the Munro family was painfully apparent.

'This is no way for a loyal ex-sergeant of the Seventy-Second to live, Lachlan. You deserve better. So does your family. Come down to the village and see me when you're up and about again. In the meantime. . . .'

Wyatt dug deep into his pockets. He was far from wealthy, but he knew he carried a half-guinea somewhere. Locating the small gold coin, he handed it to Elsa Munro. 'Take this. Use it to buy food and whatever else you need. Build up the strength of your man – and Ewan's, too. Be sure to come down to Eskaig as soon as you're able. In the meantime I'll speak to the factor on your behalf.'

Elsa Munro accepted the coin and clasped both Wyatt's hands in her own. 'God bless you, Minister. God bless you.'

'His blessings on you and your family, too, Elsa. But He'll need a little help if you're to be provided with the material things of this life.'

CHAPTER FOUR

WYATT SET OUT for John Garrett's house early the next morning. It was fine and sunny now, although there was still a bank of cloud far out over the sea to the west. Wyatt knew his meeting with the factor was likely to be a stormy one, but he had accepted that the very nature of John Garrett made a clash between them inevitable. It might as well come sooner than later.

The factor was finishing his breakfast and gruffly invited Wyatt to sit down and share a pot of coffee with him. Declining the offer, Wyatt stated that he had come to the house to discuss business — estate business.

John Garrett looked up at his visitor and frowned. 'What has estate business to do with a preacher? We've managed very well without you for a great many years.'

'*You* might have been happy with things. Lachlan Munro and his family haven't.'

John Garrett's frown deepened, then suddenly cleared. 'The ex-soldier? The man's a lazy scoundrel. I employed him on the estate for a while. So did one of the tenants over Glen Coe way. He did no more than two days' work for either of us before feigning sickness and failing to turn up for work.'

'He was feigning nothing. He suffers from the same fever that had me discharged from the Army. It returns even now to lay me low, as it does to Munro.'

'So that's it. Two ex-Army men standing together. Well, *I've* never been in the Army, and I'm concerned only with running Lord Kilmalie's estate at a profit. Lachlan Munro is nothing to me. In fact the sooner he's off Kilmalie land the better it will be for everyone. He's a thieving poacher.'

'He's also an ex-sergeant of the Seventy-Second Regiment. He served with Lord Kilmalie's son in Africa, and served well. When his Lordship learns Munro returned from Africa only to find he'd been dispossessed I doubt if he'll share your views.'

'You'll tell him?'

'A letter will be on its way by nightfall.'

Charlotte Garrett appeared in the doorway, a coffee-pot in her hand. She wanted to approach the table but could see from the stance of the two men that they were involved in an argument. Her face registered anxious uncertainty.

John Garrett stood up abruptly, only the weight of the hardwood chair preventing it from toppling to the floor. 'Come to my office.' Without waiting for a reply the factor strode to the doorway, pushing past his wife without a word to her.

Outside in the main hallway Evangeline was halfway down the stairs, a flimsy wrap thrown over her night attire. She was unprepared for her father's bellow of anger.

'What do you think you're doing? I'll not have my daughter flaunting herself like some common Highland slut in front of a stranger. Get back to your room this minute.'

Unused to being spoken to by her father in such a manner, Evangeline opened her mouth to protest. Then she saw Wyatt emerge from the breakfast room. Her jaw sagged, and she gazed at him in dismay. Her hands went to her hair, where tight curls were held in place by a multicoloured selection of rag strips. She turned and fled, her protest forgotten.

In the estate manager's office, John Garrett reached down a large leather-bound book from a shelf and placed it upon a desk.

'Close the door.'

As Wyatt complied with the gruff order, the factor turned the pages of the book until he found the one he was seeking.

'Can you make sense of figures?'

'I've kept accounts.'

'Take a look through this book. When I came here the Kilmalie estate was barely breaking even. I've brought it into profit. Allowed to do things my way, I could make this the finest estate in the whole of Scotland.'

'How? By getting rid of tenants in the same way you dispossessed Lachlan Munro?'

'Highland tenants will never pay sufficient rent to make their landlords rich. How can they? They grow hardly enough to stay alive. A fair rent is beyond them. The answer is *sheep*. Keep tenants on land and it pays pennies. Put sheep in their place and you can begin to count the profit in pounds.'

'It may make sense to the landlord. It doesn't to the dispossessed tenant.'

The factor shrugged. 'My duty is to Lord Kilmalie, not to a bunch of ne'er-do-wells who spend no more than four months of the year spoiling good pasture with their goats and pigs. For the other eight months they're content to crouch over a fire inside a hut, moving only to scratch at a flea or a louse.'

Wyatt tried to control his anger. 'I'm surprised you stay here if you despise the Highlanders so much. Especially as Lord Kilmalie doesn't share your views. He knows the Highlanders have supported their clan heads in war and peace for hundreds of years. He accepts his duty to them, as I do. That's why I've come here on behalf of Lachlan Munro. If you're not prepared to help him, I don't doubt Lord Kilmalie *will*.'

Wyatt turned to leave the office, but John Garrett called him back. 'Wait! I can't give Munro his old place back. It's been pulled down, and sheep are grazing there now.'

'Can you offer him somewhere else?'

'There's a cottage on flat land at the far end of the loch, beyond Kinlocheil. Work needs to be done on the roof, but there's good land goes with it. Too good to waste on a man who's used to the mountains, but I suppose it's better than leaving it to stand idle.'

Taken by surprise at the offer, Wyatt eyed the factor speculatively. The offer had nothing to do with the advantage to the estate of having the cottage occupied and the land worked, of this he was certain. Neither was it because John Garrett had been defeated in argument. Either Lord Kilmalie had no knowledge of his factor's methods, or he had already warned Garrett about them. Wyatt wondered how much farther he could push the factor.

'Lachlan Munro's wife said there were crops growing when she was evicted.'

'Munro will be given seed to compensate for any loss he might have suffered.'

'What about livestock?'

'Don't push me too hard, Minister. I'll arrange for Munro to be given two young pigs. If he wants a cow, he'll need to negotiate with one of his new neighbours. But I'll have no goats on the land, and he'll be charged rent, same as anyone else.'

'Not for a twelvemonth, until he's back on his feet.'

John Garrett held his breath for so long it seemed he must explode. 'Lachlan Munro is due nothing from me. I've been generous enough. *Over*-generous. Now I'll give *you* something, Minister. Food for thought. Lord Kilmalie's an old man. He'll not last for ever. Most probably his heir will think as I do, that the Highlander has no place on a modern estate. His time passed with Culloden. When he's finally gone from these parts there'll be no need for a preacher here, either. Just keep it in mind, Minister Jamieson. *I* certainly will.'

Wyatt left the factor's house well satisfied with the results of his visit. He had achieved far more than he had expected. Lachlan Munro now had a cottage, and his family had an opportunity to put their past unhappiness behind them.

Wyatt decided he would go and tell the ex-soldier of his change of fortune right away, but he did not return the way he had come. It was still early, and the clouds building over the sea had not moved any closer. It was an opportunity for Wyatt to explore another corner of his extensive parish.

At nearby Corpach was the entrance to the Caledonian Canal. It was a wonderful feat of imaginative engineering. Utilising a number of deep-water lochs, it cut Scotland in two and linked the Atlantic Ocean with the North Sea. Wyatt intended to follow this canal north-eastwards for a few miles before turning off westwards and making his way to Eskaig over the mountains.

Because of the direction Wyatt had taken, Evangeline looked in vain for him along the road to Eskaig when she ran from the house fully dressed, her newly brushed hair freed from the curling-rags. Thoroughly bad-tempered, the factor's daughter returned to the house to take her father to task for shouting at her in the hearing of Eskaig's new young minister. In the present mood of both father and daughter the confrontation boded ill for the peace of the Garrett household.

*   *   *

On the slopes above Corpach, Wyatt paused in his climb to watch a small naval vessel being raised through a series of eight locks to join the canal. Then he followed the slow progress of the ship along the canal itself before turning off.

Heading deep into the mountains for about two miles, Wyatt followed the course of a small stream that had its source somewhere in the mountains overlooking Loch Eil. It was well wooded hereabouts, and he emerged from a stretch of woodland to discover the sun had disappeared behind a layer of thin fast-moving cloud. A squall was approaching.

Wyatt toyed with the idea of turning about and returning the way he had come. He was not dressed for bad weather. His coat would not keep out rain, and his hat would take flight at the first hint of wind. He would find houses where he might shelter more easily along the canal-bank than here.

Instead Wyatt muttered a brief prayer and rammed his hat more tightly upon his head. Turning up his coat collar, he set off against the slope of the land.

For almost an hour it seemed Wyatt's prayer had been heard. Apart from a short sharp shower, the rain held off. Then, as he reached an open stretch of mountainside, the sky to the west became as black as his minister's cloak, while the wind moaned a warning that no man familiar with the Highlands would ignore.

Looking about him anxiously for some form of shelter, Wyatt saw what he took to be a small clump of bushes, about half a mile distant. It was not much, but it would be better than nothing.

Not until Wyatt drew closer did he realise it was in fact a small depression in the hillside. What he had seen was the top of stunted trees. In their midst was a long low sod-and-stone cot, its thatched roof held down with weighty stones strung together like a giant necklace.

Wyatt reached the door of the building in the same moment as the storm. There were few formalities among Highland folk. To knock on a door in time of need would have been incomprehensible to the occupants. Wyatt stumbled in through the doorway as wind and rain slammed against the low-lying cot with the noise of a cannonade.

It was dim inside, and smoke hung heavily in the air. Such light as filtered through from outside entered through two small four-pane windows, weakly supplemented by light from a peat fire burning between stone slabs in the centre of the room. An upturned bucket set in the thatch at an angle against the prevailing wind served as a chimney, but the smoke was reluctant to leave, drifting about soot-blackened beams. The living-room was divided from the remainder of the cot by a screen of rough-hewn boards, but there would be little privacy for the occupants of such a house.

A number of men sat about the fire, some on wooden stools, others on the hard earth. All were men Wyatt had last seen on the day he landed from the boat at Eskaig. Three women were in the room, too. One was grey-haired with a dark weatherbeaten skin, the others were younger. One was the dark-haired girl Wyatt had last seen casting an angry look in his direction as the militiamen drove her from the loch-edge.

The only man to stand up was the heavily bearded Eneas Ross. 'You're a long way from home, Preacher. Are you lost, maybe?'

'No.' As Wyatt spoke a fierce gust of wind hurled itself against the thatch, and the blackened beams squealed in protest. 'I had business in Corpach. I thought I'd return across the mountains. I'm glad I found your cot before the storm broke.'

As Wyatt spoke a dribble of water, peat-black from the beams, dripped down upon his head. He was reminded of other crofter cots, among the hills of the island where he had lived as a boy. The people here were not very different.

'It will be worse along the ridge than down here. Either place, it's better to be listening to it from beneath a good solid roof. Will you seat yourself?'

As Wyatt took the recently vacated stool, Eneas Ross asked: 'Was your business in Corpach with the factor?'

'It was.'

One of the two women standing at the rear of the smoke-filled room snorted derisively. Wyatt believed it to be the dark-haired girl.

As Wyatt looked at each of the men seated about the fire, Eneas Ross said: 'These are my sons – eight of them. A chief would have been proud to have such clansmen on his land in the old days.

Those times are past, Preacher. Now it seems we're taking up land the factor would rather see rented out as a sheep-walk.'

His statement brought nods and grunts of agreement from the young men about the fire, but Eneas Ross was speaking again.

'The wind will have put a chill in your bones. Mairi, bring out the "water of life" for the preacher. Mairi is my daughter,' Eneas Ross added as the dark-haired girl moved to a gloomy corner of the room. 'She's the only lass in fourteen births. Four sons survived for only a few days. Another was drowned in the loch as a lad. The other lass is Tibbie.' He pointed through the smoke. Forced back down the 'chimney' by the wind, it was now thicker than ever. 'She's a Cameron from above Loch Leven, and married to my oldest boy, Ian.'

. Mairi Ross appeared at Wyatt's side. Handing him a battered pewter mug, she commenced to half-fill it with whisky poured from a large earthenware jar. Then she went around the circle of her brothers pouring drinks for them into wooden cups. Wyatt realised that, as a guest, he had been given the family's best drinking-vessel.

'Your health, Preacher.' Eneas Ross raised his cup in a simple toast.

'God's blessing on you and yours.'

The strength of the whisky reached Wyatt's nose long before it touched his lips, and when he swallowed it drove the breath from his throat. Twice he tried to speak, but not until the third attempt did a voice that was not recognisable as his own say: 'I haven't tasted whisky like this since I left the Isles. Where's it made?'

Knowing grins about the fire gave Wyatt his answer, but Eneas Ross said: 'It was a gift, given in return for a young pig. It isn't done to question another man's generosity.'

Wyatt took Eneas Ross's point and made no further mention of the source of the illicitly distilled whisky during his chat with the men of the Ross family.

Declining a second drink, Wyatt explained that he wanted to speak to Lachlan Munro before returning home.

'You know where the Munros are?' It was the first time Mairi Ross had spoken to Wyatt since his arrival.

'They've built a lean-to on the other side of the mountain. Lachlan isn't at all well. I want to tell him I've persuaded John Garrett to give the family a cot.'

'You've persuaded Lord Kilmalie's factor to give a cot to a Highlander?' Eneas Ross's question broke the incredulous silence that fell upon the men about the fire at Wyatt's words.

'A cot *and* a piece of land. Garrett's also agreed to give Lachlan two young sows by way of compensation for what he's lost. All he needs now is a cow to provide milk for that young family of his.'

Eneas Ross's glance moved around the fire and it was answered with a nod from each son.

'We'll loan him a milk-cow until he's raised a crop or two and has money to spend.'

Wyatt beamed about him. 'Eneas, I believe the Lord has guided my footsteps this way today – ay, and sent a storm to drive me to your home. God bless you all.'

'If I made a gift of a cow to every Highlander who's been given a cot by Factor Garrett, I'd be no poorer than I am today – and you're the first preacher to give a blessing inside this house. I thank you for that.'

'Minister Gunn never came here?' Wyatt was surprised. He had been given to understand that his predecessor had been welcomed into every house in the parish of Eskaig.

'Preacher Gunn was well thought of in the communities along the loch-side, but I doubt whether he ever toiled up the side of a mountain in his life. We have no Sunday suits to wear to church, so we were never his kind of people.'

'There'll always be a place for the Rosses in my church, however you're dressed. If you don't find your way there soon, I'll need to come here again. Thanks for your "water of life". It's put the strength back in my legs.'

'One of my lads will come with you. The rain's stopped, but the cloud has lowered. . . .'

'*I'll* show him the way.' The unexpected offer came from Mairi Ross.

Her words brought Eneas Ross's bushy eyebrows together in a frown, and Mairi's chin came up defiantly.

'Tibbie and I have made clothes for Elsa's two youngest from a couple of our old dresses. If they're to be living among folk, she'll want them to look respectable.'

Eneas Ross had seen the nakedness of the youngest Munro

children. He nodded. 'You know the mountains as well as anyone, girl – better than most – and the rest of us have work to do now the rain's stopped for a while. Tell Lachlan he or the boy can come for the cow whenever he's a mind.'

CHAPTER FIVE

THE MIST OUTSIDE the thatched cottage was so thick it was impossible to see for a distance of more than ten paces, but Mairi Ross was unconcerned. Clutching a bundle of home-made clothing, she strode barefoot across the coarse Highland grass with the assurance of someone who knew exactly where she was heading. Wyatt had already gained the impression she went through life with the same confidence in herself. She moved with the long easy stride of someone used to walking long distances across the wide empty country.

'You have a freedom that's rare for a girl, Mairi Ross.' Wyatt broke a silence that had held for ten minutes after leaving the small crowded cottage.

Mairi shrugged. 'Have I? I wouldn't know. Father was so used to sons when I came along he didn't think to treat me any different. Does it bother you?'

'It's not my concern. It's your life.'

There was just a trace of amusement in Mairi's eyes when she said: 'I thought preachers weren't happy unless they were changing people. Making them all dress alike and sitting them in neat little rows in a kirk. Isn't that what being a preacher is all about?'

'Not to me, it isn't. I believe for much of the time it's possible to feel closer to God up here in the mountains than in a kirk. The important thing is to teach people to recognise God *wherever* they find Him.'

Mairi thought about this for a few minutes before saying seriously: 'That's the way I've always felt, but I could never have said so to Preacher Gunn. He certainly wouldn't have said such a thing to me – or to anyone else.' She gave him a sidelong glance. 'You're a rare kind of minister, Mr Jamieson. I'm not forgetting that you probably saved Father's life down in Eskaig the day you arrived – and my brothers', too. They'll remember. It's rare for anyone to take the part of a Highland crofter in these times. That reminds me.... How did you come to take Lachlan and Elsa Munro's part against the factor?'

Wyatt gave Mairi a sketchy explanation of his meeting with young Ewan Munro and told her what he had found when he reached the spot where Lachlan Munro had built a shelter for his family.

He was still talking when Mairi suddenly reached out and gripped his arm, bringing him to a halt.

'What is it?'

'Can't you hear?'

Wyatt listened. Above the wind he heard a distant sound that might have been surf pounding on a long sandy beach – but they were many miles from the sea up here in the mountains.

'It's a squall. A bad one.' Mairi looked about her, seemingly seeing beyond the enveloping mist. 'This way. Run!' She set an example, and Wyatt followed, hard put to keep up with her.

A couple of minutes later she scrambled into a crevice between tumbledown boulders and pulled him in after her. There was a shelter here, of sorts. A framework of branches had been driven in the ground; other branches were woven through them, and turfs and grass laid on top, weighted down with stones.

'I built it,' Mairi explained. 'I bring the cattle up here sometimes.' She needed to shout above the wind which was rising in a frightening crescendo.

Wyatt shifted his position beside her. The shelter had been built for only one person. It was very cramped with the two of them inside.

The wind increased in ferocity until it seemed it must carry all before it. The framework of the small shelter creaked and complained, and tufts of grass were peeled away. And then the rain arrived. It struck with a force that caused part of the tiny structure to cave in, and before he could raise a hand to save it Wyatt's hat was snatched away by the wind. The battered shelter groaned and distorted as its two occupants inched as far back as they could into the crevice between the rocks. Suddenly a section of the crude roof was carried away and rain poured in upon Mairi.

Removing his coat with great difficulty inside the tiny beleaguered shelter, Wyatt pulled it over both their heads as they huddled closer together. They did not talk. The sheer ferocity of the storm rendered conversation impossible, but each gained comfort in the other's presence as it raged through the mountains.

The storm passed on as abruptly as it had arrived. One moment the wind was screaming furiously about the shelter – and then it had moved on. Deserted by its powerful ally, the rain faltered and died away, leaving only the dark angry clouds to menace them.

Not until now did Wyatt realise he was holding Mairi very close to take advantage of what shelter was provided by his coat. Mairi, too, was aware of their closeness. She avoided his eyes as he released his hold on her and disentangled the sodden mass of his coat.

'I can't remember ever experiencing such a tempest.' Wyatt's voice sounded tremulous to his own ears. The sheer violence of the storm had made him acutely aware of man's insignificance in the world God had created.

'It's not over yet.' Mairi shook back her long dark hair, soaked by the rain despite all Wyatt's efforts to protect her. 'This is only a lull. Listen.'

Wyatt could hear nothing for a moment, then he caught the sound of the wind approaching once more, howling across the mountain-tops towards them. As he hurriedly wrung out his coat and placed it about them once more, Mairi said: 'I hope Lachlan and Elsa have chosen a well-sheltered spot. Where did you say they were?'

'I didn't, but they're camped well up the slope in the glen that breaks the mountains to the east of Eskaig. They're beside the stream, well down in a gully. They should be out of much of the wind, at least.'

Mairi threw off the water-heavy coat. 'Tell me where. *Exactly* where. Not beside the stream that flows through Ranald's Glen . . . the one that comes down from the mountains in a series of waterfalls?'

'It sounds like the place, but I went no farther than Lachlan's camp. . . . Where are you going?'

Mairi was squirming her way out of the narrow shelter. Reaching the entrance, she turned to look back at him. 'The stream is known as "Ranald's Lament". Many years ago, in a storm similar to the one we've just had, all the women of a small clan were swept away and drowned while summer-feeding cattle there. Water from most of the peaks on either side of the glen flows down to Loch Eil through that one glen.'

Wyatt was alarmed. 'Then, we might already be too late?'

'Yes.' Mairi was on her feet now, and Wyatt quickly followed her out into the mist and rain.

By the time Wyatt and Mairi reached the glen of Ranald's Lament the storm had whipped itself to a fury once more. They made slow progress, doubled almost in half, each with an arm crooked before their face to protect eyes from the bruising rain and battling to make progress against the wind.

The noise all about them was alarming, the wind screaming unintelligible obscenities at the intruders who dared defy its power.

During brief lulls, when it seemed the wind was gathering its breath for a further onslaught, another sound could be heard: the noise of rushing water.

Soaked and battered, Wyatt and Mairi eventually reached the shelter of the glen and began a cautious descent from the mountains. The sound of fast-running water was ominously loud here. The booming of tens of thousands of gallons of water cascading from the surrounding peaks and slopes and thundering into the glen below.

Water poured from every rocky ledge on the steep slopes about Wyatt and Mairi, and somewhere far below it joined to form a river. A great, powerful, surging, foaming, awesome river that carried before it trees, bushes, earth and rocks. Gouging a new wide path on its headlong journey to Loch Eil.

The rain had driven the mist from the mountains, and Wyatt and Mairi looked in horror at the scene below them.

'Where was their shelter?' Mairi asked the question and dreaded the answer she might receive.

Wyatt shook his head. Nothing looked the same. It would never *be* the same again. Shaking off his thoughts, he made a determined effort to locate the place where he had last seen the luckless Munro family.

'It was lower than this, I'm sure. Probably as much as five or six hundred feet farther down the glen.'

'Then, I don't fancy their chances of survival. The glen's a dangerous place after any rain, but I've never seen it as bad as this before.'

In her anguish Mairi screwed up the clothes she and her sister-in-law had made for the youngest Munro children. When she realised what she was doing it seemed for a moment she would throw them away. Instead, she set off down the slope, and Wyatt followed.

The rain had eased considerably by the time Wyatt called Mairi to a halt.

'This is where Lachlan had his shelter.'

The spot was two feet under rushing water, the debris strewn all around and caught between rocks providing clear evidence that the water had been even deeper after the earlier deluge.

'Are you sure?'

Mairi wanted to believe Wyatt was wrong – after all, he had visited the spot only once – yet she knew instinctively that Wyatt would not have declared this to be the place unless he was quite certain.

Mairi stood in the rain, dark hair hanging in long wet tresses about her shoulders and the cheap dress clinging to her body. She looked a picture of despair, and Wyatt's heart went out to her. Grasping her arm, he said: 'I'm sorry, Mairi. I wouldn't have brought you here had I realised what had happened.'

Wyatt's genuine sympathy almost broke down the flimsy barrier of self-control Mairi was trying hard to maintain. She dared not reply.

Suddenly Wyatt's grip on her arm tightened. 'Listen!'

He had heard a faint sound, almost inaudible above the background thunder of water. It might have been the cry of an eagle, returning to the mountains after being driven away by the storm. . . . Then Wyatt heard the sound again and knew it had been made by no bird. It was a child's cry for help!

Mairi had heard it, too, and already she was scrambling and sliding down the steep wet hillside towards the swollen stream.

Wyatt shouted a warning, but if she heard she chose to ignore it. He did not catch up with her until she had reached the water's edge, close to an awesome waterfall. Hundreds of tons of water thundered down from about forty feet above them, throwing up a curtain of spray that made it almost impossible to see anything. It was equally unlikely they would have heard any cries for help emanating from this spot.

Wyatt tried to explain all this to Mairi. Before he could make himself heard he needed to take her arm and lead her fifty yards away, to a spot where the rocky uneven ground split the fast-running water into a hundred interlinked channels.

Even as he was speaking they both heard the sound again – and this time Wyatt was certain. It *was* a child. Then Mairi gripped Wyatt's arm and pointed ahead.

'There . . . look!'

He saw a movement on one of the tiny islands that had been formed by the floodwater. Suddenly a small girl rose to a standing position from among the debris strewn about her. In her arms she held a baby.

'It's Kirstie . . . with Barbie!'

The child saw Wyatt and Mairie at the same time and became so excited it seemed she was about to plunge into the river and make for them.

Waving his arms frantically, Wyatt shouted: 'Stay there. Stay where you are. We'll come to you. Don't move!'

'How are you going to reach her?'

There was a wide and fast-flowing expanse of water separating them from the children, and Wyatt had no answer to Mairi's question.

'There must be a way. There *has* to be.'

Wyatt's words were more hopeful than accurate. The island was situated more than three-quarters of the way to the far side of the swollen torrent.

'We might reach them from the other side, but I can see no way of crossing. . . .'

Fed by a whole network of swollen brooks pouring from the surrounding peaks, the river gained in strength as it poured down the mountainside.

'I know a way across. Come,' said Mairi.

She shouted for Kirstie Munro to remain where she was with her young charge, then began to make her way up the slope, heading back towards the great waterfall she and Wyatt had passed a short time before. By the time Wyatt caught up with her the thunder of the water made it impossible for him to ask what she thought she was doing. Then she took his hand and headed straight for the waterfall, taking a seemingly suicidal course.

Seeing the anxiety on his face, Mairi shouted an explanation that was lost in the noise of the water. She tugged at his hand determinedly and he followed, but with increasing anxiety.

Mairi never faltered. Keeping close to the cliff-face, she walked *behind* the wall of water crashing down only feet away from them.

The noise here was deafening, and spray leaped all about them, preventing them from seeing what lay ahead. Soon they began wading through knee-deep water. Then it was waist-high, swirling back from the falls. It was cold, too, cold enough to have Wyatt gasping for breath. Suddenly the water became shallower. Moments later they were clear of the waterfall, wading through the floodwater that swirled all about them.

Stumbling clear of the water, Wyatt found he was shivering, as much with realisation of what they had just accomplished as with cold, while his head felt as though it had been resting against an anvil in a busy blacksmith's shop.

Mairi was shivering, too, but she did not release his hand. Instead she began awkwardly running over the sodden slippery ground, dragging him after her.

They located the island on which the two children were stranded, but reaching it would not be as easy as Wyatt had hoped. There were a number of deep channels between the bank and the island, and one carried a fierce current of water that reached as high as Wyatt's armpits. When he attempted to cross this channel he was swept off his feet by the current and was lucky to be deposited in shallower water some distance down the hillside.

When he made his next attempt Wyatt was secured to an improvised 'rope'. It was made from strips of cloth torn from Wyatt's shirt, the clothing made by Mairi and her sister-in-law – and Mairi's own dress.

Mairi's dress was sacrificed when it became evident that the improvised rope was still not long enough to reach the island. Without seeking Wyatt's opinion, Mairi stripped the sodden dress from her shoulders and dropped it to the ground before his startled gaze.

For a few moments, as he looked at her naked body, Wyatt's emotions were those of the soldier he had once been and not the minister of the Church he had become. Then Mairi covered her nakedness with Wyatt's discarded coat and was fastening the buttons.

'If you've done with your gawping, you can help me rip up my dress. You'd better knot it yourself; it's your life that'll be depending on it.'

Wyatt entered the water stripped to the waist, the temperature of the water causing his very bones to ache. He had one end of the 'rope' twisted about one hand, while the other end was gripped by Mairi.

Once, in mid-channel, Wyatt slipped and was carried away by the fierce current, but Mairi's grip on the cloth rope held firm until he gained a footing once more. Then he waded ashore on the island and, forcing his way through clumps of tangled brushwood, reached the two children.

Kirstie Munro, a very frightened nine-year-old, had reached the end of her endurance. When Wyatt reached her side and took the ten-month-old Barbie from her she burst into tears.

With the baby caught in one arm, Wyatt held Kirstie to him and did his best to comfort her, saying: 'It's all right now, Kirstie. You've been a brave girl. It's nearly over. Try to stay brave for a wee while longer. . . .'

Kirstie Munro had endured hours of terror and despair, despite a fervent belief that her father and mother would not abandon her. Rescue had seemed far away at the height of the storm, but she had never doubted she would be rescued eventually. Now that help *had* arrived, she realised how close she had come to death.

'In a few more minutes we'll have you and Barbie safe on the bank with Mairi. But you'll need to be a brave girl for a few minutes more. Can you do that?'

Kirstie nodded vigorously. 'I . . . I'll try.'

'Good girl. I'll send you over first. Let me tie this around you. . . .'

Wyatt knotted the end of the cloth rope about Kirstie's body and signalled for Mairi to prepare to haul the child to safety.

Kirstie was frightened of entering the water, but gradually Wyatt coaxed her to the edge of the small island. When he was quite sure Mairi was ready, he pushed the girl in.

She disappeared beneath the surface of the water immediately. A few anxious seconds later Wyatt saw her surface in mid-channel. Spluttering and coughing, she struck out for the safety of the far bank, helped along by Mairi's strength at the other end of the rope.

Soon Mairi was helping Kirstie Munro ashore, hugging the child briefly before she returned her attention to Wyatt and the baby.

Little more than thirty feet separated Wyatt and the safety of the bank, but not until Mairi knotted a large stone on the end of the rope and made a number of desperate casts did the rope reach him.

Tying the cloth rope about his waist and holding Barbie Munro in his arms, Wyatt signalled to Mairi – and plunged into the water. He lost his footing almost immediately, and as the waters closed about him felt Barbie Munro struggling frantically in his arms. It seemed an eternity before his head rose above the surface of the water and he was able to fill his lungs with great gulps of air. There were a few more anxious moments when he felt the flimsy rescue-line tear, but by then he was able to gain a foothold. Coughing and choking, he was pulled to safety by Mairi.

Overjoyed at their success, Mairi took the baby from Wyatt's arms. Then he collapsed to his knees, coughing up water he was not aware of having swallowed.

Half an hour later, when they were no more than half a mile from Eskaig, the strangely garbed quartet were met by a party of villagers making their way up the flooded glen. In the lead were Lachlan and Ewan Munro.

Lachlan Munro was not fully recovered from his illness, and his experiences in the storm had done nothing to help his recovery. He staggered rather than walked at the head of the villagers, but when he saw his two daughters he discovered new strength and was the first to reach them.

'Thank God! Thank God!' was all the veteran of the Seventy-Second Regiment seemed capable of saying as he held the baby in one arm and hugged Kirstie to him with the other.

His initial relief over, Lachlan Munro began to express his gratitude to Wyatt.

'Mairi's the one you need to thank.' Wyatt was embarrassed by the veteran's tearful gratitude. 'Without her courage and knowledge of the glen we'd never have succeeded in rescuing the girls — and I think you owe her a dress.'

'I owe the both of you far more than I'll ever be able to repay.' Lachlan Munro clasped Mairi's hands, oblivious to the curious looks of the Eskaig villagers who had become aware that Mairi was wearing nothing beneath the preacher's coat. 'We'd given Kirstie and Barbie up for dead. . . .'

Lachlan Munro's voice broke, and Wyatt laid a comforting arm across the ex-soldier's shoulders. '*They're* both all right, but what about the others?'

Lachlan Munro turned a gaunt face up to Wyatt. 'I've never known such a storm, Captain. We were all washed away — yet the whole family is safe. It's little short of a miracle.'

'That's not the end of it, Lachlan. I've more good news for you. But it's news to be shared with the family. . . . Where *is* the family?'

'In Eskaig. In the churchyard.' Seeing Wyatt's shocked expression. Lachlan Munro said hastily: 'It's best for everyone, Captain. It's eviction for anyone who harbours those who've been turned off Lord Kilmalie's land. We're camped in the churchyard, but we're not short of food.'

Anger with John Garrett welled up inside Wyatt, but this was neither the time nor the place to air his views.

'You'll not sleep without a roof over your head again, Lachlan, but let's go and find your family. You'll sleep in the manse tonight. Tomorrow? Well, that's what I want to talk to you about. . . .'

CHAPTER SIX

THE VILLAGERS of Eskaig owned few possessions, but throughout that evening small gifts of food were brought to the manse for the Munro family. Mairi was loaned a dress by a sternly disapproving matron who saw her pass by wrapped only in Wyatt's loose and ill-fitting coat. Hurrying after the dishevelled party from the mountainside, the woman caught up with Mairi as she was about to enter the manse and thrust the dress at her.

'Here, girl. I've brought a dress for you to put on. You ought to be ashamed of yourself, parading through Eskaig half-naked. It's an affront to decent Christian folk. I don't know what your father can be thinking of, I'm sure. Before I ordered him inside the house my husband had seen more of you in a single minute than he's seen of me in thirty years of marriage.'

Careful not to smile, Wyatt said: 'Bless you for the kind thought. Mairi sacrificed her dress to make a rope with which to rescue young Kirstie Munro and her sister. I'm sure the good Lord will understand.'

'Perhaps. But it will be a while before she meets with Him. In the meantime she has to live with the folk of Eskaig. She'd never have dared flaunt herself so in front of Preacher Gunn – God rest his saintly soul.'

Biting back the retort that Minister Gunn had probably never been confronted with a similar situation, Wyatt said mildly: 'I'm sure you're right – and bless you once again for your kind thought. It's something I shall remember.'

When the woman departed her expression left no one in any doubt that ensuring Mairi was 'decently' attired was of more importance to her than the approbation of Eskaig's newly appointed minister.

Settling the Munro family in the manse for the night was no easy matter. There were only two bedrooms in the small house, and Wyatt turned them both over to the large family.

The children were given the largest bedroom, and in spite of his protests Lachlan Munro was put to bed in the other. The ex-soldier was swaying with fatigue but was reluctant to give in to his weakness until Wyatt forcibly led him from the room.

Returning to the living-room, Wyatt saw Mairi running a finger along the polished-wood sideboard that had probably been donated by a previous landowner.

'It's time you started for home, Mairi; it will be dark soon. Or would you prefer to stay and share a room with the girls?'

'I'll go home when I'm ready.' Mairi looked up and saw that Wyatt's concern for her was genuine. 'It's all right. I've been out after dark before.'

She looked down again at the polished sideboard beneath her finger. 'I've never seen such a piece of furniture as this. It's beautiful. Is it yours?'

Remembering the simple earthen-floored cot on the high land above Eskaig, Wyatt shoot his head. 'I've rarely stayed anywhere for long enough to accumulate possessions.'

'Is that why you've never married?'

Had the same question come from any other woman – from Evangeline Garrett – Wyatt would have expected it to be accompanied by a degree of coyness. But there was nothing coy about Mairi Ross. It was a perfectly straightforward question.

'I suppose it is. A soldier's life was not one to share with a wife.'

Mairi's chin came up immediately. 'Neither my father nor my mother would agree with you. They met in Spain. Pa was a Guardsman.'

The information that Eneas Ross had been a soldier did not surprise Wyatt. There were few true Highland men of his age who had not served in the British army, and Eneas Ross had both the build and proud bearing of a Guardsman.

'Your mother is Spanish?' It explained Mairi's dark, almost swarthy complexion, and the haughtiness that did not accord with the status of a barefoot mountain girl.

'My mother is a good woman. As good as any around these parts.' Mairi spoke with a fierce aggressiveness, as though it was a defence she had put forward on many occasions.

'I don't doubt it for one minute. I fought under a brave commanding officer in South Africa. He met his wife in Spain. She went with him wherever he fought and as well as being extremely brave was also one of the most charming women I've ever met.'

Much of Mairi's aggression left her. 'Minister Gunn never felt that way. He always spoke of Ma as "Eneas Ross's foreign woman". I overheard him once.' The defensiveness returned again. 'Pa says she was as brave as any man on the battlefield. More than one wounded soldier owed his life to her tending.'

'She can be proud of what *you've* done today, Mairi. You saved the lives of the Munro children. I'm sorry about your dress, though.'

Mairi shrugged. 'Kirstie and Barbie are more important than an old dress.' She smiled unexpectedly. 'It was worth it, just to see the look on the face of Laura Cameron.'

'Is she related to Angus Cameron, the Eskaig church elder?'

'His wife. They make a good pair.' Mairi brushed her fingers lightly along the highly polished top of the sideboard once more. 'My ma had furniture like this in her house, when she was a girl. She said it was so highly polished you could see your face in it.'

Mairi looked at Wyatt with an expression that combined bravado and uncertainty. It was as though she was used to having such statements challenged.

'She must have lived in a very grand house.'

Mairi nodded, satisfied she had made a favourable impression.

'You must bring her down to the village some time and call on me.'

Again there was a searching look from Mairi: an expression of uncertainty that was unusual in a girl who appeared to possess such confidence in herself.

'She'd like that. I must go now.'

'Of course. Thank you for guiding me through the storm, Mairi. I'd have been hopelessly lost – or worse – if it hadn't been for you. I and the Munros have much to thank you for.'

Mairi shrugged her shoulders in a bid to hide her pleasure. 'Lachlan or Elsa would have done the same for me – or for anyone else who needed help. They're nice people.'

'You're nice, too, Mairi. I've enjoyed your company. You'll be included in my prayers tonight – and for many nights to come.'

Mairi opened her mouth as though to say something in reply. Instead she turned quickly and hurried from the house.

Wyatt was left with a feeling that he had offended her in some way, and the thought made him unhappy. Mairi Ross was a strange girl. Seemingly straightforward, yet undoubtedly complicated. She would trouble his thoughts as few other girls ever had.

The Munro family moved into their new home the next day. Word had gone around that Lachlan Munro had been given the tenancy of the small croft, and men, women and children – many from the mountains – came to see the family move in.

They were treated to the sight of their minister with his coat off, working with Lachlan and young Ewan Munro to repair at least a section of the roof in order to give the family a few square feet of shelter against the heavy spring showers.

As Wyatt attempted to lift a weighty roof-timber into position on top of the stone wall of the cot, one of the onlookers climbed up beside him to offer his help. It was difficult even with two of them, and soon they were joined by two more men. Minutes later men and boys were swarming over the cot, raising timbers or carefully handing down reusable thatch to those still on the ground. Elsewhere, women and boys began gathering branches to lay on the timbers beneath the thatch.

Taking a breather some time later, Wyatt stood back from the path to allow two women carrying an old and heavy cooking-pot to pass him. He viewed the busy scene with great satisfaction. This was how a Highland parish should be: a community where neighbour helped neighbour, and families shared each other's triumphs and tragedies, joys and sorrows.

Yet, even as he took pleasure in the scene before him, Wyatt was aware that none of the men who had gathered at the Eskaig jetty to oppose his landing was here. These were, in the main, the crofters and cottars who eked out a precarious existence in the remoter glens of the mountains around Loch Eil.

Neither was there any intimation that Wyatt had yet been accepted by them. When the roof was completed each man shook

Lachlan's hand and wished him well. Some nodded to the new minister as they went on their way, others walked off without acknowledging his presence. Their message was clear. Wyatt would need to bide his time before he was accepted as the minister of Eskaig.

But time was not on Wyatt's side. That evening he returned home tired and grubby after carrying and laying black earth divots on the now-completed roof of Lachlan Munro's cottage. When still some distance from the manse he saw two riders cantering towards him along the narrow road.

Not until the riders drew close did he recognise John and Evangeline Garrett. The abrasive and loud-voiced factor was the last man Wyatt wished to meet at the end of such a tiring day, but he managed to find a smile in response to Evangeline's greeting.

'What the devil have you been up to?' John Garrett asked. 'It looks as though you've spent the day working in a peat bog.'

'You're not far wrong. I've been helping Lachlan Munro put a roof on his cottage.'

'That's a job for a cottar, not for the minister of Eskaig.'

'You're forgetting, I haven't been inducted here yet.'

'That's what Father's come to tell you about.' Evangeline spoke quickly, determined to head off any argument between the two men. 'He's heard from the presbytery. They're coming this Sunday to induct you.'

The presbytery was a church authority composed of ministers selected to act as the Church's governing body in a particular area.

'That's right,' added the Factor, 'and don't say anything more about being "accepted". That's all attended to. There'll be enough parishioners in church to speak for you on the day.'

'From your own household, no doubt?'

'Where they come from need not concern you. The presbytery will induct you – or Lord Kilmalie will demand an explanation.'

'We've arranged a celebration afterwards at the house,' said Evangeline. 'It will be a very special occasion. One you'll remember, I promise you.'

She was determined that neither Wyatt's dogma nor her father's arrogance would stand in the way of the party she had planned to celebrate Wyatt's induction to the living of Eskaig. She intended using the occasion to impress him with her skills as a hostess and her ability to organise such an occasion. She believed both were qualities a minister would look for when choosing a wife. Wyatt was the first eligible man she had met since coming to Scotland. He also happened to be the most attractive.

Not that Evangeline was certain she *wanted* to marry Wyatt. She had no intention of spending the rest of her life in such an outlandish place as this as the wife of a minister. But Wyatt had far more to recommend him than any other minister of the Church she had met with and he was an attractive man. Married to the right woman, one with ambitions for him, Wyatt Jamieson might one day become a bishop – or whatever it was they had in the Church of Scotland.

CHAPTER SEVEN

THE MORNING AFTER John Garrett's visit, Wyatt called at the house of Angus Cameron, lay preacher and senior elder of the Church in Eskaig. He had come to inform Cameron of his induction date and to request he be allowed to address a meeting of the elders.

Laura Cameron opened the door of the elder's small house and in answer to Wyatt's polite query said unhelpfully: 'Angus is having his breakfast. You'll need to come back later.'

'Who is it, Laura?' The voice of Angus Cameron came from a rear room of the cottage.

'It's the landlord's minister. I've told him you're having your breakfast.'

There was the sound of a chair scraping on a stone floor and then the church elder appeared, a napkin tucked in the neckband of his shirt. Clicking her tongue in noisy disapproval, Laura Cameron disappeared inside the house.

Wyatt had hoped a direct appeal to Angus Cameron might improve relations between them, but he knew he had little hope of succeeding in his mission when the elder kept him at the door without inviting him inside. It was a slight that was almost unprecedented in the hospitable Highlands and Islands of Scotland. Even the most ragged stranger could expect to be invited inside and offered refreshment when he called at a house.

'You're wasting your time, Minister.' Angus Cameron became aware of the napkin. Removing it self-consciously, he tucked it hurriedly into a pocket. 'It's nothing *personal*, you understand. You may be a very good pastor down in Glasgow, or wherever it is you come from, but here in Eskaig we intend to choose our own minister. We'll not have one foisted on us by a laird who hasn't so much as bothered to ask for our opinions. It's our entitlement. One of the first principles of our church.'

'I'm in full agreement with your views, Mr Cameron.' Wyatt's manner was deliberately placatory. 'As a minister of *our* church, yours and mine, I intend to uphold those principles. That's why I'm here to ask you to speak for me before the other elders. I *want* to be Eskaig's minister.'

'You're here as the *landlord's* choice. That's an end to it. As elders of the Church of Scotland we're not prepared to weaken on such an important principle.'

'Angus!' It was an impatient shrill-voiced call, and the elder started nervously. 'Don't you let your breakfast go cold.'

'There's no more to be said now. Leave Eskaig. Tell Lord Kilmalie we'll choose our own minister, in our own good time.'

When the door shut in his face Wyatt turned and walked away. He was deeply disappointed. He had hoped he might at least persuade Angus Cameron to let him plead his case before the elders. He had failed miserably. Angus Cameron might be ruled by his wife at home, but he was an important man in both the Church and the community. Without his support Wyatt had little chance of being accepted by the Eskaig congregation – and Wyatt's own principles and pride would not allow him to accept induction unless he believed he had the approval of a large section of the community.

Eskaig formed part of the ecclesiastical district of Abertarff, which came within the jurisdiction of the Synod of Glenelg. Many of the parishes were as vast and as scattered as Eskaig. As a result, some of the ministers who made up the presbytery needed to travel to Eskaig the day before Wyatt's induction in order to witness his acceptance by the congregation.

Seven ministers would be present for the induction ceremony. Three would arrive on the day, the other four the night before. Wyatt had prepared sleeping-quarters for all four, giving up his own bed to accommodate them.

He waited with some trepidation for the arrival of the clergymen, all senior ministers of the Church. He hoped to have an opportunity to talk to them before they met with Angus Cameron.

It was almost dark before a solitary figure dressed in the sober manner of a minister and mounted on an aged donkey rode up to the gate of the manse. The rider was a tall gangling man. So tall, it seemed to Wyatt he could have stood up and allowed the donkey to walk away from beneath his legs. Instead, the preacher made hard work of dismounting. It was not until the newcomer dropped his small bundle of belongings for the second time and had the greatest difficulty in retrieving it that Wyatt realised with a sense of shock that the only sober aspect of the tall preacher was his attire!

By the time Wyatt reached the gate the visiting preacher had retrieved his bundle and stood beaming benevolently at Wyatt.

'You'll be Minister Jamieson? I'm Coll Kennedy, minister at Letterfinlay. I've had a long ride to reach you, young sir. It's given me a powerful thirst.'

Wyatt shook the strong bony hand. 'You'll find something to drink on the sideboard inside the house.' There was a whole cask of whisky, brought by one of John Garrett's men with the compliments of Lord Kilmalie. 'I'll put your donkey in the churchyard: it's just what's needed to take the thistles down.'

'I'm gratified to find you have an understanding of the needs of your fellow-men, but don't stand behind that beast of mine. He has a kick that would floor a Church of England bishop. Keep clear of the other end of him, too: he's convinced he's part-crocodile. Why our Lord chose such a creature to take him on his last ride I'll never know. Perhaps it was symbolic. Something to do with sitting upon the devil. Yes . . . I must expand that theory in my church one day.'

Wyatt grinned. It was the first time his face had known a smile for many days. 'At least you're assured of a congregation to listen to you.'

Minister Coll Kennedy looked at Wyatt from beneath unruly eyebrows, and the eyes belied his unsteady gait. 'Remember your Bible, my son. "To every thing there is a season, and a time to every purpose under the heaven . . . a time to plant and a time to pluck up that which is planted." Have faith. Your time will come, as surely as day follows night.'

'I'm not lacking in faith, Coll, only the backing of the Eskaig elders.'

'Angus Cameron, you mean? Well, could be you're right. I travelled here with three ministers of the presbytery. They're spending the night at Angus's house. I declined his invitation. I like a man to be master in his own home. Besides, Angus Cameron's wife won't allow drink in the house.'

Coll Kennedy's news that the other three ministers were spending the night with Angus Cameron caused Wyatt to forget the visiting preacher's warning. The result was that he received a painful nip on the rump from the bad-tempered donkey.

When the animal had been released in the churchyard Wyatt leaned on the gate and gazed towards the church and the Highland mountains beyond. He saw nothing of the spring colours beginning to tint the lower slopes of the mountains. Doubtless Angus Cameron had already acquainted his house-guests from the presbytery of Eskaig's opposition to Wyatt's induction. If so, the outcome of tomorrow's ceremony was a foregone conclusion. The presbytery would refuse to induct Wyatt as minister for the parish of Eskaig, despite John Garrett's arrogant assertion.

Frustration welled up inside Wyatt. If only the people of Eskaig had been willing to give him a chance. . . . He enjoyed it here, and would have been a good pastor. Since first making his decision to enter the Church of Scotland, Wyatt had dreamed of returning to the Highlands and taking charge of his own community. Following in the footsteps of his father.

Wyatt believed it was too late now. The opportunity had come – and had slipped away from him. He wondered who would be chosen by the elders of Eskaig to take his place.

Coll Kennedy had found the whisky and helped himself to a generous measure. Beaming at Wyatt, he said: 'You'll have a dram with me? I don't enjoy drinking alone.'

Minister Kennedy's whole attitude belied the statement. He looked perfectly at ease relaxing in a chair with a tumbler of whisky. The presence or absence of his fellow-men was of little consequence to him.

'I don't drink much when I'm due to conduct an important service the next day, but as I'll no doubt be preaching in a church that would be empty if it weren't for the presbytery . . . why not?'

'You've found difficulty settling in Eskaig?'

'I could settle well enough, given half a chance. But I've been appointed by the landlord. I'm "the landlord's man". That's an end to it as far as the elders of Eskaig are concerned.'

Minister Coll Kennedy savoured his whisky, gazing at Wyatt over the rim of the glass. When he eventually lowered the tumbler and set it precariously on the narrow wooden arm of his chair, half the contents had gone.

'When it comes down to the truth of it we're *all* landlord's men, in one way or another, but you've a large parish, Wyatt. It doesn't begin and end in Eskaig village.'

'My induction is dependent upon those who are in the habit of attending the kirk. From what I've heard there's not been a man, woman or child from beyond Eskaig who's attended a service for years.'

'Certainly not while Minister Gunn was here. I got out of the habit of visiting Eskaig during *his* ministry.'

Wyatt was startled by the other preacher's revelation.

'I was given to understand everyone thought the world of Minister Gunn.'

'Many of those who lived about the loch *did*. Folk never saw much of him up in the mountains.'

Coll Kennedy's words reminded Wyatt of what Eneas Ross had said to him when Wyatt visited the tiny cottage on the mountain, before the storm.

'Perhaps I should have tried to persuade some of the crofters and cottars to come in and give me their support. But, as you've said, it's a large parish, and I *do* know the people. They don't make hasty decisions. It would take time to gain their trust. More time than the presbytery's given me.'

'From what I hear, you've already made a good start with some of those folk whom Preacher Gunn never met.' Coll Kennedy grinned at Wyatt's surprise. 'There's little goes on in the Highlands that a *good* minister doesn't know about within twenty-four hours. I think you should also know that the presbytery is here so quickly because we've been called in by the Eskaig elders. They're in agreement with you about one thing, at least. They say the kirk will be empty for the induction service tomorrow – and for every service held there until you're gone. It seems they're in an awful hurry to get you out and appoint a minister of their own – and I suspect Elder Cameron has some ambitions in that direction. You'd better pray that the good Lord has a wee miracle to spare for you tomorrow, Wyatt Jamieson.'

*　　*　　*

Sunday dawned grey and misty – and it did not get off to a good beginning for Wyatt. His first task of the day was to chase Coll Kennedy's donkey from the manse kitchen garden, but by the time he came out of the house the animal had devoured every scrap of greenery to within a finger's breadth of the ground.

Wyatt also had a throbbing headache. He had stayed up drinking and talking with Coll Kennedy until the early hours of the morning and was paying the penalty. Shivering and round-shouldered with cold, Wyatt thought it felt more like judgement day than induction day.

Coll Kennedy did not emerge from his room until a full hour later. In a voice that might have sawed a branch from an oak-tree he declared that unless he was conducting a service he made it a rule not to talk before ten o'clock.

At the hour when Coll Kennedy had promised to break his silence, Wyatt was standing in the shadows at the rear of the little Eskaig church, having spent some minutes on his knees by the grave of his father. Only the first two rows of pews were occupied. Seven seats were occupied by the church presbytery, the remainder by John Garrett, his family and household.

The factor, fully aware that the morning was likely to bring a showdown between the landlord he represented and the presbytery, was white-faced with anticipation. He was also seething with an anger aimed at the residents of Eskaig, each of whom was a tenant of Lord Kilmalie.

Aware of her father's mood, Evangeline managed to smile reassuringly at Wyatt whenever he glanced in her direction.

Wyatt did not return her smiles. He had never felt less inclined to a display of happiness. His fears about the residents of Eskaig were justified. They were rejecting him – and it seemed the presbytery were aware of the mood of the villagers. The three members who had spent the night in Elder Cameron's house had acknowledged Wyatt with only the most perfunctory of nods, apparently anxious to save themselves from later embarrassment.

'Are you quite certain you informed folks of the time of your induction, Mr Jamieson?' The question came from a bowed bespectacled preacher who was stricken with an advanced muscular disease that had caused a crippling curvature of his spine. In spite of such a disability, the preacher had set out before dawn that morning to walk ten miles to Eskaig from Spean Bridge.

'They know the time.' Wyatt battled with a foolish urge to brazen things out, to accept nomination from the handful of retainers brought to the church by John Garrett for the occasion. 'The people of Eskaig have made their thinking clear. I'll not oppose them. You can inform the presbytery I'll leave the manse and return on the next boat to call at Eskaig. . . .'

John Garrett could contain his impatience no longer. Unable to hear what was passing between the two preachers he rose from his seat and approached the pulpit beneath which Wyatt was standing, while the bent and twisted preacher made his painful way to where the other presbytery members sat quietly talking among themselves.

'What's happening? Why hasn't the induction begun?'

'There'll be no induction. The Eskaig people have made their wishes clear.'

'Damn the people of Eskaig!' The factor's outburst echoed from the walls of the church and caused the heads of presbytery members to turn in his direction, shock registered upon their faces.

If John Garrett noticed, he ignored their outrage. 'What the people of Eskaig want doesn't matter. The courts of this country have made that quite clear. They're tenants, every one of them. They'll do whatever Lord Kilmalie tells them — and he's sent *you* here as his minister.'

'The Church of Scotland acknowledges only one Lord — and He's not a peer of any *earthly* realm.'

Hot blood suffused the angry factor's face, but before he could say more Coll Kennedy suddenly cried: 'Hush, everybody! Can you hear what I hear?'

For a moment Wyatt could hear nothing. Then a sound was carried to the church on the wind. It was a sound that had always been capable of stirring his blood, no matter where he heard it. But never before had it carried such meaning as it did now.

What he could hear was the sound of that most ancient of Scots musical instruments, the bagpipes. But this was not the instrument played by lowlanders, or at weddings or clan festivities. The sound he heard came from the great war-pipes, the instrument used to lead Highland regiments into battle, and the piper was playing a 'gathering' tune: a summons for all men within hearing to assemble in readiness for war! It was a sound that had last echoed across the waters of Loch Eil almost a hundred years before, when Prince Charles Stuart returned to Scotland to claim the throne that was rightfully his.

Wyatt was the first out of the church. John Garrett was a close second, with the presbytery a straggling third.

Uncharacteristically speechless, John Garrett's mouth dropped open at sight of the motley throng advancing along the road through Eskaig, heading towards the church.

'What the devil. . . .' John Garrett found his tongue, but could think of no more words to say.

'It has nothing to do with the devil.' Wyatt was fighting hard to maintain some composure as the piper turned off the road to the church and the crowd followed. 'I believe you're looking at a God-sent army. His answer to a humble man's prayer.'

Beyond the advancing 'army', Wyatt could see residents at every door along the single narrow street of Eskaig.

At the church entrance the stirring notes of the 'gathering' died a discordant death as the piper removed the pipe from between his lips and the crowd came to a halt. Among them and well to the fore were Eneas Ross, his wife and eight sons, as well as Mairi and Tibbie. Lachlan Munro was here, too, with his whole family. Lachlan, holding himself proudly erect, was being imitated by his son.

There were many other men, women and children, too, most of them strangers to Wyatt. When the pipes fell silent there was a brief moment of uncertainty before Lachlan Munro stepped forward and approached Wyatt.

'We've come to see you inducted, Captain, and to sign the call for you if need be.'

Angus Cameron and half a dozen men of similar age had hurried to the church in pursuit of the piper and his followers. They arrived in time to hear Lachlan Munro's words. The church elder elbowed his way through the Highland cottars until he confronted the ministers of the presbytery who stood together in a bemused huddle.

'You can't listen to the cottars. Not one of them has seen the inside of a kirk for years. Their children haven't been baptised – and half are wedded only by declaration, not by the Church.'

'Then, it would seem Eskaig has sore need of an active minister,' commented Coll Kennedy drily. 'Unless the cottars have been excluded, they've as much right as anyone else in Eskaig to sign the call.'

'Minister Gunn would have had to know of our existence before he could exclude us,' said a heavily pregnant Highland woman. 'He never came up to the hills to find us – and we all knew there was no welcome for us down here.'

'Do you live within the parish? All of you?'

The presbytery minister's question was answered by Eneas Ross in a voice that defied all argument.

'There have been Rosses in the mountains about Loch Eil for longer than there's been a village of Eskaig. We prayed to God before ever Lord Kilmalie raised a kirk here.'

'The Rosses have never been anything but outlaws and sheep-stealers. You may live here, Ross, but you're not one of us and you never will be – not while you share your house with a papist woman.'

Encas Ross stretched out both his arms to hold back his angry sons before advancing upon Angus Cameron. He stopped when no more than a forearm's length separated him from the other man.

'We're both old men, Angus. Neither of our lives is worth a hanging. If it wasn't so, I'd slit you from belly to throat just to prove there's no more in you than I'd expect to find in a chicken. Magdalene has a name you'll find in your bible and when I married her she wasn't old enough to know the difference between a papist and a Methodist. Her lack of knowledge never prevented her from saving my life and the lives of many good Christian Highlanders on the battlefields of Spain. Some of the men she saved are here today to testify to the truth of what I'm saying. Since then she's given me eight live sons and a daughter. *All* would have been baptised inside the Church of Scotland if it hadn't been for you and Preacher Gunn. Magdalene is as good a Christian as any Scots man or woman here – and better than many. Minister Jamieson is the first preacher from Eskaig – or anywhere else for that matter – to step over the threshold of my cot and already he's done more for Kilmalie tenants than Preacher Gunn did in all his years at Eskaig. We're here to sign the call for him. He's the man *we* want.'

The presbyters looked uncertainly at the elder who had been host to three of their number the previous night, but Coll Kennedy was the first to speak.

'It's a good shepherd who can return such long-lost sheep to the fold, brethren. We came to Eskaig to induct a new minister. Shall we go inside and perform our duty?'

Avoiding looking at the Eskaig elders, the ministers of the presbytery filed inside the small church, followed by a congregation large enough to occupy a full half of the pews. Soon only Wyatt and the elders remained outside the church, Angus Cameron standing apart from the others, an ageing and disconsolate figure.

Acting on a sudden impulse, Wyatt crossed to the senior Eskaig elder. 'I don't expect you to sign the call for me, Mr Cameron, but won't you at least come inside for the service? You're an elder. It's *your* church. . . .'

'Yes, I'm still an elder and I've supported the Church in Eskaig all my life. . . .' There was deep bitterness in Angus Cameron's voice. 'I never thought I'd live to see the day when papists and unbelievers would be welcomed into the kirk where I was baptised and married, and where I expected to have a prayer said for me when I died. I'll not set foot inside this kirk again until Eskaig has a minister who's been called by the elders – his call witnessed by decent God-fearing folk.'

Angus Cameron had suffered an unexpected and humiliating defeat, but when he turned his back on the small grey-stone church and walked away he maintained a fragile dignity.

All except two of the elders followed Angus Cameron, and those who stayed seemed uncertain of what to do. Then, with glances directed at the ground beneath their feet, they walked past Wyatt and into the church. With one last regretful glance after Angus Cameron and his companions, Wyatt followed, to accept his call as minister of Eskaig.

CHAPTER EIGHT

OVER THE NEXT FEW WEEKS Wyatt steadily consolidated his position as Eskaig's pastor. Cottars still came down from the surrounding hills to attend Sunday services in the lochside church, but their numbers were not as great as they had been for Wyatt's induction day. He knew, too, that when winter weather closed in on the Highlands they would remain in their cottages, cut off from the outside world. But now the villagers from Eskaig were beginning to return to their church. On Sundays when Wyatt stood in his pulpit and looked down at the upturned faces of his congregation he was able to count all but two of the Eskaig elders in the congregation.

Wyatt had won his unsought battle with Angus Cameron, but the absence from church of the most senior of the Eskaig elders gave him no pleasure. However, Wyatt had little time to fret about the stubborn Angus Cameron. There were many other matters to claim his attention. The boundaries of Wyatt's parish were no more than lines drawn with a pen on a far from accurate map in the offices of the Moderator of the Church of Scotland. In secret glens among the mountains, far from roads and tracks, were men and women who had never been visited by a minister and children who had never seen the inside of a church. It was a situation Wyatt was determined to rectify. His was a Highland parish, peopled by a hardy and independent people. Wyatt was determined that God would be as proud of them as he was.

There was also work of a more mundane nature to be undertaken. Preacher Gunn had been a weary and dispirited old man for the last few years of his life, and the garden of the manse had been sadly neglected. Wyatt set out to restore it to some form of order.

One warm evening he was clearing brambles from what he intended would one day be a vegetable patch. It was hot work, and Wyatt was working stripped to shirt and trousers.

Suddenly, Wyatt heard a shout. Looking up from his work, he wiped perspiration from his eyes and saw young Ewan Munro running towards him along the loch-side track. The speed with which the boy moved was proof that his leg had healed well. By the time Ewan reached the manse he was hotter than Wyatt, perspiration vying with dirt on his face, and so excited and breathless that his speech was unintelligible.

Wyatt suggested that Ewan recover his breath before attempting to explain his excitement, but after a breath-holding half-minute the boy would have burst had he not spoken.

'Minister . . . there's a man . . . down by the loch . . . caught . . . in one of the factor's man-traps. He's . . . lost a foot.'

Wyatt looked at Ewan in appalled disbelief. 'A *man-trap*! Are you sure?'

Ewan Munro nodded his head vigorously. 'Factor Garrett sets them . . . along the edge of the loch. Everyone knows where they are . . . but this man's a stranger. He . . . he swears well.'

'Show me where you saw him.'

Wyatt propelled Ewan Munro from the garden with a hand on his shoulder, then set off after him at a trot. He was horrified to learn that Lord Kilmalie's factor was setting man-traps. No amount of poaching justified such methods of prevention.

It was hardly surprising that Ewan Munro had been out of breath by the time he reached the manse. The boy led Wyatt alongside the loch for more than a mile. Skirting Eskaig village, he plunged into the undergrowth that grew to the edge of the loch.

There were many gorse-bushes, but by now Wyatt could hear a man's voice raised in what sounded like extreme pain. Ignoring the needle-like leaves of the yellow-flowering gorse that drew blood from his bare arms, Wyatt forced his way towards the victim of John Garrett's anti-poaching methods.

The gorse parted in front of Wyatt, and he stumbled into a large clearing at the water's edge. Here he found the man-trap 'victim'.

Squatting upon the ground, one of the man's trouser-legs hung in tatters. He had certainly lost the lower part of one leg. Yet he seemed more concerned with removing pine-needles from his hand and was cursing in the manner of a man more angry than hurt.

Wyatt looked again at the empty trouser-leg and observed there was not a speck of blood to be seen.

The unknown stranger looked up and scowled as Wyatt approached. He was a hairy man, and it was difficult to see where the man's red beard ended and his hair began. Even the man's eyebrows seemed to entangle themselves in the hair about them. But the blue eyes beneath the hairy brow were bright blue, alert – and angry.

'Was it you who set that abominable machine?' He pointed to where a huge rusting trap lay upon the ground, its ugly teeth of tempered steel clamped tightly together.

Wyatt shook his head, still puzzled. 'Ewan came to me with a story that there was a stranger here who'd lost a foot in a man-trap.'

'And so I have! Why else do you think I'd be crawling around like a baby, getting gorse-needles in my hands and knees?'

As the man spoke he moved to a more comfortable sitting position, and a splintered wooden stump emerged from the torn trouser-leg.

'It's a *wooden* leg!' Wyatt's frown cleared, and a slow grin filled with relief took its place.

The stranger's fleeting grin matched Wyatt's own as he looked across the clearing to where Ewan Munro stood in wide-eyed puzzlement. 'Did you believe it was my *real* leg I'd lost? No, laddie. I lost my leg under a Glasgow cart many years ago – and made enough fuss when it happened to be heard up here. Even so, without my peg-leg I'm as helpless as a landed tadpole.'

'Let me give you a hand to stand. Put an arm about my shoulders, and I'll help you back to the manse. Thank God it wasn't the leg He gave you that was caught in that contraption. I'll have words with the factor about this.'

'You're a *minister*?' Now it was the turn of the one-legged man to be surprised.

'That's right.' Aware of the manner in which he was dressed, Wyatt added: 'I was doing a spot of gardening.'

When the other man was standing balanced on his good leg and leaning heavily against him, Wyatt said: 'I don't think I've seen you hereabouts. Who are you, and what are you doing here?'

'If you were anyone else but a minister of the Church, I'd tell you to mind your own business. As you're who you are, and as likely as not will let me fall to the ground if I offend you, I'll answer your questions. The name's Alasdair Burns. I'm a migratory creature, like the birds of the air. Once I, too, was a factor, though I set no man-traps. More recently I've been a man of letters. In winter you'll find me teaching school in Glasgow, but in summer I'm a free man. Free to roam the Highlands and enjoy God's handiwork.'

'Not to mention the proprietor's salmon.' Wyatt nodded to where a neatly wound fishing-line lay in the grass.

'I've never seen it before, Minister. But as it would appear to have been abandoned it would be a sin to leave it to rot away. Boy . . . you'll find a bag beneath the bushes. Put the line inside and bring the bag to me – and close your mouth, or someone is likely to mistake *you* for a fish and feed you a hook.'

Ewan Munro had never seen a man with a peg-leg before and he had been gaping in wonderment at Alasdair Burns. Now he hurried to obey the stranger's orders.

Shrugging the bag to his shoulder, the Glasgow schoolteacher leaned heavily on Wyatt and said: 'Lead me where you will, Minister. Without my leg I'm no more than a human wheelbarrow, going in whichever direction you've a mind to push me. But if you've a good piece of cherrywood at your manse, or oak even, I'll carve myself a new pinion. Then I'll give the best young runner ten paces' start and catch him over a hundred yards.'

As they forced their way clear of the undergrowth, Alasdair Burns asked: 'What manner of man is this proprietor of yours that he'd set man-traps around the edge of a loch? It might as easily have been a wee child trod on that thing. A bairn's leg is worth more than all the salmon in Scotland.'

'This is the factor's doing. He has more power than is good for any man in his position. Ewan, do you know of any other man-traps?'

'Every one of them. I followed Garrett's men when they set them.'

'Go and spring them with a stout stick. But be careful. We want no more accidents.'

Ewan Munro looked scared, and Wyatt added: 'If anyone sees

you doing it, tell them you're acting on my instructions. *I'll* take it up with John Garrett. He knows they're illegal as well as do I.'

As Ewan Munro hurried away, relishing the thought of carrying out Wyatt's instructions, the one-legged man came to a halt.

'I need to rest for a moment or two. Sit me down on that rock over there.'

Seated on a boulder at the edge of the path, Alasdair Burns took out a coloured kerchief and mopped his brow. Looking curiously at Wyatt, he said: 'There are few ministers in Scotland who would take such a bold stand against their patron's factor – especially when the law is on the other side. Those traps were on the proprietor's land, and set to catch poachers.'

'As you said yourself, what are a few salmon when compared with a child's leg? Such traps are fiendish.'

'Not when used against Highlanders, surely? Most landlords have yet to be convinced Highlanders are human.'

'*I'm* a Highlander.'

'Then, I've no need to tell *you* what such folk think, Minister. You'll know it well enough for yourself. All right, I'm ready to go on now.'

Alasdair Burns needed to rest on a number of occasions before being helped inside the manse. Wyatt realised that the Glaswegian schoolteacher was neither as strong nor as fit as he pretended to be. Easing the bag containing his belongings to the floor, the one-legged man lowered himself to the dubious comfort of a wooden armchair and laid his head back gratefully.

'I'll find some whisky for you. That should make you feel better.'

'Give me a fine cup of tea instead and I'll be dancing a reel for you within the hour.'

Collapsed in the chair with head thrown back and eyes closed, Alasdair Burns's appearance belied his brave words.

The kettle was steaming gently at the edge of the fire, and Wyatt made a cup of strong sweet tea and handed the cup to the weary one-legged man.

'Get this down you. While you're drinking I'll look for some wood in the barn. I think I saw some unused roof-timbers there. I don't know what wood it is, but it's well seasoned.'

'Ah! You're a true man of God, Minister. May He shower blessings upon you.'

Alasdair Burns knocked back half the scalding-hot tea in one long swallow and made appreciative noises. He was downing the second half when Wyatt left the house and made his way to the barn.

As Wyatt searched for a piece of wood that would be suitable for a wooden leg, he thought about his strange visitor. Alasdair Burns's speech and vocabulary confirmed his story that he was an educated man, but his clothes and general health were not those of a man who had been in a well-paid and prestigious post until recently.

When Wyatt returned to the manse with a piece of good seasoned wood Alasdair Burns had drunk his tea. He agreed with no show of reluctance to a second cup and declared the piece of timber would provide him with an artificial limb far superior to the one he had lost in the jaws of Factor Garrett's man-trap.

That evening Wyatt tackled Alasdair Burns as the one-legged man was sitting on the doorstep of the manse fashioning his new artificial leg. Wyatt put the questions that had been bothering him since receiving the brief explanation of his visitor's history prior to his arrival at Eskaig.

'Where was it you said you were teaching school this past winter?'

Alasdair Burns's knife ceased whittling at the wood momentarily, then it resumed working with increased vigour.

'You're an inquisitive man, Minister. I didn't say.'

Wyatt waited for the one-legged man to amplify his terse matter-of-fact statement. When it became evident that nothing more was forthcoming, he asked: 'Where *were* you teaching?'

'Glasgow Green.'

Wyatt frowned. 'I can recall no school at Glasgow Green – although I visited the gaol there on more than one occasion.'

'I see you're familiar with Glasgow, Minister.'

'I'm also familiar with Glasgow politics, Mr "Burns". I recall a certain Chartist meeting being broken up by the Army because the speaker was preaching sedition. If my memory is not at fault, there were at least three deaths and as many injuries. The speaker was himself seriously hurt, falling under a wagon and losing a foot when pursued by cavalrymen. I understand it was this alone that saved him from transportation – or the gallows. He was sentenced to imprisonment instead. His name was Alasdair, too, but not Burns. It was . . . Anderson, I believe.'

'There's nothing wrong with your memory, Minister. The name was indeed Anderson. Alasdair Burns Anderson. For the time being I find it more expedient to use the name my mother brought with her into matrimony, rather than the proud name my father believes I have irrevocably besmirched.'

'How true is the remainder of your story?'

'True enough. Since I stopped serving landowners I've been teaching school in winter and spending my summers here in the Highlands. At least, that's what I did before I went to prison. Now there's not a school in the country would employ me.'

'How do you manage to live?'

Alasdair Burns shrugged. 'By poaching fish from the lochs or snaring deer or rabbits when I'm in the hills. I get by during the summer months and worry about winter when it happens. For the moment I'm simply enjoying my freedom. A prison cell is hard on a man used to breathing the free air of the Highlands.'

When Wyatt made no further reply, Alasdair Burns began whittling the piece of roof-timber once more. Frowning in apparent concentration, he asked: 'What happens now you know my secret? Shall you be telling the authorities about me? Or will you leave me to go on my way in peace as soon as I've fashioned a new leg?'

'Your presence is of no interest to the authorities hereabouts. You're a free man now and can go wherever you've a mind. But I've a proposition I'd like you to consider.'

'A proposition?' Alasdair Burns eyed Wyatt cautiously. 'I'm a mite suspicious of ministers' "propositions". A preacher in Glasgow gaol "proposed" I should write a full confession – implicating my fellow-Chartists, of course. He suggested it was "for the good of my soul".'

'I'll tackle your soul in due course. Right now I'm more interested in your skills. We're in sore need of a teacher in Eskaig. If I can persuade Lord Kilmalie to pay for a school and a house to be built, would you stay here and teach?'

Expressions of disbelief and pleasure struggled with each other for possession of Alasdair Burns's face. 'You'd trust me, a convicted Chartist, to teach school in your parish?'

'I've never considered Chartism to be particularly treasonable, although I'd expect you to keep your beliefs to yourself and not take them inside the classroom.'

'You need have no fear of that, Minister. Your Highlanders have troubles enough without me adding to them.'

'Then, you'll stay on in Eskaig?'

Forgetting his artificial leg was broken, Alasdair Burns made a move to stand up. When realisation came he clung to the door-frame and extended his hand to Wyatt.

'You won't regret your trust in me, Minister. I'm a good teacher. A *damned* good teacher — begging your pardon. Eskaig will have the finest school in the Highlands.'

Wyatt accepted Alasdair Burns's hand. 'I don't doubt it. But you'll need to trim that beard and your hair before I introduce you to my church elders. At the moment you look more like a marooned pirate than a teacher.'

CHAPTER NINE

WYATT SHARED LOCH EIL and a fine Highland morning with a pair of sea-eagles. Perched in the moss-covered skeleton of a waterside tree, the birds contemplated the prospects of a new day's hunting on the sparkling loch. On either side the mountains had shed the last vestiges of winter snow. Only Ben Nevis, aloof and superior, retained its white-capped dignity.

But the beauty of his surroundings failed to influence Wyatt's mood as he made his way to the factor's house. Ewan Munro had sprung seven man-traps the previous evening. Wyatt was angered by the thought of what might have happened had a small child strayed into the powerful jaws of the undiscriminating device.

It was still early when Wyatt reached John Garrett's house, but he was surprised to be informed by a dour, heavily built servant-woman that the factor had not yet left his bed.

When Wyatt asked whether Evangeline and Mrs Garrett were also in their rooms he was told, equally dourly: 'Mrs Garrett and Miss Evangeline have gone to Glasgow on a visit. If you want to know any more about the family's business, you'd best wait and ask the factor for yourself. I'm only a servant – and in this house a servant learns to keep her own counsel. I'll knock on Mr Garrett's door and tell him you're here, that's all.'

With a sniff that expressed disapproval for the world in which she lived, the heavily built servant waddled away to haul herself up the stairway with the aid of the ornate balustrade.

Waiting downstairs in the hallway, Wyatt heard voices from somewhere on the first floor. First the servant's voice, then John Garrett's – and another he did not recognise. There was the sound of a door slamming, and moments later the servant made equally heavy work of descending the stairway. She paused at the bottom to say breathlessly: 'Mr Garrett knows you're here. He'll no doubt be down in a minute or two.'

It was in fact a full ten minutes before John Garrett made his way down the stairs to the hallway. Puffy-faced and dark-jowled, the factor's first words provided evidence of his ill-humour.

Addressing Wyatt, he snapped: 'What the devil are *you* doing here at such an hour? Has there been an earthquake that's tumbled Eskaig in the loch? No, that's *too* much to hope for. Well, spit it out, man, what is it?'

'Your first words weren't far off the mark, Mr Garrett. I'm here to talk about instruments of the devil. Man-traps.'

John Garrett stiffened. 'What about man-traps? Don't tell me *you've* stepped in one. No, of course you haven't, or you'd not be standing here on two good legs.'

'Those traps of yours could sever a child's leg. They're diabolical. I've had them all sprung. If I hear of any being set again, I'll personally heave them into the loch.'

'You'll do *what*?' His face flushing angrily, John Garrett took a pace forward, and for a moment Wyatt thought the factor would lay hold of him.

Instead John Garrett thrust his face to within inches of Wyatt's and said angrily: 'Lord Kilmalie's appointed you to look after souls. I'm here to take care of his lands and business interests. I haven't interfered with your duties, Minister – and, by God, I'll not have you interfering with mine. Poachers are robbing Lord Kilmalie of his fish and his deer. My job is to prevent them, using whatever means I believe best.'

'There's no beast or fish worth the leg of a child, and that's what your traps will claim before long. I've told you of my actions; I'll explain my reasons in a letter to Lord Kilmalie. I'll be asking for land and money to build a school at the same time. Meanwhile you can recover your traps from the loch, when you've a mind.'

Wyatt reached the door before John Garrett found his voice again. 'What's all this about a school?'

'It's time there was a school in Eskaig. I intend opening one.'

'What for? There's nothing in Eskaig for an educated Highlander. There's nothing here for *any* Highlander. Their time is over.

Educating them will only cause discontent. Let them go to where there's work for an educated man and get their learning there.'

This time Wyatt was out of the house before Garrett called to him again. 'Look, Jamieson, I'm not an unreasonable man. I'm willing to meet you halfway. Drop your idea of a school and I'll take up all the man-traps.'

Wyatt was intrigued yet puzzled to know why the factor was so opposed to having a school at Eskaig, but he was not prepared to drop the idea.

'I'm not an unreasonable man, either, Garrett, but there *will* be a school in Eskaig *and* I'll see there are no traps around the loch or anywhere else on Lord Kilmalie's lands.'

'Then, you can go to hell! But remember: it's not only ministers who can write letters.'

The door of John Garrett's house slammed shut behind Wyatt, but he did not look back. Neither did he return immediately to Eskaig. Once on the rough road, out of sight of the factor's house, but within view of the gate at the end of the long drive, Wyatt settled down to wait.

Twenty minutes later a young girl walked from the driveway and turned in Wyatt's direction. Small and slightly plump, she had the freckles and pale colouring that often went with light ginger hair. She also had a bold glance and turned it upon Wyatt when he rose to his feet and fell in beside her.

'I didn't ask for your company.' She spoke in Gaelic.

'Neither did John Garrett. I expect he found you a much more agreeable companion.'

'Oh! Then, you'll be Minister Jamieson?'

'That's right. Who are you?'

'Seonaid. Seonaid Fraser. And you've cost me a good breakfast.'

'I doubt you'll fade away from hunger. But you're not from Eskaig.' Wyatt had not seen the girl in the village or in his church.

'I'm from up there.' Her hand waved vaguely in the direction of the mountains behind Eskaig. 'My father has a croft.'

Albeit vaguely, the girl had indicated the high lands to the east of the Ross holding. Wyatt had heard this area had been cleared of tenants long before his coming to Eskaig. He said as much to Seonaid Fraser.

The girl turned a bold look on him again, and this time it also held a challenge. 'You heard right. Everyone was turned off the land — except my father. He'd have gone along with the rest, had I not gone down on my knees to the factor. He let us stay — for a price.'

'I see. . . . And you're the price?'

There was defiance in the boldness now. 'I suppose you're going to tell me it's wrong to want my father to end his days in the house where he was born. To stay in the only home he's ever known, and be buried beside my mother when he comes to the end of his days.'

'You don't need *me* to tell you you're doing wrong, Seonaid, whatever the reason. You're breaking God's commandments. Surely your father can't want this for you? What happens when he dies? What will you do then?'

'I'll probably stick a knife in the factor and take to the mountains.' Seonaid Fraser spoke matter-of-factly, but with a vehemence that suggested she might do exactly as she said. 'That's if his wife doesn't do it first. She's crazy enough at times.'

'Does Garrett's wife know what's going on?'

The Highland girl snorted derisively. 'I doubt if there's anyone about here except you who doesn't know what I'm doing — or *why* I'm doing it.'

Wyatt was shaken by Seonaid Fraser's admission and her candidness. Highland girls in general led a more free-and-easy life than lowland girls or those who lived in towns or villages, but they rarely flouted convention so openly as this girl.

'I'll leave you here, Minister Jamieson. That's my way home.' Seonaid Fraser pointed to a path that wound its way towards a saddle between two peaks.

Troubled with his thoughts, Wyatt knew he should have said far more to the freckle-faced girl. Should have been able to present an infallible argument against what she was doing. But the argument eluded him for the moment.

'I'll come to visit you and your father soon.'

'You won't tell him what I'm doing?' Suddenly the brazen woman of the world disappeared and a young concerned girl stood in her place.

'So *he* doesn't know, either? Where does he think you were last night?'

'Nursing a sick friend.'

'What would happen if he came to Eskaig looking for you and someone told him the truth?'

'He never leaves home. He's been totally blind since the year I was born.'

'Oh!' Wyatt looked again at the young freckle-faced girl, and this time he saw the worry-lines around her eyes. 'Nothing can make what you're doing right, Seonaid, but I'll not be the one to tell your father.'

Deeply troubled by his thoughts, Wyatt had turned to go when Seonaid Fraser's voice brought him to a halt.

'Minister. . . .' When Wyatt responded to her call the girl appeared embarrassed, as though not certain she ought to have spoken.

'What is it?'

'The factor sent me away because he said he has a letter to write to Lord Kilmalie . . . about you.'

'I never doubted that's what he would do, but thank you.' Garrett was wasting no time in putting his case before Lord Kilmalie.

'He's a dangerous man. He hounded Preacher Gunn to his grave. He'll try to do the same to you.'

Her warning delivered, Seonaid Fraser walked away from him and struck out up the side of the mountain, heading for her home and the blind father waiting for her there.

CHAPTER TEN

LORD KILMALIE'S REPLIES to the letters sent by both Wyatt and John Garrett were brought to Eskaig by Evangeline. In Edinburgh with her mother, the girl had paid a courtesy call on the Eskaig landowner and had been closely questioned about happenings on the Highland estate before being asked to act as Lord Kilmalie's messenger.

This news was told to Wyatt by Evangeline when she delivered his letter on the evening of her return. The tone of the letter was almost abrupt. The absent landlord told Wyatt he had not been sent to Eskaig to begin a war with the factor. John Garrett was entrusted with the running of the estate; Wyatt was expected to take care of the spiritual needs of the tenants.

Having made this clear, Lord Kilmalie went on to say he did not agree with the use of man-traps and had ordered John Garrett to destroy all those he had. As for the school, the landlord had suggested at least ten years before that a school should be provided for the local children. He had authorised both land and funds for this purpose. He had not realised until now that his suggestion had not been implemented, but he accepted the factor's excuse that no teacher had been available at the time. Now Wyatt was authorised to choose an acre of land for the school and grounds. Lord Kilmalie had instructed his factor to arrange for a school and schoolmaster's house to be built on the land, all expenses to be met by the estate.

There was a strange, rather rambling paragraph at the end of the letter which Wyatt did not fully understand. The Eskaig landowner decreed that the land required for the new school and house would be given to Wyatt and not to the Church. He gave as his reason the fact that the Church was no longer an unchanging institution upon which both State and people could rely implicitly. Lord Kilmalie ended by saying he felt quite certain Wyatt would understand what he was saying and, when the time came, would act accordingly.

Wyatt did *not* understand, but he was delighted that the landlord had granted his request for a school. It was an important step forward for the people of Eskaig and the surrounding district.

When Wyatt showed the letter to Evangeline she hinted that it was couched in friendlier tones than the letter received by her father. Evangeline also expressed her support for Wyatt in the matter of the man-traps. She had been deeply shocked to learn her father had been party to their use, and the incident had provoked an unusually heated argument between father and daughter.

All the time Wyatt was reading the letter, Evangeline had been clutching a small wrapped package. Now she thrust it at Wyatt and said, almost shyly: 'I've brought you a present.'

'You've brought a present for *me*? What is it?'

'Open it and you'll see.'

'You shouldn't have spent your money on me. . . .' As he spoke, Wyatt was removing the paper from the carefully wrapped package. 'Evangeline, it's a *wonderful* present. How can I possibly thank you enough . . . ?' In his hand he held a prayer-book bound in dark red leather and embellished with gold.

Wyatt leaned forward and kissed Evangeline on the cheek, and for a few moments her cheeks were the colour of the prayer-book.

'What induced you to buy such a lovely thing for me?'

Evangeline's shrug could not hide the pleasure she felt. 'I remembered the old prayer-book you carried for your induction. I thought you'd like a new one.'

The prayer-book used by Wyatt for his induction had belonged to his father, but he did not enlighten Evangeline.

'When will you make a start on your school?'

'Right away. There's a site next to the church that will be ideal. I'll speak to your father about it tomorrow.'

'There's no need. He said that as far as he's concerned you can build it wherever you like. He didn't use such polite words, but that was only to be expected. He was upset by Lord Kilmalie's letter. But where will you find a teacher?'

'I have one staying in the manse with me right now. He's from Glasgow.'

'Oh!' This time Evangeline was slower to hide her feelings, and Wyatt realised with a sense of surprise that she was disappointed.

'Come and meet him. He's an interesting man.'

'I . . . I don't think I will.'

'Come on. I'm sure you'll find him as intriguing as I do. . . .'

At that moment Alasdair Burns solved the problem of whether or not Evangeline would meet him. Evangeline and Wyatt had been standing inside the garden gate of the manse, and suddenly Alasdair Burns appeared at the door of the house.

'I've a brew of tea made if you've a mind for— Oh! I'm sorry, Wyatt. I didn't realise you were talking to someone.'

'That's all right, Alasdair. I was about to come in to fetch you. I'd like you to meet Evangeline Garrett, the factor's daughter.'

Alasdair Burns's smile froze. 'The daughter of the man whose trap took off my leg?'

An expression of horror came to Evangeline's face as her glance dropped to Alasdair Burns's false leg, and Wyatt hastened to explain.

Angry at her own wasted sympathy, Evangeline snapped: 'I strongly disapprove of their use, but I believe the traps were set in places frequented by poachers. What were you doing there, Mr Burns? It's a long way from Glasgow, and there are no schools about Loch Eil.'

'That's a situation we're fortunately able to rectify,' Wyatt said hurriedly. 'Evangeline's brought me a letter from Lord Kilmalie. He's agreed we can have our school.'

Alasdair Burns was delighted. As Evangeline looked on in disapproval at his familiarity, he gripped Wyatt's hand and said enthusiastically: 'It's *wonderful* news, Wyatt. A triumph, no less. I never expected your Lord Kilmalie to agree – not after all else you had to tell him in your letter. It's wonderful news indeed.'

A warm friendship had grown up between the two men during the two weeks Alasdair Burns had been staying at the manse, and the travelling schoolteacher was genuinely pleased for the Minister. In secret he had feared that if it came to a showdown Lord Kilmalie would rule in favour of his factor, as most landlords were wont to do.

'Who'll be coming to this school of yours?' Evangeline's voice was chill.

'Every child in the district, if I have my way.'

'Girls as well as boys?'

'Of course.'

'I'll not teach girls.' The surprising statement came from Alasdair Burns. 'They're trouble. Too imaginative by far.'

'How very *interesting*.' The Glasgow schoolteacher seemed able to strike sparks from Evangeline, and her eyebrows were raised in an exaggerated manner. 'Perhaps you'd care to draw on your experience and tell us more, Mr Burns?'

'I've said all that needs saying. If you want to know more, I suggest you visit Glasgow gaol next time you're there. You'll find thirteen schoolteachers lodged inside. Eleven as a result of teaching girls.'

Wyatt stepped in hurriedly, before Evangeline could question Alasdair Burns further about his knowledge of the inmates of Glasgow gaol.

'That's in a city. Things are different here in the Highlands.'

'Not for me. Trouble has never had any difficulty finding me. I don't need to go looking for it. I'll not teach girls.'

'I will. Boys, too, if Mr Burns feels he'd rather go off and teach elsewhere.' The triumph in Evangeline's voice was tinged with irritation. She was aware this man aroused totally unreasonable anger in her, but she did not know why it should be so.

'Alasdair will remain in Eskaig.'

During the couple of weeks he had known the one-legged schoolteacher, Wyatt had developed respect for the man's knowledge and learning. The pupils of the lochside school would have an exceptional teacher in Alasdair Burns. Wyatt had no intention of letting him go – and parents might not be so keen to send their children to school if they were to be taught by the daughter of their factor.

To Evangeline, he said: 'If you're really serious about wanting to teach, there's no reason why our new school shouldn't have *two* classrooms. One for Alasdair and the boys, the other for you and the girls. But what will your father think of you teaching Eskaig children?'

Evangeline's chin came up in a defiant attitude that reminded

Wyatt of her father. 'I'm old enough to make decisions for myself. Anyway, I don't doubt he'll be more than happy to have me somewhere where he isn't tripping over me the whole time.'

Something in her voice made Wyatt wonder whether she, too, knew about Seonaid Fraser.

Wyatt was taken aback by the explosion of enthusiasm among his parishioners when he announced from the pulpit of the church that Eskaig was to have a school. When he left the church he was besieged by parents anxious to enrol their children as students. By the time the last parent had departed for home, Wyatt and Alasdair Burns had taken the names of thirty boys and seventeen girls who would be attending classes when school began.

There was equal enthusiasm when Wyatt called for men to build the school and a teacher's house on the plot of land Wyatt had chosen, alongside the churchyard.

Wyatt had expected John Garrett to place difficulties in his way in respect of the school. However, it seemed Lord Kilmalie's letter to his factor had left no room for argument. Wyatt went to the Garrett house to inform the factor of his choice, only to be informed that he could 'do what the hell he liked'. John Garrett added that if Lord Kilmalie wanted to give away land without consulting his factor it was entirely the landowner's business.

The school and schoolhouse were built in eleven days. It would have been ten, had work not ceased for one day as a mark of respect for the area's oldest inhabitant who died on the day the foundations were laid for the school.

Archibald Mackinnon died in the week of his hundred and third birthday, in a remote crofter's cottage many miles to the north of Loch Eil. His passing broke the last human link with the area's glorious past. As a young boy, Mackinnon had shaken hands with Prince Charles Stuart. The occasion had been the Young Pretender's triumphal procession along the banks of Loch Eil, on his way to make a near-successful bid to win back the throne of his ancestors.

Mackinnon was nine years of age when the proud young prince became a hunted fugitive, leaving his bloodied and defeated supporters to straggle back to their homes about Eskaig after the horror of the battlefield of Culloden.

Archibald Mackinnon survived the English wrath that scythed through the Highlands in the wake of Culloden when the Duke of Cumberland set out to destroy the heritage of the clans. He saw the pipes and the tartan banned, and survived to witness the restoration of at least a vestige of ancient Highland pride.

The grand old man had also become something of a legend in his own right. It was said his illicit still produced a whisky that had no equal in the whole of Scotland.

When news was brought to Wyatt that the old man had died, he immediately set out to visit the Mackinnon home. It was the dead man's wish to be buried in the Eskaig churchyard, alongside long-forgotten ancestors, and Wyatt wanted to discuss the funeral with the man's relatives.

Wyatt found the family with their relatives and neighbours holding a 'mourning party'. It was an event that Archibald Mackinnon would have greatly enjoyed. The dead man was in his bed in the centre of the cot's earthen-floored living-area. The body was not lying down in repose, but propped up in sitting posture, as though not to miss any of the activities going on about him. At one end of the long low cottage was the byre, separated from the living-area by only a flimsy wooden fence. On the other side pigs grunted and squealed noisily, squabbling over the occasional titbit disposed of in their direction.

When he arrived, Wyatt quickly discovered he was the only sober man present. The pungent reek of whisky hung on the air, and those who had been subjected to its fiery potency for too long were sprawled on the floor about the dead man's bed.

The arrival of the minister created a temporary diversion. A heavily bearded man who declared he was the dead man's great-grandson cleared a zigzag path to the deathbed, shouting: 'Make way for the preacher. Clear a way to the corpse.'

Anyone who was slow to remove himself from the path of the bearded man's unpredictable course was roughly shoved aside. One man who lay in his path on the mud floor was kicked until he crawled away and disappeared beneath the dead man's bed.

By the time Wyatt reached the bed only the unconscious 'mourners' were unaware of his arrival. The remainder gathered about him, clutching a wide variety of drinking-vessels and staring, slack-mouthed. Wyatt had the uncomfortable feeling he was expected to provide his watchers with some form of miracle. Perhaps breathe new life into the dehydrated body of the man who occupied the bed.

Wyatt cleared his throat noisily. 'Er ... shall we say a prayer together for the soul of our dear departed brother....?'

'Brother? Brother? What's he talking about? Archibald's been nobody's brother since Dougall died thirty years since.' A small toothless dumpling of a woman, with a face almost as wrinkled as the dead man's, peered belligerently about the room, defying anyone to argue with her.

'That's Great-Aunt Flora,' explained Wyatt's guide in a whisper that was heard by every conscious man and woman in the cot. 'Great-Grandad's only surviving child. She's a wee bit simple....'

'I heard that! I heard every word, you ungrateful devil. I'm not so simple that I didn't know you were robbing my poor dead father of his sheep when it got so he couldn't get out to count them for himself. And what's this *ministear* doing here? If you'd spent more time with your great-grandpa, you'd have known he couldn't stand the sight of a preacher. He always said if heaven was going to be full of preachers he'd take his chance with the devil. Go back to Eskaig, *ministear*. We'll be at the village by noon tomorrow and you can say your piece over him then – but be sure he's laid in the ground next to his father and those brothers you were just mentioning. Put him anywhere else and I swear he'll haunt you to the end of your days....'

There was a movement from beneath the bed, and a voice began to bemoan the fact that someone had stolen his whisky. There was a bump as the unknown speaker struggled to rise to his feet. The bed shook and suddenly tilted to one side, pitching the body of Archibald Mackinnon to the floor.

Wyatt made his escape during the ensuing mêlée. Once outside he leaned against the side of the cottage and mopped his brow. It sounded as though a clan war had broken out within the cottage, but Wyatt wanted no part of it. Had the whisky not been flowing quite so freely, he would have returned and tried to restore some dignity to the scene, but he knew better than to interfere in a Highland family dispute when all the participants were fired with drink.

Stepping over a body that lay across the path, Wyatt set off across the springy upland turf on the three-hour return walk to Eskaig.

CHAPTER ELEVEN

THE FUNERAL SERVICE for Archibald Mackinnon was a memorable occasion for Wyatt in many ways – and one he would have been happy to forgo. The centenarian's links with Highland history brought clan heads, landowners and Scots title-holders from as far away as Inverness. How the news of the death and time of Mackinnon's funeral reached them, Wyatt would never know, yet all morning they poured into the small lochside village, completely swamping the facilities of Eskaig's single, somewhat disreputable inn. The shore of Loch Eil and the adjacent hillside were dotted with colourful groups of Highland gentry, sporting a variety of tartans, although few wore the predominantly red sett of the Mackinnon.

At eleven-thirty the visitors began to file into the small church. By noon the church was full and villagers were standing in the aisles and crowding around the doorway – but there was no sign of the funeral cortège.

By twelve-thirty Wyatt was remembering the events of the previous day, and beginning to wonder whether any of the Mackinnons had been left alive after their altercation.

By one-thirty most of the exalted guests had forsaken the church and were seeking refreshment at the Eskaig inn.

Two hours after the funeral service should have begun, it was suggested a horseman be despatched to learn what had happened to the funeral cortège of the late Archibald Mackinnon. One or two of the gentry, more irascible than the others, decided to call it a day and went home.

Then one of the village boys who had been stationed along the road the funeral procession would take shouted: 'Here they come!' A few minutes later the drone of pipes could be heard and the procession came into view.

Funerals were always special occasions in the Highlands and Islands, and Wyatt had seen a great many, but never one like this. There were many more mourners than had been present at the Mackinnon croft the previous day, men and women having joined the procession during its long progress. But it was not its size that made such an impression on Wyatt. The procession had the air of a retreat by the vanquished from a battlefield. Cuts and bruises were much in evidence, and the mourners at the head of the procession walked as though defeated in body and mind. Then Wyatt observed a number of flagons being passed from hand to hand and he realised that the Mackinnons were still inebriated.

It was with a sense of deep misgiving that Wyatt stood back at the churchyard gate to allow the Mackinnon family through. Only when most of them had passed by did a significant omission become apparent.

Wyatt looked anxiously down the long line of mourners before hurrying to the church entrance and tackling the bearded great-grandson who had welcomed Wyatt to the Mackinnon croft.

'Where's the coffin? I can't see it. . . .' Wyatt had to repeat his question three times to the glazed-eyed Highlander before it provoked a response – and then a furious argument erupted among the family mourners.

'You should have been carrying him. . . .'

'We carried him for the first half-mile; it was your family's turn.'

'Who brought him down the most difficult part . . .?'

'Where did you see the old man last . . .?'

Doing his best to contain an increasing sense of panic, Wyatt questioned one of the more sober mourners and discovered the coffin had last been seen about a mile back along the track, when the party crossed a small stream. This, at least, was a relief. Wyatt had thought for one ghastly moment that the procession had left the body of the centenarian in bed at the croft, high in the mountains.

A party of villagers volunteered to return along the way the mourners had come in a bid to locate the missing coffin, and Wyatt went inside the church to seat the family of Archibald Mackinnon and explain the latest delay to the congregation.

It was another fifty minutes before six perspiring Eskaig villagers entered the church bearing the coffin containing the body of Archibald Mackinnon. In a hurried aside one of the men informed Wyatt they had found the coffin tilted on its end against a tree, a number of bearers lying about it in various stages of intoxication.

By this time many more of the congregation had left the little church and such was the state of the Mackinnon family that Wyatt cut the service short and hurried them outside to the fresh air of the churchyard. Here, as swiftly as decency and dignity would allow, the centenarian was laid to rest among his ancestors.

It was with a great sense of relief that Wyatt saw the Mackinnon family straggling back towards their croft in the high lands. After a potentially disastrous beginning, the funeral service had ended comparatively well – if one overlooked the bearded grandson who overbalanced and fell into the grave on top of the coffin and had to be lifted out by other family members.

Preacher Coll Kennedy stood beside Wyatt as the Mackinnons disappeared into the distance. He had arrived shortly before the funeral service began, having heard of the old man's death only that morning. He had ridden to Eskaig as fast as his aged donkey would travel. Coll Kennedy had known Archibald Mackinnon for most of his life and was, he said, distantly related to the Mackinnon family.

The preacher from Letterfinlay had managed to sample some of the whisky carried by his distant kinsmen, but he was by no means drunk. As the last Mackinnon reeled out of sight, he shook his head sadly. 'You're witnessing the turning of a page of history, Wyatt. Things will never be the same in the Highlands now that Archibald Mackinnon has gone. His family looked on him as an anachronism, a man who had long outlived his usefulness, but now they'll learn the truth. It was only old Archibald who held the Mackinnons together, here where their roots lie. In five years' time – no, *three* – there won't be a Mackinnon left in this part of Scotland, you mark my words.'

'There are no doubt some who'll be pleased to see the back of them. They're a wild lot.'

'True, but it's men like the Mackinnons who taught the world the meaning of loyalty to their own. They're true clansmen.'

Wyatt conceded the truth of Coll Kennedy's argument, and the tall gangling Letterfinlay preacher rested a hand on Wyatt's shoulder. 'You've had a hard day, Wyatt. There will be few days when you have to bury a centenarian, deal with his drunken family and tug your forelock to every family of note living within twenty miles of Eskaig. Talking of drink . . . would you have any of that fine whisky left? I need something to take away the taste of "The Mackinnon". . . .'

Inside the manse Wyatt allowed himself the luxury of sitting down to enjoy a glass of whisky with his guest. Alasdair Burns also sat with them, but he drank nothing stronger than tea. He was much tidier these days, his hair and beard trimmed neatly and more in keeping with his new status as Eskaig's proposed schoolteacher. Coll Kennedy looked at the one-legged man as though he had questions he would like to ask, but for the time being he kept them to himself.

'I didn't see Angus Cameron at the funeral.'

'He hasn't attended the kirk since I came here. I've tried to persuade him to come back, so have the other elders, but Cameron is a stubborn man.' Wyatt had seen Angus Cameron on his knees in the roadway outside Eskaig as Archibald Mackinnon's coffin was carried through the village.

'He's also a man of considerable stature. We're going to need men like him in the near future, Wyatt. Things are happening in the Church. Serious things that threaten to tear the Church of Scotland apart. You've heard?'

Wyatt shook his head. He had been so tied up with parochial matters that there had been no time to keep up with national issues.

'You've solved the problems you had when you arrived in Eskaig, and the result is satisfactory to everyone. Other parts of Scotland haven't been so fortunate. Landowners have appointed ministers totally unacceptable to the people and refused to listen to the objections. Recent court cases have made matters worse. The courts have decreed that a *landowner* is entitled to appoint a minister to a living, no matter what the people think. It's an issue that eats at the very foundation of our way of worship, Wyatt. It's split the Church in two. Half believe the matter of a minister's acceptance should be settled by the people themselves. The others say we must go along with whatever the courts decree.'

'Where do you stand?'

'I'm with the people. Sometimes, as in your case, they may need a little persuading that they have the right man, but it's for the minister to do the convincing, not the landowner – or the courts of the land.'

'I agree. There was a time when I thought I would have to leave Eskaig for those very reasons. It's for the people to decide who they want. But what can be done if a minister is appointed by the landowner and refuses to respect the wishes of his parishioners?'

'If the people make it clear they don't want a minister, the Church must step in and refuse to induct him.'

Alasdair Burns entered the conversation for the first time. 'If they do, the landowner can now take the matter to the courts knowing they'll decide in his favour. There *is* another course of action, but it's so radical I can't see many members of the established church even considering it.'

Both ministers looked at Alasdair Burns in surprise. Coll Kennedy was the first to reply.

'You're a schoolteacher, Mr Burns. Are you also an expert on church matters?'

'I studied for the Church for two years,' came the surprising reply. 'I left when I foresaw the very problem you have now. In an *established* church you have to accept that ultimate power within that church rests with the establishment. If you intend a church to be administered by its members for the benefit of its members, then you must have a *free* church.'

'Radical views indeed, Mr Burns – and how do you suggest the Church should go about disestablishing itself without destroying all it is and all it represents?'

'I didn't say it would be easy, Minister Kennedy. Your church members would need to make a great many sacrifices – particularly the ministers – but isn't that how true Christianity began?'

'Sacrifices are sometimes necessary, perhaps. Self-destruction is foolhardy.'

'If what you say is true, you would be forming your brave new free church with a strong nucleus of worshippers all feeling as you do. They'll provide you with a stout foundation for your new movement. A base upon which to build and go forward. Do nothing and you'll find your ideals crumbling about your ears. You'll end up losing not only your church, but your integrity as well. It's often easier to destroy something by doing nothing than by reaching out and grasping a problem firmly before it becomes too big to tackle.'

'You argue in the manner of a reformer, Mr Burns. Altogether too strong for the classroom, surely?'

'I've never denied I'm a reformer – and never will. Wyatt knew that when he asked me to teach school here. I promised him I wouldn't air my views to my pupils and I'll keep that promise – but I'm not in the classroom now.'

Minister Coll Kennedy continued to stare at Alasdair Burns for many moments, but it was difficult to tell from his expression whether he was in agreement or disputed the one-legged schoolteacher's views. Suddenly he nodded vigorously. 'You're right, of course. It takes an outsider to see exactly what's needed.'

Raising his glass to Wyatt for a refill, Coll Kennedy said: 'I envy you, Wyatt. I'd give a lot to have someone like Alasdair Burns to argue with on a long winter's night. One of these days I'll come and spend a full day with you and learn something of his history. Right now I think I'm better off knowing nothing. No man who argues so well against the establishment can have reached his age without running headlong into trouble.'

CHAPTER TWELVE

THE ESKAIG SCHOOL was a huge success from the very first day. Children from the village arrived clean and tidy, glowing with excitement at the thought of their great new venture. Those who arrived from the surrounding mountains and glens had no 'Sunday best', but they, too, were eager to obtain the mystic benefit of 'an education'. The Highland families were asked to contribute two pence for each child sent to the school. Few possessed even such a trifling sum, but no child was turned away.

Much to Wyatt's relief the teaching arrangement proved highly successful. Within a matter of days the mutual antagonism between Evangeline and Alasdair Burns had changed to a grudging respect. Evangeline was impressed by the red-bearded man's knowledge and she admired his ability to impart it to his pupils. For his part, Alasdair Burns recognised that Evangeline had a natural teaching talent and she worked hard to overcome her lack of teaching experience.

Wyatt was well pleased with this, his first major project on behalf of his parishioners. He led prayers at the school on three mornings a week and on his latest visit had read a letter to the pupils from Lord Kilmalie. The Eskaig landlord promised a bible to each pupil when he, or she, was able to satisfy Wyatt they had reached a satisfactory reading standard. A race to be the first to receive a bible appeared to be developing between Ewan Munro and one of the older girls in Evangeline's class.

Wyatt believed every child in Eskaig was attending school, but one day, as he passed through Eskaig on his way to visit the Munro family, he heard a child's voice on the other side of a garden wall.

Peering over the wall, he saw a boy of about the same age as Ewan Munro. Seated on a small patch of grass, the boy was throwing a stick for a small black and white dog to retrieve and return to him. Both boy and dog were enjoying the game. Each time the boy threw the stick the dog would race off in pursuit, barking in excitement. Snatching up the wood, the dog returned it to the young boy, tail wagging in triumph.

'That's a fine game you're enjoying there, young man, but wouldn't you rather be at school?'

The boy looked around, startled at the sound of Wyatt's voice. The dog dropped the stick, a growl rumbling at the back of its throat.

The dog rushed towards the garden wall, barking furiously and causing Wyatt to lose the boy's reply. The animal continued its din until a woman came from the house and ordered it inside. The dog obeyed her, but only when a closed door shut off its barking was it possible to hold a conversation. Wyatt repeated his question to the boy's mother.

'Yes, he'd rather be at school. He'd prefer to be *anywhere* rather than here on his own. Unfortunately, before you can do any of the things other boys take for granted you need to be able to walk – and Jimmy hasn't walked since he was four years old. He has the palsy, Minister. There . . . do you see?' As she spoke, the woman lifted the child easily from the ground and swung him about to face Wyatt. The child's legs were thin and emaciated, incapable of supporting the weight of the smallest child. '*Now* you know why he isn't at school with the other children.'

'I'm sorry, I didn't know. . . .'

'That's right, Minister Jamieson. You *don't* know. There are a lot of things you don't know about Eskaig folk, so why go around hurting people with your ignorance? Pack up your things and go back to wherever it is you've come from.'

The bitterness in the woman's voice took Wyatt by surprise. The boy was looking at Wyatt wide-eyed as the woman scooped him up. She was about to carry him indoors when Wyatt called to her again.

'I hadn't finished talking. I didn't realise Jimmy was a cripple – but that's no reason why he shouldn't attend school.'

The woman stopped and looked back at Wyatt. She seemed to

have some difficulty in digesting what Wyatt had just said to her, but Wyatt was looking at the expression on the face of the crippled boy.

Wide-eyed, the boy's glance went from Wyatt to the woman. 'Can I go, Ma? Can I go to school?'

'Hush now. That was *cruel*, Minister. You know full well a boy like Jimmy can never attend school. He can't take a step for himself. . . .'

Wyatt's gaze had never left the face of the small boy, and he watched as the hope and joy seeped away.

'Have you heard of a Bath chair? It's a chair with wheels, and a handle enabling the occupant to steer it while he's being pushed along. If Jimmy had one of those, he'd not only be able to attend school, but also be the envy of every boy there.'

'A *Bath* chair, you say? I've never heard of such a thing. And where would we be getting one here, in Eskaig?'

Wyatt was remembering how cleverly Alasdair Burns had manufactured his wooden leg. 'I think I know someone who might be able to make one for him.'

The young boy was squirming in his mother's arms. 'Does it mean I can go to school, Ma? Please. . . .'

When the woman still looked doubtful, Wyatt said quietly: 'He'll learn to read. Books will open up a whole new world for him.'

'I'm a widow-woman. I doubt if I could raise the money for his lessons. Buying books would be quite out of the question.'

'No child has been turned away from my school because a fee hasn't been paid. As for books . . . when I think he's able to read and understand them, I'll find him books to read.'

This would pose no problem. The boatman had recently delivered two trunks containing all the books Wyatt had collected during his years at university.

The woman still seemed doubtful, but it would have taken a hard-hearted woman to deny the child she held in her arms.

'All right, Minister. I'll let Jimmy attend your school if you can provide one of these wheeled chairs. . . . And thank you.'

Alasdair Burns was less enthusiastic about Wyatt's promise that the teacher would be able to make a Bath chair. 'I've seen one,' he confessed, 'but it was made from a basketware chair, and it had wheels so small they'd need to be specially made.'

'The chair poses no problem,' said Evangeline promptly. 'We have one at home. I'll have it sent down in the pony trap this evening.'

'The wheels might be more difficult to obtain,' conceded Wyatt. 'They'd need to be as light as possible, but strong.'

Alasdair Burns snapped his fingers. 'I've just thought of a man who has exactly what we want. Kirkpatrick Macmillan is a black-smith living down Dumfries way. He's been experimenting for years with velocipedes – they're a sort of two-wheeled hobby-horse. When I last met him he showed me one that could be propelled through a series of rods connected to the back wheel while keeping both feet off the ground.

'With only *two* wheels?' Evangeline looked at Alasdair Burns accusingly, believing him to be making an untimely joke. 'How could he keep his balance with both feet off the ground?'

'I don't pretend to understand his ideas,' confessed Alasdair Burns, 'but when I was in his smithy I saw wheels of all sizes adorning the walls. If I wrote him a letter, do you think the boat-man who calls here would see it was delivered?'

Wyatt nodded. 'Donald McKay works the full length of the west coast. He'll know how to get a letter to this Macmillan.'

Donald McKay proved Wyatt's confidence in him was not misplaced. Not only did he deliver the letter in person, but he also brought back three wheels made to the specifications requested by Alasdair Burns.

The one-legged schoolteacher had built a frame, complete with steering mechanism, and attached it to the basket-chair supplied by Evangeline. An hour after the wheels arrived at the manse, the home-made Bath chair was heading for the village, pushed by Alasdair Burns. Wyatt went with him.

By the time they reached the house where Jimmy lived the Bath chair was at the head of a growing procession of villagers. When the excited Jimmy was carried from the house by his mother most of the Eskaig residents were out of doors and a cheer went up as the excited boy was placed in the wheeled chair for the first time.

Ensconced in the chair, Jimmy was delighted with his new-found mobility. Weaving the Bath chair from one side of the narrow village street to the other, he was soon shrieking to be pushed faster.

Eventually Alasdair Burns brought the fun to a halt, fearful that the Bath chair might be smashed before it had a chance to perform its intended purpose. Hot but very, very happy, Jimmy reluctantly steered his new vehicle back to the garden gate, there to be lifted out and hugged by his mother.

Scarcely able to control her emotion, Jimmy's mother choked on her words as she thanked Wyatt.

'Alasdair Burns is the man you should be thanking. It was his skill that built the chair for Jimmy.'

'I do thank him, from the bottom of my heart, but it was *you* who made it possible. I won't forget this, Minister. I said some unkind things to you when we first met. I'm sorry. Eskaig is fortunate to have you here.'

Embarrassed by the woman's gratitude, Wyatt made his escape after telling Jimmy he expected to see him at school the following day.

'Your skills have made one small boy and his mother very happy,' commented Wyatt as he and Alasdair Burns made their way back to the manse.

'I trust that's *all* that's been done.' There was a concerned frown on the face of the red-bearded teacher as he limped along beside Wyatt. 'Kirkpatrick Macmillan sent a letter to me with the wheels. It was addressed to Alasdair Burns *Anderson*. When I went to the jetty the letter was in the hands of John Garrett. He *said* nothing to me at the time, but I've an uncomfortable feeling that won't be an end to the matter.'

One Sunday, soon after the opening of the school, Wyatt found Mairi waiting for him when he left the Eskaig church at the end of his service. He had seen her inside with Donnie, the youngest of her brothers, but there was no sign of Donnie Ross now.

'Mairi! I was delighted to see you at my service,' Wyatt greeted the Highland girl warmly. It had been a few weeks since they had last met. 'Will you come to the manse and have some tea with me? Donnie, too, of course.'

Such an invitation extended to a young girl from an unmarried preacher would have shocked most of Wyatt's Eskaig parishioners. Having her brother along would make it *almost* acceptable.

Wyatt was disappointed when Mairi shook her head. 'I must catch up with Donnie; he's gone on ahead. I wanted to speak to you. To ask a favour.'

'If it's within my power, I'll be delighted.'

'It's to do with your new school. I'd like to come to it.'

Wyatt was taken aback. He *had* toyed with the idea of starting reading classes for the older parishioners, in order that they might learn to read the Bible, but he had intended it to be more in the nature of a Sunday school. He asked Mairi if perhaps she would not prefer to attend such classes.

Mairi shook her head emphatically. 'No. I want to learn to read and write. To do sums . . . and learn about things, and places. Places where Pa and Ma . . . and you have been.'

'I only teach twice a week, Mairi, and then it's religious instruction, not geography.'

'Oh!' She managed to make her disappointment sound like surprise. 'That doesn't matter. It'll be all right as long as I'm not taught by *her*.'

'If by "her" you mean Miss Garrett, then I'm afraid it's "her" or nobody. Alasdair Burns won't teach girls of any age, and I find I'm too busy to take all except two classes a week.'

For some moments Mairi fought an inner conflict. Then she shrugged. 'As long as she teaches me all the things I want to know, it'll be all right, I suppose.'

Wyatt was even less certain about the idea than Mairi herself. She would be far and away the oldest pupil in the school. Almost Evangeline's own age in fact. He was still mulling the matter over in his mind when Alasdair Burns came through the churchyard from the school, heading towards the manse. He and Wyatt made a habit of eating together at Sunday lunchtime.

'You're just the man I want to see, Alasdair. Mairi has asked if she can attend our school. What do you think?'

'It's a splendid idea. It might encourage other young men and women to come. I'd like to see the whole Highland community educated. They'd be less open to exploitation by all and sundry. . . .'

Catching Wyatt's warning glance, Alasdair Burns grinned. 'All right, Wyatt. One sermon in a morning's enough for anyone.' To Mairi he said: 'Classes begin at nine in the morning – on the dot.

The fee is two pence a week for those who can pay. Most can't, so you won't be barred on that count.'

'No Ross has ever had to rely upon charity,' declared Mairi, head in air. 'I'll pay my way.'

'Then, you'll be most welcome at my school. You can begin tomorrow.'

'Will you be staying in Eskaig during the week?' Wyatt asked the question, aware it took more than two hours of gruelling walking to reach the Ross cottage.

'Coming to school won't mean I'll be let off my chores. I'll come from home each day.'

'Then, you'd better bring a change of clothing with you and leave it at the manse. On a wet day you'll get soaked. You can't sit in a classroom all day in wet clothes.'

'You're very solicitous about that young lady's well-being.' Alasdair Burns looked at Wyatt with a curious expression on his face as Mairi hurried away to catch up with her brother. 'Is there something I should have been told about her before accepting her in my school so eagerly?'

'No, but the decision came easy to you. You won't be teaching her. I hope Evangeline accepts her presence in school as readily.'

Evangeline did *not* accept the presence of Mairi Ross in her class. The Kilmalie factor's daughter conceded that Mairi was intelligent and quick to learn, but these were the only points she made in her new pupil's favour.

'She's disruptive, insolent and . . . *disrespectful*!'

Evangeline's complaint was her sixth in the three weeks Mairi had been attending the Eskaig school.

'I can't teach children with someone like her in the class. She's undermining my authority. You should have known better than to allow a crofter-girl of that age to come to school – *especially* a Ross. Many of the parents of the other girls are complaining. They're beginning to wonder whether you have a particular reason for allowing her to take lessons.'

'What is that supposed to mean?'

They were talking in one of the classrooms after school. Wyatt had been hammering nails in the wall and he now began hanging half a dozen framed paintings, donated by Annie Hamilton, the woman who owned the Eskaig inn.

'Well, whether or not you are aware of it, there was a lot of talk in the village after you came down from the mountains with Mairi Ross in a state of undress. . . .'

Wyatt dropped the painting he was trying to hang. He managed to slow its progress with his foot, but it was not enough to prevent a sliver of gilded wood from breaking away from the frame when it hit the floor. Wyatt took a deep breath. It was on occasions such as this that he regretted his status as a minister. It meant he could not resort to a well-known old army swearword to express his feelings.

Picking up the broken piece of wood, Wyatt tried to attach it to the damaged frame, but there seemed to be a piece missing. After turning it this way and that, he threw it through the open window.

'Mairi Ross's dress was sacrificed to rescue two young children from certain death. It would take an evil mind to think ill of her for *that*.'

'I'm only telling you what I've heard.' Evangeline stooped and picked up the missing sliver of wood from the floor and handed it to Wyatt. 'But I'm not surprised at such gossip. *I've* heard her talking about the furniture in the manse as though she's familiar with every piece that's there.'

'If you saw her home, you'd understand why. They lead a very simple life in the mountain crofts. Any furniture *they* have is made from rough wood, by her father. It's no more than a childlike trait to boast of what she's seen.'

'But she's *not* a child, Wyatt. Such gossip will do you no good at all.'

'Very well, I'll speak to her.' The second sliver of picture-frame followed the first through the window, and Wyatt hung an artist's romanticised depiction of a stag at bay without further trouble.

It was one thing to tell Evangeline he would speak to Mairi about her behaviour at school, but quite another to bring the matter to the attention of Mairi herself.

Wyatt had hoped to tackle Mairi after his Sunday-morning service, but none of the Ross family attended church that week. Then, between lessons on Monday afternoon, Wyatt received a complaint that Mairi had totally disrupted a lesson by correcting Evangeline about Wellington's campaign in the Iberian peninsula.

Mairi quoted both her parents as authorities on the subject.

That evening, when Mairi left school Wyatt was waiting for her outside Eskaig, at the point where she would leave the road and make her way through the mountains to the remote croft.

Mairi's pleasure at seeing Wyatt was short-lived. As soon as he asked her how she was enjoying school she knew why he had been waiting for her.

'*She's* sent you to speak to me, hasn't she?' Wyatt needed to stride out across the wiry low-growing heather in order to keep up with her. 'I *knew* she would. She thinks *she's* the only one who knows anything. . . .'

It was impossible to conduct a sensible conversation walking at such a speed. Reaching out, Wyatt took hold of Mairi's arm and brought her to a halt.

'Mairi, Miss Garrett's at the school to *teach* you and the others. It's not easy for her, especially as she knows so little Gaelic. From what I hear, you're not making it any easier.'

'From what you hear from who? Her? She's not likely to tell you the truth.'

'Then, perhaps you'd like to tell me *your* version of what's been happening.'

Mairi looked at him intently for some moments, but then she shrugged. It doesn't matter what I say. You're bound to take her side even if she *is* wrong. Like you say, *she's* the teacher.'

'I'm not taking *any* sides. All I want to do is resolve a classroom problem to everyone's satisfaction.'

Once again Mairi gave him a long hard look. 'You'll never resolve anything as long as I'm in *her* class. She wants me out of the school and she won't leave me alone until she's succeeded.'

'That's foolish talk, Mairi. Why should she want you to leave the school? You're older than the rest, it's true, but you're just as eager to learn as the others. More so, probably.'

'You *really* don't know why?' Mairi's disbelief seeped away when she saw his puzzlement. 'No, I don't believe you do. All right, I'll try not to upset her, but I don't think it's going to work. Now I must hurry. The cows have to be milked before dark.'

Wyatt watched Mairi and returned her wave just before she disappeared from view around the hillside. He wanted to believe he had resolved the problem that existed between Mairi and

Evangeline, whatever the truth of it, but he feared he had not heard the last of the matter.

True to her promise, Mairi tried hard not to antagonise Evangeline during the ensuing week, even when during a geography lesson she believed the factor's daughter was unnecessarily scornful of the crofting method of farming.

Then, during a history lesson, continuing the story of Wellington's campaign in Spain, Evangeline made a remark about the women who followed the English troops. She called them 'camp followers', adding that they were no better than the name implied.

Mairi jumped to her feet immediately. She informed Evangeline Garrett that most of the 'camp followers' were married to soldiers. They travelled with the army for no other reason than to be near their husbands, providing them with what little comfort they could on the march. Carried away by her anger, Mairi scornfully told Evangeline she could never imagine *her* staying by her man in battle or rescuing a wounded husband and carrying him to safety under fire.

Evangeline chose not to take issue with Mairi over the matter. Instead she ordered Mairi to leave her class, declaring she would no longer tolerate her interruptions and arrogant behaviour.

Pretending not to care, Mairi said: 'I don't *want* to stay in a school with a teacher who makes up her own history as she goes along. That's not learning.'

'We've heard quite enough from you, Mairi Ross. Get out *now*, if you please.' Evangeline was white-faced, but there was a hint of triumph in her voice. Coming on top of her previous outbursts, Wyatt would have no alternative but to confirm Mairi's dismissal.

Head held high, Mairi maintained her dignity, although her eyes burned with the ignominy of being ordered from school by the factor's daughter. 'It'll make no difference, you know. You won't get him.'

'I don't know what you're talking about. What's more, I don't care.' Evangeline's face had suddenly changed from white to scarlet.

'I'm talking of Preacher Jamieson. You can set your bonnet at him if you like, but he'll not have you, whether I'm around or not.

And that's the *real* reason you're getting rid of me; we both know that.'

'Get out! *Get out!*' Evangeline was beside herself with rage, acutely aware of the grinning faces of Mairi's late classmates who were enjoying the discomfiture of the factor's daughter.

'I'm going.' Mairi was desperately miserable at being expelled from the Eskaig school. She had wanted so much to receive an education. Without it there could be no escape from the grinding seasonal toil of the croft. However, she had no intention of allowing Evangeline to see how unhappy she was. 'I hope you'll tell the preacher the truth of why I'm going. . . .'

Alasdair Burns passed Mairi in the doorway and understood immediately the cause of the din coming from Evangeline's classroom. Taking a deep breath, he stomped into the room and bellowed for silence.

Providing the means for young Jimmy Gordon to attend school produced an unexpected bonus for Wyatt. One evening he received a visitor at the manse. In answer to a knock, Wyatt opened the door to find Angus Cameron standing hat in hand on the threshold.

'Elder Cameron! This is indeed a surprise. Come in.'

Behind Wyatt, Alasdair was in the room and he heard Wyatt speak the elder's name. He was so surprised he tried to remove the hot kettle from the fire without using a cloth to protect his hand. Dropping the kettle hastily, he cursed his carelessness.

'I won't come inside.' Angus Cameron was ill at ease in the presence of the man whose appointment as minister he had opposed so vehemently. 'But I would like to have a word with you, Minister Jamieson. Could we walk awhile, maybe?'

'Of course.' There was a fresh northerly wind blowing, and Wyatt took a coat from a peg inside the door before stepping outside. 'We'll walk to the kirk. The wind's rising, and I should check that all the windows are closed.'

'That will do fine.' Angus Cameron replaced the hat on his head and held it in place with one hand. The wind blew fiercely in the gap between manse and church. 'It's a while since I saw inside the kirk. I've missed it sorely.'

'No one has forced you to stay away, Elder. I've always made it quite clear your presence in the kirk would be very welcome.'

'It's that I've come to talk to you about. . . .' They reached the church porch, and Angus removed his wide-brimmed hat once more. He stood turning it in his hands as though it were a ship's wheel. 'First, I would like to thank you for what you've done for Jimmy – Jimmy Gordon. He's my grandson. Janet, his mother, is my daughter. An only child. We've all been worried about Jimmy. Apart from that dog of his, he'd seemed interested in nothing at all. Yet tonight he's had me pushing him all around the garden in that wheeled chair you gave him and he's bubbling over with enthusiasm about going to school with the other children. You've given him a new lease of life, Minister, and I'm here to offer you an apology. I still don't agree with the way you were appointed, but you're proving yourself a good pastor.'

The two men entered the church, and while Angus Cameron was talking he looked about him with the air of a man who had come home after a long absence.

'Nothing's changed here, Elder Cameron. Everything is just the way you left it – but it would be all the better for a sermon or two from you.'

Angus Cameron looked at Wyatt incredulously. 'Do you mean that?'

'I do. You're sadly missed here. It would make me very happy if you resumed your place in the kirk . . . *our* kirk.'

In the elder's hands the hat-brim was curled so tightly that Wyatt feared it might never resume its original shape. Suddenly Angus Cameron nodded vigorously, momentarily incapable of speech.

'Good! Can I put you down for the sermon on Sunday afternoon? There's another matter I would like to discuss with you, too. There's a need for another chapel, at the far end of the loch, near the Munros' cottage. I couldn't consider it unless I had help with my own preaching duties. Do you think there is something you might be able to do. . . ?'

CHAPTER THIRTEEN

WYATT HAD SEEN NONE of the Ross family for almost four weeks, since Mairi stormed out of the school building. He told himself he was concerned about the whole family, but honesty forced him to admit he missed speaking with Mairi. On a visit to Lachlan Munro, Wyatt asked about the high-mountain family, but the ex-soldier seemed unusually vague.

'I expect the womenfolk are at the shielings, summer-grazing their cattle. That's where they make their cheese and butter to see them through the winter – but you know that, Captain. They must have done the same thing on the Islands.'

'*You're* talking of the women, Lachlan; *I'm* asking of the whole Ross family. That includes nine men, I believe.'

'Ah, well, it's a short summer up here. There's plenty to do at this time of year.'

Wyatt had a feeling that Lachlan Munro was not telling him all he knew of the Ross men. He would need to find out for himself what was happening on the high lands above the loch.

Wyatt chose his day well. The wispy early-morning mist promised a fine day. Sure enough, by the time Wyatt had toiled up the steep slope of the mountains behind Eskaig and reached the glen where the two Munro children had been involved in their frightening adventure, the sun was rising in a cloudless sky.

Surrounded by all that was best in the Highlands, Wyatt walked along beneath a loose-linked chain of skylarks, each bird hanging far above him, their unending repetitive song always with him.

It was not quite so green on the high lands as it was at the lochside. The soil was thinner here, and sun and wind dried the ground quickly, but the land supported a wide variety of animal and bird life. He saw many mountain hares, long-eared high-leaping animals, fast-running on erratic courses between hiding-places, well aware of the presence of a silent gliding eagle commanding the skies overhead. Once Wyatt saw a magnificent stag using a low rocky ridge as a plinth. The proud animal slipped swiftly from view when it spotted the alien presence of a man in its domain.

Eventually, without hurrying, Wyatt came in sight of the Ross cottage. Smoke was seeping from the crude chimney, but there was no other sign of life immediately apparent about the place. He eventually located Eneas Ross and his Spanish wife working side by side, backs bent, on a vegetable plot some distance from the house. The plot was hidden from view by low stone walls that protected the plants against the cutting wind.

Magdalene Ross waved in response to Wyatt's call, but she carried on working. Eneas Ross straightened his back slowly and stiffly and waited for Wyatt to reach them.

'You're a long way from Eskaig, Minister. What brings you up here this time?'

'I've missed you and your family at my services. I thought I'd come and satisfy myself you were all right.'

'It's a busy time of year for us, Minister. Crofters slipped the good Lord's mind when He decreed man should work for only six days of the week. During winter, when the snows are with us, we can find time to pray every day, but we need to work like two men through the summer if we're to survive. Now, where are my manners . . . ? Away to the house with you, woman, bring the whisky and a piece of new cheese for Minister Jamieson.'

Eneas Ross's words were loud and dictatorial, but the look that followed Magdalene Ross towards the cottage contained a gentleness seldom seen in such a man. When his wife was beyond hearing, Eneas Ross said: 'She's been carrying on something awful about not coming to your kirk, Minister. She'd have come on her own, but she's not so steady on her legs these days. If I let her go, I'd get no work done for worrying about her.'

'How about your boys? Couldn't one of them have brought her to the kirk?'

A strange expression crossed the face of Eneas Ross, but it was gone again so quickly Wyatt wondered if he had imagined it.

'The boys aren't here. They've gone down to the lowlands to fetch back some sheep – all except young Donnie. He's at the shielings, hunting food for the womenfolk. He'd rather be with his brothers, I dare say, but if that young Fraser girl's there I doubt he'll be too unhappy.'

Wyatt wondered whether Eneas Ross knew of Seonaid's association with John Garrett. But he had not come here to cause trouble.

'I would have thought there were sheep enough about here.'

'There are, but those who own them are robbers. They've robbed our people of land for their sheep-walks and they'd rob blind any man who tried to strike a bargain with them. I'll not deal face to face with any man who runs sheep on cleared land in the Highlands.'

Magdalene Ross arrived with the whisky-jar, a half-loaf of coarse bread and a great chunk of newly made cheese, brought from the shielings by Mairi on a visit a few days before.

The talk turned to the summer grazing-lands, and Wyatt expressed an interest in paying them a visit.

'Why not?' Eneas Ross agreed. 'You'll find Mairi and Tibbie there. You'll also meet a great many womenfolk you'll not have met before. Mind, you'll not make it back to Eskaig by nightfall. Either get the women to make a shelter for you there or come back here for the night.'

Wyatt had not intended going to the shielings quite so soon, but the more he thought about it the more sense it seemed to make. He had no urgent tasks waiting for him in the village, and it might be a long time before he had another such opportunity.

Thanking Eneas Ross and his wife for their hospitality, Wyatt took directions and set off for the shielings. The way would take him past the home of Seonaid Fraser. He intended to call on the girl's blind father.

Unlike the Ross cot, the Fraser home occupied an exposed position on the slope of one of the highest peaks in the area. It also had a sad air of neglect about the place, although a small vegetable plot was the equal of the one Wyatt had just seen at the Ross croft.

There were a couple of tethered goats here, too, and as Wyatt approached he was surprised to see Seonaid at home milking one of the animals.

She stopped when she saw Wyatt and, setting aside the wooden bucket, hurried to meet him

'What are you doing here? You've not come to tell my father about me and John Garrett? Please don't. It will kill him.'

'He'll learn nothing from me,' Wyatt reassured the girl. 'I'm on my way to the shielings and thought it was time I called and paid your father a visit.'

Behind them in the cot doorway a man appeared. He looked directly to where Wyatt was standing with Seonaid, but the cloud of blindness was in his eyes and Wyatt knew he could not see them.

'Who's that, Seonaid? I heard voices. Who are you talking to, girl?' The voice was querulous and somewhat peevish.

'It's the minister from Eskaig here to see you. He's on his way to the shielings. I'll be taking him with me when I go.'

'A minister? What's he doing all this way from Eskaig? We've never had one here before.'

'All the more reason to make him welcome. You're always complaining no one ever comes calling on you.'

'That Ross boy is here often enough, although we're better off without the likes of him. I never trusted a Ross when I could see them. I trust them even less now I can't.'

'Minister Jamieson hasn't come all this way to hear what you think of your neighbours. You've often said how you'd like a prayer said for Ma . . . well, now's the chance. I'll finish milking the goats and then I'll need to get back to the shielings. Our cows will want milking, and no one else will do it for me if I'm not there. Will half an hour do you, Minister?'

Wyatt nodded, and as he followed Hamish Fraser inside the cottage Seonaid returned to the goats.

Once inside there was little to distinguish between this cot and the one occupied by the Ross family, although the Fraser home was not as clean. It also lacked an indefinable warmth that was present in the Ross household.

'Don't you find it lonely up here, Mr Fraser? Have you ever thought of moving to Eskaig?'

'The answer to both your questions is No. Why should I find it lonely? Besides, I've lived here so long I don't need eyes to find my way around and I've got Seonaid to think of. I know all about Eskaig and the wicked ways of folk who live there. Seonaid's mother came from Eskaig. She had me to thank for removing her from temptation. She realised that, Minister. Realised it and was grateful.'

'Seonaid told me her mother is dead. Is she buried in Eskaig? If you tell me where her grave is, I'll tidy it up for you. Perhaps you'd like me to take you down there some day . . .?'

'She's not buried in Eskaig – and I keep her grave tidy for myself. I visit it every day, sometimes twice.'

'I don't understand. There's not another burial-ground for miles. . . .'

'Preacher Gunn wouldn't bury her in the churchyard because she killed herself. Down in the stream it was, the first year I went blind, and with Seonaid no more than a wee bairn at the time. I buried her myself, close by where she died, next to the stone where she always kneeled to do her washing. That was the closest she ever came to praying, Minister, on her knees by the stream. I've prayed for her – Seonaid too, I've seen to that. But no preacher's ever put his hands together on her behalf.'

'Then, we'll rectify that straightway. Show me the place.'

Hamish Fraser walked from the house with the confidence of a man who knew the position of every item of furniture.

Once outside, he called: 'Seonaid, come with us, girl. The minister's going to say a prayer at your mother's graveside. Come now.'

'You go on. I've been down there once today. I need to finish milking the goats if I'm to get back to the shielings.'

For a moment it seemed Hamish would insist on his daughter accompanying them. Then he shrugged his shoulders apologetically. 'I'm sorry, Minister. She's a good girl, but since those Rosses started calling she's grown a mite too independent.'

'You don't like the Ross family?' Wyatt asked the question of Fraser as he followed the blind man down a well-worn path towards a stream.

'I do not. During the early years of my marriage they would have turned my own wife against me had I not put a stop to it. They've tried the same thing with Seonaid. When she was a child she'd sometimes run away. I knew where she went to, but since I was blind I could do nothing. I had to wait until they brought her back to me – and they wouldn't have cared had I starved in the meantime. It's hard being blind, Minister. Had I not lost my sight, I'd have settled matters once and for all with Eneas Ross and those boys of his. I'm surprised Lord Kilmalie allows them to remain on his land. The Rosses have never been anything but renegades with no regard for another's property – be it wife, daughter or livestock.'

Wyatt would have liked to know more, but he said nothing. It would not do for a minister to become involved in family feuds.

The stream-bank at the end of the path had been worn away by many generations of usage, and a small dam built lower down meant that a wide and deep pond had formed. The fast-moving stream kept the water fresh and clear. At the very edge of the pond was a large flat laundry-boulder, the surface worn smooth by generations of washerwomen.

Six feet away was the grave of the late Mrs Fraser. There was no cross. The simple, slightly raised plot was little more than five feet long, and less than half as wide, the whole grave encircled by stones of varying sizes. There was also a sprig of freshly picked heather placed on the mound, and Wyatt remembered that Seonaid had admitted to visiting the grave earlier.

Both men sank to their knees beside the unconsecrated grave, and after a short prayer Wyatt recited a portion of Psalm 103: '. . . he remembereth that we are dust. As for man, his days are as grass: as a flower of the field, so he flourisheth. For the wind passeth over it, and it is gone; and the place thereof shall know it no more.'

After Wyatt closed his bible, Hamish Fraser remained on his knees for some minutes, tears coursing down his cheeks. When he stood up again, he clasped Wyatt's hand in both his own. 'Bless you, Minister. She's waited many years to have a man of God say a prayer over her. She'll rest easier now, I know.'

'I'll have a prayer said for her in the kirk this Sunday, too – but I still believe you'd be better off living in Eskaig village.'

Hamish Fraser reverted to his earlier, abrupt manner. 'You'll never get me near that place. *Never.* I'd kill myself same as my Mary before I'd go, because I'd surely die once I got there. It's not my sort of place. One cottage leaning against another; neighbours with their ears to the walls to hear all that's going on; women gossiping behind a man's back the minute he's passed by. . . .'

'It's not as bad as that, Mr Fraser. I can see that you'd miss all you have here, but one day Seonaid will want to go her own way – and you won't be able to stay here alone.'

'She'll not leave me. Seonaid will always come back.' Hamish

Fraser spoke fiercely, causing Wyatt to look at the man sharply.

At that moment Seonaid called: 'Are you ready, Minister? I have cows to milk when I reach the shielings, and it's a three-hour walk.'

'I'm ready.' Wyatt turned to bid farewell to Hamish Fraser, but the blind man had gone inside his home.

CHAPTER FOURTEEN

'THANK YOU for not telling Father about me . . . and the factor.'
Seonaid Fraser's thanks came as she and Wyatt left the high-land
cottage behind them and struck out across the mountain-tops.

'I wish I felt I'd done either of you a favour by remaining silent.
Had I said something, your father might have decided to leave the
cottage and move closer to people. He spends too much time on his
own.'

'That's the way he likes to be. He doesn't get on with other
people. He'd kill himself rather than move – kill me, too, if he was
to learn what I've been doing.'

Wyatt knew he would soon have to do something about the
relationship between Seonaid and John Garrett. He wished he possessed the experience to accomplish what he wanted without hurting any of the innocent parties concerned.

He was still contemplating the problem when Seonaid Fraser
asked: 'Why are you coming up here to the shielings? Has it anything to do with Mairi Ross?'

The question took Wyatt by surprise. 'Mairi Ross? Of course
not. Why should it have anything to do with her?' Even as he spoke
the words, Wyatt realised he had come very close to telling a lie. He
may not have come to the shielings *specifically* because of Mairi
Ross but, having learned the reason why the Ross family had not
attended church for some weeks, he would not have carried on to
the shielings had she *not* been there.

'She talks of you a great deal. I thought there might be some sort
of "understanding" between you. She's a very nice girl, you know.
If she didn't live up here, among the hills, some man would have

come along and snapped her up ages ago. Why haven't *you* married?'

Aware that Seonaid Fraser was giving him a long sidelong glance, Wyatt changed the subject. 'Your father doesn't seem to like the Ross family. Why?'

'He doesn't like anyone, I've already told you that.'

'I feel it goes deeper than that – and I don't think I'm wrong.'

Now it was Seonaid Fraser's turn to sink into a silence, but it did not last for long.

'Yes, you're right, Father *hates* Eneas Ross and anyone who bears the Ross name. It all happened years ago . . . because of Ma. Both Eneas Ross and my father were sweet on her, but it seems she liked Eneas better. Before he went off to join Wellington's army she promised to wait for him. When he came back with a Spanish wife she was heartbroken, but a couple of months later she married my father. It couldn't have been an easy life for her up here. She was used to Eskaig, where she'd had neighbours and other women to talk to. Father wouldn't have helped much; he's never known any life but the one we lead up here. I believe they quarrelled a lot. Sometimes when it became too much for her she'd run off to the Ross place – as much for protection as for anything else, I suppose. Father can be a very violent man. I believe he was even worse when he discovered he was going blind. I was born by then, but it didn't seem to make any difference to the way he behaved. Magdalene Ross has said my Ma spent more time with them than she did at home. That wouldn't have pleased Pa much, because he's also a very jealous man. It seems that one day, after a particularly bad row, Ma went off, leaving me behind. When she hadn't returned after five days, Father took me with him and somehow found his way to the Ross place. Ma wasn't there, but Eneas and his oldest boys went out searching for her. They found her in the pond, dead. Instead of being grateful for their help, Father swore that if Eneas Ross hadn't encouraged her by letting her stay at the Ross house whenever she'd had a fight with him she'd have settled at home. There were harsh words on both sides, and Father and Eneas haven't spoken to each other from that day to this.'

'That hasn't stopped at least one of the Ross family from coming to visit you.'

'Donnie? I like him, but I haven't encouraged him. It's just nice to have someone my own age to talk to sometimes, that's all.' Seonaid Fraser hesitated a moment before speaking again. 'The only trouble is he's too serious. Every other week he's asking me to marry him.'

Wyatt remembered the youngest Ross boy. He was a tall, clean-shaven, open-faced young man.

'You could do a lot worse, Seonaid.'

'I'll do a sight better — or I'll not get wed at all. If I were to marry Donnie, I'd never get to leave the Highlands. I'd spend the rest of my life either at the Ross home or where I am now. I want more than that from life, Minister Jamieson. I'll do anything if it means I can get away from the life of drudgery I have here.'

'What does Donnie think about you and John Garrett?' Wyatt put the question to her bluntly.

'He believes it's all malicious gossip. I told you, Minister. Donnie's a very nice boy.'

Seonaid Fraser's words troubled Wyatt. She was a bright intelligent girl, but she had led a tragic lonely life. No doubt she was flattered by the attentions of John Garrett, but Donnie Ross was a red-headed volatile Highlander. Wyatt hoped the young Ross boy would do nothing foolish when he learned the truth about Seonaid, as one day he surely must.

For the remainder of the long walk to the shielings their talk was of less contentious matters, during the course of which Wyatt learned a great deal about the men and women of his Highland parish.

When they were still some distance from the shielings they were met by Donnie Ross. He was carrying a long-barrelled flintlock musket. The tall young man's explanation was that he was out hunting and just happened to be in that spot. However, he was too young to be able to hide his disappointment at finding Seonaid Fraser had company.

After an initial greeting, the trio walked in silence until Wyatt said: 'That's a fine old gun you're carrying, Donnie. Is it your own?'

Donnie Ross looked down at the musket with great pride. 'My great-grandfather carried it at Culloden and gave it to Pa. It's still more accurate than any other gun I've ever fired. It's taken out by anyone in the family when they go hunting.'

'What have you shot for the pot so far today?'

'No more than a rabbit or two, and a couple of pigeons. My

'main task seems to be to keep foxes from the newborn calves.'

'Is that so? It's a pity you didn't meet up with us sooner. I saw a fair-sized buck not half a mile back.'

'All deer belong to the landowner. There are laws against shooting them. At least, there are for people like us.'

'There were laws against owning muskets after Culloden, but you're carrying a Jacobite musket. It's a pity you're not interested in shooting a buck for the pot. Lord Kilmalie told me I was welcome to hunt a deer or two if I could find the time.'

Donnie Ross was torn between his desire to walk Seonaid Fraser to the shielings and a rare opportunity to stalk and shoot a deer without fear of retribution.

'Go off and shoot a deer for us. We could do with a good meal up at the shielings.' Seonaid Fraser helped Donnie make up his mind.

'All right. Make sure there's a good cooking-fire ready for when we get there.'

'You shoot a deer before you start giving me orders about cooking it, Donnie Ross!' Seonaid Fraser was peeved that Donnie had not argued about leaving her and going off to hunt a deer.

'Don't worry,' Wyatt said to the uncertain young man as he turned to look back at Seonaid Fraser for the third time. 'She'll be the proudest girl at the shielings when you return with a fine buck for the pot, but we'll need to hurry if we're not to lose the opportunity.'

Wyatt had seen only one buck, but in fact it was in the company of two does. They were roe dear, not quite as wary of humans as the larger red deer but still not easy to approach. The two hunters came to within a hundred paces of the animals, but here all cover ended.

'It's now or never,' said Wyatt. 'Do you think you can down the buck from here?'

Donnie Ross looked doubtful. 'I'll try, but I'm not as good a shot as some of my brothers.'

The three deer were edgy, and suddenly the buck raised its head and took two short paces forward. The does, too, seemed to be on the point of flight.

'Now . . . shoot!'

Donnie put the gun to his shoulder, aimed quickly and fired, but the three animals were on the move before the sound of the shot echoed around the mountains. By the time the thick pall of black powder-smoke was tugged away by the wind the deer were bounding away, each fast-moving leap putting another twenty feet between them and the hunters.

'Damn!' Donnie Ross swore softly and immediately apologised. 'I'm sorry, Minister.'

It was not clear whether the disconsolate hunter was apologising for his language or for missing his target.

'Better marksman than you would have missed such a shot. The deer had taken fright and started running before your musket-ball was halfway there.'

Donnie shrugged unhappily. 'Pa wouldn't have missed it. Neither would Mairi.'

'Mairi can handle a gun?' Wyatt was genuinely astonished. Shooting was not usually included as one of a young woman's accomplishments.

'Pa says she's as good as he is. She learned because she was fed up with being told she *couldn't* do things because she's a girl. When she puts her mind to it she can do most things as well as any of the rest of us.'

Once more Wyatt warmed to the uncomplicated honesty of Donnie Ross.

'Let's go and find this extraordinary sister of yours and confess to our failure as hunters. She'll forgive us, I'm sure.'

'She'd forgive *you*, no matter what you did,' declared Donnie Ross. 'I don't know what she'll say to me, though.'

The two men talked easily as they walked towards the shielings. They took a different path from the one Wyatt had walked with Seonaid Fraser, the younger man guiding Wyatt across the heather-covered shoulder of a mountain that rose high above them.

They had been walking in silence for a while when Wyatt suddenly reached out and gripped Donnie Ross by the arm, bringing him to a halt.

Instead of offering an explanation, Wyatt pointed silently to the mountainside above and to one side of them.

The young Ross's glance searched the hillside for a full minute before he detected a movement and drew in his breath sharply.

'It's a stag!'

'There's more than one up there. It's a small herd.'

'They're red deer. I'm surprised they haven't seen us.'

'They probably have, but we're too far off at the moment to pose any threat.' As he was speaking Wyatt was studying the terrain — and he saw what he was seeking. If he and Donnie Ross dropped down the slope a short distance, a belt of gorse would hide their progress from the sharp-eyed stag.

Keeping the gorse between themselves and the grazing animals, the two men worked their way slowly and cautiously along the mountain slope, not risking so much as a glance towards the spot where they had last seen the deer. But eventually the gorse came to an end and there was nothing ahead but low-growing heather. Signalling for his companion to remain low, Wyatt slowly — very slowly — raised his head above the level of the bushes.

There was not an animal in sight.

Wyatt conveyed the news to Donnie Ross in a hoarse whisper. The young man surveyed the scene with equal caution before crouching beside Wyatt once more.

'There's a slight ridge about fifty feet above us. I believe they must be grazing on the other side.'

Wyatt looked again. 'I think you're right. Let's go and find out.'

Leaving the cover of the gorse, the two men made their way to the ridge with even more caution than before. Wyatt was the first to reach it and he chose a spot where there was a small outcrop of rock. Raising his head very, very slowly, he suddenly froze, his hand motioning for Donnie Ross to remain perfectly still.

When he pulled back again, Wyatt whispered excitedly: 'There's a young stag no more than a hundred paces away. Is your musket loaded and primed?'

Donnie Ross shook his head. 'Can I take a look?'

'Yes, but be careful.'

Moments later the younger Ross was back beside Wyatt. 'It's too far. I couldn't hit it from here.'

'We'll never have a better shot. They're grazing away from us. . . .' Wyatt hesitated for only a moment more. 'Pass me the gun. Powder and shot, too.'

Donnie Ross's mouth dropped open. '*You're* going to try a shot?'

Wyatt was already measuring a quantity of coarse black powder in the palm of his hand. He added a pinch more before pouring it carefully into the end of the long barrel. A ball wrapped in a small canvas patch followed and was rammed down carefully and silently.

Donnie Ross followed the loading ritual closely and shook his head. 'You'll probably miss. Pa's the only man I know who might score a hit at this range.'

Wyatt completed his preparations for firing from the ancient flintlock and made a last-minute check on flint and pan. All was as it should be. It felt 'right'. The feel of a well-loaded musket. Something that no training sergeant could impart to a recruit. It was a feeling he had forgotten until now.

Replacing the ramrod beneath the long-barrelled musket, Wyatt peered over the rocks. There were five deer altogether and, if anything, they had moved farther away, grazing the new season's heather higher up the slope.

Wyatt carefully slid the long barrel between two small rocks and took careful aim at the nearest stag. It was an animal of no more than two years of age with immature straight antlers. His finger tightened on the trigger . . . and the animal moved.

Wyatt moved the weapon to follow the stag's progress, and as he did so the barrel of the musket struck one of the rocks.

In an instant five heads came up, and Wyatt knew that in another few moments they would be gone. It was now or never. He pulled the trigger. There was a loud report, and for a brief moment neither man could see anything through the cloud of acrid gunpowder-smoke. When it cleared they could see all five deer running.

'You've missed!' Even as Donnie shouted the words the stag nearest to them stumbled to its knees and then fell on its side.

Donnie Ross let out a yell that might have been heard all the way to Bannockburn, adding still more speed to the hoofs of the surviving animals.

'That was a *great* shot. You wait till I tell Pa that our preacher downed a stag at a hundred and fifty paces with Great-Grandad's gun.'

'I can't help feeling there might have been an element of luck involved. . . .'

Donnie Ross's expression showed that he, for one, dismissed the possibility of it being a lucky shot. Wyatt had to admit to himself that he, too, felt none of the humility he ought to have shown after downing one of the most beautiful of God's creatures.

CHAPTER FIFTEEN

SHRILL CRIES OF DELIGHT greeted Wyatt and Donnie Ross when the two men entered the shielings. The women had been expecting Wyatt since Seonaid Fraser had arrived and told them the minister of Eskaig was on his way to visit them.

'You've done fine to bring in a deer for us, Donnie,' said Tibbie Ross, avoiding looking directly at Wyatt. 'Although I hope the factor doesn't get to hear you've been shooting the laird's deer. He'd not be too happy with the Ross family.'

'It was the preacher who shot it, not me.'

Donnie Ross was in the middle of a group of admiring women, and Wyatt thought he might have been excused had he sought to take some of the glory, albeit unearned, for a while longer. 'Preacher Jamieson has Lord Kilmalie's permission to hunt whenever he wants.'

'Well! Our minister has a great many unexpected talents. How long are you staying with us, Minister Jamieson?'

There was such a wealth of implied familiarity in Seonaid Fraser's voice that many of the older women looked to Wyatt to observe his reaction.

'I'll be staying long enough to help eat the stag – and to hold a service for you all. I trust you'll surprise me, Seonaid, by being able to say all the prayers along with me.'

His reply brought a chorus of hoots from the women, aimed at Seonaid Fraser, and Wyatt knew he had successfully stepped over the trap she had placed before him.

Wyatt could not see Mairi among the women. In fact there were very few faces he recognised.

'If it's our Mairi you're looking for, you'll find her down at the stream with the butter-makers.' The information was volunteered by Tibbie Ross and accompanied by a knowing smile.

'I'll no doubt see her before I leave. I went to the croft to see why none of the Ross family has been to my kirk lately. As I was so close I decided to come on to the shielings. I'm glad I did; there are many here I've never seen before. Certainly not in Eskaig for a Sunday service.'

One of the listening women, her face weathered from many years of outdoor working, said sharply: 'Highland folk are closer to God up here in the lands He made than they ever were in Preacher Gunn's kirk in Eskaig.'

There were many murmurs of agreement – proof once again that, although Wyatt's predecessor might have had a strong following around Loch Eil, he had none up here among the crofters and cottars of the mountains.

'It was no more Preacher Gunn's kirk than it is mine. It belongs to the Lord. You're as welcome there as anyone else. It's my intention to learn something about each of you while I'm here, then I'll look forward to meeting your menfolk in Eskaig one Sunday soon. But don't let me stop you from working. You'll need to have all your chores done if we're to enjoy a good meeting tonight.'

The Highlanders were a polite people, and Wyatt had toiled all the way from Eskaig to meet them. They would attend the service and hear what he had to say to them. However, not everyone would be able to attend the proposed prayer meeting, and it was noticeable that the herd-boys suddenly took an unprecedented interest in their charges, vying with each other to perform what were usually unpopular evening chores.

Wyatt wandered about the shielings talking to the women. Some came to Eskaig once or twice a year in order to buy those household items they could neither make nor improvise. Others had never left the mountains during their lifetime. If it was not possible to make an exchange for something they wanted, they went without. Most of these were cottars, or sub-tenants. They rented their primitive cots in exchange for labour and a percentage of their crops from tenants who were themselves almost as poor. It was an archaic and inefficient method of husbandry that was still prevalent in both Ireland and the Highlands of Scotland. The method needed to be brought up to date. There had to be change, but it would take time to alter customs that went back hundreds of years — and time was not on the side of the Highlanders.

It was more than an hour before Wyatt reached the stream where Mairi and a few other girls were making heavily salted butter for the whole of the shielings. He had glanced in her direction more than once as he moved around, but she always seemed to be busy.

There were a number of different types of butter-churn in use by the women. Mairi was working a plunger type, the buttermilk being agitated by means of a plunger attached to a long stick which she worked two-handed. The churns had been brought in hand-pulled carts, or packed on the backs of ponies from remote Highland cots. Keeping the heavy wooden plunger moving inside its tall iron-banded churn was warm work, and Mairi was both hot and bad-tempered.

'Nice of you to drop by, *Minister* Jamieson,' she retorted in answer to his greeting. 'I'm surprised you have the time to come visiting *us*, what with your kirk, the school . . . and the factor's daughter.'

Mairi brushed back a tress of black hair with her hand and attacked the butter-churn with renewed vigour.

'What's Evangeline Garrett got to do with anything?' Mairi's verbal attack had taken Wyatt by surprise. He was not to know Mairi had mentioned his name so often at the shielings that he had become known, even to those who had never met him, as 'Mairi's minister'.

His unexpected visit to the shielings had provoked much comment, and the sly glances cast in Mairi's direction did not pass unnoticed by her. When Wyatt had chosen to speak to most of the other women first, not approaching her until he had been in the glen for more than an hour, the sly innuendoes assumed a new and more spiteful nature. Wyatt was paying the penalty for his tardiness.

'I thought you might have had to ask her permission before coming up here on a visit.' Mairi's anger was subsiding as swiftly as it had erupted, leaving her feeling rather foolish, but she was determined Wyatt should not know. 'She seems to decide most other things in your life — like who can go to your school. . . .'

So that was it. Wyatt was vaguely relieved. 'Evangeline is the teacher. It's for she and Alasdair Burns to decide who they're going to teach. Otherwise they could say with justification that I am running *their* lives for them. Besides, as I recall, it was *you* who made the decision to leave.'

'That was only so she wouldn't have the satisfaction of throwing me out.' The plunger thumped on the base of the churn as Mairi attacked her task once more. 'You'd better hurry up and start your prayer meeting. It will be dark before you get back to Eskaig as it is.'

'I'm not returning to Eskaig tonight – and you'd better go easy, or you'll knock the bottom out of that churn.'

As the plunger thumped against the base of the butter-churn, Wyatt walked off to help two women carry a wooden tub that must have contained at least eight gallons of milk.

Life at the shielings was well organised. Women and young boys had been coming here for longer than anyone could remember, and they all knew what was required of them. Without the summer grazing, those who lived among the high mountains could not survive. During the all too brief summer months nature was bountiful here. Beef cattle were fattened for the late-autumn sales held in Fort William and Inverness. They might even be driven to lowland areas if their numbers and the prevailing price made such a journey worthwhile. Dairy cattle, too, enjoyed the lush grass, and their milk was shared between calves and butter-maidens. Hopefully the cattle would leave the shielings with enough fat on their bones to survive the long hard Highland winter, sharing a cot with their owners. Not *all* would survive. In a bad winter four out of five might perish and there would be hardly enough meat on their bones to flavour a good stew.

This was the background to the days spent at the shielings, but the grim reality of survival in the mountains was not allowed to spoil the comparatively carefree life the women enjoyed here. Through the dark cold days of winter, beleaguered by penury and privation and with even basic survival hanging in the balance, the shielings provided happy memories of the past and hope for the future.

Until about an hour before dusk, Wyatt moved about the shielings talking to cheese-makers, herd-boys, milkmaids and cooks. Except for Donnie Ross, all the boys were beneath the age of fourteen. By contrast, the women were of all ages, ranging from the youngest girls to old women who sat hunched in disapproval, glowering on the scene about them as they knitted or worked tapestry. These doyennes of the shielings missed nothing that their own kinswomen were doing and frequently called out a warning if the behaviour of the younger women did not meet with their approval.

There was singing, too. Songs of the herd-boys farther along the glen; the singing of the cheese-makers and the women tending the cooking-fires. . . . But most beautiful of all was the singing of the dairymaids as they went about the evening milking. There must have been thirty or forty girls milking cows, and each song began with one clear voice singing a low, lilting, haunting tune that had been sung in this glen by many generations of milkmaids. The words would be taken up by others, and it was a sound that no listener would ever forget.

Wyatt had heard the same songs many times before when he was a boy in the Isles. They brought back memories he had thought were long forgotten. Yet he had never heard them sung as they were this evening, and he knew he never would again.

'It's such beautiful music. It always makes me want to cry when I hear it.'

There was no anger in Mairi now, but her voice startled Wyatt. He turned and saw her standing close behind him. She looked cooler, having washed in the cold Highland stream, and her dark hair had been brushed and tied back behind her neck.

'It's very moving,' agreed Wyatt. He cast another glance at Mairi. She had changed her dress, too. She still wore working-clothes – no one would have any different here at the shielings – but they were clean and fresh. 'You seem to have left your ill-humour back there with your butter-churn.'

Anger sprang to Mairi's face momentarily, but as Wyatt caught his breath in anticipation of another explosion she saw the humour in his eyes and smiled ruefully.

'I'm sorry. I don't even know *why* I was so rude to you.'

'You've been working very hard, and it's a hot day. We're all entitled to be bad-tempered sometimes without a need to explain it.'

'Perhaps. All the same, it wasn't *all* my fault that I didn't get along with Miss High-and-mighty at your school.'

'I never thought for one moment it was. That's why I've brought some books up here for you. Most are school books, but there's a bible, too. It was my mother's. I'd like you to have it.'

Feeling suddenly embarrassed, Wyatt said: 'I think more people must have learned to read and write using a bible than from any other book that will ever be written. I'll find time before I go to help you get started on a few lessons.'

Mairi could only murmur her thanks, because at that moment one of the older women came to tell Wyatt that now would be the best time to hold a prayer meeting, before the women had supper ready.

'You'll be eating with us,' said Mairi as word was passed for the women and boys to gather for the service. 'The best cut from an animal is always given to the hunter, and my mouth is watering at the thought of sharing it with you.'

Wyatt kept the prayer meeting brief and simple. A show of hands provided him with the information that only a few of his congregation had ever seen the inside of a church and not many of these had attended a service in recent years.

Even so, it was a prayer meeting that Wyatt would never forget. The shielings were located in a beautiful spot. The slopes were lush with rich green grass, and beyond them were rugged mountains shaded in every colour imaginable. Wyatt's prayers and the responses were made to an accompaniment of lowing cattle, bleating calves and the music of a fast-flowing shallow burn. Over it all hung the scent of peat fires and the aroma of cooking venison.

There was an undignified scramble among the herd-boys to be first in line when Wyatt gave a final blessing on the congregation, but their supper was assured. They were well looked after at the shielings, especially as after the meal some of them would be going off to guard the cattle throughout the night. There were many foxes in the area bold enough to attack a sleeping calf. Apart from the loss of a precious animal the noise was likely to cause a stampede, scattering the cattle for miles across the Highlands and causing many injuries among them.

As dusk settled upon the glen Wyatt sat at a peat cooking-fire, sharing a meal with Mairi, Tibbie and Donnie Ross. All about them were many other fires, most with their own family groups. Some were celebrating the occasion with song, others sat in silence; but tonight, at least, no one would go to bed hungry.

'Does Seonaid Fraser have any special friends with whom to share a cooking-fire?'

Wyatt asked the question in all innocence and was unprepared for the reaction of the others. Donnie jumped as though someone had fired a shot alongside his ear, while Tibbie's snort was heard at the next fire, thirty paces away. Mairi fixed him with a look that was packed with questions.

It was Tibbie who eventually gave him an answer.

'She'll share a fire with anyone who needs a pair of hands and isn't fussy who they belong to.'

'That isn't true!' Donnie Ross sprang to Seonaid Fraser's defence immediately. 'Lots of folk are happy to have Seonaid help around their cooking-fire. She's a good worker. Better than both of you, I don't doubt.'

'The part of Seonaid Fraser that works hardest is something *you* should know nothing about, young Donnie. It's a good thing this will be your last year at the shielings. I told your father you were too old to come here. He should have listened to me.'

'Tibbie! Donnie! That's enough from both of you.' Mairi brought the quarrel to an abrupt end. 'Donnie, we need more water. Go to the burn and fetch some. Tibbie, we'll be needing more peat for the fire in a minute or two. We might as well have it now. Off you go.'

When brother and sister-in-law had gone off in different directions, Mairi explained to Wyatt: 'Tibbie knows Donnie's sweet on Seonaid. She shouldn't tease him so.'

Carefully turning a sizzling piece of venison on a wooden spit, Mairi looked across the fire to where Wyatt sat nursing a gently smoking pipe. 'What's *your* interest in her?'

'I feel sorry for the girl, I suppose. I called in to see her father on my way up here. She can't have the easiest of lives.'

'No,' Mairi agreed. 'But she doesn't go out of her way to make it any easier for herself.'

Before Wyatt could ask Mairi what she meant, Tibbie returned to the fire with an armful of half-dried peat turf.

'We'll need to cut more turfs tomorrow. We've at least six more weeks up here and hardly enough peat for three.'

'We've used more than usual tonight.' Mairi arranged a number of turfs about the burning fire, taking care not to disturb the glowing ashes immediately beneath the spitting meat. 'You must go easy on Donnie, Tibbie. You know how he hates to be teased – especially about Seonaid.'

'You'd be doing him more of a favour if you were to "tease" him yourself. If we're not careful, he'll be marrying the girl and bringing her home. Then we'll *all* know the meaning of trouble. I wouldn't leave her alone in the house with my Ian, I can tell you. I worked hard to get him; I'll not lose him to her.'

Wyatt would have liked to ask Tibbie what she meant, but Mairi said softly: 'Hush now, here's Donnie back.'

As though he was aware that the women had been talking about him, Donnie was scowling when he came into the firelight. He dropped the wooden bucket heavily to the ground, spilling some of the water.

By the time the water Donnie had spilled began hissing and steaming on the hot stones at the edge of the fire, he had gone off into the night once more.

'I'll go and find him. . . .' Wyatt rose to his feet. But Mairi said: 'Leave him. He'll be back for supper all the better for being left alone for a while.'

'I need to speak to him. To find out where he's sleeping and ask if he'll share his shelter with me.'

'Yours is already made. It's not much, but it will keep the wind off you, and we won't be having any rain tonight. It's over there, close to where Tibbie and I are sleeping. Donnie is a little farther away.'

The light from the fire was just strong enough for Wyatt to see a small lean-to shelter, no more than four feet high and perhaps seven long.

'You'll be comfortable enough on your bed,' said Tibbie mischievously. 'Mairi made it herself from fresh new heather. I've never known her take so much trouble over anything before. You should sleep like a newborn babe.'

CHAPTER SIXTEEN

SUPPER was a very pleasant meal. Donnie returned to the fire in a better humour, and Tibbie refrained from criticising him about Seonaid Fraser. One of the older women sent across a generous jar of whisky 'for the minister', and there was enough to be passed around among the four of them.

After the meal was over, Tibbie wearily announced that hard work, a meat supper *and* a prayer meeting were all too much for her to take in one day and she was going to bed. She had been gone only a few minutes when Donnie picked up his flintlock musket and said he would check the herd-boys. There had been a fox on the prowl for a few nights.

'Has he really gone to check on the herd-boys?' Wyatt asked the question of Mairi when Donnie had gone.

'He'll check every one,' confirmed Mairi, adding what Wyatt already knew: 'Donnie's incapable of telling a lie. It doesn't mean he'll come straight back here, mind you. . . .'

'You're not as set against Seonaid as Tibbie is?'

'Seonaid's no better and no worse than a girl with her background ought to be.'

'You mean, because her mother committed suicide and she has a blind father to cope with?'

'There's few up here in the mountains who believe Seonaid's mother committed suicide. Hamish Fraser could see well enough at that time to have followed his wife when she went off on one of her "visits" – or so I've heard said. But I'm only repeating gossip. As for Seonaid . . . I don't believe all I've heard, but I wouldn't care to see her marry Donnie. He deserves better.'

'Does Donnie know of John Garrett's interest in the girl?'

Mairi's surprise was too great to keep hidden. '*You* know about that? You *have* worked hard on getting to know what's happening here, Minister Jamieson. No, I don't think Donnie's heard the rumours about Seonaid and the factor. If he has, he's dismissed them, just as he has all the other rumours about her. As far as Donnie's concerned, Seonaid can do no wrong.'

'I've known far worse girls than Seonaid Fraser who've made very good wives. . . .' Wyatt hesitated. 'And I'd like you to call me Wyatt. I feel we know each other well enough for that.'

Wyatt's words gave Mairi a warm glow inside, but instead of allowing her feelings to show she said: 'You must know a great many people "well", *Minister Jamieson*. I seem to recall that you and Miss Garrett are on first-name terms.'

'You have a wonderfully selective memory, *Mairi Ross*, but we were talking about your brother and Seonaid. No doubt the situation will resolve itself by next year when Donnie goes off with his brothers . . . for the sheep.'

'What do you know of the sheep? Who told you?'

Mairi's questions came back too quickly, confirming the suspicion Wyatt already held. The sons of Eneas Ross had gone to the lowlands not to *buy* sheep but to *steal* them.

'Your father told me only that your brothers had gone to bring back some sheep. The inference was they would be buying them, but I suspected the truth. When I was in Glasgow I heard talk about Highlanders reverting to the old ways. Raiding sheep-farms in the lowlands and bringing the animals back here with them.'

'I'm not saying that *is* what the boys are doing but, if they are, who has the right to say they're doing wrong? The sheepmen come here to graze their sheep on the mountains, offering the landowners more money than they've ever seen before – on condition the crofters and cottars are cleared. They're stealing our lands, our homes, our whole way of life. Are we wrong to fight back?'

'What your brothers are doing is not "fighting back", Mairi. It's *stealing*, and stealing is wrong.'

'So you side with the landowners? I should have expected it, I suppose. At first I thought . . . I *believed* you were different.'

'I'm pointing out that stealing is wrong. It's against God's law and it's contrary to the laws of the land. The good Lord may be prevailed upon to forgive sinners, but the law isn't so understanding, and it's the law I'm particularly concerned about right now. I told you I heard talk in Glasgow about sheep-stealing. It was said the government had agreed to use the militia to guard the flocks. What happens if your brothers come up against militiamen instead of unarmed shepherds?'

'Do you really think they might?' Mairi's eyes were deep dark shadows in the firelight.

'I think it's highly likely. Is it possible to go after them and bring them back?'

Mairi shook her head. 'They've been gone too long. They're due back any day now.'

'Then, I trust for everyone's sake they haven't been caught. A sheep-stealing raid originating on Kilmalie land would give Garrett all the excuse he needs to clear every tenant from these mountains.'

'Ian's with them. He won't let them do anything stupid.' Mairi's words expressed more confidence than she felt. Ian, Tibbie's husband, liked to think things through before doing anything, but he would not be expecting militiamen to be guarding the lowland sheep.

'I'll go home and have a word with Pa tomorrow. He'll know what can be done. Now I must take these dishes to the burn and clean them ready for the morning.' Mairi wanted something to take her mind off her concern for her brothers.

'I'll carry them down to the burn for you.'

Mairi looked at Wyatt quizzically. 'I hardly need help to carry four plates.'

'All the same, I'll carry them.'

It was a moonless night, but the sky was liberally sprinkled with stars. These, coupled with the many cooking-fires dotted about the shielings, made progress to the stream easy. Along the way they passed a number of women returning, and Wyatt wondered whether it was his imagination that put a depth of meaning in their polite 'Good night to you, Mairi. Good night, Minister'.

He knew it had not been imagination when Mairi said: 'Your reputation will be in tatters after this . . . Wyatt.'

Mairi's use of his Christian name for the first time gave Wyatt a ridiculous sense of pleasure. 'If that's true, you'll need to make an honest man of me and stop their tongues wagging.'

He regretted the weak joke as soon as he had made it. Mairi made no reply and did not speak again until they were both kneeling in the darkness at the edge of the stream.

'Is this what camp life was like when you were a soldier?' Mairi's soft-voiced question broke her long silence.

'On the good nights, perhaps, although the company often left much to be desired.'

'What of the women Ma has told me about?'

'She remembers the Peninsular campaigns. My active service was spent in Africa. The few women who accompanied us there were left in a township on the coast.'

'Has there never been a woman in your life?'

'No one in particular. There *was* one, a distant cousin. I expected to see more of her when I returned from Africa, but she married and moved to America while I was away.'

'Were you very upset?'

'Not that I can recall. A little disappointed, perhaps, but by then I had my mind set on the Church.'

'You're an unusual minister, Wyatt. Very different from Preacher Gunn. You can shoot, you take the side of the Highlanders – and you're not eager to condemn.'

'We all have our own way of doing things. I've seen too much of life and men's weaknesses and strengths to think I know everything. I don't doubt that many of those who live in Eskaig wish they had a minister more like their last one.'

'I like your way of doing things much better. You make God sound like someone *real*. Someone who *cares*. Preacher Gunn made Him sound like someone who was watching just so He could catch us out when we did anything wrong.'

Wyatt stood up and placed the plates on the grass while he wiped his hands on the kerchief he carried. 'I learned about God from my father. He never doubted for one minute of his life that God cares deeply for each and every one of us. He was right, although it sometimes wasn't easy to believe when I watched men dying in agony on a battlefield.'

Mairi rose to her feet, too, and as she did so put a hand on Wyatt's arm. Whether it was an expression of sympathy, or because she felt herself slipping on the soft wet earth, was uncertain, but slip she certainly did. If Wyatt had not caught her, she would have fallen into the stream.

Regaining her balance, she laughed. When Wyatt made no move to release her she fell silent. When he drew her close she did not pull away. Then he was kissing her as he had never before kissed anyone, and she responded with an ardour that equalled his own. For a few minutes the lust of the flesh became a reality to the man of God.

Wyatt pulled back from her, his thoughts in a turmoil. 'Mairi . . . I'm sorry.'

He was still holding her, and she said: 'If you really feel you need to say sorry, then I'm sorry, too.'

'I shouldn't have done that. . . . It wasn't right. . . .'

Mairi pulled herself free of his grasp. 'You needn't worry yourself. I won't tell anyone. Your reputation may be dented by what the other women are thinking, but that's all. Anyway, it was only a kiss. . . .'

'I don't care what anyone says or thinks about *me*. Right now I'd happily shout it from the pulpit that I've kissed you.'

Despite the darkness, Wyatt knew Mairi was smiling again.

'I think that's the way I feel, too, so what is there to be sorry about?'

'I didn't want it to *end* there, Mairi. I had thoughts I've never had before. Thoughts I stand in my kirk and preach against. . . .'

Suddenly Mairi kissed him again, but she stepped back quickly before he could take hold of her. 'I'm glad, Minister Wyatt Jamieson. It means you're human, the same as anyone else. I'd hate to grow over-fond of a man who planned to become a saint.'

Before the import of her words had fully registered, they both heard a sound from nearby and fell silent instinctively. A minute or so later two people passed by at some distance, talking quietly. It was too dark to see any more than that the couple were very close to each other, but their low voices gave them away.

'It's Donnie,' hissed Mairi.

'And Seonaid,' agreed Wyatt.

'I knew it! I knew they'd be up to no good if I didn't keep watch on them every minute of the day and night.'

'Where are you going?' Wyatt caught Mairi's arm before she could hurry after the young couple who had now passed from hearing.

'To find out what she's been up to with Donnie. . . .'

'Will you tell them what *we* were doing here when we heard them?'

'Had they been doing no more, I wouldn't be concerned, but they've done more than kiss, or her name's not Seonaid Fraser.'

'You don't know that, Mairi. Folk who saw us here might say the same about us.'

'Oh, no! Donnie isn't a minister of the Church, and Seonaid Fraser isn't a Ross – nor will she be if I have anything to say about the matter. Come on, I've things to say to that young brother of mine.'

Mairi's questioning did not take place that night. Wyatt and Mairi were no more than halfway back to the cooking-fire when a shout went up from farther down the glen. It brought the occupants of the shielings running from their makeshift shelters. A fox, or probably two, had eluded the herd-boys and attacked a calf born only that evening. Before the boys drove off the attackers the calf's throat had been torn open, and the unfortunate animal lay gasping out its brief life on the turf.

The rumpus so frightened the other cattle that a number of them stampeded along the glen. They met the Highland women running towards the scene and split up, running in half a hundred different directions.

It was close to dawn before the last animal was returned to the shielings, and the moment of reckoning for Donnie Ross had been put off until another time.

CHAPTER SEVENTEEN

MAIRI WALKED as far as her home with Wyatt. There was a vague feeling of embarrassment between them, although all the long silences originated with the Eskaig preacher. Mairi chattered about the problem of Donnie, her worries about the other brothers, life at the shielings. . . . Anything except her relationship with the man walking beside her.

Not until they were in sight of the stunted trees sheltering the Ross cot did Wyatt mention the incident that had kept him silent during the long walk from the shielings.

'Mairi, I want to speak to you. About what happened last night.'

Mairi stopped walking and turned to look at him.

'Do you mean the attack on the poor calf by the foxes?' she asked innocently. 'They've found the foxes' lair. Donnie will lie in wait for them today. It won't happen again.'

'That isn't what I want to talk about.'

'Oh? Then, perhaps you have an answer to the problem of Donnie and Seonaid Fraser? I'll be obliged to you if you have.'

'Mairi, you know very well it's *us* I want to discuss.'

'Are you going to tell me you're sorry once again?'

'No . . . well, *yes*. . . .'

Never in all his life had Wyatt been so tongue-tied and confused. Mairi did not suffer the same problem.

'I don't want to listen.'

She began to walk on, faster than before. When Wyatt caught up with her and tried to speak again, she cut him short.

'You're so anxious to apologise that I can only believe you wish nothing had happened. All right, forget it, if that's what you want. I won't tell anyone that "the minister" kissed me. Anyway, I expect you kissed so many girls when you were a soldier that forgetting one more won't matter too much to you.'

When Wyatt brought her to a halt Mairi looked up at him defiantly, only her eyes giving any hint of the solid cold unhappiness inside her.

'I'm not apologising for kissing you. I *wanted* to. I . . . I just don't think it should have happened the way it did, hidden by darkness. I ought to have said something to you first. I don't want you getting the idea . . . the idea you *have*. There have been few women in my life. You're very special to me. I wanted you to know this.'

It was the most difficult speech he had ever put together, far harder than the sermon at his induction as minister of Eskaig, but the expression on Mairi's face told Wyatt it had been a success.

'Thank you for saying that, Wyatt. About it being special, I mean. It was special for me, too. *Very* special. As for it being dark when you kissed me . . . it's not dark now.'

He kissed her, and she clung to him to make it last as long as the breath in her would allow. When they reluctantly drew apart, she said shakily: 'I hope you're not going to apologise again.'

'No.' He took her hand and began walking towards the hidden cot. 'But I think we need to talk a little.'

Their talk had to be deferred. They had walked no more than a few paces when a voice hailed them from the direction of the cot. They looked up to see a tall young man waving to them.

'It's Dugald!' Mairi released Wyatt's hand and returned the greeting. Dugald was one of her brothers. 'The boys must be back.'

However, all the Ross brothers had not yet returned from their sheep-'buying' expedition to the lowlands. When Mairi enquired about the others Dugald replied vaguely that they had sent him on ahead to let their father know of their plans. They should be arriving with the sheep in a few days' time.

'You had no trouble?' Mairi put the question as her father came from the house and greeted the Eskaig minister with a nod.

'It was the easiest trip we've ever made,' replied her brother proudly. 'You've never seen such sheep. You'd think we'd rounded up cattle by mistake!'

Silencing his son with a frown, Eneas Ross asked Mairi: 'What made you think there might have been trouble?'

When Mairi hesitated, Wyatt said: 'I told Mairi of something I heard before leaving Glasgow. The authorities were planning to deal with an increase in sheep-stealing by mustering the militia. They believe the Highlanders are resorting to their old ways. They are determined to put a stop to it.'

'If there's a drought in the lowlands, it's blamed on the Highlanders,' retorted Eneas Ross. 'If they come here seeking their sheep, they'll end up chasing their own tails. They'll find nothing.'

Eneas Ross's manner was scornful, but Wyatt knew the ex-Scots Guardsman was no fool. He would heed Wyatt's warning and take whatever action might be necessary.

Dugald Ross was absent from the meal of bread, cheese and new-made butter brought from the shielings by Mairi. No excuse was made for the young man's absence, but Wyatt had seen father and son engaged in earnest conversation a short while before.

Later, when Wyatt was preparing to leave the cot, Magdalene Ross called from where she was working at the kitchen table beneath a window, to say that two horsemen were approaching from the direction of Eskaig.

With thoughts of the militia uppermost in his mind, Wyatt was first to reach the door. Magdalene Ross had been only partly correct. The riders were still far off in the distance, but it was possible to see that one of them was mounted upon a donkey.

It was Coll Kennedy. The other rider was well wrapped in a cloak and a hat and was unrecognisable at this distance. Not until the horse was urged forward at a brisk trot was Wyatt able to see that its rider was not a man, but a woman. It was Evangeline Garrett.

Wyatt was even more surprised when the horse was pulled to a halt only a few paces from the gate where he was now standing. Evangeline leaped to the ground and ran to embrace him warmly, an expression of great relief on her face.

'Wyatt, where have you *been*? We were all so worried when you never returned last night. I wanted to organise a search party for you. I would have, too, had Alasdair not persuaded me to wait until today. At this very moment he and the Eskaig villagers are searching around the banks of Loch Eil. What have you been doing?'

'I've been at the shielings. I held a prayer meeting there yesterday evening.'

'Why didn't you tell someone where you were going? When

Preacher Kennedy rode over from Letterfinlay this morning I made him ride straight out with me again to help search for you. It was he who suggested we come up here. Didn't you realise how worried we'd all be? Oh, it doesn't matter. You're safe, that's the important thing.'

Evangeline hugged him again, and Coll Kennedy's eyebrows disappeared beneath the wide brim of the hat he wore pulled low down on his forehead.

Breaking free from the factor's daughter, Wyatt extended a hand to the mule-riding minister. 'I'm sorry if I've caused you to extend an already long ride.'

'No one need apologise for bringing me up here. Quite apart from the beauty of the mountains hereabouts, I know the identity of the man who supplies Eneas Ross with his whisky. There's not a distiller in Scotland to compare with him.'

'You'll be treated to new-baked bread and butter fresh from the shielings, too, I've no doubt. Mairi brought some home not two hours since.'

'You've been to the shielings with the Ross girl?' Evangeline Garrett's delight at having found Wyatt suddenly vanished.

'With Mairi and about a hundred others.' Wyatt would not allow Evangeline's disapproval to make him feel guilty. 'It's the first time a minister's been there to hold a prayer meeting. It was a great occasion.'

'No doubt. Are you coming to Eskaig now to help me explain how I've made a fool of myself?'

'I'm deeply touched by your concern for me, Evangeline, but before I return to Eskaig there are a few things I want to say to the Ross family.'

'I see. Well, I doubt if I am very welcome here. Thank you for accompanying me, Minister Kennedy. I expect I shall see you again in Eskaig.'

Mounting her horse, Evangeline Garrett cast an angry glance in Wyatt's direction before tugging hard on the reins and heading her horse back towards Eskaig.

'A young lady with a mercurial temperament, I fear,' commented Coll Kennedy. 'But attractive enough. She'll no doubt tempt some besotted young man into wedlock one day.'

'No doubt,' agreed Wyatt. 'But you haven't ridden all this way to gossip about the marriage prospects of the factor's daughter. On the way inside you can tell me why you came to visit me.'

'We'll need longer than that to discuss my news, Wyatt. Things are happening in our church that are making thinking men uneasy. The time is coming when a decision must be made. It's vitally important that it's the *right* one. We'll discuss it on the way back to Eskaig. First, I intend to enjoy an hour or two of traditional crofting hospitality.'

Eneas Ross met the two men at the door of the cot and gravely shook hands with Coll Kennedy. 'We met at Preacher Jamieson's induction, but I never expected to welcome you to my house. *Two* preachers in one day! The good Lord must be making amends for all the years when we never saw a one.'

'I'll leave the saving of your soul to Minister Jamieson, Eneas. I came up in the mountains to find him and I'm resting here a while out of respect for the man who keeps you supplied with whisky. He has no equal anywhere in the Highlands.'

Eneas Ross's face split in a wide smile. He recognised in the Letterfinlay minister a man who understood the essentials of life, minister of the Church or not. 'I've something inside I know you'll enjoy, Preacher. It's supposed to be twenty years old. I wouldn't swear my life away on its age, but I promise you'll never have tasted a finer dram anywhere.'

As Eneas Ross talked, Wyatt was waiting for Mairi to appear. When the whisky arrived and she had not put in an appearance, he asked where she was.

'Gone back to the shielings.' The surprising reply came from Magdalene Ross. 'She followed you out when you went to meet your friend, then came back to the cot and said she was going. Why she should be in such a hurry I don't know. Didn't she say goodbye to you?'

Wyatt was deeply hurt that Mairi had returned to the shielings without speaking to him first. He wanted to have another talk with her. Then he remembered the enthusiasm with which Evangeline Garrett had greeted him. He thought he knew why Mairi had returned to the shielings so abruptly, and the knowledge would trouble him until they met again and he was able to explain. . . .

CHAPTER EIGHTEEN

ON THE WAY BACK to Eskaig, Coll Kennedy told Wyatt what had brought him from Letterfinlay. The donkey-riding minister had consumed an astonishing quantity of Eneas Ross's whisky, declaring it to be quite as good as had been promised. However, the news he had to impart to Wyatt would have sobered even the most drunken preacher.

There had been another court ruling about the right of a parish to elect its own minister. A man who had achieved notoriety for paying close attention to other men's wives when their husbands were absent was presented to a living by the landowner, in spite of strong local objections. When the time came for his induction only the local innkeeper signed the minister's call. At the same time, every male member of the parish put his name to a petition calling for the landowner to nominate someone else.

So unsuited for his post was the new minister that when the landowner refused to heed the wishes of his tenants the Church itself set aside the unwanted preacher's appointment.

Determined not to be beaten, the landowner placed the matter before a secular court. The court found for the landowner. Disinclined to flout the law of the land, the presbytery responsible for the area agreed to the induction.

The Assembly, the 'supreme court' of the Church, immediately brought its full weight to bear upon what had become a power struggle between Church and State. The Assembly issued an order prohibiting the presbytery from settling the unwanted minister upon the objecting parishioners.

When it became clear that the presbytery intended to put State before Church, the Assembly took the unprecedented step of suspending the ministers of the presbytery, thus prohibiting them from conducting any services.

Ignoring the orders of the Assembly, the dismissed presbytery went ahead with the induction. At the ceremony the parishioners gathered at their church and petitioned the presbytery to reconsider its action. When their plea was ignored, the people rose as one and left their place of worship, never to return.

The action of both sides had split the Church of Scotland apart. When the House of Lords, the highest court in the realm, upheld the findings of the lower courts a vast body of opinion within the Church was dismayed. It was a very strongly held belief that only the parishioners themselves could tie the pastoral knot that bound a minister to his flock.

Even now battle-lines were being drawn, with ministers lining up on both sides of the argument. A meeting of those who objected to State interference in the Church was to take place in Edinburgh in November. The decisions made here would decide the future of the Church of Scotland. Coll Kennedy had come to ask Wyatt where he stood, and whether he would accompany the Letterfinlay minister to the Edinburgh conference.

Wyatt had no hesitation. The conflict had been bubbling for a long time, and he knew what he had to do.

'You already know where I stand, Coll. I was ready to give up the living of Eskaig when I believed the people didn't want me. It's *they* who must decide who they want as their minister. That's the rock on which our church is built. If we don't fight this issue, we're only one step short of having the State appoint ministers without reference to either Church *or* people. The State won't give way on this question, and the Church *can't*. Only the Lord himself knows the answer to the problem. Where does our own presbytery stand?'

Coll Kennedy changed position on his donkey, easing some of his aching muscles. 'They are no more united than the Church itself. Half are for carrying on as though nothing has happened. The others want to break away and form a free church, based upon Presbyterian principles.'

Coll Kennedy was echoing the view put forward by Alasdair Burns when the subject had been brought up soon after the teacher's arrival at Eskaig. It was a radical solution, not the fruits of reasoned argument among churchmen.

'I would be happy if it were possible to settle matters within the Church itself, but I fear it's already too late for reconciliation.'

That evening Alasdair Burns joined the two ministers for a meal in the manse, and the crisis within the Church was the sole subject of conversation.

Alasdair Burns was of the same opinion as the two ministers.

'I can't see that you have any alternative but to break away and form a new church. The sooner you face facts and take action, the better it will be for everyone. The longer you leave it, the harder it will be. You're merely giving the "Establishment" time to make a Disruption as difficult as possible.'

'It will be difficult enough anyway,' declared Wyatt. 'Imagine the decision facing a minister who has given a lifetime to the Church. He'll need to rebel against all he has worked for and begin a new life at a time when he should be looking forward to peaceful old age. This without a home or a kirk. What of the wives and dependants of ministers? How will they react to being turned out of their homes?'

'A man must be true to his beliefs,' said the schoolteacher. 'Nothing worthwhile has ever been achieved without suffering and sacrifice.'

'Sacrifice is worthwhile only if it fully achieves its end,' said Coll Kennedy. 'Unfortunately, I fear many of our older ministers might go to their graves believing their sacrifices to have been in vain.'

'I thought Christianity promised us nothing in *this* life, all the rewards being saved for the next? Surely your ministers will find their answers waiting for them in the great world to come?'

'I'm sure they will,' said Coll Kennedy. 'But even those who are about to achieve that happy state will want to know those they leave behind will enjoy a degree of comfort and security.'

'Don't underestimate the strength of the wives and families of our ministers,' said Wyatt. 'Many have been the strength behind the Church for years. You'll not find them wanting when the call for action comes.'

'I think there's one thing you're both overlooking,' said Alasdair Burns. 'When the smoke of battle has cleared the only winners are likely to be the landowners. All over the Highlands all that's standing in the way of wholesale clearances is a few articulate ministers.

Take away the backing of an established church and the clearances will resume on a scale that will empty the Highlands of people faster than sheep can be driven in.'

Factor John Garrett rode up to the Ross croft in company with the sheriff-substitute, ten constables and a party of twenty sore-footed militiamen who formed a ragged line in front of the cot gate and leaned heavily upon their muskets.

The constables dismounted, and they and the militiamen stood in two groups, talking nervously as John Garrett rode his horse through the narrow gateway and up to the door of the cot, the sheriff-substitute behind him.

In the doorway Eneas Ross stood silently watching their approach. His position in the doorway also prevented any of the hot-headed younger members of his family from leaving the cot and coming into contact with the forces of the law.

'Ross.' John Garrett spoke above the sound of a dog which darted from the house and was snapping at the legs of the factor's horse, causing it to back off nervously, trampling through the greenery of a vegetable patch. 'The sheriff-substitute's here to investigate a serious case of sheep-stealing. Damn you, man! Call off the dog or I'll have one of the militiamen put a musket-ball where its brain should be.'

Eneas Ross growled out a low command, and the dog returned to the cot immediately, pausing in the doorway to glance up at the crofter with a look that might have been accompanied by a wink had it been human.

'Those sheep out there. . . .' The factor leaned forward and indicated a flock of sheep grazing not far from the house. 'Are you going to claim they arrived in the dead of night and you know nothing of them?'

'Why should I say such a thing? They belong to me.'

John Garrett sank back in his saddle, looking pleased with himself. 'I think we've found your stolen sheep, Sheriff. Eneas Ross has never run sheep in his life. You'll have the culprits here, too. Ross's sons will be skulking not far away. They'll be the Highlanders who were seen driving sheep in this direction. Take the lot of them. The Kilmalie estate will be well rid of them.'

As the sheriff-substitute turned in the saddle to call orders to his men, Eneas Ross said: 'You've always been a man given to hasty decisions, Factor. It would no doubt have brought you trouble long ago had you not enjoyed the protection of the landlord.'

To the other man, Eneas Ross said: 'I expected more of a Scotsman – even a lowlander such as yourself. A "sheriff", did I hear the factor say?'

'Sheriff-substitute,' corrected the horseman. 'But the offices carry the same powers. If you have something to say, you'd better make it quick, before I call up my constables and the militiamen.'

Eneas Ross was unperturbed by the sheriff-substitute's threat. 'If I've understood correctly, you've come seeking stolen sheep. You'll not be finding them here, even if you brought a thousand men with you. There are seventy-nine sheep out there. What's left of one that broke its leg is in the stewing-pot. I have a receipt for eighty sheep from Andy Graham of Inverness, dated only a week ago.'

'Where did you get the money to buy eighty sheep?' The factor made no attempt to hide his scorn, but it was lost on Eneas Ross.

'My rent has always been paid on the day it's due to you, Factor. How I manage my holding is my own business.'

The sheriff-substitute spoke to Eneas Ross without looking at John Garrett. 'We're looking for two hundred sheep, Mr Ross. I can see without having to count there are no more than eighty sheep out there. Show me your receipt and we'll be on our way with apologies for having troubled you.'

The mere suggestion of an apology being made to the Highland crofter had John Garrett writhing in his saddle, but he said nothing. His own power, great as it might be, was limited to the estate of Lord Kilmalie. The sheriff-substitute exercised all the powers bestowed upon him by law, and it extended over a much wider area. It would not be wise to offend him.

'Mairi, will you bring that bill of sale to me.'

Mairi had come to the cot with more cheeses from the shielings earlier that day. Things were going Eneas Ross's way, and he would not put his advantage at risk by having one of his sons come from the house and make an unthinking comment to antagonise the sheriff-substitute.

Mairi brought the bill of sale and handed it up to the sheriff-substitute.

As she stood waiting for the lowland man to read it John Garrett stopped his angry fidgeting. He had seen this girl on a number of occasions before today, but realised he had never really *looked* at her before. She was tall and slim, and the sun she had acquired at the shielings went well with her long black hair.

'Thank you, young lady.' The sheriff-substitute handed back the bill of sale to Mairi and inclined his head to Eneas Ross, who had not moved from the doorway. 'We need trouble you no more, Mr Ross. My thanks for your patience. May my men have some water before we leave?'

'There's a burn just down there.' Mairi pointed to where the slope of the land dropped from view. 'It's where we fetch water for the cot – and kindly keep your horses from trampling down the banks about the laundry-stone.'

'Of course.' The sheriff-substitute nodded to the barefoot but haughty crofter girl, amusement taking the place of offence.

John Garrett remained looking down at Mairi for a moment or two more. He had jerked his horse around to follow his companion when Eneas Ross called: 'Sheriff! When my boys brought our sheep down from Inverness they said a flock of sheep, maybe two hundred or more, had crossed the Great Glen near Laggan, maybe ten days before, heading north. They were being driven by Sutherland men. You've a deal of riding yet if they're the men you're after.'

A wave of the sheriff-substitute's hand signalled acknowledgement, but it gave the groaning militiamen no indication whether they would be required to trek for another hundred miles or so across the mountains in search of the missing lowland sheep.

Pulling his horse to a halt beside Mairi, John Garrett said softly: 'A girl like you is wasted up here in the mountains. Come down to Corpach and I'll find work for you in my house. It won't be too arduous, I promise you.'

'I'll also be expected to warm your bed, no doubt? No thank you, Factor. I don't much care for some of those who've been there before. If I *do* come to your house, it'll be to present you with a bill calling for payment for the backache that went into planting the vegetables your horse has trampled on today.'

John Garrett put finger and thumb inside a waistcoat pocket. Pulling out a golden half-sovereign, he flicked it to the ground at Mairi's feet.

'That should make good any damage. Keep it for yourself. It will serve as a reminder that there's more to be had at Corpach if you change your mind.'

As the horsemen and the militiamen moved away, Eneas Ross needed to use all his paternal authority to keep his sons from whooping with glee before the party passed beyond hearing.

When their father relaxed his restraint, the sons of Eneas Ross made so much noise it set the dog barking once more.

'Put me down!' Mairi beat futilely at the shoulders of one of her brothers as she was lifted in the air and swung around. 'You're fools, all of you. How you did it, I don't know. If it's ever discovered that bill of sale is a forgery, you'll all rot in gaol. Me, too, I've no doubt.'

'A forgery! My dear sister, that bill of sale is perfectly genuine. We purchased eighty sheep from Andy Graham. Neither the sheriff-substitute nor Kilmalie's factor need know he's a kinsman of ours.'

Mairi looked from one grinning face to another, thoroughly perplexed. She had returned from the shielings only an hour before and knew nothing of what had gone on in her absence. When she had seen the sheriff-substitute and his men arrive and the sheep grazing nearby she was quite certain all the Ross men were about to be arrested.

'We've Preacher Jamieson to thank for not being caught with stolen sheep,' explained her father. 'You'll remember his last visit here?'

Mairi *did* remember, and the memory brought a blush to her face, but Eneas Ross was far too elated to notice. 'He told us that steps were being taken against sheep-stealing. I sent Dugald to tell Ian not to bring the animals here.'

'That doesn't explain how we've got eighty sheep and a bill of sale.'

'Ah! That was Ian's own idea.' Eneas Ross smiled proudly in the direction of his oldest son. 'He didn't need to go to no school to think it up, neither. He took the sheep up to your Uncle Andy Graham and made him a proposition that no right-thinking Highland sheep-farmer could refuse. He offered him two hundred prime sheep that would lose themselves in his own flocks, in return for half that number with a bill of sale.

'Andy's always been a hard man at bargaining, so Ian came away with only eighty, but you'll not hear me complain. I'll even send one of the boys down to Eskaig with a beast for the preacher. Had you not brought him home with you from the shielings, we'd all be facing the prospect of life in a prison hulk now. I've always said he's the best preacher we've ever had. He understands our ways.'

Mairi tried not to think too hard about Wyatt and his 'understanding ways'. Instead, she said: 'What was that talk of two hundred sheep and Sutherland men driving them north?'

Eneas Ross's grin widened. 'It was true enough. What I *didn't* say was that the sheep belonged to a lowlander who was having them taken north to a cleared area. I'll let the sheriff find that out for himself. Mind you, I doubt if they'll enjoy themselves on the way. There's a lot of rain coming in. The best thing we can do is close the door, bring out the whisky and drink the preacher's health. Let the sheriff and his men take care of themselves!'

CHAPTER NINETEEN

WHEN WYATT AGREED that Alasdair Burns and Evangeline should share the teaching in the Eskaig school, he feared the personalities of both teachers were likely to cause problems. Both had explosive and volatile natures, and they came from widely differing backgrounds.

Evangeline was a member of an established society, where wealth and birth represented power and an automatic assumption of authority. Her father was paid to maintain the wide gap that existed between landowner and tenant. Consequently, her whole upbringing was conditioned by a pattern of life that was comfortable and secure for all those who represented authority.

Alasdair Burns despised those who claimed unearned privilege. He espoused Chartism, the universal suffrage of all men, and he championed every man's right to have a voice in his own future. He was a man with passionate Radical beliefs, who had been prepared to go to prison for espousing them.

At first it seemed Wyatt's fears would be justified. The two teachers rarely spoke to each other, and any policy decisions were made through Wyatt. Even so, the school ran extremely well and it was not long before each teacher developed a grudging respect for the other's capabilities.

When Wyatt fell out with Evangeline as a result of his visit to the shielings, the mutual respect between the two teachers burgeoned into a warm and growing affinity that was as surprising as it was unexpected.

Evangeline had not inherited her father's unforgiving nature, and her anger with Wyatt was soon forgotten. Indeed, their relationship improved now much much of the adulation she had felt for him was transferred to Alasdair Burns.

In the evening when school ended the two teachers met to discuss their day. Often they would stay to take tea with Wyatt and keep him informed of the progress – or otherwise – of their pupils.

A favourite with them all was Jimmy Gordon, Angus Cameron's crippled grandson. A strong bond had grown up between Alasdair Burns and the young boy, partly owing to their respective disabilities. In recent days the teacher had become increasingly concerned about Jimmy Gordon's condition. Mentally a match for any boy or girl in the Eskaig school, the boy's physical condition was deteriorating at a truly alarming rate.

It was a matter of great concern to everyone and became the subject of discussion whenever Wyatt and the two teachers met over tea in the manse. Then the day came when the crippled boy had to be sent home to rest after complaining of feeling unwell.

Alasdair Burns was clearly upset, and Evangeline tried to reassure him. 'He puts so much *in* to each lesson. That's probably the reason he's so tired, nothing more. He does enjoy school. These past few months have been the best of his poor young life.'

Her colleague shook his head. 'I've seen other children with palsy. Sooner or later it affects the heart and lungs as well as the limbs.'

'What does the doctor say?' Wyatt put the question.

'He won't have seen anyone but the physician from Corpach,' replied Evangeline. 'I wouldn't let that man treat Coll Kennedy's donkey – and that's the most obnoxious creature I've ever known. The man's a charlatan. He couldn't hold down a practice anywhere but here, in the Highlands. Unfortunately, there's little alternative, because the Fort William physician is little better.'

'This isn't a matter for an *ordinary* doctor.' Alasdair Burns spoke thoughtfully. 'Jimmy needs to be seen by a surgeon. A man who's seen dozens of similar cases. Who knows if there's anything likely to improve his condition.'

'You'll not find someone like that outside of Edinburgh,' said Wyatt.

'You're right.' Alasdair Burns became suddenly brisk. 'I know just the man. He's at the Edinburgh teaching hospital. His son's there, too, and he and I attended school together.'

'You can't take Jimmy Gordon to Edinburgh. He has no strength for such a long journey.'

'I'll bring the surgeon here. Oh, you needn't look so surprised, Evangeline. I've yet to meet a professional man from the city who doesn't jump at an opportunity to visit the Highlands. He's able to dine out for months on tales of the "quaintness of the Highland folk". As for a surgeon who comes here to *treat* one of them ... why, he'll be a celebrity.'

'It's quite true,' agreed Wyatt. 'That's one of the things that most annoyed me in both Edinburgh and Glasgow. You'd think we were all fairground freaks to listen to them.'

'I tend to forget *you* are a Highlander,' said Evangeline. 'But, then, you're different somehow.'

'I've seen the world outside, that's all, but so have thousands of Highlanders who served as soldiers. Lachlan Munro and Eneas Ross are two who immediately spring to mind.'

Evangeline stiffened at mention of the Ross family, and Wyatt thought she was thinking of Mairi, but when she spoke it was of the old crofter himself. 'Don't mention the name of Eneas Ross in my father's hearing. Old soldier or not, he'll never be forgiven for making my father look foolish in front of the sheriff's assistant – or whatever he's called. My father is still convinced some sheep that were in Eneas Ross's possession had been stolen from the lowlands, but the sheriff thought differently. He had Father guide him over half of Scotland in appalling weather looking for those wretched animals. It wasn't until the militia and the constables threatened to mutiny that the search was called off.'

Wyatt smiled but said nothing. He knew the true story and had enjoyed the mutton sent down from the mountains by Eneas Ross. Changing the subject quickly, he asked Alasdair Burns: 'You'll write to the surgeon? Donald McKay will deliver it himself if you explain what it's about.'

'No, I'll go to Edinburgh and speak to the surgeon in person. I might be able to persuade him to come earlier than he otherwise would.'

'Is that wise?' Wyatt was thinking of Alasdair Burns's past associations, but he caught a signal from the teacher to say no more.

'It will be all right. I may only have one good leg, but I can get about as well as any other man. You've said it's time the children had a holiday from school. Call it from the end of this week and I'll take next week's boat.'

Evangeline gave a sudden laugh. 'I'd love to be travelling in that boat myself. Father's taking it to attend the annual estate meeting in Edinburgh. I doubt if either you or father will be able to look at each other without falling out. Be careful of him, Alasdair. He's my father and I love him, but he's quick to take offence and he bears a grudge for a very long time.

The news that Alasdair Burns was making a journey to Edinburgh on behalf of young Jimmy Gordon captured the imagination of the Eskaig villagers. Although scornful of most of those who came to the Highlands from outside, the villagers regarded the cities to the south with considerable awe. Medical men who lived and worked there had to have been touched by the hand of God. As for a city *surgeon.* . . .

Almost overnight the teacher became a celebrity in the small community. The Eskaig tailor found a part-bale of cloth in his workroom that had been taken in settlement of a debt many years before by his tailor father. It had been kept to make a suit for the landowner when he paid his next visit to Eskaig, but the landowner never came. Now the cloth was unwrapped, generations of dust carefully blown from its surface, and a suit was cut for Alasdair Burns to wear to Scotland's capital.

A collection was also taken, begun with a generous donation from the landlady of the village inn. Eskaig was a poor community, but it was a caring one. When Alasdair Burns swung his wooden leg from the rickety jetty to the wooden deck of Donald McKay's steam-launch he had enough money in a pouch beneath his shirt to secure accommodation in Edinburgh and pay the return fare for himself and the surgeon.

The three-day voyage to Glasgow went almost exactly as Evangeline had predicted. It was impossible for two men to travel in such close proximity without talking to each other. Unfortunately, each conversation served only to confirm their widely diverging views on life.

It might have been wiser had Alasdair Burns held his tongue when the factor poured scorn on the 'foolishness of teaching the children of Highland peasants to read and write', suggesting it gave them ideas above their station in life and served only to make them discontented. Unfortunately the one-legged schoolteacher had never been a man to avoid an argument.

'Would their "station in life" be the one designated for them by the landowners, or the one these "peasant" parents envisage for their children, Factor?' Alasdair Burns put all the reasonableness he could muster into the question.

'It's the place in life that God himself has allotted them,' announced John Garrett pompously. 'Some of us are born to lead, others to follow. That's the natural order of things. To put any other ideas into people's heads is to stir up discontent. I blame the Church — yes, and the teachers, too. You teach children all sorts of nonsense that they don't need to know. It's not only unnecessary, but at times downright seditious.'

'Perhaps you'd like to see slavery brought back and extended to the Highlands, Factor? Blind obedience, or the whip — with man-traps for those with a mind to go where they will?'

John Garrett looked at Alasdair Burns sharply, but he could read nothing from the other man's expression. The factor had lost the argument with Wyatt over the man-traps, and it still rankled with him. He wondered how much this teacher knew.

'I'm not saying the lot of the tenant should be made harder. On the contrary, a tenant who knows his place and doesn't try to rise above it is a happy man. He doesn't need education or any such nonsense.'

'He's also likely to end up in Canada or Australia. Evicted from his home because he trusted a landowner. If he has some learning, he'll know that by fighting back he might remain in the place where he *wants* to be. If he hasn't, he'll no doubt watch his home torn down and the land he and his forefathers toiled trampled by the cloven hoofs of an animal that was surely designed by the devil himself. No doubt you're happy to have sheep on your land, Factor. After all, they don't think, don't answer back and they don't attract schoolteachers or ministers to question your way of doing things. You're quite right, we *do* stir up discontent. We teach the people to recognise injustice and not offer blind obedience. Through learning a man's likely to discover he's inferior to no one. That he, too, has a God-given right to live life the way it should be — and actually *enjoy* it! If that's sedition, Factor, then I'm for it, by God I am!'

This was the last discussion between teacher and factor. Fortunately other passengers were picked up from small villages on the lochside and the coast along the way. It meant the two men from Eskaig were not obliged to travel in a smouldering silence for the remainder of the voyage.

However, the nights were spent on shore. After navigating the Crinan Canal to Loch Fyne on the second day of the voyage, the passengers were accommodated in a harbourside tavern in the busy fishing port of Tarbert.

That evening John Garrett was sharing a table with a noisy party of Englishmen, travelling northwards to join a shooting party in the Highlands. Impressed by his importance as Lord Kilmalie's factor, and eager to gain the benefit of his knowledge of the Highlands, Garrett's companions were keeping him liberally supplied with drink.

The drinkers became increasingly boisterous, and at the height of their celebrations, John Garrett rose to his feet and lurched towards the door leading to the tavern yard, with the intention of relieving himself. On the way he passed the table where Alasdair Burns was seated alone, finishing his evening meal.

When Garrett saw the teacher he halted, looked down at him belligerently, and made a mumbled unintelligible remark. Alasdair Burns ignored him, devoting his attention to the meal on the table in front of him.

The teacher's indifference infuriated John Garrett beyond all reason, and he shouted: 'I'll not be insulted by a crippled Scots teacher. You'll show respect when I speak to you, d'you hear?'

The words were at least understandable now, but the factor's actions were not. Leaning across the table unsteadily, Garrett rested his weight upon his hands. It was impossible to tell whether his next move was deliberate or an accident, but suddenly one hand slid across the scrubbed boards of the tavern table and sent Alasdair Burns's plate crashing to the stone-flagged floor.

As all heads in the room turned towards the sound, Alasdair Burns struggled awkwardly from his chair and *he* was in no doubt that the incident was deliberate.

'Damn you, Garrett! You did that on purpose. You're a drunken oaf.'

John Garrett pushed himself up from the table, his face contorting angrily. The brandy he had consumed might have had an effect on his speech, but his hearing was unimpaired. He took a half-pace backwards and his fist swung in a ferocious arc that missed its target by half an arm's length.

Alasdair Burns was sober, and his return blow was accurate. It struck Garrett high on the cheekbone, and the factor took two involuntary paces backwards before sitting heavily upon the stone floor.

'I say.... That was unnecessary, surely....' The three men who had been drinking with Lord Kilmalie's factor came across the room. One helped the fallen man to his feet, while the other two turned their attentions upon Alasdair Burns. They advanced upon him, their intentions clear, but the one-legged teacher stooped and picked up the knife with which he had been cutting his meat. It was a wicked-looking piece of cutlery with a pointed twelve-inch blade. The knife would have been equally at home in the hand of a fighting man. It was sufficient to make the two Englishmen forget all thoughts of taking the part of their drinking acquaintance.

When John Garrett regained his feet he shook off the man who had helped him and dabbed the back of one hand to the spot beside his eye where Alasdair Burns's fist had landed.

'You'll regret this evening's work, Teacher.' In sharp contrast to his drunken mumblings of a few minutes before, John Garrett now spoke with only a barely discernible slur in his voice. Alasdair Burns's punch had sobered the factor astonishingly quickly. 'You'll regret it more than anything you've ever done in your unremarkable little life.'

'Go to bed, Factor, before you insult someone with less restraint than I have.'

Alasdair Burns threw the knife on the table and limped his way from the room as the landlord put in a belated appearance to call on all the parties involved to calm down and enjoy a drink 'on the house'.

CHAPTER TWENTY

JOHN GARRETT was absent from the Eskaig estate for two weeks. When he returned he seemed well pleased with himself. This news was brought to Eskaig by a villager who had seen the factor land from the weekly boat at Corpach.

The villager was more concerned about the continued absence of Alasdair Burns. The teacher was not in the boat, neither was there a letter from him to explain why he had not returned with the Edinburgh surgeon.

The disappointment of the villagers was coupled with concern by those closest to Jimmy Gordon's family. The sick boy had been greatly heartened by the concern shown to him by Alasdair Burns and the villagers. He was convinced the teacher would bring a surgeon from Edinburgh with a cure for his illness.

As the days became weeks and the young boy began to lose hope, his already serious condition worsened. His weakness became more pronounced, and he needed to be cajoled and bullied into taking an interest in the things going on about him.

The day after John Garrett's return the factor summoned Wyatt and the Eskaig church elders to a meeting at his house. He gave no reason for wanting to speak to them, and speculation was rife among the men as they walked from Eskaig in a cold drizzle which had settled over the loch and the surrounding mountains. It was felt that the factor must have brought important news for the village from Lord Kilmalie's estate office in Edinburgh.

The men were kept waiting in the hallway of John Garrett's impressive home for almost twenty minutes before the factor put in an appearance. Much to Wyatt's surprise Garrett was accompanied by his daughter, and Evangeline apologised to the delegation for keeping them waiting in the hallway.

'What's this about?' Wyatt asked Evangeline the low-voiced question as her father led the elders to the estate office situated at the rear of the house.

'I don't know. He just said he wanted me to hear what he has to say. I know no more than you.'

Wyatt was apprehensive. He believed the factor's disclosure might have something to do with the state of Lord Kilmalie's health – and he was convinced it would not be good news.

The factor's disclosure had nothing to do with the landowning peer. When Wyatt and the elders were lined up in front of the factor's desk, John Garrett waved his daughter to a seat beside him. Leaning back in his own chair, he eyed each of the elders in turn before settling his gaze upon Wyatt.

'I've called you all together because I have some *very* interesting news for you. It concerns the teacher that Minister Jamieson appointed on your behalf.'

The factor seemed to find Wyatt's surprise very satisfying, but it was Elder Cameron who spoke, asking eagerly: 'You have news of Mr Burns? Is the surgeon coming to Eskaig to see young Jimmy? He's talked of nothing else since his teacher left.'

John Garrett knew nothing of the purpose of Alasdair Burns's mission to the Scots capital. For a moment he appeared puzzled, but almost immediately dismissed the question as being of no importance.

'I know nothing of any surgeon, but I know a *great* deal about your precious teacher. Do you know he's a gaolbird? He spent two years in prison before coming to Eskaig. He's well known to the authorities in Edinburgh and Glasgow for preaching sedition and trying to sow the seeds of revolution. This is the man who's been allowed to put his ideas into the heads of your children. The man who was chosen to be a teacher by Minister Jamieson. His name's not even Burns, but Anderson.'

The factor leaned further back in his chair, and the face of every man in the room was turned towards Wyatt. Evangeline sat staring in front of her, pale and round-eyed.

'Alasdair is as entitled to use Burns for his name as Anderson. Both names are his by birthright. As for his past. . . . I was aware of it when I offered him the post of teacher at the Eskaig school. . . .'

'A gaolbird,' muttered John Garrett. 'You employed a *gaolbird*!'

'A man who went to prison not for wrongdoing, but because he preached sound Christian principles,' said Wyatt firmly. 'The principle that man is created in God's image and so is entitled to a dignity befitting his status.'

'It's one thing talking such nonsense here in this room among men sensible enough to know the truth for themselves. It's quite a different matter for a man like Anderson – or Burns, call him what you will – to fill the minds of children with dangerous sedition.'

'Alasdair Burns has been giving the children of Eskaig an education. The ability to take a worthwhile place in the world in which they'll grow up. He was putting no Chartist ideas in their heads. This was a promise he made to me when I appointed him and he's kept his word – as Evangeline knows. Alasdair Burns is a *fine* teacher. Eskaig is fortunate to have him.'

The fact that Wyatt knew of the teacher's background and was not prepared to make excuses or apologise for his appointment chagrined John Garrett. However, he could see the church elders were less certain of Alasdair Burns's qualities than Wyatt.

'Well, he'll not teach in Eskaig again. He's back where he belongs – in an Edinburgh gaol.'

'In gaol? On what charge?'

'What about the surgeon? Jimmy's expecting him to come and make him better—'

'What's he done? *What has he done?*'

Above the hubbub that greeted John Garrett's startling announcement, the voice of Evangeline rose shrill and demanding.

'That need not concern you. You'll be able to carry on teaching at the school when Minister Jamieson gets another teacher – if that's what you want to do. Mind you, I didn't pay for your schooling in order that you might teach a lot of *Highland brats*—'

'I asked you a question. *Why is Alasdair Burns back in gaol? What has he done?*'

'That's a question I'd like answered, too.' Wyatt leaned across the desk and glared angrily at the factor.

'The police in Edinburgh are questioning him about his part in the serious Chartist riots that have occurred this year in Lancashire, Yorkshire and Stafford—'

'That's ridiculous! Alasdair's had no part in any rioting. He's been in Eskaig for most of the summer. He must have set out for the Highlands as soon as he was released from prison.'

'Then there's the matter of an assault upon *me*, when we lodged at the Tarbert inn, on the way to Glasgow.'

John Garrett spoke loudly enough for everyone in the room to hear, then sat back again, satisfied with the sensation his latest revelation had caused.

'Alasdair *assaulted* you? Why should he do such a thing? He hardly knows you.'

John Garrett shrugged smugly. 'The man was intoxicated ... causing trouble. I reported it to the police in Edinburgh.'

'After you learned about his background, and in order to provide the police with a reason to arrest him, no doubt.'

The factor gazed at Wyatt with an expression of mocking innocence. 'I told the police I'd been assaulted by a drunken man and identified him to them. What they do with him is their business. I didn't think it necessary to ask their intentions—'

'*You're a liar!*'

The words, hissed in fierce anger by Evangeline caused every sound in the room to cease.

'What did you say?' Ashen-faced, John Garrett stood up and faced his daughter, who was also on her feet and trembling with the intensity of her anger.

'I said *you're lying*. Whatever else he might have done, Alasdair Burns was not intoxicated. He's never touched a drop of alcohol in his life.'

'I don't care whether he drinks or whether he doesn't. I'll not be called a liar by my own daughter in front of strangers. Go to your room this instant!'

John Garrett was used to ordering men to do his bidding and having his orders obeyed. However, this was no Highlander fearful of losing a tenancy upon which his life and the life of his family depended. Garrett was confronted by an angry daughter whose temper was a match for his own.

'You heard me, girl. *Go to your room!*'

'I'll not move until I've heard the truth of Alasdair's arrest.'

Catching her father out in a blatant lie had shaken Evangeline, but she was deeply concerned. She stood in the centre of the room, hands on hips, glaring at her father with anger vibrating from her whole being.

John Garrett would have known exactly what to do had one of his tenants defied him in such a manner, but if there *was* a weakness in him it was the affection he held for his only daughter.

'I'll speak to you later. The rest of you can go. I've said everything you need to hear. If you have any other questions about your late teacher, I suggest you direct them to your minister. He employed the man.'

Striding to the door, Garrett bellowed: 'Binnie! Where is that girl? Why I keep a servant who's never around when she's wanted, I don't know. Binnie! Show these men out. Damn the girl! Where is she?'

As John Garrett stamped along the corridor shouting for the servant-girl, Wyatt spoke to Evangeline.

'Are you going to be all right? You've made your father very angry.'

'He's made *me* angry. More angry than he realises. If he starts any of his nonsense with me, I'll walk out of the house. I've threatened to do it often enough before.'

'He might not have been quite so angry with you before.'

'Then, you'd better leave the manse door open for me. Don't worry, I'll find out all I can about Alasdair and let you know tomorrow. You'll go to Edinburgh and see if you can do anything for him?'

Wyatt nodded. He had grown to like and respect the one-legged schoolteacher. He believed Alasdair Burns was in desperate need of a friend.

CHAPTER TWENTY-ONE

THE ESKAIG VILLAGERS were dismayed by the news of Alasdair Burns's imprisonment. A few felt the Edinburgh authorities must have some lawful reason for his arrest and some were shocked to learn their minister had taken on a teacher who had already served a term of imprisonment. Many others were sympathetic to the Chartist cause. They believed Alasdair Burns was being victimised for his past and did not doubt his latest arrest had been engineered by John Garrett. They were aware of the factor's opposition to Highland children attending school. They argued that this was his method of having the school closed without incurring the wrath of Lord Kilmalie.

Jimmy Gordon was too hurt and bewildered to apportion blame. Alasdair Burns had promised to bring back a surgeon to help him and he had not kept his promise. The thought of one day being able to do the things other boys did had given Jimmy Gordon just enough strength to hold on during the last few difficult weeks, even though the pain in his twisted body had become almost more than he was able to endure.

With all hope of a cure gone, Jimmy Gordon slid into a sharp decline, alarming his mother and doting grandparents. When Wyatt paid a visit to the Gordon home at the request of Mrs Gordon he was shocked by what he found. The small boy was lying in his bed and there was a new frailty about him that Wyatt found alarming.

Talking seemed only to tire Jimmy Gordon, and after a few minutes Wyatt left the room, promising the boy he would go to Edinburgh himself and return with both Alasdair Burns and the promised surgeon.

'Will you really go to Edinburgh?' Jimmy's mother asked the

question outside the room where her son lay. She clung desperately to the hope that a city surgeon could work a miracle. Hope was all that was left to her.

'I'll be on the next boat,' Wyatt assured her. 'In the mean time do your best to keep him cheerful. Don't allow him to give up. There are marvellous doctors and surgeons in Edinburgh. They make new discoveries every day. Perhaps they will have something to cure Jimmy. A surgeon will certainly be able to ease Jimmy's pain. I'm going away to pray for him now. I hope everyone in Eskaig will do the same.'

As he walked from the house, Wyatt was acutely aware that no surgeon, however brilliant, was capable of performing miracles. Only God himself could help the crippled Jimmy Gordon.

There were a small number of villagers at the jetty to see Wyatt leave in Donald McKay's fussy little steam-launch. Among them was Angus Cameron. The elder would take Sunday services in the kirk during Wyatt's absence, but his presence at the lochside owed more to concern for his grandson than to respect for Wyatt.

Nevertheless, the elder's farewell was sufficiently warm for Donald McKay to comment upon it as the steam-launch fussed clear of the jetty and headed back down the long narrow Loch Eil.

'You've done well, Minister. I never doubted you'd convince the folk of Eskaig they had the minister to suit them. I didn't expect you to win Angus Cameron to your side.'

'I'm not yet certain I have,' commented Wyatt. Angus Cameron still disapproved of the Highlanders from outlying crofts and cots attending his kirk. 'We've come to an understanding, no more. Right now he's very concerned about his grandson. I'm hoping to bring a surgeon back to see the lad when I return, but first I must try to free Alasdair Burns.'

'The one-legged teacher? The man I took to Glasgow not three weeks since?'

Wyatt nodded. 'He's in trouble. They have him in gaol in Edinburgh. I'm convinced there's been some mistake. Hopefully I'll have it sorted out in time to return with you on your next voyage.'

Donald McKay looked thoughtful for some minutes before saying: 'Would the teacher's trouble have anything to do with the argument he had with the factor in Tarbert?'

'It's more than likely. John Garrett claims Alasdair assaulted him. He reported the matter to the police in Edinburgh.'

'The teacher assaulted Garrett? Like hell he did. . . . Begging your pardon, Minister. It was the other way around.'

'You *saw* what happened?'

'Everything. The teacher was sitting having a meal by himself and minding his own business when Garrett went up to him. The factor had been drinking with some fancy Englishmen, up here for the shooting. He'd had about as much drink as he could take and was his usual argumentative self. He picked a quarrel with the teacher and began swinging punches at him. The teacher did what any red-blooded man would do. He hit Garrett – just the once, mind you. The next minute the factor was on his backside on the floor. It was a blow that a man standing on *two* legs might have been proud of. It would have delighted many a Highlander to see it, though I doubt any other man would have let Garrett off so lightly. He's not the best-liked man in these parts.'

'Would you repeat what you've just told me in a courtroom?'

Donald McKay hesitated, suddenly wishing he had not been quite so eager to tell the minister about the incident in the Tarbert inn. 'I've a living to earn, Minister. One day in court and I've lost a round trip of six days.'

'A man's future depends on what you could tell the sheriff, Donald. Alasdair Burns has been in trouble before because of his Chartist views. This could well mean his being transported.'

After a further hesitation, Donald McKay nodded. 'You're right, Minister. I'd much rather be kept out of this, but if it's the only way of preventing the teacher being sent away I'll tell what I saw.'

'Good man! You've lifted a load from my mind. Now I believe I have a real chance of freeing Alasdair Burns.'

The prospects were certainly much brighter now, but there was still the matter of Alasdair Burns's alleged involvement in the Chartist riots.

The little steamer had almost reached the Narrows, the descriptive name for the stretch of water linking Loch Eil and Loch Linnhe, when Donald McKay muttered: 'It looks as though we've another passenger, though why she couldn't walk on to Corpach, I don't know.'

As the steam-powered launch eased carefully towards the bank against the tricky current, Wyatt looked up to see Evangeline standing on the bank. She was dressed in town clothes, a small canvas-bound trunk at her feet.

As the boat grated on the shingle and Donald McKay jumped ashore to fetch the trunk, a securing rope in his hand lest the boat drift away, Wyatt helped Evangeline on board.

'Where do you think you're going?' Wyatt asked the question, although he knew there could be only one answer.

'To Edinburgh – with you. To see what can be done for Alasdair.'

'It's foolishness! I can do everything that needs to be done. There's no reason why you should travel all that way for nothing.'

'I have no intention of arguing with you about it. I'm going to Edinburgh. That's an end to it.'

'How did you persuade your father to let you make such a journey alone?'

Glaring defiantly at Wyatt, Evangeline said nothing.

'He doesn't know!' Wyatt's disbelief was tinged with grudging admiration. 'He'll be absolutely furious when he finds out where you've gone.'

'He can be as furious as he likes. I'll not be treated as a child, or ordered around as though I were one of Lord Kilmalie's tenants. I'm going to Edinburgh and I'll see Alasdair released even if it means Father never speaking to me again!'

Wyatt repeated what Donald McKay had told him of the events in Tarbert, and Evangeline nodded her head vigorously in agreement. 'That's what I *thought* must have happened. Knowing both men as I do, I don't doubt they began arguing before they'd been on the boat together for half an hour. Father is unused to having anyone question what he says. Since Lord Kilmalie's been too ill to take any real interest in the estate Father's made all the decisions for himself. Sometimes he's so convinced he's right about everything it frightens me. It's bad enough when he's sober. After he's been drinking heavily he becomes impossible.'

'Donald McKay said your father had been drinking when he and Alasdair came to blows in Tarbert.' Wyatt gave Evangeline a shrewd look. 'Are you doing this just to spite your father – or is there another reason? One I should perhaps know something about?'

The defiant look returned to Evangeline's face for a moment. Then her eyes met his, and she relaxed. 'I can tell you. I've grown very fond of Alasdair during these past few weeks. He's a fine teacher, and a good man. We may not always agree about politics, but he's sincere in his beliefs. I . . . I admire him very much.'

Evangeline spoke with a sudden fierce passion. 'Alasdair has a keen mind – a *brilliant* mind. One day his talent will be recognised and he'll teach at a university or somewhere. . . .'

As Evangeline ran out of words, Wyatt reached out and took her hands in his. 'I'm happy for you, Evangeline. Happy for *both* of you. Alasdair *is* a good man.' He released her hands. 'However, before we can talk about your future we need to extricate Alasdair from the mess he's in. . . .'

At the Tarbert inn Wyatt tackled the landlord about the incident that had occurred there three weeks before. Although quite as reluctant as Donald McKay to become involved in any court proceedings, the landlord agreed the trouble had been none of Alasdair Burns's making. Evangeline went to bed that night upset in the confirmed knowledge that her father had deliberately lied to have Alasdair Burns arrested.

Wyatt and Evangeline clattered into Edinburgh on board a fast carriage, the evening sun still high enough to pick out the battlements of the great castle dominating the skyline.

Evangeline intended to lodge with the family of the lawyer who administered Lord Kilmalie's estate. She was particularly friendly with a daughter of the family and always stayed at the house whenever she visited the Scots capital.

Wyatt would stay at the house where he had lodged during his student days, but they both agreed it was important they should first learn what was happening to Alasdair Burns.

The prison was as grim and forbidding as any Wyatt had ever seen – and he had visited a number of them in his capacity as a Church of Scotland minister. His previous parish in Glasgow had been home for many of that city's habitual criminals.

Evangeline edged closer to him as they were escorted along a dark corridor, followed by the echoing clang of steel-barred doors being closed behind them. There was a vile smell in here, the smell of many unwashed bodies kept in close confinement. It was noisy, too, as though an inmate needed to raise his voice in some primitive attempt to boost his courage and prove his manhood in such an emasculating environment. Some had already given up the struggle. They sat on the straw-strewn floor, with bodies bowed to captivity, only their minds free to wander the byways of the past, where 'hope' and 'promise' were not words that left a bitter taste on the tongue.

Once Wyatt and Evangeline stood aside for a poor wretch who shuffled past, heavily manacled and fettered, his chains dragging on the uneven flagstone floor.

'He's being hanged in the morning,' explained the warder with proprietary pride. 'Killed his wife, mother and three children with an axe. He's mad as May butter. The hangman'll be doing him a favour.'

Evangeline shuddered and whispered to Wyatt: 'Poor Alasdair. Imagine being locked up with such people.'

Another protesting door was swung open, and the warder said cheerfully: 'Here we are. This is where we keep those who're waiting to go on trial. They've windows here *and* an exercise yard.'

The windows were tiny barred apertures, at least twelve feet from the floor, and the 'exercise-yard' was a small paved area beyond the cell. No more than twenty feet square, it had walls so high the sun's rays could not touch the faces of the men who walked there.

It would be some time before it became dark in the streets of Edinburgh, but in here the light from a few oil-lamps hanging in the corridor cast grotesque shadows on the walls of the communal 'remand' cell.

'It's later than usual for visitors,' explained the warder. 'If you hadn't been a minister of the Church I wouldn't have allowed you in, but so long as you only stay a wee while I can't see it will do anyone any harm.'

The warder smiled ingratiatingly when Evangeline slipped a silver coin into his ready hand. Touching a hand to his forehead, he turned towards the bars of the cage-like cell. Raising his voice, he called: 'Burns, or Anderson, or whatever it is you're calling yourself today, show yourself. You've got visitors. Come, move yourself before I have to take 'em out again.'

There was a movement at the back of the cell, and Alasdair Burns appeared. Forcing a way through the crowd of prisoners who were gathered about the bars, he came to where Wyatt and Evangeline were standing.

'Can't we see him on his own? Without all these ... others?' Evangeline was dismayed that she and Wyatt would have to try to talk to Alasdair with so many prisoners listening.

'Sorry, miss. It's against regulations to allow a prisoner out of his cell to talk to a visitor.' The warder lowered his voice and gave Wyatt a sly wink. 'Mind you, if you was thinking of *compensating* me for all the trouble it'd cause, I just *might* be able to have him put in a *comfortable* cell for the next time you was here. One with a chair for the lady. I've even been known to let a prisoner have use of a cell with a *bed* to entertain. . . .' The warder suddenly remembered to whom he was talking and hurriedly backtracked. 'Not as that would be at all appropriate in this case, of course. I can recognise a *real* lady when I see one.'

Evangeline missed the last part of the turnkey's dissertation as she reached through the bars and grasped Alasdair Burns's hand.

Alasdair was grubby and unkempt, his beard almost as wild as when Wyatt had first met him on the banks of Loch Eil. His clothes were crumpled and dirty, with straws of various lengths attached to them.

For his part, Alasdair Burns could not hide his distress at having the factor's daughter see him in such surroundings.

'Alasdair, are you all right?' It was as much as Evangeline could do to fight off tears at his plight.

Watching the pair of them, Wyatt wondered what John Garrett's reaction would have been had he been able to witness the same scene.

'What are both of you doing here in Edinburgh? Don't tell me you've come all this way just to visit a one-legged Chartist troublemaker?'

Wyatt suspected the unwarranted description was Alasdair Burns's way of preparing Evangeline for the charges he might have to face. 'We've come here to secure the release of a dear friend. We intend setting about it as soon as possible. You're needed to teach school in Eskaig.'

Alasdair Burns released his hands from Evangeline's grasp as gently as he could. 'You're talking of another world, Wyatt. I was another man there. I thought I might escape from the past, but it's caught up with me.'

'You mustn't talk like that, Alasdair. Mustn't even *think* that way.' Evangeline reached through the bars and grasped one of the imprisoned man's hands once more. 'You're a good man. The people of Eskaig know this and they want you back.'

Struggling to keep control of the self-pity welling up inside him, Alasdair Burns said: 'Talking of Eskaig people, how's young Jimmy Gordon?'

'He's a very sick little boy,' said Wyatt. 'Were you able to speak to the surgeon you hoped might be able to help?'

Alasdair Burns shook his head angrily, his own problems forgotten. 'Surgeon Murdoch is a busy man, but I managed to find his son, the one I was in school with. He was going to speak to his father. I was to call back and see him. That was three weeks ago. I've been locked up here ever since.'

'Tell me where I might find this friend of yours. I'll go to him tonight, when I've seen Evangeline settled in with her friends.'

'You've only just arrived in Edinburgh and came straight here to see me?' Alasdair Burns was deeply moved. 'Thank you. Thank you both; you're good friends indeed.'

The other inmates of the cell nodded their heads vigorously. They had been following the conversation with great interest.

The warder chose this moment to return. 'You'll have to leave now. The chief warder's very strict about not having visitors inside these walls after dark. Besides' – the warder lowered his voice to a dramatic whisper – 'there's things as goes on inside a prison at night that no respectable young lady should ever know about.'

After giving Alasdair Burns a few shillings and learning where his doctor friend was to be found, Wyatt and Evangeline left the prison. It would have put the schoolteacher's life in jeopardy had they given him more money. As it was, Evangeline would never forget the scene in the remand cell when she looked back as she and Wyatt reached the first iron-grille gate and saw the ragged prisoners clamouring about Alasdair.

Evangeline vowed to herself that she would not rest until Alasdair Burns was a free man.

CHAPTER TWENTY-TWO

THE NEXT MORNING Wyatt rose early to see Hamish Murdoch off on the dawn coach to Glasgow. Surgeon Murdoch was too busy to make a six-day round journey to a remote Highland village to treat one small boy. However, his physician son had worked as his father's assistant for two years and was willing to undertake the journey. He would stay at the manse in Eskaig and treat the journey as a holiday. If, after examining Jimmy Gordon, he felt anything more might be accomplished in Edinburgh, he would return with the boy and his mother to the city hospital where his father practised.

The details had been thrashed out at a meeting held in Surgeon Murdoch's house the previous night and lasting until well after midnight. Wyatt guaranteed to reimburse any expenses incurred by the physician. The villagers of Eskaig had already offered financial help if it was found to be necessary for the boy to come to Edinburgh.

It seemed everything was in hand in respect of young Jimmy Gordon, but the problem of Alasdair Burns had yet to be resolved.

At ten o'clock that morning Evangeline and Wyatt met at the office of the sheriff, to enquire into the circumstances of Alasdair Burns's arrest. Wyatt had hoped to enlist Lord Kilmalie's aid in securing the schoolteacher's release. Unfortunately, the Eskaig landowner was in London, undergoing medical treatment. However, Charles Graham, the Kilmalie estate administrator, had given Evangeline a letter of introduction to the sheriff. It was this, preceding them into the sheriff's inner office, that secured them an interview with the guardian of the city's laws.

The letter lay open on the desk before him as the sheriff peered at his visitors over the top of his pince-nez, frowning from one to the other.

'Good morning. Will you be seated, please?' Sheriff Buchanan spoke in a quiet, almost deferential voice, belying the reputation he had of being a firm, albeit fair, dispenser of the Queen's justice.

When Wyatt and Evangeline were both seated on wooden chairs, the width of a highly polished desk-top away, Sheriff Buchanan said: 'I understand you wish to discuss the arrest of Alasdair Burns Anderson with me? You do realise, I suppose, he is a convicted lawbreaker?'

'I accept he's served a term of imprisonment for expressing Chartist views.'

The sheriff gave Wyatt another penetrating stare over the top of his pince-nez. 'Anderson was convicted of inciting disorder. We are currently investigating the possibility that he was also involved in very serious Chartist disturbances in England only this year.'

'Alasdair Burns — or Anderson, as you prefer to call him — has been teaching school in Eskaig, in the Highlands, since early summer. He's become a valued member of the community there. When these riots occurred Alasdair was in the village. I'll vouch for this, as will every inhabitant of Eskaig.'

When the sheriff said nothing, Wyatt added: 'My story can be confirmed by Lord Kilmalie's estate office, here in Edinburgh. I informed them at the time Alasdair was taken on as a teacher.'

Sheriff Buchanan conceded the strength of Wyatt's argument. Lord Kilmalie was a powerful landholder. 'If what you say is true, I have no doubt Anderson can be quickly cleared of involvement in the disturbances in England. However, there remains the matter of an assault upon a Mr Garrett, factor of Lord Kilmalie's Highland estate. It happened in a tavern, I believe. Apparently Anderson was the worse for drink at the time. Nevertheless, drunkenness is not accepted as an excuse for breaking the law.'

'Alasdair Burns doesn't drink.' The interruption came from Evangeline. 'I think a mistake has been made. I *know* a mistake has been made.'

When Sheriff Buchanan raised a sceptical eyebrow, Evangeline said stiffly: 'I am the daughter of John Garrett, Lord Kilmalie's factor.'

A brief blink was the only indication of Sheriff Buchanan's surprise. 'Unfortunately it was your *father*, and not yourself, who laid a complaint against Alasdair Burns Anderson, Miss Garrett. I regret therefore that only *he* can withdraw the charge. In the circumstances I suggest you ask him to call in and see me. If other charges are to be dropped, I will need to speak to him.'

Outside the sheriff's office, Evangeline said desperately: 'Now what do we do? My father will never agree to return to Edinburgh to secure Alasdair's release from prison. He's more likely to make himself "unavailable" unless he's *forced* to put in an appearance.'

'I doubt if Sheriff Buchanan's patience will last that long,' commented Wyatt. 'Neither will my own. Let's go and see Charles Graham. He's a lawyer; he must know of something we can do.'

It was not necessary to wait for Sheriff Buchanan's patience to wear thin, or for Charles Graham to find a legal loophole through which to secure the release of Alasdair Burns Anderson.

John Garrett arrived in Edinburgh that same afternoon. He stormed into the Kilmalie estate office hot and dusty and in a foul mood.

When he had returned home in the evening, four days before, John Garrett had been informed by his tearful wife that Evangeline had packed a bag and left home. His first thought was that she had moved to Eskaig as a result of the bitter quarrel that had taken place over his part in the arrest of her one-legged colleague.

Then Garrett learned from a maid that Evangeline had packed only her *city* clothes. What was more, she had left firm instructions to the domestic staff about caring for Charlotte Garrett while she was away.

Nevertheless, John Garrett still expected to find his daughter in Eskaig and he set off to bring her back. His mood was conciliatory. He would apologise for the way he had spoken to her in the presence of the Eskaig minister. Promise her a trip to Edinburgh with money to buy clothes. She would forgive him, as she always did, and he would promise to try to remember she was a woman and no longer his 'little girl'.

On the road to Eskaig, John Garrett encountered one of his water bailiffs, and from him learned the truth. Evangeline had been seen boarding Donald McKay's boat, bound for Glasgow. Minister Jamieson was on the boat with her.

John Garrett knew immediately where they were bound, but he misinterpreted Evangeline's reason for making the journey. He believed it was a misplaced gesture of support for Minister Wyatt Jamieson, rather than any concern for the imprisoned Eskaig teacher.

Early the following morning John Garrett obtained a passage in a Russian steamer which was clearing the Caledonian Canal *en route* for Glasgow. It was an uncomfortable voyage. The ship was filthy, every surface above and below decks coated with black dust from the coal that fed its fires. It also stank from its cargo of raw whale oil. The cargo had been badly stowed, and the ship had a severe list which caused it to yaw badly in all but the calmest sea. To cap it all, there was a knife-fight among the crew shortly before the vessel berthed in Glasgow. Two seamen were badly hurt, and passengers and officers were terrified for almost two hours.

All these experiences fuelled the anger that exploded when John Garrett saw his daughter and Wyatt seated side by side in Charles Graham's Edinburgh office.

Towering above them, he roared: 'What the hell do you think you're playing at? I've had to chase you halfway around the Scottish coast. . . .'

'Now, John, take it easy.' Charles Graham moved quickly around the desk to take the angry factor by the arm.

Shaking the administrator's hand away, John Garrett jabbed a finger at Wyatt: 'You! What do you mean by bringing my daughter here? Are you out to cause a scandal? I know why you'll say *you're* here, but I don't give a damn for your one-legged schoolteacher. It's my daughter's reputation I'm concerned with. I'll have you thrown out of the Church. . . .'

'Father, stop being so *dramatic*. Wyatt had no idea I was coming to Edinburgh until I boarded the boat at Corpach. He certainly didn't know I hadn't told you.'

John Garrett was momentarily dumbfounded, but his daughter's words did little to calm him. He had set off from Loch Eil filled with anger, and it had grown along the way. It was going to take more than a few placatory words to restore him to anything approaching normality.

'I'll deal with you later, my girl. Right now I've a few things to say to *him*.' Jabbing a finger at Wyatt, the factor cried angrily:

'You're a minister of the Church, supposed to be a responsible man. You're lucky I haven't sworn out a warrant against you on a charge of kidnapping. . . .'

'Father! Will you listen to me? My coming here has nothing to do with Wyatt. I'm glad he *was* with me for the voyage, but I was coming anyway.'

'Don't lie to me, girl. Why would you come to Edinburgh without telling me? If you'd said you wanted to come shopping, I'd have sent your mother with you.'

'My coming to Edinburgh has nothing to do with shopping – or anything else I'd expect you to understand. I came here to help Alasdair Burns.'

As John Garrett stared at his daughter, open-mouthed in disbelief, the Kilmalie estate administrator said: 'Come now, John. Let's discuss this calmly and rationally. Evangeline has a mind of her own. You've told me so many times in this very office – and with considerable pride, I might add. If she'd decided to come to Edinburgh, then neither the minister nor you nor I could have stopped her.'

Leaning forward in his chair, Wyatt said: 'I'd like to hear more of the factor's habit of swearing out warrants on trumped-up charges.'

Although angry, John Garrett knew to what Wyatt was alluding. He possessed sufficient self-control to fall silent, wondering exactly how much knowledge Wyatt had.

'I think I should leave the three of you to talk things over,' said Charles Graham. 'I am a lawyer and I feel you have things to say to one another it's better I know nothing about. I shall be in the outer office. Call me if I am needed.'

With these words, he scooped a bundle of documents from his desk and made a hurried exit.

When the lawyer had left, John Garrett looked at his daughter accusingly and shook his head, signifying bewilderment. 'Anderson . . . a one-legged schoolteacher . . . and you? I can't believe it. This is a nightmare. A ghastly nightmare. I'm going to wake up in a minute and have a good laugh about all this.'

'You've tried the "I'm your father and you're my little girl" plea far too often. It isn't going to work any more. Let's talk about the false charges you've laid against Alasdair.'

'I don't know what you're talking about. The man's being

charged with treason. Plotting against the Queen . . . *our* Queen.'

'The authorities were making enquiries about Chartist riots, not treason, and we can prove Alasdair Burns was in the Highlands when they took place. There will be no charges,' Wyatt corrected the Eskaig factor. 'That leaves only this so-called assault on you.'

Evangeline suddenly slumped down upon a chair and looked up at her father. 'Alasdair never assaulted you, Father – or anyone else, for that matter. He has strong convictions, but he's a gentle man.'

'Is my own daughter calling me a liar now?' John Garrett's anger flared up once more. 'I tell you the man assaulted me. He was raging drunk.'

'As I told you in Eskaig, Alasdair doesn't touch alcohol. As for the assault . . . we've spoken to two witnesses, one the landlord of the inn where you were staying. Both will testify that *you* assaulted *Alasdair*.'

'They're probably both Chartists, too. None of them is to be trusted.'

John Garrett's blustering might have intimidated one of his Eskaig tenants, but it had no effect upon his daughter – or Wyatt.

'I do hope you won't stand by that story, Factor. If you do, I'll be obliged to call the witnesses. I don't doubt there are more than the two who have already spoken to me. I suggest you go to see the sheriff and tell him you've made a mistake. Ask him to withdraw the charges you've made against Alasdair Burns.'

'I'll do no such thing!' John Garrett was blustering in desperation now. 'The man's a *scoundrel*. If he's transported, it will be the best thing that could happen – for everyone.'

'Except Alasdair Burns.' Wyatt stood up. 'You know what has to be done, Factor. Do it today. I'll not stand idly by and let Alasdair Burns spend another night in prison for something he hasn't done. If he's not freed by four o'clock, I shall give the sheriff the names of the witnesses to this so-called "attack". You might well find your-self taking Alasdair's place in gaol.'

To Evangeline, Wyatt said: 'No doubt you'll be wanting to talk to your father. I'll wait outside with Mr Graham.'

'I have nothing more to say to my father. Not after all he's done. I'll come with you.'

'Evangeline. Wait . . . *please!*'

It was the first time Wyatt had heard the word used by the factor.

'I need to talk to you. We *must* talk. All right, I'll drop my charge against this Chartist – although I strenuously deny I was entirely to blame. If I'm willing to do this for you, then I hope you'll listen to something *I* have to say.'

Evangeline hesitated for a few moments. 'All right – but I'm not prepared to listen to a catalogue of my sins. Nor to hear how ungrateful I am after all you've done for me. We'll talk seriously about the future – and I warn you in advance it means talking about Alasdair Burns.'

For a moment John Garrett seemed to swell with renewed anger. Then he looked at his daughter's determined expression, and the anger turned to a pain he could not hide. He nodded.

'Thank you, Father. It gives me no pleasure to quarrel with you.'

Evangeline smiled at Wyatt, and he could see how much of a strain the argument with her father had been for her. 'Wait for me outside. We'll go to the prison together and give the good news to Alasdair.'

CHAPTER TWENTY-THREE

EVANGELINE was not in Edinburgh to see Alasdair released. She had left Edinburgh only hours before, accompanying her father to London. It was part of a reluctant agreement reached by father and daughter when John Garrett agreed to withdraw his charges against Alasdair Burns.

John Garrett explained to Evangeline that he needed to go to London to discuss urgent business with Lord Kilmalie. He played upon his daughter's sense of duty, declaring he would be expected to return at least part of the hospitality extended to him during his visit. There was no time to call Evangeline's mother from Eskaig to act as hostess for him – even were she strong enough in body and mind to undertake such a task. He added that the visit would also afford Evangeline a rare opportunity to view fashions in the world's most exciting city.

However, it was Alasdair who convinced her she should go. Evangeline was reluctant to leave Scotland while he was still behind prison bars, but the teacher had been officially informed that his release awaited only the signature of the sheriff when he ended his involvement in a long trial in the criminal court.

'You must go,' repeated Alasdair. 'He *is* your father – and this prison is no place for you to be spending so much of your time.'

At Wyatt's insistence, and helped by a sizeable donation from Evangeline, Alasdair had been moved to a small cell where he had privacy and a modicum of comfort. Yet the sounds and smells of the gaol were ever present and, visiting Alasdair on her own, Evangeline had been forced to run the gauntlet of prisoners who reached out from communal cells and expressed foul-mouthed resentment of those more privileged than themselves.

'But what if something should go wrong and you're *not* released?'

'Nothing will go wrong. I'm as good as a free man already. Besides, Wyatt will ensure I'm released.'

Alasdair had heard some of the abuse hurled at Evangeline as she walked along the prison corridors, and it disturbed him deeply.

'Evangeline, you've been a wonderful friend these last few days. More. Were it not for you, I would be facing a bleak future in a prison colony. But it distresses me to have you come here.'

He felt uncommonly emotional and tried to dismiss the feeling with a weak joke. 'One visit to prison is enough for a social experience. Too many tends to harden the heart.'

'Is that how you see me, Alasdair? No more than a friend who comes to see you for an "experience"?'

Evangeline spoke quietly, her eyes not leaving Alasdair's face.

Alasdair stood up so abruptly he almost fell and he grimaced with momentary pain. 'I'm a crippled man, locked inside a prison cell – and with two years of imprisonment behind me. I'm known to the authorities as a Chartist, a reformer and a *troublemaker*. There needs to be only the slightest whiff of discontent in the air and I'm arrested for questioning. It will always be so. It's as certain as the knowledge that I'll never grow a new leg and be a whole man again. Yet you ask me if I see you as "no more than a friend". Look at me, Evangeline. Look at me *honestly*.'

Alasdair sank to the stool once more. 'I'm deeply grateful to you for all you've done. To feel more than gratitude would be folly.'

Evangeline was quiet for some moments, before saying: 'I *am* looking at you, Alasdair, and there's more true honesty in me at this moment than ever before in my life. I see a good and honourable man. A man who is concerned for others, and for whom I care very deeply. I may not fully understand your views yet, but I respect them, and I would like you to teach me more when we're back in Eskaig. Will you promise you'll do this?'

Alasdair rose to his feet once more, without a trace of unsteadiness this time. He looked at her for a few moments, and then held out his arms.

When he held her, he said: 'At this moment I could forget where I am and promise you the whole world – but it would be only the delirium of a very happy man.'

'I don't crave for the world, Alasdair – although I believe you could make it yours if you set your mind to it.'

Alasdair's hand came up to stroke her hair. 'We'll talk more about it when you return to Eskaig from London. If you return from all the great city has to offer you and can still look at me as you are now, I'll believe in miracles. I'll even pray for one to happen.'

There was *some* truth in John Garrett's story. There *were* some estate matters needing the landowner's personal attention. But Garrett had also learned that Lord Kilmalie's heir, a distant cousin, was making a rare visit to London. Brought to England from his home in Australia by the news that his titled kinsman was seriously ill, the heir to the Kilmalie title and lands had no intention of remaining in London for long. As soon as a number of legal documents had been drawn up and signed confirming him as heir to Lord Kilmalie, he would return to Australia.

Father and daughter travelled part of the way to London on the newly constructed railway. Evangeline found it a dirty and uncomfortable mode of transport. Black smoke and ashes entered the open windows of the teeth-rattling carriages, making clothes and skin filthy.

As they reached a recently completed section of rail, the train slowed to a walking pace. Suddenly, on both sides of the train there was a crowd of many thousands of excited men and women. The dress of many of the men showed them to be 'navvies', the labouring 'navigators' employed to build the railway.

When John Garrett called to ask the reason for the assembly, a dozen men pointed to where a platform had been erected beside the line. On the platform stood perhaps a dozen men, among them a clergyman, a uniformed army officer and several well-attired gentlemen. There was also a young pale-faced man, no older than Evangeline. His arms were pinioned and he stood between two men who were dressed in the uniform of the warders Evangeline had seen in Edinburgh prison. Behind the group was a stout wooden frame from which dangled a noose.

'It's a hanging. . . . He killed a ganger.'

Even as the words rang out a dark-coloured linen hood was

placed over the young man's head. His body twisted and contorted as he fought against his executioners, while the crowd howled for him to accept his punishment 'like a man'.

As the noose was passed over the shrouded head, Evangeline turned away in horror, but not before she had seen the expression of almost gleeful anticipation on her father's face. It made her shudder. She remembered the chained and manacled man in the Edinburgh prison. . . .

Her distress went unnoticed by her father and the other passengers who crowded the windows for a better view of the execution. The train slowed to a snail's pace now, the engineer as keen to witness the spectacle as his passengers. Moments later a great roar rose from the throats of the crowd, and Evangeline knew the law had taken revenge upon the young man. She closed her eyes and wished Wyatt was with her to say a prayer for the young man's soul. Or Alasdair Burns, to comfort her and explain why it had been necessary to take a young man's life.

The train gathered pace again, and the passengers returned to their seats. Evangeline kept her eyes closed, not wishing to be part of their excited chatter. She hoped they would soon find a topic of conversation that did not include the scene they had just witnessed.

Although Alasdair remained in the forefront of Evangeline's thoughts, London did much to dull her memory of the railside execution. She found herself caught up in an exciting whirl of carefully planned social activities, arranged for her by her father. Escorted to the theatre by attentive young men, she visited salons and at afternoon tea-parties met young women of her own age. She was even encouraged to purchase fashionable clothes that should have been far beyond the reach of her factor father.

John Garrett was determined to show Evangeline there was a whole new and exciting world beyond the Highlands. By doing this he hoped she would come to see Alasdair Burns for what he really was and to realise how much more the world had to offer.

Six months earlier, the factor's scheme would have succeeded. At that time Evangeline had been thoroughly dissatisfied with Highland life and forever finding excuses to visit Glasgow and Edinburgh. Much had happened since then. Evangeline found herself thinking more, and not less, of Alasdair Burns while she was in London. She *missed* him.

It was strange, really. She had felt only scorn for the one-legged Glasgow man when they first met, viewing him as less than a whole man. Then, as time went by and their work brought them increasingly together, her feelings had undergone a dramatic change. She learned to admire his patience and saw the many kindnesses he performed, with no expectation of reward or even recognition. As she warmed towards him she learned that Alasdair Burns possessed a keen intellect, a more able brain than any man she had ever met. He also had an indomitable courage. His disability was not so much a handicap as a challenge. An opportunity to prove how much he *could* do.

Evangeline had fallen in love with Alasdair Burns. What was more surprising, she loved him for what he *was* and not for what she believed he might one day achieve with *her* as his wife.

It did not mean Evangeline had lost all ambition. She honestly believed Alasdair would one day become a university lecturer. Unless he did, the country would miss the opportunity to learn from a great free-thinker. Chartism was only *one* of the many causes in which Alasdair Burns passionately believed.

Thinking of Alasdair Burns and the look in his eyes when they had parted in his Edinburgh prison cell brought a warm glow to the whole of Evangeline's body.

She would enjoy the pleasures of London to the full. She would also accept the unprecedented generosity of her father. But when the time came to return to Scotland she would happily hurry back to Eskaig . . . and Alasdair Burns.

Knowing nothing of his daughter's thoughts, John Garrett believed everything was finally going his way. Evangeline was obviously enjoying all that London had to offer. She was also meeting many highly eligible young men. Far more than she would meet in Scotland. It was costing a huge sum to dress her in the fashion of those about her, but he was convinced the results would repay him many times over.

Evangeline's début in London society had been made possible by the future Lord Kilmalie, 'Major' Jock Skene. Deeply tanned, and rough-skinned, with manners to match his appearance, Skene was an unlikely socialite. Now in his mid-fifties, he had been sent to Australia by the family as a 'remittance man', after abandoning a brief army career and leaving many debts behind him. On Kangaroo Island, off the coast of South Australia, Jock Skene became a seal-hunter. Helped by a series of Aboriginal 'wives', he shipped the skins of fur seals and kangaroos to Europe. This venture ended when Skene maimed a man in a drunken knife-fight for the favours of one of the Aboriginal women. He was forced to flee.

Jock Skene next surfaced in Eastern Australia as an employer of convicts, engaging them upon land-improvement projects. It was here, amidst fears of a convict uprising, that a small militia unit was mobilised and Jock Skene assumed his dubious rank of 'major'.

Things went well for Skene from this time on. He acquired a great deal of land in Eastern Australia and was among the first to drive cattle and sheep overland to the newly colonised Province of South Australia. He bought more land here, stocked it well and then assisted in surveying the interior of the province.

Jock Skene was a tough, coarsened outdoor man, totally out of place in a London drawing-room – but he *would* be the next Lord Kilmalie. London society moved over to make room for him.

John Garrett and Jock Skene discovered a common interest at their very first meeting. Jock Skene had ridden to wealth and respectability on the woolly backs of a moving tide of sheep. There was no disagreement on the course that would be followed to restore the flagging fortunes of the Highland estate when Jock Skene came into his inheritance.

The future policy for the Kilmalie estates was formulated over numerous bottles of brandy in the London house Skene had rented for his stay. For three weeks schemes were made and documents drawn up which were to shape the future of thousands of acres of Kilmalie-owned Highlands.

Jock Skene returned to Australia knowing it would not be long before he assumed a title and enough property in Scotland to make him a leading British landowner.

John Garrett would have preferred the heir-presumptive to remain in London until the title was secure, although in some ways the departure of Skene came as a relief. Supporting Evangeline's social activities had made alarming inroads into the factor's savings and, for all his high hopes, he could see few results of the expenditure. One or two of the 'eligible young men' had expressed more than a passing interest in Evangeline, but none seemed to interest her. However, John Garrett hoped the experience she had gained would make her see the men in Eskaig – Alasdair Burns in particular – for what they were. Uninteresting *little* men who could give her none of the pleasures she had enjoyed in London.

Garrett returned to Scotland with documents he would deliver to the Eskaig estate administrator on the death of Lord Kilmalie. They contained detailed instructions on the policy to be pursued on estate lands when Jock Skene came into his inheritance. The letters confirmed John Garrett as factor and invested in him the authority to implement the proposed changes.

CHAPTER TWENTY-FOUR

WHEN THE LITTLE STEAM-BOAT with Wyatt and Alasdair Burns on board increased speed to negotiate the narrow entrance to Loch Eil, Wyatt could see the whitewashed houses of Eskaig in the distance. He experienced a feeling of coming home. It was very different from the uncertainty of his arrival only six months before. Yet Wyatt's future here was still threatened, but now it was by events that were happening elsewhere in Scotland.

While working to secure Alasdair Burns's release from prison, Wyatt had found time to meet with senior ministers of the Church in Edinburgh, and pay a visit to his former tutors at the university. All were deeply disturbed at the course being pursued by both Church and State. If a collision could not be averted, they agreed that the Church as they knew it could not survive.

On one side the so-called 'moderates' accepted the State's right to dictate church policy. In opposition were those who declared their consciences would not allow them to accept State interference in religious affairs.

The contentious issues that had been festering for many years were finally coming to a head. The next few months would decide what would happen – and whether Wyatt would remain as Eskaig's minister.

Putting these thoughts behind him, Wyatt looked to see if there was a 'reception committee' at the jetty. He could see only one man seated on the ground beside the flimsy jetty, and the shrill note of the steam-boat's whistle failed to bring anyone else hurrying from the village.

'That's strange.' Donald McKay frowned as he pointed the

stubby bow of the steamer shorewards. 'There's usually at least half a dozen villagers to meet me. Something must be wrong.'

'There aren't even any children. With no school to attend, I'd expect to see them racing each other to meet us.'

'Who's that at the jetty?' Donald McKay swung the wheel, manoeuvring his boat against the current that was sweeping them too fast towards the low shoreline.

Wyatt shook his head. 'We're still too far away. I don't recognise him.'

'I do.' Alasdair's voice was filled with foreboding. 'It's Hamish Murdoch.'

For a moment the name meant nothing to Wyatt. Then he remembered: Hamish Murdoch was the Edinburgh physician who had come to examine young Jimmy Gordon.

The physician's half-hearted wave when they drew nearer fuelled the fears of the two passengers. They were confirmed when Wyatt stepped ashore and asked about the young patient.

'There was nothing I could do for him.' Hamish Murdoch's disconsolate shrug was an expression of the helplessness he felt.

'Is Jimmy . . . dead?' Alasdair Burns put the question.

The physician nodded a reply.

Alasdair Burns was deeply distressed. He stood with fists tightly clenched for some minutes before he would trust himself to speak. 'It's my fault. Had I not been arrested. . . .'

Hamish Murdoch shook his head vigorously. 'It's *nobody's* fault. I could have done nothing for the boy had I arrived weeks – or even *months* – earlier. I made this clear to the child's mother, and his grandfather. I've seen too many children with this particular form of palsy. *Far* too many. We haven't yet found a cure. One day, perhaps. . . .'

'I'm sorry you've had a wasted journey.' Wyatt could think of nothing else to say.

'Not *entirely* wasted.' The physician reached in a pocket and pulled out a piece of lead shaped like a tiny musket-ball. 'I extracted this from the leg of a small boy. It's one you missed, I believe, although you did an excellent job on the others. I examined the boy's father, too. I'm not an expert on tropical diseases, so there was little I could do to prevent his recurrent fevers. However, the man also has a serious chest complaint, and I fear it will grow worse. I told him he should really move to a place with a more congenial climate. I doubt if he'll consider my advice. He's a stubborn Highlander.'

The Edinburgh doctor threw his bag in the boat. 'I also treated a number of your people who came to me at the manse with their ailments. Some I was able to help, others I could not. One of the latter was a rather forward young lady named Fraser – Seonaid Fraser. I'm inclined to believe she came to the manse seeking your advice, rather than my medical diagnosis. Be that as it may, the girl's pregnant.'

Wyatt called on Janet Gordon before going home to the manse. Angus Cameron and his wife were also in the house, together with a number of villagers who had come to pay their respects to the little boy.

On the voyage from Glasgow, Wyatt had told Alasdair Burns the villagers had been informed of his past. The schoolteacher was nervous of his reception when he returned to Eskaig. He need not have worried.

When he asked hesitantly if he might go to the room where Jimmy lay in order to pay his last respects, the grieving mother agreed immediately.

'Of course! You did more than anyone in Eskaig to make Jimmy's last months happy. He thought the world of you. You've suffered for him, too. You'd not have been thrown into prison by the factor had you not gone to Edinburgh for a surgeon. You'll always have a place at the table in this house, Mr Burns. In every other house in Eskaig, too, I dare say.'

The nod of agreement from Angus Cameron surprised Wyatt. Highlanders were an unpredictable people. Fiercely independent and frequently scornful of the laws of the land himself, the Highlander was inclined to distrust others who broke the law. Wyatt had anticipated trouble in having Alasdair Burns reinstated as Eskaig's principal teacher. Janet Gordon's words, backed up by Angus Cameron's approval, meant the villagers had accepted Alasdair Burns as one of 'their own'. He would be free to do as he wished as long as he remained loyal to the closely knit little community.

It was a great relief. Not having to fight for the teacher's future left Wyatt free to tackle the many other problems beginning to press in upon him. He carried a letter for Charlotte Garrett from her daughter, explaining why she had left home so hurriedly and giving the reason for the continuing absence of father and daughter. Evangeline trusted the servants to take care of her mother, but Mrs Garrett was unpredictable.

Wyatt walked to the factor's home the following morning. He had the funeral of Jimmy Gordon later in the day, but Evangeline had been concerned for her mother. Wyatt had promised to deliver the letter personally at the very earliest opportunity.

For once Wyatt walked along the edge of the loch without either noticing the beauty of his surroundings or pausing to admire the soaring eagles crying to each other as they maintained a hunter's vigil above the surrounding mountains.

Wyatt was thinking of the duty he had to perform later in the day. A funeral was always a sad occasion. That of a child such as Jimmy Gordon, who had experienced so few of God's blessings during his young life, particularly so. Doubtless the young boy who had suffered such affliction in this life would reap a just and welcome reward in heaven. Unfortunately, few grieving parents gained immediate comfort from the promise of *heavenly* riches when God had withheld so much from their young child in *this* world. Wyatt admitted *he* did not always understand God's workings, but he had a faith that could accept even those things he found confusing.

The door to the Garrett house was opened to Wyatt by the same dour, heavily built servant who had greeted him on earlier visits. She had never been unduly impressed by the presence of a visiting minister of the Church, and this morning was no different. Before he had time to utter a greeting, she said: 'The factor's not at home, and if it's Miss Evangeline you're after, then you probably know more of her whereabouts than *we* do.'

The servant's unwelcoming words were accompanied by such a sniff of disapproval that Wyatt was left in no doubt about her opinion of *him*.

'I'm here to deliver a letter to Mrs Garrett, to tell her about Evangeline and her father.'

'Who is it, Binnie? Don't stand there with the door open. It's costing a fortune to heat the house as it is. Send them about their business.' The shrill voice of Charlotte Garrett came from the top of the stairs leading from the hall behind the servant.

Rolling her eyes in an exaggerated expression of overstretched patience, the servant's large bosom heaved a great sigh and she turned back into the house.

'It's the minister from Eskaig. He says he's got news of the master and Miss Evangeline.'

'Tell him my husband's not in the house at the moment and I don't know when he'll be back. He must try again this evening — and send Evangeline to my room. She's to stop hiding from me. She knows how it upsets me.'

Charlotte Garrett's voice was shrill and complaining. There was something more in the voice, too. . . .

Wyatt stepped past the servant into the hall. Charlotte Garrett stood at the top of the stairs dressed in her nightdress, over which she was wearing an old jacket. Her hair was so untidy it could not have come in contact with a hair-brush for many days.

'It's me, Mrs Garrett. Minister Jamieson. I've brought you a letter from Evangeline. She asked me to deliver it to you personally. She and her father have gone to London together, from Edinburgh.'

'Edinburgh? London?' Charlotte Garrett seemed totally bewildered.

'Will you come down? I'll explain it to you.' Wyatt moved to the foot of the stairs and, still confused, Charlotte Garrett descended very slowly.

The servant had closed the front door. Crossing the hall to stand hardly a pace away from Wyatt, she said: 'She's worse than ever this time. She shouldn't be left alone. The factor knows well enough what she's like. He should have someone looking after her.'

Charlotte Garrett reached the hall and gave Wyatt a smile as though he was an invited guest and she suitably dressed to receive him. 'Shall we go to the breakfast room? There's a nice fire there. You must be feeling the cold after your journey. Binnie, we'll have some tea, if you please.'

Scotland was enjoying an unusually warm late summer, but there was a roaring fire in the large grate in the breakfast room.

Charlotte Garrett stood with her back to the fire and beamed at Wyatt. 'Please take a seat. I'm so sorry John isn't here to greet you. He won't be long, I don't suppose. . . .' Suddenly a worried expression came to the face of the factor's wife. 'I *do* wish I knew where

Evangeline was. She shouldn't be absent when we have guests. That girl worries me, Minister. Do you have any children of your own?'

Wyatt shook his head. 'No . . . but I've brought you a letter from Evangeline. She says you're not to worry about her. She's thrilled about going to London and promises to write to you from there.'

'London? No, you must be mistaken. We were talking together only this morning. . . .' Breaking off the conversation, Charlotte Garrett put a hand to her head. 'It's this silly game she's playing with me. Hiding away. Pretending she can't hear when I call. I do wish she wouldn't. She knows how I worry. . . .'

Suddenly Charlotte Garrett looked at the letter in her hand. Casually she turned, and before Wyatt could prevent her she had thrown it into the flames of the fire.

'If you'll excuse me, Minister.' Charlotte Garrett held a hand to her forehead, her face contorted with pain. 'Excuse me, please. It's this headache. Stay for tea. . . . Evangeline will be here in a moment or two, I'm sure. . . .'

Charlotte Garrett crossed the room and hurried out through the doorway, almost colliding with the servant-girl who entered carrying a laden tea-tray.

Clucking her disapproval, the servant put the tray down on a small table.

'How long has Mrs Garrett been like this?'

'As long as I've been here – and that's a sight longer than anyone else. Sometimes she's worse than others. She's always at her best when Miss Evangeline's about. I don't think that girl believes me when I tell her what her mother's like sometimes.'

'Has a doctor seen her?'

The servant gave Wyatt another of her smirks. 'She's been seen by half the doctors this side of the border – and a great many on the other side, too. None of 'em has done her any good. She's some medicine upstairs, but it's the devil's own job to get her to take it. Not that it helps her. If you ask my opinion, I'd say that more than anything else she needs a husband to care for her – *really* care, I mean.'

'Does she have a personal maid?'

'Not any more. Poor Mary was almost as simple as *she* is. Anyway, she left last week.'

'See if you can find another maid for her from the village.

Someone who'll help with her hair and ensure she dresses properly. I'll account for what I've done to Evangeline when she returns.'

'I don't mind explaining it to *her* myself — but it's that father of hers. *You* explain it to him.'

Wyatt did not relish the thought of telling John Garrett why he was interfering in the domestic affairs of the Garrett household, but he nodded. 'I'll take care of it. You find a girl — and be sure she understands she's employed to look after Mrs Garrett. I'll look in tomorrow to see how things are going.'

'Thank you, Minister.' It was more civil than the servant had been upon his arrival, but as Wyatt turned towards the door she called him back.

'Minister . . . if you see that draggletail Fraser girl on the road between here and Eskaig, will you tell her what you know of the whereabouts of the factor?'

'She's been here seeking him?'

'If I had a sovereign for every time I've opened the door to her, I wouldn't need to work any more. She's been here three times this past week. She won't believe *me* when I say I don't know when the factor will be back. You tell her; she might take more notice of you.'

'What does she want with John Garrett?' Wyatt was thinking of what Hamish Murdoch had said before he left Eskaig.

'That's none of my business.' Suddenly the plump house-servant gave Wyatt a malicious smile. 'But if the factor doesn't return for a month or two I doubt whether you'll need to ask such a question.'

CHAPTER TWENTY-FIVE

THE FUNERAL of Jimmy Gordon was in sharp contrast to that held for centenarian Archibald Mackinnon. It was sober and solemn, and none of the Highland gentry was among the many mourners.

However, there was no shortage of tears. Genuine grief from his family and young friends from school and village. The graveside service was conducted by Angus Cameron. Tears coursed down the Eskaig elder's face as he read from the book of Revelation: 'And God shall wipe away all tears from their eyes; and there shall be no more death, neither sorrow, nor crying, neither shall there be any more pain: for the former things are passed away.'

Lining up to commiserate with their colleague and his daughter, the other elders agreed they had never attended a more moving funeral service than the one conducted by Wyatt and Elder Cameron that day.

Most of the Ross family were at the funeral, and Wyatt thought Mairi would remain behind to speak to him. He looked forward to chatting to her once again. It would be a few moments of pleasure in an otherwise depressing day.

To Wyatt's surprise, he saw Mairi walking away along the road with the rest of her family while he was still talking at the graveside.

By the time the last of the mourners had left the churchyard and Wyatt had caught up with the Ross family they were already on the track leading to their mountain home.

'Mairi . . . wait! I want to speak to you.'

'If it's about the books you loaned me, I'll have one of the boys drop them in at the manse when they next come to the village.'

'It has nothing to do with your lessons. . . .'

Magdalene Ross said something in a low voice to her husband. He gave a nod to Mairi, and the remainder of the family began to walk on along the path.

For a moment it seemed Mairi would follow them, and Wyatt said hurriedly: 'I thought you'd stop and talk a while to me, back there.'

Mairi shrugged. 'I didn't think it was right. Not at Jimmy's funeral. . . .'

Mairi blinked rapidly, and Wyatt saw she was close to tears. 'Anyway, you had lots of your friends around you. I was surprised your precious Evangeline wasn't there, too.'

Wyatt frowned. 'I'm sure she would have come, had she not been away. She was very fond of Jimmy. We all were. But what has Evangeline to do with anything?'

'After you both went off in a boat to Glasgow together I thought you probably couldn't bear to be parted – or wasn't she all you expected her to be? Perhaps you'll be trying someone else now.' Mairi's scorn should have shrivelled him. 'And you a minister, too. It's a fine example you're setting, I must say.'

'Mairi Ross, I do believe you're jealous.' Wyatt spoke quietly, but he found it difficult to keep the pleasure he felt from showing in his voice. Mairi would not show jealousy unless she really cared for him. She was hurt by what she believed to be his duplicity.

'Jealous? You have a very high opinion of yourself, *Minister Jamieson*. Why should I be *jealous*, for goodness' sake? Because I let you kiss me? If I were jealous of everyone who did that, I'd never have time to attend to anything about the croft and Pa would soon want to know all about it. *Jealous* indeed!'

'You're jealous, Mairi Ross, and it pleases me that you should be. Yet you have no cause. Certainly not where Evangeline Garrett is concerned.'

'Oh? Are you saying you *didn't* go off to Glasgow in Donald McKay's boat with her, when I heard Donald McKay himself say so on his very next trip?'

'I caught the boat from Eskaig, yes, but no one was more surprised when she boarded the same boat at Corpach. . . .'

Mairi's snort of derision would have been the envy of Binnie, John Garrett's house-servant.

'I was even more surprised when I learned we were both going to Edinburgh for the same reason. *To have Alasdair Burns released from gaol.*'

There was no derision in Mairi's expression when she spoke again. 'It was her father had Burns put *in* prison. Why should she want to help him get out?'

'Perhaps for the same reason you're so upset at the thought of me going off with Evangeline Garrett.'

Mairi coloured up, but there was no anger in her now. 'As I said before, you have too high an opinion of yourself, Wyatt Jamieson. If I'm pleased that there's nothing between you and that Garrett girl, it's for *your* sake. She's not for you. Her father will be nothing but trouble for any man who marries her.'

'I'll pass your warning on to Alasdair.'

'I must catch up with the family now. I have work to do at home.'

'I'll call in to see you tomorrow. I'll be coming to visit Seonaid Fraser and her father.'

Mairi's manner underwent another rapid change.

'Why?'

'I'm the pastor here. I like to visit all my parishioners as often as I can.'

'The news that she's carrying Garrett's bastard hasn't taken long to reach you.'

Her words jolted Wyatt. It seemed Hamish Murdoch was not the only person to recognise her condition.

'If she's in trouble, I must see what I can do to help.'

'Seonaid's never been short of men ready to help her when she's wanted them.' Mairi's next words explained much of her bitterness. 'She's got young Donnie staying at her house to help with the chores and the animals. Don't tell Pa you've been to visit them when you come to the cot tomorrow. He's barred Donnie from coming home for as long as he's carrying on with Seonaid.'

'I'll have a chat with Donnie and see what I can do.'

'Thank you.' Mairi laid a hand on Wyatt's sleeve for a moment. 'Tell Donnie to get word to me if he needs anything. Tell him . . . he'll always be my favourite brother, whatever happens.'

Wyatt called at the factor's house before heading into the mountains. Charlotte Garrett looked better than she had on his previous visit, although she was still confused about the absence from the house of her husband and daughter. Binnie had succeeded in finding a girl from Corpach village to work as Charlotte Garrett's personal maid. She seemed a sensible girl, and Wyatt felt happier when he left the factor's house this time.

The sun was hidden from view behind a thin layer of high cloud, and there was an autumnal chill in the wind blowing across the slopes of the high lands. Wyatt shrugged himself farther inside the turned-up collar of his coat and lengthened his pace. He had an uneasy feeling the day ahead was going to prove difficult.

Donnie Ross and Seonaid Fraser were coming from a small thatched stone shed when Wyatt approached the Highland cot. Donnie, looking thinner and even younger than when Wyatt had last seen him, was bloodied from fingertips to elbow. Seonaid, noticeably plumper than before, was also spotted with blood.

When Wyatt expressed consternation, Seonaid explained: 'One of the cows had trouble calving. I thought we'd lose both cow and calf, but Donnie saved them.'

Donnie shrugged. 'I've done it before. The cow came from Cameron of Loch Lochy. Most of his animals have the same trouble calving. We've two of them at home.'

'He's just being modest, Minister. Donnie has a way with animals, as he has with all things on a holding. Even the vegetables seem to grow twice as fast for him. Me and Donnie can make a go of things here, I know we can.'

Donnie Ross was embarrassed by Seonaid's praise. Extending his bloody arms, he said: 'I'll go and wash this off. I'll bring some water in the bucket for you, Seonaid.'

She nodded, and Donnie Ross made his way to the stream that ran close beside the grave of Seonaid's mother.

'You once told me you wanted more out of life than you'd find in the Highlands.'

Seonaid peered down at her bare and dirty feet. 'That was before I got to know Donnie better. He wants to marry me. He's really very kind, Minister. I've decided I *will* marry him.'

'What about the child you're carrying? Garrett's child, if rumour and my own eyes are to be believed.'

'Donnie knows about the baby — but there's no reason to believe it's Garrett's. It's just as likely to be Donnie's.' Seonaid spoke defiantly, as though expecting Wyatt to argue with her.

Instead Wyatt asked: 'What does your father think of you wanting to marry a Ross?'

Wyatt was looking towards the stream, to where Donnie Ross had finished washing off his arms. Skimming the excess water from his skin with the heel of each hand, he filled a wooden bucket with water and began climbing back up the hill towards the cot.

'My father won't speak to Donnie. Won't even allow him to sleep in the house. It'll be different when we're married – and we *will* be married. I've told father about the baby. If he tries to stop me marrying Donnie, I'll refuse to name the child's father. Then I'll be sent to prison and he'll starve to death left here on his own.'

'If I'm to marry you, I'll need to speak to him, Seonaid – if that's really what you want.'

Seonaid Fraser said nothing until Donnie Ross was almost within hearing, then she nodded. 'I want you to marry us. You'll find my father in the cot, lying on his bed, sulking. That's how he spends most of the day since we had words. If he starts any of his nonsense, you can remind him of what I've just said.'

Advancing to meet Donnie, Seonaid Fraser took the bucket from him. As she carried it inside the house, she called: 'I won't be long, but I need to change out of this dress and wash it before the blood dries. You speak with Donnie, Minister Jamieson. He'll tell you when we'd like the wedding to be.'

Donnie Ross seemed unable to find words to talk about anything once Seonaid had disappeared from view inside the cot.

'You were supposed to be telling me when you and Seonaid would like me to marry you,' Wyatt prompted, after a long silence.

'As soon as you can. . . . This week?'

Wyatt smiled. 'You'll need to wait at least a month, Donnie. We'll read the banns from the pulpit on the next three Sundays. But, first, I'll need to talk to Hamish Fraser and your father.'

Donnie Ross stiffened. 'Pa doesn't want me to marry – but he won't stop me. I'll marry Seonaid by declaration if I have to.'

'Marriage by declaration', a formal statement made before witnesses, was valid in Scottish law, but it was a custom that was frowned upon among traditional Highlanders. Many families felt deeply ashamed if their offspring were not 'decently' married, in a church.

'I doubt if that will be necessary, Donnie. Your father's only thinking of you – and you *are* both very young.'

'Age has nothing to do with it. I've wanted Seonaid to marry me for as long as I can remember. Anyway. . . .' Donnie dropped his gaze to the ground at his feet. 'We must be married as soon as possible. There's a baby to think of now.' Donnie looked up at Wyatt, and the simple honesty of the young man was almost painful to see. 'I do love her very much, Minister Jamieson.'

Wyatt put a hand on Donnie's shoulder. 'I know you do, Donnie. I believe Seonaid is very fond of you, too. Don't worry; things will work out, I promise you.'

Walking beside the prospective bridegroom on the way to the Ross croft, Wyatt hoped he had not made a rash promise.

It had not been difficult to obtain Hamish Fraser's agreement to the wedding. Lying on a feather-filled mattress in the darkness of the cot, Seonaid's father told the Eskaig minister his daughter could do whatever she wished, adding: 'She will anyway.'

He wanted to know nothing of the wedding plans, neither would he attend the Eskaig church. The two young people would have his grudging consent to wed, but they would not enter into married life with his blessing.

Wyatt anticipated even stronger opposition to the proposed union from Eneas Ross.

The head of the Ross family was seated on a stool inside the doorway of his cot. He had been watching the approach of his youngest son and the Eskaig preacher for many minutes.

Mairi had seen them, too, and ran to meet them before they reached the house. Greeting Wyatt with a warm smile, Mairi gave her young brother a hug and a kiss that left him in no doubt where her sympathies lay.

'Is all the family at home?' Donnie asked the question anxiously.

'They're all about somewhere. Pa sent Tibbie to find them all when he first saw you coming.'

'Does he need their support against me?' Donnie asked bitterly.

'You know Pa better than that.' Mairi linked her arm with his and took his hand, squeezing it affectionately. 'He doesn't need *anyone's* support once he's made up his mind about something. I think he's sent for them in the hope they'll be able to change your mind about Seonaid. He *is* upset, you know. He really does believe you're doing the wrong thing.'

'He *won't* change my mind.' Donnie spoke fiercely to hide the hurt he felt at his father's opposition. 'I intend to marry Seonaid.'

'*I* know that. So does Ma. And Dugald and Stewart. I don't want you to marry Seonaid; I don't think she's good enough for you – but I'd probably think that about anyone you wanted to marry. It's your decision, and you're my brother. I'll stand by you.'

'So it's to be Ma and her four youngest against Pa and the rest of the family?'

'I suspect you've also got Wyatt on your side.' Mairi looked past her brother to where Wyatt walked beside them in silence. 'The odds could be far worse.'

'I hope your father will look upon me as an impartial third party,' said Wyatt. 'If he believes anything else, we're not likely to get anywhere with him.'

'You can stop right there, young Donnie.' The powerful voice of Eneas Ross halted them at the gate. '*You* can come in, Minister. I'll have you in the house, too, Mairi. But Donnie knows he's not welcome in my house while he's living under the roof of Hamish Fraser.'

'Eneas! He's your own son. *Our* son. You have no right to turn him away when he's come to see you – and with the minister, too!' Magdalene Ross came to the doorway, the apron she was wearing twisted into a tight knot in her hands.

'Don't tell me what rights I have in my own house, woman. If you want to greet him, I'll not stop you – but you'll do it outside. As for Donnie bringing the preacher to the house . . . you know *why*, the same as I do.'

Magdalene left the house and ran to where Donnie, Mairi and Wyatt stood. Gathering her son in her arms and giving him a kiss, she said: 'You're thin. You should stop this foolishness. Come home to let me feed you again.'

'I'm eating as well as I ever have, Ma. As for coming home . . . I'll do it willingly when I can bring Seonaid here, too.'

'You'll not bring the Fraser girl to this house, Donnie Ross,' said Eneas Ross. 'Words of welcome would turn to bile in my mouth if I tried to speak them.'

'Can we talk about this calmly and reasonably, Eneas?' Wyatt decided it was time he intervened between father and son. 'Donnie and Seonaid have asked me to marry them. In view of Donnie's age I'd like your consent.'

'There's nothing to talk about. I'll not have a son of mine marrying a daughter of Hamish Fraser.'

'Then, you'll have to live with the knowledge that you're responsible for sending me to prison. I doubt if Hamish Fraser would do such a thing.' The angry words came from Donnie.

As Magdalene Ross let out a wail of anguish, Eneas Ross said sharply: 'Prison? What are you talking about, boy? Why should *you* of all people go to prison?'

'You know how severe the bastardy laws are. If I can't marry Seonaid and support the child she's having, I'll go to prison.'

Eneas Ross leaped to his feet. 'Seonaid Fraser's having a bastard? *Your* bastard?'

There was a sound from behind Wyatt. When he looked round he saw that most of Donnie's brothers and Tibbie had returned to the cot.

'*Garrett's* bastard, more likely.' The speaker was Ian, the eldest of the Ross brothers.

Donnie rounded on his brother, and his mother caught his arm, fearing brother would strike brother.

'You had no call to say that, Ian.' Donnie sounded more hurt than angry. 'You wouldn't like anyone to say such a thing about Tibbie.'

'Tibbie's never given me or anyone else cause,' retorted Ian Ross. 'Rumours have never stopped about Seonaid and Garrett – yes, and other men before him.'

Donnie looked bewildered and hurt, and Wyatt stepped in quickly. 'Such foolish talk is getting no one anywhere. From what I hear, the girl has been more sinned against than sinner. I've spoken to both Seonaid and Donnie at some length. I'm satisfied they know what they're doing. What's more, I'm convinced they love each other, too.'

'*Love?* What nonsense is this you're talking, Preacher? When it comes to taking a wife there's far more than *love* involved. A man must take his family's wishes into consideration *and* think how his wife will get along with *them*.'

'Did *you* think of all these things when you married Magdalene?

A Spanish Catholic in the Highlands of Scotland? Did you make certain *your* family would approve before you decided to take her for your wife?'

Wyatt asked the question quietly, but it was heard by every member of the Ross family and they fell silent as they waited for Eneas to answer. None awaited his reply with more interest than Magdalene.

'That was different,' Eneas said after a couple of false beginnings.

'Was it? I, too, was in the Army, Eneas. I know what's said about girls who marry soldiers on a campaign march. Are you telling me you didn't trust your own judgement — just as Donnie is?'

'If you weren't a man of God, you'd regret speaking of Magdalene and Seonaid Fraser in the same breath, Preacher Jamieson.'

'I'm saying nothing against Magdalene, Eneas — and I wouldn't. There's not a man I know who has a better wife. All I'm saying is that Donnie is your son — yours and Magdalene's. Trust him; he's a sound, sensible young man.'

'He's a boy . . . hardly more than a child.' Eneas glared at his son, uncomfortably aware of his wife's eyes on him.

'You were a year younger than me when you joined the Army, Pa. You've told me so many times.' Donnie hesitated. 'I want to go into marriage with your blessing, Pa. Yours and Ma's.'

'You'll never get my blessing to a marriage with Hamish Fraser's child. Nor will she ever set foot inside this cot again. I can't speak for your mother, and I won't try.'

'Does Donnie have your permission to marry?' For Donnie's sake Wyatt wanted to hear Eneas Ross say the words.

'He can do whatever he pleases. You've been telling me how much of a man he is. Very well, I'll not interfere in his life again. He must go his own way now.'

'Pa!' Donnie took a step towards his father, but Eneas Ross turned away and walked inside his cot without another look at his youngest son.

CHAPTER TWENTY-SIX

DONNIE ROSS and Seonaid were married in the little Eskaig church four weeks after Eneas Ross turned his back on his youngest son.

Donnie Ross arrived at the church looking self-consciously resplendent in a new kilt and plaid, preceded by a piper and flanked by two of his brothers, Dugald and Stewart.

The church was well filled by villagers. Many of the older women had attended every wedding conducted in the Eskaig church during their long lifetime. They would not miss this, the most talked-about ceremony for very many years.

When the three young Ross boys entered the church, Donnie looked eagerly among the congregation, hoping other members of his family might have had a last-minute change of heart. None was there, and the watching villagers did not miss the fleeting expression of unhappiness that touched his honest young face.

Donnie and his brothers were not kept waiting long. There was a stir in the church as Seonaid arrived. She was accompanied by Mairi, who had set aside her misgivings about the marriage for the sake of her younger brother.

As the two Highland girls walked down the aisle towards the waiting bridegroom there were nudges, smirks and many knowing looks among the congregation. Seonaid's dress, newly made for the wedding, could not hide the swelling of her body about the waist.

If Seonaid was aware of the unkind interest being taken in her figure, she did not allow it to spoil the occasion. She kept her gaze firmly fixed on the spot where Donnie waited at the front of the church. His nerves and curiosity overtook him, and he turned once to check on her progress. When he saw his bride, Donnie gave her a smile that Wyatt later swore would have lit up the darkest kirk.

Seonaid reached Donnie's side, and the bride and groom walked forward together. When they stood before Wyatt the ceremony began.

A great stillness fell upon the congregation when Wyatt called for any man to come forward if he could show just cause why the young couple might not be joined together in matrimony.

It was rumoured that John Garrett had returned late the previous evening, travelling from Glasgow, as he had once before, on board a Scandinavian ship bound for the Caledonian Canal.

Wyatt's call to the congregation passed without a response, and a sigh went through the crowded church that might, spitefully, have been interpreted as disappointment. The moment soon passed.

Donnie's responses were made in a strong clear voice. After a surprisingly faltering start, Seonaid's responses gained in strength until they matched those of her bridegroom.

When Wyatt pronounced the young couple 'man and wife' in the sight of God and the Eskaig community, there was not a man or woman present who did not respond with a fervent 'Amen' on their behalf.

Outside the church a reception party was waiting. Salutes were fired over the young couple from guns that had survived the ban placed upon them after Culloden. When Donnie and Seonaid emerged from the clouds of black powder-smoke rolling across the church path they were met by a fiddler. The musician led the way to the schoolhouse, which had been suitably bedecked for the celebrations that were to follow.

In the grounds of the school three fires were burning. Over each a whole sheep was being turned on a spit. As fat from the animals dripped on slow-burning peat fires, yellow flames leaped about the slowly rotating carcasses and a mouth-watering aroma filled the air.

Soon lines of excited villagers formed a large square, and Donnie and Seonaid led the dancers in a wild reel that thumbed its nose at Seonaid's condition. The dances were fast and furious. A few perspiring dancers attributed this to the fact that the fiddler, a Corpach man, was being paid at the rate of a penny a dance – plus as much whisky as he could drink.

It was a celebration that would continue until well into the night. Indeed, once darkness fell and the mutton was carved and distributed, the celebrations grew in intensity. By now the fiddle-player was flagging in spite of the incentive to keep playing, and pipers were brought in to take his place.

When more whisky was brought up it became noticeable that more men and fewer women were taking part in the dancing now.

When many of the older girls and boys began to wander off hand in hand together into the darkness, Wyatt felt it advisable to lock the doors of his kirk. The young couples might otherwise be inclined to take advantage of the shelter afforded by the church against the night wind.

On the road outside the school he met a horseman sitting in his saddle, watching the festivities from a distance. Wyatt could make out no more than the outline of the man, but he said: 'Come and join the celebrations. There's food and drink for one more.'

A startled white face was turned towards Wyatt, and a voice that was the last he would have wished to hear tonight exclaimed: 'Eh? Oh, it's you, Jamieson. What's going on? The music and drunken singing can be heard four miles away, at Corpach.'

'It's a wedding, Factor. Two young people have been married today. The villagers are celebrating in true Highland fashion.'

Wyatt hoped John Garrett would accept the explanation without demanding further details, but the factor was not a man to take half-statements without question.

'Who's been married? If it's a Kilmalie tenant, it's usual for me to be informed.'

'Donnie Ross has married Seonaid Fraser — and you haven't been here to be informed.'

The long silence that followed Wyatt's announcement was finally broken by the factor.

'Seonaid's married . . . young Ross? I don't believe it.' The words came out in a hoarse incredulous whisper.

'It's quite true, I can assure you. I married them myself, this afternoon.'

Again there was a long silence, broken this time by Wyatt. 'It's customary for a landowner to give his good wishes, at least, to a young couple. Is there anything you would like to contribute on Lord Kilmalie's behalf?'

'Damn your Highland customs! I'll not be taken for a fool. I should have been told of this. I should have been told. . . .'

Wyatt waited for the factor to add to his surprising statement, but John Garrett had said all he intended to say this evening. Jerking his mount around, he dug the heels of his riding-boots into the flanks of the horse and clattered back the way he had come.

As Wyatt stood alone on the darkened road the sound coming from the school grew even louder. The newly wed couple had decided it was time to bring the celebrations to an end – for them, at least. They were to spend the first night of their married life at the Eskaig inn. A room had been placed at their disposal by Annie Hamilton, the somewhat disreputable landlady of Eskaig's only tavern.

The only Englishwoman in the village, Annie Hamilton had made her appearance in Eskaig at the end of the Napoleonic Wars, with her crippled ex-soldier husband, son of the inn landlord. Although there was always some doubt, she insisted she *was* legally married. Such was her character that no one in the small village possessed the courage to challenge her statement.

She had met the landlord's son when he was a soldier in the 79th Regiment, passing through London. She, like Magdalene Ross, had accompanied her husband on the campaign that took the 79th Regiment from Portugal through Spain and on to the final battles inside the French border. It was rumoured Annie Hamilton had carried her wounded husband on her back from the final battlefield and ensured he received immediate treatment from the overworked military surgeons.

She continued to nurse her semi-invalid husband when he took over the inn from his father. After she was widowed, Annie Hamilton ran the Eskaig inn herself, despite vociferous opposition from the scandalised village elders.

Annie Hamilton had heard every one of the rumours about Seonaid's morals and the probable father of the baby the young bride carried. She paid no heed to them. Annie Hamilton had never been one to accept the narrow views of the others. She was one of the few villagers to have visited Magdalene Ross in the isolated Highland croft, drawn there by the common experiences both women had shared.

Annie Hamilton knew what Magdalene Ross would have wished

or her son and his bride. Loyalty to her husband might have prevented Magdalene from attending the wedding, but the inn landlady determined the young couple would want for nothing on their wedding night.

Led by two pipers and the inebriated fiddler, the young couple made their way to the inn surrounded by revellers. At the inn someone crumbled a cake over the head of the bride and there was a scramble among the unmarried girls to retrieve the pieces. Superstition had it that the girl who picked up the largest piece of cake would be the next to wed.

Then it was the turn of the men of Eskaig who claimed the right to kiss the bride. Bowing to custom, Seonaid stood by the inn door. Unfortunately, fuelled by whisky and Seonaid's reputation, some of the 'well-wishers' crossed the bounds of propriety. Wyatt saw what was happening and plunged into the excited crowd to go to Seonaid's aid – but Annie Hamilton was there first. Wielding a long-handled copper warming-pan, she emerged from the doorway behind the young couple and quickly drove off the liberty-taking revellers.

Reaching the doorway where Annie Hamilton stood on guard in the manner of an avenging Britannia, Wyatt said: 'You wield a handy bed-warmer, Annie.'

Annie Hamilton brandished the long-handled 'weapon' menacingly. 'Had there been a bayonet attached, I'd have driven them all the way to the lowlands. You'd have done the same if all I've heard of your past service is true.'

'I've seen bayonets wielded to less purpose than your warming-pan,' countered Wyatt. 'There'll be a few bruised heads in the morning. You'll be closing the inn now, no doubt?'

'Closing? Not on your life, dearie. This lot have got the taste for drink now. I'll stay open until the last man drops to the floor. I expect to do more business tonight than in any two weeks of the year.' She looked up to where a lamp shone dimly through the curtained window of the 'bridal suite'. There will be little sleep tonight for them, but I doubt if they'll be complaining in the morning, poor dears.' The lewd wink she gave Wyatt would have shocked many ministers. Wyatt only grinned. 'If you'd like a drop of *good* whisky yourself, I've a quiet room at the back. It will be on the house.'

Wyatt shook his head. 'I need to be up early. Lachlan Munro is ill again. I've promised I'll pay him a visit.'

'The poor man. With such a nice little family, too. Until you came to Eskaig he'd received scant reward for serving his country well. Call in to see me before you go. I've a bottle of something that will cheer him up. There should be plenty of food left over from this lot, too. It'd be a pity to see it go to waste. There'll be more than you can carry, I've no doubt.'

Thanking Annie Hamilton for her generosity, Wyatt set off for the manse. He had gone only a few paces when Mairi fell in beside him.

'It was a fine service you gave for Donnie and Seonaid. It got their marriage off to a good start, in spite of their circumstances.'

'They're not the first young couple to have found the restraints urged upon them by the Church hard to accept. I doubt if they'll be the last.'

'I wish I could accept the child as Donnie's.' Mairi looked towards her companion, but it was too dark to make out his expression. 'You're no fool, Wyatt. You know what's been going on between Seonaid and the factor. What do you think?'

'I've just married two very nice young people who have to face a great many difficulties together in the months and years ahead. I think we should give them all the help we can.'

'They'll get that from me. From Ma and Pa, too, if they ever get into any *real* trouble. But you haven't answered my question.'

'And I don't intend to.' Wyatt changed the subject abruptly. 'I didn't see you scrambling for the cake back there at the inn door.'

'If marriage depends upon a piece of cake, I don't think I'll bother.' Mairi spoke scornfully, at the same time uncomfortably aware that she carried a large piece of cake carefully wrapped in her handkerchief. She had snatched it up unnoticed from inside the inn doorway, while other girls were scrabbling on the ground in the street outside.

'How are your lessons coming along?' Wyatt asked the question as the silence that fell between them began to lengthen.

'I can read well enough now, and my handwriting is much improved.' Mairi spoke nonchalantly, as though what Wyatt thought did not much matter. Yet the thought of earning his praise had driven her on for long firelit hours after a hard day's work at the shielings and, more recently, by candle-light in the mountain cot while the rest of the family slept.

'You can *read* already?' Wyatt's admiration was genuine. He had not forgotten the many night hours he had put into studying – and he had been fortunate enough to have a literate and enthusiastic father to give him help and encouragement. 'You've done marvellously well. Better than if you'd stayed at the school, I don't doubt.'

It was exactly the response for which Mairi had been working so hard. She was determined to prove *she* could learn without tuition from Evangeline Garrett.

Behind them a discordant wail rose upon the night air as a set of bagpipes was brought into use. The wedding revellers would not end their celebrations for a long time yet. There would be little sleep for the newlyweds or for anyone else in Eskaig tonight.

'You're not on your way home to the croft?' Wyatt asked the question as they left the lighted windows of the last house behind and were engulfed in the darkness of a starless night. The way to the mountain croft would take Mairi past the manse, but to attempt to find the faint mountain path on such a night would be foolhardy.

'I'm staying in the village, with a married friend. Why do you ask?'

'I didn't like to think of you walking across the mountains in the darkness. It's dangerous. I also wondered whether you would come with me to visit the Munro family in the morning. Lachlan's ill again. Annie Hamilton's promised as much food for them as can be carried.'

'Poor Elsa. Her family are a constant worry to her. Yes, I'll come, if that's what you would like.'

'I would.'

Mairi stopped walking, and Wyatt stopped, too. They stood in silence, no more than a foot apart, each aware of the other's closeness.

'I'd better get back to the village. . . . Not that I'll be missed with all that's going on. . . .'

Mairi waited for a reply. When none came, she said: 'I'll see you in the morning.'

'Yes.'

'Goodnight, Wyatt.'

'Mairi. . . ?'

'Yes?'

'Don't go. . . . Not yet.'

Then he was holding her and kissing her as he had kissed her once before in the darkness, at the shielings. They kissed for long minutes, and when he held her close she clung to him. They were both aware of the hunger of their bodies. For Mairi it was a new and wonderful, yet frightening, experience. Suddenly she wanted Wyatt with a ferocity that allowed no restraint. She forced herself against him and gasped as she felt him respond. There were moments of near-ecstasy as body explored clothed body – and then they both heard the sound of someone approaching along the road.

They stood self-consciously apart as the 'clump and drag' of the approaching steps identified the unseen man as Alasdair Burns.

The schoolteacher sensed rather than saw them in the darkness and he stopped when still a few paces away.

'Who's there?'

'It's me, Alasdair.'

'Wyatt! What are you doing standing here in the darkness? I would have thought you'd have been in Eskaig, bible in hand, warning your flock against at least three of the deadly sins. Neglect your duty tonight and you'll end up with a whole crop of brides, all carrying their past before them. . . .'

There was a slight sound from the darkness, but it was missed by the chuckling schoolteacher. When Wyatt reached out he discovered Mairi had gone.

When Alasdair Burns, still laughing, had gone on his way to the schoolhouse, Wyatt retraced his steps to the village, but there was no sign of Mairi. Wyatt made his way home to the manse, deeply troubled.

CHAPTER TWENTY-SEVEN

WYATT THOUGHT IT PROBABLE Mairi would find an excuse
for not coming with him to the Munro croft in the morning. Not
until he came face to face with her at the Eskaig inn did he realise
just how much he had wanted her to be there. He needed to talk to
her. He, better than she, knew how close they had been to commit-
ting the sin he had warned others against on so many occasions
from the pulpit of his kirk.

Each carrying a heavy sack of food, they said very little to each
other until the village was well behind them and they stopped for a
brief rest.

'I'm ashamed of myself for what happened last night.' Wyatt
knew he had not found the right words, even before Mairi replied.

'*Nothing* happened last night – at least, nothing to make either of
us ashamed.'

'It was no thanks to me, Mairi. If Alasdair hadn't come along
when he did. . . . And after all I've had to say to others about
resisting "the lust of the flesh".' Wyatt's face contorted in self-
recriminatory anguish.

Mairi turned to face Wyatt. 'Since arriving in Eskaig you've
endeared yourself to many people – especially those from the
mountains – because you've come among us as someone who's as
human as anyone else. All the other preachers we've seen – and
there haven't been many – have set themselves up as the closest
thing to God that Highland folk are ever likely to see. Minister
Gunn was one. You're different. You've never tried to impress us
with being *better* than any of us. You've simply pointed out what's
right and what's wrong. Telling us what God would *want* us to do.

That's why you're well liked. That's why *I've* grown so fond of you. There's nothing to be ashamed of in being mortal, surely?'

Mairi struggled to lift the heavy sack to her shoulder. She did not succeed until Wyatt came to her aid. Shrugging the burden to a more comfortable position, Mairi added scathingly: 'If it was only *lust* you were feeling, then perhaps it *is* a good thing Alasdair Burns came along when he did.'

With this observation, Mairi made off along the edge of the loch, setting such a pace that by the time Wyatt shouldered his own sack and caught up with her he was puffing and panting like Donald McKay's steam-launch. When he tried to correct the erroneous impression he had given to Mairi, she told him curtly: 'Save your breath for walking, *Minister Jamieson*; you sound as though you haven't too much to spare.'

Wyatt planned to make his peace with Mairi when they next rested, but fate in the form of Ewan and Elsa Munro and the youngest Munro girl interceded.

They were gathering wood close to the loch. When they recognised Wyatt and Mairi they waved cheerfully and hurried to meet them.

Elsa Munro took possession of all the wood that had been collected, and Ewan relieved Mairi of her load.

The boy had sprung up during the summer months and he looked far healthier than when Wyatt had first met with him.

When Wyatt commented upon this, Elsa Munro smiled. 'Ewan's a different boy, Minister, thanks to you. He's doing a man's work on our land and enjoying every minute. He's felt especially good since that doctor from Edinburgh put his leg to rights. Not that *you* didn't do a good job in removing the rest of the lead shot,' Elsa Munro added hurriedly. 'The doctor said if it hadn't been for you Ewan would probably have lost his whole leg. . . .' Elsa Munro shuddered. 'I dread to think what would have become of us if that had happened. Ewan's the man about our house, and no mistake.'

'Lachlan's no better, then?'

Ewan Munro had dropped behind to readjust the position of the heavy sack on his bony young shoulder. With a quick glance in his direction, Elsa dropped her voice. 'Lachlan will never be any better. The Edinburgh doctor said we could expect bad days and *very* bad days. All the good ones are behind us.'

Mairi was carrying the young Munro girl, but she put an arm about her friend's shoulders and gave her a sympathetic hug. 'Lachlan's a good man, Elsa. He deserves better fortune.'

'So does Ewan. He's enjoyed the school, Minister, but we need him to work the land now.'

Wyatt nodded. It was a problem that educationalists were having to face throughout the land. By the time a boy or girl reached an age where they could benefit most from schooling they were needed to contribute to the support of the family. 'I'll bring some books along for him to read in the evenings. It would be a pity if he wasted all he's learned. He's a bright boy.'

Lachlan Munro was in the garden of the croft, directing his daughters in a hunt for caterpillars among an impressively sprouting crop of late greens. Leaning on a stick, the ex-soldier looked frail, emaciated and much older than his years.

He was genuinely pleased to see the Eskaig minister. When food and whisky were produced from the sacks the sick man's gratitude was overwhelming. Although it was not yet mid-morning, Lachlan made his wife set out the food on the only table in the house. When it was ready the young family sat down on home-made benches and ate. With a pewter mug of warming whisky in his hands, Lachlan Munro watched happily as his family tucked in to the best meal they had ever eaten. He declared Donnie and Seonaid must have had a fine marriage feast indeed in Eskaig.

Later Wyatt sat with Lachlan on the low freestone wall that encircled the garden, enjoying the winter sunshine. Each man held a pot of whisky in one hand, and blue smoke from two clay pipes drifted lazily upwards from where they sat.

Looking about him, Wyatt said: 'You've put in a lot of work here, Lachlan. It's a different croft from the one you took over.'

'Ewan and Elsa have done most of the work. Ewan's a good boy. He's a hard worker and he loves the land.' Lachlan Munro knocked out his pipe against the wall beside him. 'My biggest worry is what's going to happen to them all when I'm gone.'

Wyatt began to protest that Lachlan Munro would outlive them all but, shaking his head, the ex-soldier waved him to silence.

'I knew the truth better than anyone, Captain — and I include your Edinburgh doctor. I'll be lucky if I see another planting-time. I don't mind so much for myself; I've had a good life. Seen places that most Highlanders have never heard about. Besides, I've outlived this body of mine. It's not comfortable to live in any longer. You know all about it, Captain. You've gone through it yourself. Can you imagine what it's like living with such pain day and night, week after week, month after month? It will be a relief for me when the time comes. It's Elsa and the children I'm worried about. Do you think you can help them?'

'How? Do you have something particular in mind?'

'Speak to Garrett. See if he'll let Elsa take this place on when I'm gone. She and Ewan can make a go of it, helped by the girls. They're doing it now in all but name.'

Wyatt doubted whether the factor would be willing to grant *him* any favours, especially after the humiliation Wyatt had caused him in Edinburgh. Wyatt doubted, too, whether he would be able to call on support from Lord Kilmalie again. Then he looked at Lachlan Munro's face. There was an expression of fevered pleading there. 'I'll try, but I can't promise anything.'

'Thank you, Captain. If anyone can help them, it's you. It's likely every crofter and cottar will need all the help he can get before long. A flock of sheep came through near here last week, driven alongside Loch Shiel so as to avoid any trouble around Corpach and Eskaig, I reckon. Ewan watched them crossing the shallows. He said they were ten and twelve deep and it took most of the daylight hours to drive them over.'

'Where were they heading?' Wyatt asked the question sharply. Sheep in such numbers spelled trouble for someone.

'They were on their way to the slopes beyond the Fraser cot. It's Kilmalie land that was cleared a few years ago, but some of the animals are bound to spill over on to worked land. It's my opinion that Garrett's looking to create trouble.'

'You could well be right. I'll have a word with him when I speak about Elsa taking over the rent here. I'll be back to let you know how I fare, Lachlan. Right now there's someone else I must talk to.'

As Wyatt stood up to leave, Lachlan Munro followed the minister's glance. Mairi was in the doorway of the cot, surrounded by the children. She was saying her farewells.

Lachlan Munro gave Wyatt a tired smile. 'Mairi's a fine girl, Captain. A good, strong, loyal girl who takes after her mother. You remember the women who'd follow their men into battle, Captain? Right up to the enemy lines? No, of course you don't. You were too young to have been some of the places I've been to. A good one would go into hell to bring her man back – and Mairi's a good one. She'd make a fine wife for a soldier – or for a minister who's fighting his people's battles.'

'I believe you.' Wyatt never took his eyes from Mairi. He thought she might try to slip away without bidding him a proper farewell. He was right. A wave of the hand and Mairi was out of the garden, swinging barefoot and long-legged across the turf, not heading towards Eskaig, but making for a stream-fed glen that curved deep into the mountains in the direction of the Ross croft.

By the time Wyatt had said goodbye to the entire Munro family and caught up with Mairi she was half a mile from the croft and well into the wooded glen.

'Have you lost your way? Eskaig is in that direction.' Mairi waved an arm to where the high shoulder of a mountain ridge stood between the glen and the road to Eskaig.

'Why did you run off as you did? With no more than a wave?'

'I thought you'd prefer it. There's little temptation in the wave of a hand.'

Wyatt realised that Mairi was mocking him. He probably deserved it, but there were things that had to be said.

'I want to talk to you before you return home.'

'Oh? Are you going to warn me against leading any other poor man into temptation? Just in case he doesn't have your own God-given strength of mind?'

'That's enough, Mairi.'

'No, it isn't, *Minister*. You won't ever need to feel ashamed again because of me, I promise you.'

Mairi had taken at least ten paces before he caught up with her again and took her arm. She tried to shake his hand away, but he held her fast. When she turned to remonstrate with him she found herself pulled into his arms – and he was kissing her once again. She continued to struggle for only a few moments before responding as she had twelve hours before.

When Wyatt stopped kissing her Mairi's whole body was trembling. His hand came up to touch her hair, but suddenly she shook herself free.

'Why, Wyatt? Why do you do it when you know you're going to regret it afterwards?'

'I regretted what I did because I believed I had no right. Because I felt I wasn't certain enough. Now I *am*. In fact, when I think clearly about it, I've known since I first stepped ashore at the Eskaig jetty and saw you.'

'Known what?' Mairi hadn't intended the words to come out as a whisper.

'I love you, Mairi. I want you to marry me.'

Mairi tried hard to hold her own emotions in check. Only she knew the true extent of her feelings for Wyatt. For this very reason she wanted to be certain he meant what he was saying.

'You're being foolish, Wyatt Jamieson. Marriage is out of the question for us.'

'Why?'

Her reply was not at all what Wyatt had been expecting. Her reaction to his kisses had led him to expect a very different answer.

'Why? It should be perfectly obvious to you. I'm a simple Highland girl who owns little more than I'm wearing right now. I've never had shoes on my feet, can only just read and barely write. Sums are beyond me. You're a *minister*. The most important man in the whole area after the landowner – and many would say more important than him. You've served as an officer in the Army and been to a university. . . . Do I need to go on?'

Wyatt looked at her in genuine surprise. 'What's any of that got to do with us getting married? *My* mother was a cottar's daughter. She died before I was old enough to know her well, but my father swore she was the best wife any man ever had – even though *she* never learned to read or write.'

Wyatt looked so hurt and bewildered that Mairi wanted to hug him. Instead she said: 'It would be foolish, Wyatt. If you weren't a minister with such high principles, we could do the same as Donnie and Seonaid did at the shielings. The same thing other young courting couples do when they want each other badly enough.'

'You know I can't do that, Mairi. The *soldier* in me is sorely tempted, but I'm a minister now. Although I find it hard at times, it's what I want to be. Besides, that would be no answer at all, for either of us. I want to *marry* you. To have you for my wife. Nothing less will ever be enough.'

'Marrying our Donnie to Seonaid has addled your brain, Wyatt Jamieson. If I said Yes, you'd wake up in the night in a cold sweat, wondering whatever made you do anything so stupid.'

'That isn't true, Mairi. I *want* to marry you. I thought.... I *hoped* you felt the same way,' Wyatt was pulling his thoughts together now.

He was hurt because Mairi seemed not to be taking his offer of marriage seriously. For the first time he wondered whether there was anyone else in Mairi's life. After all, Wyatt had not been the minister in Eskaig long enough to know all that had gone on before his arrival. There could be a strong contender for the hand of the Highland girl. Someone he knew nothing about. The thought dismayed him far more than the possibility he might have made a fool of himself.

'I've told you what I think, Wyatt. I'm far too fond of you to let you do something you might regret later.'

Secretly, Mairi felt incredibly happy. She did not doubt that Wyatt *believed* he loved her – and she loved him so much it was an ache inside her that only he could cure – but *marriage* was not in itself a goal for her. She wanted to have a relationship with Wyatt that would be something very special for both of them. A union that would stand the strain of the many pressures it was likely to come under in the future. A marriage such as her Scots father and Spanish mother had.

'You *are* fond of me?' Wyatt was grasping at straws, but he was not prepared to give up all hope.

'I'm more than *fond* of you, Wyatt.'

'Then . . .?'

Before he could say more Mairi's hand was raised to his lips and cut off the words.

'Think of what *I've* said, Wyatt. Think about it very carefully.'

Briefly her mouth replaced her fingers. Then she turned and walked away.

As Wyatt watched her go, admiration was added to the love he felt for the self-styled 'simple Highland girl'.

There would be few situations that Mairi could not handle as a minister's wife. One day she *would* marry him. It was only a question of time.

CHAPTER TWENTY-EIGHT

WYATT CALLED ON John Garrett the next day. He had two reasons for the visit. One was Lachlan Munro's wish that his wife might take over the croft on his death. The other was to learn what Evangeline intended to do. Although she had returned with her father, she had not yet put in an appearance at the Eskaig school.

One look at the factor's face when Wyatt was shown into the office at the back of the house was sufficient to tell Wyatt he had not chosen the best moment to call and ask favours.

'What do you want, Jamieson?' The factor's greeting was all his scowling expression promised.

'I came to ask after your wife, and Evangeline. . . .'

'What the hell has my family got to do with *you*?' Garrett's manner was more than usually obnoxious and held no pretence of good manners.

'I've called once or twice while you were away. Your wife was unwell, and her maid had walked out. I sent to the village to hire another. . . .'

'So it was *your* idea to employ that slattern. I suggest you ought to pay any wages due to her. I've just dismissed her. Fortunately I was able to persuade the last maid to come back. She's worth three of any of the church-going trash to be found in Corpach. God! That stupid girl came into the bedroom unexpectedly, caught sight of my bare backside and damned near went into hysterics. The way some of your people behave, you'd think the human body was created by the devil, instead of in God's own image. I prefer to have sensible mature girls working in my home.'

'Your wife was very sick. As her minister I was concerned for her.

did what I believed was best.'

'I won't have you interfering in my household, Jamieson, do you hear? From what I've been told, your church needs to heed what's happening in its *own* house. You don't seem to be making a very good job of *that* at the moment.'

Wyatt bit back a cutting retort. Speaking as politely as he felt able, he asked: 'Did Evangeline return with you?'

'What have my daughter's movements to do with you? I'm still not satisfied with the story you gave me about the two of you going off to Edinburgh together. If I ever learn there's more to it than you've told me, I'll have you thrown out of your church, Jamieson, you mark my words.'

Ignoring the factor's threat, Wyatt persisted: 'I'd like to know whether Evangeline will be returning to teach at the school. We can't bring the girls back without someone to teach them.'

'Is Anderson – or Burns, or whatever you call the man – still teaching there?'

'Of course. Without him there would *be* no school.'

'Then, you've answered yourself. My daughter will never teach in the same school as that convicted troublemaker. If the elders had an ounce of sense, they'd have got rid of the man when I gave them the opportunity. If you've nothing else to say, you can get on your way. I've work to do.'

Wyatt's wasted journey had done no more than give the factor an opportunity to be even more rude than usual. He turned to go. At the door he paused and turned back in time to catch the self-satisfied smile on John Garrett's face.

'Did you hear anything of Lord Kilmalie before you returned?' Wyatt asked.

'I saw him. He's a dying man.' There was no hint of respect or sorrow in the factor's expression. Indeed, the smugness was more pronounced than before. 'Go back to your church and pray for him, Jamieson. When he dies you'll see changes around Eskaig; that I *can* promise you.'

Wyatt found John Garrett's smug confidence disquieting. He wondered what had occurred in London.

Wyatt was halfway along the driveway from the house when he heard his name being called. He turned to see Evangeline running after him.

When she caught up with him she hugged him affectionately before reproving him. 'You were leaving the house without seeing me? I'm deeply hurt, Wyatt. Why didn't you send word to me you'd come calling? I'd have rushed down to see you immediately. I was upstairs with Mother. The servants told me you've been to the house to see her while we were away. I'm very grateful, Wyatt. She's obviously been very confused, but she's getting better. It seems as though I've been away for *months*. How is Alasdair? And young Jimmy Gordon? Was the physician able to help him?'

Wyatt remembered Evangeline had not returned to Eskaig on board Donald McKay's steam launch. Passengers who did usually arrived in Eskaig knowing more about village matters than those who lived there.

Assuring the factor's daughter that he and Alasdair were both well, Wyatt broke the news of Jimmy Gordon's death.

It came as no unexpected shock, but Evangeline was very upset and shed a few tears on his behalf. After borrowing Wyatt's handkerchief, she handed it back and said: 'I'm sorry. Would he have lived if Father hadn't had Alasdair arrested and put in prison?'

Wyatt shook his head. 'It would have made no difference. Jimmy was dying when I first saw him. Alasdair and the school gave him a reason for *wanting* to live, no more.'

'I must call on Jimmy's mother when I return to teach at the school.'

'Your father swore he wouldn't allow you near the school as long as Alasdair was there, too.'

'Father says a lot of things he'd *like* to see happen. He took me to London to find me a husband, but that didn't succeed, either. If he tries to stop me teaching, I'll threaten to run off somewhere with Alasdair. That should frighten him enough to make him change his mind. I'll be back as soon as Mother's more settled. At the moment she panics if I'm out of her sight for very long.'

'There's no need to run off anywhere with Alasdair. Weddings are popular in Eskaig this year. I married Donnie Ross to Seonaid Fraser on the day you returned.'

Evangeline drew in her breath sharply. 'Does my father know about this?'

Wyatt nodded. 'He rode into Eskaig during the wedding celebrations.' He hesitated. 'You know . . . about Seonaid?'

'I'm closer to my father than anyone, Wyatt. Did you think the whole of the Highlands knew of his affair with Seonaid and I didn't? She isn't his first mistress, and she won't be the last, but I *do* believe he was fonder of her than he was of the others. This would explain the foul mood he's been in since our return.'

Evangeline seemed almost to be talking to herself. Suddenly she said: 'Wait here for me. I'm coming to Eskaig with you. I think we should tell each other all that's happened during these last few weeks. I have a lot to tell you about London – and Lord Kilmalie's heir. . . .'

By the time Eskaig was reached Wyatt knew as much as Evangeline about her father's frequent meetings with the heir to the Kilmalie title and estates. Her information left him sorely troubled.

Evangeline knew nothing of the details of the two men's talks, but John Garrett's arrogance and assuredness were significant. The factor must have come to an agreement with the Kilmalie heir about the estate's future. Wyatt wished he knew more. It might prove to be of vital importance to the residents of his Highland parish.

The reunion of Evangeline Garrett and Alasdair Burns would not have met with the approval of Evangeline's father. They clung to each other for some minutes, oblivious to the presence of the Eskaig minister. The warmth of their greeting took Wyatt by surprise. He had thought Evangeline to be joking when she made the remark about eloping with Alasdair. Now he was by no means certain.

When the two teachers separated they continued to hold hands and chattered about Alasdair's incarceration in the gaol in Edinburgh as though it had all been a huge joke. Yet Wyatt knew they were both aware how serious it had been – and the man responsible for Alasdair's arrest was still capable of coming between them.

Wyatt also remembered the factor's threat made to him only that morning. He did not doubt that John Garrett would go to great lengths to break up his daughter's relationship with Alasdair Burns.

CHAPTER TWENTY-NINE

THE NEWS OF THE DEATH of Lord Kilmalie reached Eskaig only weeks after John Garrett's return from London and Edinburgh. It pushed all other issues into the background. The news was brought to the Highland village by Charles Graham, the Kilmalie estate administrator. He arrived in a specially chartered steamer with surveyors and clerks to reassess the estate assets. The arrival of so many 'outsiders' caused great unease among the villagers and those whose futures leaned heavily upon the Kilmalie estate.

The party disembarked at the rickety Eskaig jetty on a Saturday morning under the curious gaze of many children and villagers. The new arrivals recruited the older boys to carry their baggage to the inn, paying them generously. Although nothing was said of the reason for their visit, the news of Lord Kilmalie's death was in the village before the luggage.

Word was brought to the manse by a breathless village boy. He had sprinted all the way from Angus Cameron's house, spurred on by the urgency in the voice of the church elder.

Wyatt abandoned the sermon on which he was working and hurried to the inn where the villagers were beginning to gather, Elder Cameron among them.

'Have you been told officially of Lord Kilmalie's death?' Wyatt put the question to the solemn-faced elder when he reached him.

'It's true enough. The administrator's here with his staff to value the estate for the new landowner. One of the crew of the boat that brought them is a Corpach man. Oh, yes, it's true enough. I fear we'll see more changes than we want hereabouts. I've heard the new laird's from Australia, the place where the British government sends all its convicts. We can't expect such a man to have *our* interests at heart. Giving him a title's not likely to make him a gentleman overnight. No, Minister, Eskaig will regret the passing of the old Lord Kilmalie before any of us is very much older.'

Wyatt remembered the resentment against 'the old Lord Kilmalie' when the landowner had appointed him as minister of Eskaig. He did not remind the elder. Instead he said: 'I'm going in to see the administrator now. Will you come with me?'

'I will, although it will be the first time I've ever set foot inside such a place.' Angus Cameron led the way determinedly to the door of the Eskaig inn, the crowd parting respectfully before him.

The Kilmalie estate administrator greeted Wyatt cordially and shook hands with Angus Cameron.

'My visit to Eskaig is a sad occasion, I fear,' said Charles Graham when the visitors had seated themselves in his room. 'You know, I presume, that Lord Kilmalie is dead?'

When Wyatt and Angus Cameron nodded, the estate administrator exclaimed: 'Of course you do. I'd forgotten how effective the information service is in a small Highland village. I came straight to the inn from the boat without saying more than "Good day" to anyone, yet the news was here before me. Be that as it may, Lord Kilmalie died seven days ago and has been buried in London. His heir was in the country until recently, but is now *en route* to his home in Australia. It will be some time before he can be contacted and instructions received. In the meantime I imagine things will continue much as they have in recent years. I need to conduct a survey of estate lands and property. It's necessary in order to set a value on the new Lord Kilmalie's inheritance and assess the income and liabilities with which he'll be faced. I'll be sending a messenger to John Garrett, inviting him to meet me here this evening. We need to discuss both my survey and the prospects for the future. . . .'

At that moment both visitors were forced to move to make way for a number of inn servants. They were bringing in luggage from the boat.

When the servants had gone, leaving the room cluttered with the administrator's belongings, Charles Graham said: 'I fear any attempt at serious conversation is doomed right now. Perhaps you gentlemen will join the factor and myself for dinner this evening.'

As Wyatt and Angus Cameron left the inn, luggage was being

carried through the passageways of the inn and more was piled up on the roadway outside. Angus Cameron stopped to gaze at the luggage, and his bushy eyebrows met across a deep furrow.

'There's an awful lot of luggage for such a small party. They would seem to have come prepared for a long stay.'

'No doubt. Many of the bags will contain instruments belonging to the surveyors. Anyway, we'll hear more of their plans this evening. But come to the manse with me first, Angus. We must discuss a memorial service for Lord Kilmalie. You can tell me of some of the benefits he has brought to the village.'

Angus Cameron nodded seriously. 'There's maybe not so many as there might have been. Yet I'm afraid time might show the *worst* thing he ever did for Eskaig was to die.'

Every man and woman in Eskaig and in the mountains beyond the village knew how important to them was the accession of a new landowner. Their future lay entirely in his hands. A good landlord could ensure happiness and security. A bad one had the power to dispense misery, poverty and an end to their very way of life. The new Lord Kilmalie could squeeze Eskaig out of existence, if he so wished. Every householder in Eskaig and the surrounding mountains was a tenant of the new inheritor.

Aware of the great importance of the evening meeting, many tenants gathered in the road outside the inn. They stood in silence, or conversed in low serious tones. When Wyatt and Angus Cameron arrived a path was quickly made for them and a few of the men directed low-voiced instructions to Wyatt.

'Don't let them put up our rents too much, Minister.'

'Invite the new laird to meet us.'

'We're relying on you to speak for us, Minister.'

Wyatt was aware of the responsibility he carried upon his shoulders. He was also painfully aware how misplaced was their faith in him. He had been invited to 'discuss' the future of the Kilmalie tenants, but he had no power to influence any of the parties involved. However, nothing could be finally decided until the new Lord Kilmalie had made his wishes known – from his home many thousands of miles away.

The meeting was to take place in a private room beyond the taproom. Charles Graham, his clerks and the senior surveyor were already seated about a large fire. The days were growing shorter, and the evenings had a chill about them that heralded an early winter.

Charles Graham suggested a drink as they sat by the fire and waited for the factor to come from Corpach.

Wyatt accepted, but Angus Cameron declined both seat and drink. He believed that sitting too close to a fire aged the skin of a man. As for strong drink ... the elder had *never* touched a drop during all the years of his life. He intended his entry into the Lord's kingdom to be as a lifelong abstainer.

Cameron's frown of disapproval would have disconcerted most men, but Charles Graham merely smiled and poured a glass of water for the church elder.

'Your stand against alcohol is admirable, Elder Cameron, but I read my bible regularly and I expect to find the good Lord waiting to greet me at the gates of heaven with a glass of superb wine in his hand.'

'If all men had the same strength of will as our Saviour, strong drink might indeed be a blessing, Mr Graham. As it is, the devil uses it for his own works.'

'I respect your convictions, Elder. However, I believe you're missing one of life's rare pleasures. ... Ah! This sounds like your factor. Now we can get down to business.'

John Garrett's loud voice could be heard outside the room. He seemed to be in an unusually jovial mood. Entering the room, Garrett ignored the two Eskaig churchmen. He nodded to the lesser members of the Edinburgh party and extended a hand to the Kilmalie estate administrator.

'Charles! It's good to see you in the Highlands at last. But there's no need for you to lodge here, in the back of beyond. You must come to the house.'

Charles Graham declined the offer. 'We have much work to do in and around Eskaig. We'll be calling on your services, of course, and I trust I'll be a welcome visitor to your home. However, my business will be more conveniently carried on from Eskaig.'

Accepting a drink from one of the clerks, John Garrett frowned. 'What sort of business? It must be extremely pressing to have brought you from Edinburgh with such a large entourage.'

'As I explained in my note to you, I'm here as a result of the sad death of Lord Kilmalie. Unfortunately, his passing means rather more than the loss of a fine man. We're witnessing a period of great change in Scotland. Values are changing, too. It's been felt for very many years there should be a reassessment of the estate's value. Now it has become necessary in order to ascertain the *extent* of his successor's inheritance. Would you believe the boundaries of the Kilmalie estate have never been accurately defined? We must progress with the times, I'm afraid.'

'Today's world overtook Lord Kilmalie many years ago, but he refused to face the fact,' declared John Garrett callously. 'Things will change now, and I for one am not sorry. . . .'

A servant appeared at the doorway and waited patiently until he caught Charles Graham's attention. Graham held up a hand to silence the factor. 'It seems our meal is ready, gentlemen. Shall we resume our discussion over the dinner-table? Let me lead the way.'

As they walked together from the room, Angus Cameron shook his head gloomily. 'I don't like it, Minister. "Change" and "progress" are words that mean very different things to landowners and tenants. To them it means making more money. To us it's just another way of saying "clearance" and "hardship".'

'Let's wait to hear what everyone has to say before we make a judgement, Angus. We have a thriving little community here. The new Lord Kilmalie won't want to destroy it. We might even find an improvement in the quality of our lives.'

Wyatt was aware there was a hollow ring to his words. Angus Cameron was right. Enthusiasm for change usually spelled disaster for the inhabitants of the Highlands.

For much of the meal the talk about the table was light-hearted. Both the Kilmalie administrator and the chief surveyor led busy social lives and they possessed a wealth of anecdotes about life in Scotland's capital city. Only Elder Cameron maintained a sombre and unsmiling demeanour throughout the meal. Wyatt suspected much of this stemmed from unfamiliarity with the variety of cutlery placed on either side of his plate. In many parts of the Highlands a knife and wooden spoon were the only dining implements deemed necessary. In the mountains the spoon itself was scorned as an unnecessary luxury.

Not until the port was circulating and tobacco-smoke drifting up to form a blue haze above the table did the talk turn to business matters, prompted by Charles Graham. He was seated at the far end of the table from Wyatt, flanked by John Garrett and the chief surveyor.

'Minister Jamieson, are you aware you're a benefactor under Lord Kilmalie's will?'

The information, called the length of the table, took Wyatt by surprise. Lord Kilmalie had been so generous during his lifetime, Wyatt had not considered he might benefit by the landowner's death.

'Do you mean I benefit personally? Or is it a gift to my church?'

'It's a gift to *you*, Minister. In recognition of your heroism in saving Lord Kilmalie's son. The man who *should* have been his heir. I'm not at liberty to inform you of the details, the will has not been officially read yet, but I can assure you it's a substantial sum.'

'Has his Lordship been equally generous to his Eskaig tenants? I'm rather concerned about these "changes" you're forecasting.'

Seated beside Wyatt, Angus Cameron was nodding vigorous agreement with his minister's words.

'I'm more concerned with gathering facts about the estate, Minister. It will be for the new Lord Kilmalie to act upon my findings as he thinks fit, of course. However, I don't foresee any immediate changes. I gather he has no intention of leaving his home in Australia and taking up residence in this country, so administration is likely to prove difficult for a while.'

'Not as difficult as you think, Charles. I have some papers I would like you to read.'

John Garrett rose from the table abruptly and left the room.

He returned carrying a leather satchel from which he produced a number of papers. He handed them to Charles Graham with a triumphant flourish.

Graham frowned when he glanced down at the papers, and his puzzlement grew as he read them. He read the first paper thoroughly and then glanced quickly through the remainder. Suddenly looking up at John Garrett, he said sharply: 'Where did you get these . . . and when?'

'I met Major Skene – the new Lord Kilmalie – when I was in London. We spent a lot of time together. He gave me these papers shortly before he left for Australia. A solicitor was consulted before they were drawn up. I think you'll find they're all perfectly legal.'

'I don't doubt it. I'm less concerned with the legality than with the manner in which this whole matter has been conducted. Why was I not informed of this before?' Charles Graham threw the papers down on the table in front of the factor. 'Such an underhand "arrangement" is disgraceful.'

John Garrett shrugged. 'You'll have to speak to the new Lord Kilmalie about that. It was *his* duty to inform you, not mine.'

'I'm not talking of anyone's *duty*, John. I'm talking of trust – and honesty. You and Evangeline stayed at my house when you were on your way home from London, yet you never gave me a hint that you had these documents in your possession. Documents that make my position as administrator for the Kilmalie estates damned near untenable!'

The factor seemed genuinely startled by Charles Graham's anger. 'Nothing has changed as far as *you're* concerned. You're still the administrator for Lord Kilmalie's estates, no matter who holds the title.'

'An administrator with very little power of administration. It's an intolerable situation.'

Charles Graham stood up from the table, pushing back against his chair so hard it crashed noisily to the floor behind him. 'My obligations to the estate of the late Lord Kilmalie mean I must carry out a survey. It doesn't decree that *I* need be present. I shall return to Edinburgh first thing in the morning.'

'Will someone please explain what's happening?' Wyatt had been a confused onlooker until now.

'Yes, tell him, John. The minister has a right to know. Mr Cameron, too. Tell them how you've persuaded the new Lord Kilmalie to give you absolute power over the Kilmalie estates – and its tenants. Full executive powers "for as long as you are making a profit", I believe is the wording. Answerable to no one but a man in far-off Australia! Here. . . .'

Charles Graham picked up the documents and threw them down the table towards Wyatt. 'Read for yourself how one man's ruthless ambition has been achieved. Read it – and then warn the people of the estate what they can expect from a man who does this to his friends. God help them, Minister. I doubt if anyone else can.'

CHAPTER THIRTY

THE SNOWS reached the Highlands earlier than usual in the winter of 1842. Travelling from the Arctic circle, the wind piled cloud upon dark grey cloud. Then one day the wind suddenly dropped and the clouds no longer sped across the sky but hung over the mountain-tops, swollen and menacing. The Highlanders waited anxiously as the gap between sky and land closed. It seemed that when a sharp mountain-top touched the plump belly of the grey mass overhead its contents would empty upon the Highland landscape.

This was exactly how it occurred. As the grey of day became the black of night, the cloud sagged upon the heights of Ben Nevis. An eerie silence gripped the land, and when Eskaig awoke the next morning four feet of snow blanketed the village and surrounding mountains.

Wyatt had seen Mairi only once since their visit together to the Munro home, and it had been an unsatisfactory meeting. Mairi came to church with her mother, father, six brothers and Tibbie. Somehow, Wyatt never seemed able to speak to her without one of the others being present. Now he knew they would probably not meet again until the spring.

The weather was not allowed to interfere with the important church conference held in Edinburgh halfway through November. Minister Coll Kennedy came from Letterfinlay by boat, travelling along Loch Lochy and the lower reaches of the Caledonian Canal to Corpach. Here he joined Wyatt and two other local ministers in Donald McKay's steam-launch for the passage to Glasgow, *en route* to Edinburgh. With the future of the Kilmalie tenants so uncertain, Wyatt had thought of cancelling his trip to Edinburgh. However, Garrett was unlikely to make a move against the Highlanders in such weather, and the conference was vitally important to the future of the Church in Scotland.

It was a rough and uncomfortable voyage, almost as though the Lord was putting their resolution to the test. For the whole of the journey the four preachers discussed the future of the church to which they had dedicated their lives. From all over Scotland hundreds of ministers were doing the same as they converged upon the Scots capital.

Arrangements had been made for the ministers to be lodged in houses of church members. Coll Kennedy and Wyatt were billeted with a very elderly widow who was terrified when one of the Edinburgh elders informed her that her charges were from the Highlands. Her relief when she saw they were not coarse, armed or red-bearded was evident. However, Coll Kennedy was disgruntled when she informed the two clergymen she did not allow drinking, smoking or swearing inside her house.

'If I come here again, I'll wear my tartan, carry a claymore with me and walk in shouting my clan motto. She'll not care what I do afterwards, just as long as I keep quiet.'

'What is the motto of the Kennedy clan?' Wyatt was curious. As far as he knew, his own family had neither tartan nor motto.

Coll Kennedy had said more than he intended and he appeared slightly self-conscious. 'It's French. "Avise la fin." '

' "Consider the end." ' Wyatt grinned. 'It's very apt, Coll. Our landlady's rules might succeed in saving you for greater things.'

'I don't think the family is particularly noted for observing the motto. One of them, some centuries ago, roasted the Abbot of Crossraguel in his castle. It couldn't have enhanced his chances of a place in heaven, although it *did* vastly increase his temporal land-holdings.'

The two men were sharing a room, and Wyatt paused in his unpacking. He realised he knew very little about the happy-go-lucky preacher from Letterfinlay.

'Which of your ancestors *lost* the family fortunes and made it to heaven?'

'Oh, it was never lost. The sixteenth earl is my brother. Another brother is a baronet. We're also distantly related to the lords of Kilmalie.'

Wyatt's open-mouthed astonishment brought a smile to the face of Coll Kennedy. 'Don't let it overawe you, Wyatt. *I'm* never likely to have a title. There are six older brothers between me and the earldom. My father was in the habit of telling his friends I'd joined the Church in order to gain a heavenly inheritance, because I'll never have one here on earth.'

'With such a background why are you fighting the landowners – people like your own brother – over the issue of patronage?'

'Being well-bred doesn't mean I have no principles.' Coll Kennedy's indignation lasted only a matter of seconds. 'While we're on the subject of principles, I *refuse* to set off on an unknown journey without drinking to whatever lies ahead. . . .'

With a wink at his companion, Coll Kennedy produced a bottle of whisky from his baggage. 'Share this with me, Wyatt. God knows – and He alone – it's certainly an unknown road we'll all be travelling if the Convocation votes to stand or fall on the patronage issue. There's no way we can retreat with honour.'

On 17 November 1842, 474 dissatisfied ministers of the Church of Scotland assembled in St George's Church, Edinburgh, to listen to Dr Chalmers, one of the Church's most respected ministers. He took as his text 'Unto the upright there ariseth light in the darkness'. He proceeded forcibly, and with great skill, to relate his text to the darkness that had caused the Church to stray from the path wherein lay its duty.

It was the largest gathering of ministers Edinburgh had ever witnessed, and the people of the Scots capital sensed they were bearing witness to an historic occasion. When the service was over the ministers adjourned to Roxburgh Church, close to the university where Wyatt had been a student. Along the route the pavements were lined by silent members of the Church, most with heads bowed in prayer, calling for wisdom to prevail at the Convocation.

The ministers were anxious to reach the right decision. Their livelihood and the future of their families were at stake, along with their Christian principles.

The facts before them were starkly simple. The highest courts in the realm had ruled that the Church of Scotland must accept the rights of patronage. The choice of a preacher rested with the patron – in practice, the landowner – and not with the community he would serve. Furthermore, in the final analysis it was the State and not the Church that was the arbiter of pastoral matters.

If the Convocation agreed this was unacceptable to them, they had no alternative but to break away from the mother church and form a 'free' church. By so doing they would give up home, income and their status in the community.

Yet, as Wyatt realised on the very first day of the Convocation, no other decision was morally possible. Others thought the same. On the third day a vote was taken on an ultimatum to be delivered to the British government: 423 ministers voted with their conscience.

The die was cast. Unless the British government changed its mind, there would be a new, 'free' church in Scotland.

The handshakes exchanged among departing ministers were firm and warm. Here in Edinburgh there was comfort in their numbers and a shared determination. With such unanimity no man could have doubts about the future.

Squatting on the wet deck of Donald McKay's steamer as it battered a blunt-nosed passage through the choppy waters of the Firth of Lorn, Coll Kennedy passed a pewter flask to Wyatt, pulled the high collar of his coat about his ears, and shivered.

'We've difficult days ahead of us, Wyatt.'

'There can be no other way.' Wyatt wiped the lip of the flask on his sleeve and returned it to his companion. 'We both knew it. So did the Convocation.'

'Will you be able to convince your elders and parishioners that you've done the right thing?'

'The elders should need no convincing. I sometimes feel they still resent my appointment by Lord Kilmalie. I'm not so certain of the people. They shy away from change. The Church has always been a safe haven in uncertain times. They'll be confused.'

'You'll be able to convince them. You're closer to the Highlanders than any minister in these parts.'

Wyatt hoped Coll Kennedy was right. If the Highlanders failed to follow him into the breakaway church, it would be an empty personal victory for him.

*   *   *

The mountains around Loch Eil huddled beneath a thick blanket of undisturbed snow. Wyatt wondered yet again how Mairi and the Ross and Fraser families were faring. He intended to pay them a visit at the earliest opportunity.

The snow was not so deep at the lochside. The constant passage of people and animals had trampled a network of tracks reaching out from the village.

One such cleared path extended as far as the small jetty, and many people were making their way here to meet the small vessel. They had to be coming to meet Wyatt. He was the only passenger in the steam-launch, Coll Kennedy having left the vessel at Fort William.

'One thing I'll say for you, Minister. Your arrivals in Eskaig rarely go unnoticed.' Donald McKay spoke past his pipe, only a few inches of face being visible between the damp fur of his beaver hat and the turned-up collar of his oilskin coat. 'As I've said before, you're more welcome today than when I first brought you here.'

'I hope I'll still be welcome when they hear the news I'm bringing. Unless the English Parliament has a change of heart there'll be an end to the Church as we've all known it.'

'I wouldn't trouble yourself overmuch about it,' was Donald McKay's surprising reply, 'Highlanders have known centuries of following a particular clan. Clans have split and thrived all the better for it. It'll be the same with the Church. You'll find, as with the clans, it's the *man* they'll follow. If they respect *you*, they'll follow you to hell, if that's where you say you're going. You don't need me to tell you this, Minister. You've served in a Highland regiment. . . .'

Donald McKay broke off to wrestle with the wheel as the steamboat caught the current and swung off course.

Wyatt thought of what the Glaswegian boatman had said. It could be he was right. Wyatt had known Highland soldiers follow a respected officer without falter when they knew they had been given orders that would lead them into the very jaws of death. He believed the ministers attending the Convocation had been right to take the stand they had. He sincerely hoped his parishioners respected him enough to agree – and to follow.

'What happened, Minister?'

'Did you reach agreement?'

'Will the British government listen?'

The questions came across the water as the steam-boat was edging in towards the jetty. Wyatt waited until the boat bumped heavily against the flimsy structure and Donald McKay thrust the engine into neutral.

'The Convocation has set out the terms on which the Church can discharge its duties. The resolution was signed by more than four hundred ministers. It's to be hoped the Government will take it seriously.'

'What if they don't?' The question came from one of the older villagers.

'Then, there will need to be a Free Church. I'll be reporting to the elders tonight. Tomorrow I'll call a meeting in the kirk and tell everyone what went on in Edinburgh.'

All the way back to Eskaig the villagers bombarded Wyatt with their questions, receiving no more than a series of half-replies from Wyatt. They deserved more – they were *entitled* to more – but, first, Wyatt wanted to discuss every aspect of the Convocation's decision with the elders. He had gone to Edinburgh with their support; they needed to know that what lay ahead was nothing less than the tearing asunder of the Church of Scotland.

Alasdair Burns was in the manse, kneeling beside the fire and cursing with scant respect for his surroundings.

'It's this damned wind. Any other direction and the fire roars away faster than you can pile on the peat. When the wind's coming off the loch it will blow smoke in your face without producing a single flame.'

A large pot was suspended on a chain over the fire with heat enough for the contents to be boiling merrily, each burst bubble releasing an appetising smell into the room.

'Where's Mrs Kerr?' The deaf woman usually came to the manse to prepare Wyatt's main meal. Perhaps she had not realised he was returning.

'Someone's giving birth in the village. Mrs Kerr's not only the church cleaner and minister's cook; she's also Eskaig's midwife. It seems there's not a woman for miles around will give birth unless she's there.'

The mention of childbirth set Wyatt to thinking of Seonaid Ross once again. He hoped Mrs Kerr would not need to attempt to struggle through the snow to the mountain cot just yet. Once more he determined he would go into the mountains as soon as the weather permitted.

'This smells as though it's almost ready. How did Convocation go?'

Wyatt gave his companion a summary of the Convocation proceedings, and the ultimatum they had delivered to Parliament in London.

'There must be a rare strength of feeling within the Church. It's the first time I've heard of a gathering of more than one minister reaching agreement on anything. Of course, your ultimatum will get nowhere. Parliament is elected to look after the vested interests of landlords and landowners. It will agree to nothing that takes one jot of power from *them*. You might as well break away now.'

'I don't doubt you're right, but can you save the hot air for the pot? I'm starving.'

'I'll have it ready now. Find yourself a bannock or two from the bin. Mrs Kerr baked some only this morning. There's some beef in the stew today. Ewan Munro brought some in for you. Their calf died while you were away.'

Wyatt winced. The Munros could do without any more bad luck. 'Did Ewan say how his father was keeping?'

'He's poorly. This weather is hard on his lungs.' Alasdair Burns ladled steaming-hot stew into a deep bowl and carried it carefully to the table. 'Was Angus Cameron among those meeting you at the jetty?'

Wyatt thought. 'No – and that's surprising in view of the importance of my journey to Edinburgh. Is he ill?'

'He's well enough to have walked to the factor's house – at Garrett's invitation.'

Wyatt paused with his spoon poised above the bowl in front of him. 'Why should Garrett want to speak to Angus Cameron?'

Putting his own bowl of stew on the table, Alasdair Burns lowered himself to a seat. 'Only Garrett and Cameron have the answer to that question. Evangeline told me both men were looking well pleased with themselves by the time Cameron left to return to Eskaig.'

Wyatt was baffled. What could John Garrett want with the Eskaig elder? It had to be something to do with church affairs, of course. Angus Cameron could offer nothing else of interest to the factor. Wyatt wondered whether it had anything to do with the imminent Disruption of the Church of Scotland. No doubt the senior elder would enlighten him when they met that evening.

The meeting between Wyatt and the church elders was a solemn affair. It took place in the tiny meeting-room that had been added to the church building by Wyatt's predecessor. Even the crackling of a warm fire brought little cheerfulness to the occasion.

After Wyatt had given the elders a résumé of the Convocation's proceedings there was a long silence among his listeners.

'What do *you* think will happen?' The question came from the oldest and most frail elder, a man Wyatt had seldom heard utter a word in his presence.

'I fear Parliament will reject the demands of Convocation. If it does, those preachers who think as I do cannot in all conscience remain in a church where spiritual authority has been usurped by the State.'

'Who will take on the pastoral responsibility given up by you and the others who resign their livings?'

'If the people of Eskaig agree with what I'm doing, I will stay and work for them – as a minister of the 'free' church. No doubt the present church will make some attempt to carry on here, too.'

Wyatt looked seriously at each man in turn. 'I wish there had been another way, but unless there is a change of heart in London men of conscience have no alternative.'

'I don't agree with patronage, but wouldn't it have been better to fight against it from within?' The speaker was Angus Cameron.

'Sadly, no. The Church has tried without result to free itself from the dictates of the State. It has resulted in *increased* government control. If we are to worship in the way we wish, we must be a "free" church.'

'Who will pay your salary in this brave new "free" church?'

'Convocation suggested a levy of a penny a week from each family.' Wyatt found himself puzzled by Angus Cameron's opposition to Convocation's decision. The senior elder had been the most intransigent of all the elders when Lord Kilmalie had appointed Wyatt to the Eskaig living. 'It shouldn't prove beyond the means of most families.'

'Is Eskaig to have a "penny preacher"? Would you bring the Church to *this*, after the sacrifice and hard work of generations of dedicated churchmen? We're respected by landowners and the highest authorities in the land. Would you set this at nought? I say we must remain within the established church. If there are any wrongs, they are best righted from *within*.'

'Would you have discussed this with John Garrett, Angus?'

The senior elder's reaction was immediate and angry. 'What are you suggesting? That I've been influenced by something Garrett's said?'

'I'm suggesting nothing. I heard you've been to Garrett's house while I was in Edinburgh. It would be natural enough to discuss the state of the Church while you were there. I thought he might have given you his views.'

'I went to Corpach with the church accounts. It's usual for the minister to take them about this time of year. You weren't here, so Garrett asked me to deliver them. We discussed the accounts. No more, and no less.'

Wyatt did not believe the senior elder. He was far too defensive. But why should he lie – and about what?

After the meeting, Wyatt pinched out the candles that had illuminated the room and checked the doors and windows. Fierce gales were likely to spring up suddenly in the Highlands at this time of year.

Outside the church Wyatt thought there might be some justification for accusing him of being over-cautious. Not a breath of wind disturbed the few brown leaves that hung dry and lifeless from the trees. It was cold and cloudless, and the ring of light encircling the full moon promised a heavy frost. The night was made lighter by the reflection of the moon on mountain snow. So still was it that the soft whistle of an otter a mile or so up the loch sounded noisy.

Wyatt crossed to the corner of the little churchyard where a holly-tree sheltered his father's grave. Dropping to his knees, Wyatt shared his thoughts with the man who had been forced to make many unpalatable decisions during his own lifetime. Then he prayed that he, too, might have the strength to do what he knew to be right.

When he brought the brief graveside sojourn to an end, Wyatt stood up, shivering in the chill air of the night. He glanced up towards the snow-covered mountains towering high above Loch Eil.

Beyond those peaks lay the Highland moor on which lived Mairi Ross. He wondered what she was doing tonight. He wished it were possible to see her. To speak to her. He found he was missing her more and more as the days and weeks passed. It would be a long lonely winter.

CHAPTER THIRTY-ONE

IN THE HIGH MOUNTAINS in a harsh winter such as this life was reduced to a basic determination to survive, and the provision of sufficient food and warmth for humans and animals. Both suffered the hardships of Highland living, and both shared the minimal comfort of a Highland cot.

Outside the back door, if there was one, peat was piled to the level of the roof, and stacked as deep as a castle wall. Above the door turfs came together in the manner of a badly built igloo. The occupants could keep their fire alight by reducing the width of the peat walls, even when snow lay about the cot deeper than a man.

Part of the cot was partitioned off from the family. In here lived the cows and pigs that would provide the heart of next summer's stock. Sometimes there would be a sheep or two, but they were not intended to survive the winter snows. They would be killed and eaten when the time was right.

Other sheep remained outside, taking their chances with the weather. Most would survive in the shallow glens to which instinct had driven them. They sheltered from the icy blast in tunnels and holes formed in the snow by the heat of their bodies. When the weather improved the cottars would go in search of them, hoisting them from their life-saving prisons, by which time they would be no more than fleece-hung skeletons. Inside the cot, if the occupants had calculated correctly, they would survive on a monotonous diet of salted meats and fish, used to flavour oatmeal cooked in as many ways as ingenuity would allow.

If the calculations had been seriously wrong, or the winter exceptionally harsh and long, it might become necessary to bleed the cattle. The blood would give extra nourishment to the mess of oatmeal that by now would be the sole food left to beleaguered crofters and cottars. If the weather had not relented by the time the cattle were weakened to the point where they could no longer stand, then lean and tough beef was added to the menu. If, as had been known to happen, there was still no let-up in the weather, one of the household would need to set out through the deep snow to seek help. The remainder of the family would sit with hunger gnawing at their entrails, awaiting succour. If none came ... they perished.

It was this environment that made the Highlander what he was. His hardiness in surviving the harshness of winter bred a soldier who had become a legend in the British army. Stalked by death from birth, he had cheated him so many times that death was no longer a stranger to be feared, but an opponent to be outwitted and frequently defeated.

Eneas Ross had met the ultimate enemy many times, in the Highlands and farther afield. He knew better than most how to keep him at bay. The Ross cot was snug and well stocked to withstand the harshest winter. The animals that occupied a full half of the cot added a pungent aroma to the smell of a peat fire, damp thatch and unwashed bodies. The smell passed without comment. It was possible to live with a stench, and *living* was what it was all about.

The Ross family were more fortunate than most. They had bread, cheeses, salt butter and beef to eat, and sheep to kill if required. They had whisky, too, and many stories to tell as they sat around the fire.

There were tales of Wellington's campaign through Portugal and Spain, and across the Pyrenees into France; memories of Magdalene's childhood among the sun-kissed orange-groves of Spain; accounts of how constables and militia had been outwitted when raiding for sheep in the lowlands. Stories, too, of the long-ago, when all Englishmen were enemies and men of the mountains and glens forgot their centuries-old feuds and joined together to follow their prince and drive the forces of a Hanoverian king southwards from Scotland.

Mairi listened with one ear to stories she had heard through nineteen Highland winters as she struggled to master the arts of reading and writing. Sometimes she would read to the family from the bible Wyatt had given to her. This gave particular pleasure to her mother. Magdalene Ross would sit nodding approval of the bible stories that had been told to her in her own language when she was a child.

At night, with only the faint light of the peat fire to keep the darkness inside the cot at bay, Mairi would lie in bed, listening to the whisky-induced snores of her father and brothers. Occasionally there would be other sounds from the cupboard-like box bed shared by Ian and Tibbie. The sounds embarrassed Mairi. The whole family knew what they were doing, and she felt no young married couple should need to make love surrounded by parents and family. That was not how she wanted it to be when she married.

She wondered what life in a manse with Wyatt would be like. The thought caused her to squirm on the heather-filled mattress. It was all a foolish dream, of course. She lacked the background and the education to become a minister's wife. All the same. . . .

A moan from Tibbie brought her back to earth. She wondered how many other members of the family were lying awake listening to sounds that were never meant to be shared with more than one other person. . . .

Christmas in Eskaig was almost lost in a howling blizzard that swept in from the mountains. Not until evening was it possible for Wyatt to clear a way to the church, assisted by a grumbling but hard-working Alasdair Burns.

The Christmas service was held in a candle-lit church and attended only by those few Eskaig residents who had been able to dig a way from their houses. After the service they stood around in the church porch, seemingly reluctant to leave the shelter afforded by the building. All agreed it was the worst winter weather in living memory.

Then, early in January, an unexpected warm spell of weather brought about a partial thaw – on the loch's edge, at least. People emerged from their houses to take advantage of the break in the winter weather and repair some of the ravages of winter storms.

Evangeline rode to Eskaig from Corpach, and classes were held in the school for the first time in many weeks. The factor's daughter was pale-faced and looked very tired when she and Alasdair came to the manse for a midday meal. When they were all seated at the table, Wyatt asked her if she was feeling ill.

Evangeline shook her head. 'No, but Mother has become a worry. She's more confused than ever. She really needs to have someone with her for every hour of the day and night. When the weather improves I'll take her to Edinburgh again. There's a doctor there who has helped her in the past.'

'Couldn't you take advantage of the good weather and take her now?'

'I can't leave the house with only the servants there. Father went to Edinburgh himself yesterday. He boarded a boat at Fort William.'

Wyatt wondered what business the factor had in Edinburgh, but he said: 'Couldn't he have taken your mother with him?'

'He hasn't taken her anywhere for at least ten years. If he had, she might never have become as she is now. I spoke to him about her, but he said his business was too important to be wasted on matters that could very well wait.'

There was a deep bitterness in Evangeline's voice, and Alasdair Burns looked sympathetically in her direction. 'If there's anything I can do, you have only to ask.'

Evangeline reached out and rested her hand on the teacher's arm. 'Thank you, Alasdair. Just being able to tell you my troubles this morning has helped.'

Evangeline toyed with her knife for a few moments before saying: 'Actually, I think my father is up to something. He's spent hours in his office, studying the maps of the Eskaig estates produced by Charles Graham's surveyors. He's been writing many letters and notes and goes to Fort William whenever weather permits. Once the Fort William magistrate came to the house, and he and my father spent the whole day in the office together.'

'Maps and magistrates. . . ? It sounds to me like the recipe for a clearance.' The comment came from Alasdair Burns.

Wyatt lowered his spoon to the unfinished meal. Food had suddenly lost all taste for him. 'It should surprise no one. The factor has never made any secret of his thinking. He's always saying it's sheep and not tenants that make profits for an estate.'

Wyatt stood up from the table. Walking to the window, he gazed up at the high mountains. The thaw was beginning to touch them, too. Here and there a dark outcrop of rock protruded from the white snow.

'If the weather holds, I'm going up into the mountains tomorrow.'

'Be careful. The mountains are dangerous after a thaw,' warned Alasdair Burns.

'I'll be careful.'

Wyatt thought of the first occasion when he had been in the mountains. Of Mairi, the rescue of the Munro children – and the disapproval of some of the villagers when he brought Mairi back to the manse dressed only in his coat. The thought made him smile.

'If there's another change in the weather, you might be marooned in the mountains for weeks – months, even. Perhaps you might even return to us as a married man! Can a minister conduct his own wedding?'

There was an exchange of glances between the two teachers.

'It's another married couple I'm particularly concerned about. Donnie and Seonaid Ross weren't wed long enough to plan for a winter such as this.'

Evangeline's face stiffened at the mention of Seonaid, but Alasdair Burns did not notice. 'No doubt you'll be looking in upon the Ross croft, too? Just to make sure they're surviving the winter?' he asked.

Wyatt looked up at the mountains again before replying: 'Of course. It's on the way to the Fraser cot, after all.'

Eneas Ross and his family did not waste the unexpected break in the harsh winter weather. Able to leave the house for the first time in weeks, they turned the animals out of the house and cleaned up after them. Doors and windows stood open, washing was draped over a freestone wall to dry, and Eneas Ross's many sons were scouring the still-deep snows of the high area, searching for sheep.

When the animals were located in their body-width caverns they were hauled out unceremoniously. Carried to a patch of land, their diligent nuzzling uncovered winter grass that was promptly grazed to its roots.

Sound travelled far in the clear air of the mountains, and Wyatt was still half a mile from the Ross croft when one of the sons saw him. Shielding his eyes, the young Ross identified the unexpected visitor, and his voice carried clearly as he called to the croft.

'Mairi! You've just time to put on your best gown. The preacher from Eskaig's coming calling.'

A moment later Mairi's face appeared at the window, her long hair loose about her face. Even from this distance Wyatt could distinguish the smudges on her face. She was working as hard as any other member of the Ross family.

Wyatt raised his hand to wave to her, but she disappeared from view before his hand reached shoulder height. The greeting was returned by the brother who had first seen him.

Mairi had not reappeared by the time Wyatt reached the croft, but the remainder of the family were gathered outside to welcome him — and Wyatt's appearance was the subject of immediate concern. The sun was quite warm up here in the mountains, and the snow had been reduced to a depth of no more than two or three feet in most places. However, where the path ran through a shaded place the snow still lay man-high. Wyatt had also been forced to wade through some of the many mountain streams which tumbled from the peaks. As a result his clothing was sodden and it was as much as he could do to stop shivering.

Magdalene Ross tut-tutted about him, while Eneas Ross suggested a practical solution.

'You'd better get out of those clothes, Preacher, before you catch your death of cold. Come into the house by the fire. I've a shirt that will fit you well enough. Ian, you're about the same size as the preacher. Let him have those new trousers you bought for your wedding. Malcolm, you have the best pair of shoes in the house — bring them quickly. All you women can leave the house — and don't come back until you're told. I'll be pouring you a wee dram, Preacher. What are you doing coming up here in the middle of winter? I doubt if there's ever been a preacher here in January before.'

Wyatt passed Mairi in the doorway. Clean-faced, her hair was tied neatly at the nape of her neck, and she wore a clean dress. She smiled at him, and in that moment the long and arduous climb to the high lands became worthwhile.

As he changed from his wet clothes, Wyatt spoke to Eneas Ross. 'I came up here because I've been worried about the effect the bad weather might have had on you.'

'We've had bad winters before. Not for such a long spell at one time, perhaps, but I've lived up here far too long to let any weather take me by surprise.'

'I'm worried about the Frasers, too. Donnie hasn't been there long enough to have things properly organised, and Hamish Fraser wouldn't have been able to prepare for winter.'

Eneas Ross's face showed concern for a brief unguarded moment. Then his expression hardened. 'Fraser has managed well enough all these years. I don't doubt he'll be better off this year.'

Wyatt put on the last of the borrowed clothing, and Eneas Fraser called the women back inside the house. As they returned, Wyatt said: 'You're probably right about the Frasers, Eneas. All the same, I'll go on to see them as soon as my clothes are dry and I've a dram or two of your whisky inside to warm me on my way.'

'Please yourself, but you'll not visit Fraser and get back to Eskaig tonight. Return here and stay with us. There's so many of us already that one more will make no difference, and I fancy you'll have better company than you'll find there.'

Wyatt hesitated for only a moment. 'I'd like that. Thank you. Now, where's that whisky? I'm chilled through to the bone.'

While Eneas Ross half-filled a pewter mug with whisky and Magdalene began cooking dough bannocks on a barred 'girdle-iron' set on the fire, Mairi began arranging Wyatt's clothes, placing them so close to the fire that very soon steam began rising from them, drifting upwards until it was lost among the smoke-black-ened beams. She had heard Wyatt give notice of his plans, and the thought of having him sleeping beneath the same roof excited her more than she would allow the others to see. It meant poor Tibbie and Ian would lose the scant privacy of their box bed for the night, but they would survive.

'Did I hear you say you were going to see Donnie and Seonaid?' They were the first words she had spoken to Wyatt since his arrival.

'Yes. They're the first couple I've wed since coming to Eskaig, and I'm taking a personal interest in them. I want to assure myself they're all right.'

'I'll come with you. . . .' Seeing the knowing smiles of her brothers, Mairi added heatedly: 'I've been forced to stay inside the cot with this lot for weeks. It will feel good to get away from them all for a couple of hours.'

'You could always take a walk to see if there are any sheep beneath the ridge. That way you'd be free of *everyone*. Wouldn't you prefer that, little sister?' a young Ross suggested.

'I'll go where I want to go. Right now I've had enough of foolish brothers. Your clothes will be dry in about half an hour, Wyatt. I'll be outside enjoying the sunshine.'

Mairi left the cot to a chorus of good-natured catcalls from her brothers. When she had gone, Tibbie crossed to the fire and adjusted Wyatt's wet clothing unnecessarily.

While she was close to Wyatt, she said softly: 'Mairi's very fond of you, Minister.'

'I'm very fond of her, too, Tibbie.'

Tibbie's warm smile transformed her pale and tired face. 'I'm glad. I was beginning to think Mairi would never find someone like you. She's a very special girl, Minister. She's worked hard on the schooling you gave her. You'll not find a better wife in the Highlands — or anywhere else.'

CHAPTER THIRTY-TWO

'AREN'T your feet cold?' Wyatt looked aghast at Mairi's bare feet as he set out with her for the Fraser cot.

Mairi seemed surprised at the question. 'A little. But they'd be just as cold if I were working outside the cot.' She shifted the bundle she carried to a more comfortable position. 'I'll be able to dry my feet when we get there. What will you do about your shoes?'

Wyatt had his own clothes on again. The coat, shirt and trousers were dry, but his shoes were still wet and uncomfortable. He had to admit that Mairi had made a good point.

They were both carrying bags of food for Donnie and Seonaid and her father. Eneas Ross might have disowned his youngest son, but Magdalene Ross had not. Cheese, butter and newly baked bannocks were in the bags, together with salted beef, and a quarter of a sheep that had been found injured beneath the snow.

'I've missed you, Mairi. There have been many moonlit nights when I've looked up at the snow on the mountains and prayed you were safe and well up here.'

'We were snug enough to have seen out another month of snow. I don't know whether it was due to your praying, or to Pa's sound planning!' There was the faintest trace of humour in the sidelong glance Mairi gave him.

All conversation ceased for some fifteen minutes while they scrambled up a steepish slope of broken rock in order to avoid a low-lying area where snow had drifted. On the far side of the ridge was an area of broken rocks which gave some shelter from the wind. Here Mairi dropped her bundle to the ground. Standing with her back to a large boulder, she rubbed the shoulder which had borne the weight of her load and watched as Wyatt flexed aching arms.

'You've lost weight, Wyatt. You haven't been ill with that fever you told me about?'

'I wasn't too well for a few days after Christmas, but it wasn't as bad as the last time. Each attack seems to be less serious than the one before.'

'Poor Wyatt. You really should have someone to look after you.'

'I agree. . . .' Wyatt took a deep breath. 'Have you thought any more about the discussion we had after Donnie and Seonaid's wedding?'

'What more was there to think about? I told you then what I thought. Look at me, Wyatt. What sort of wife do you think I'd make for the minister of Eskaig?'

'The sort of wife *I* want – and I'll not settle for any other.'

When Mairi did not reply immediately, Wyatt added: 'Anyway, I may not be the minister of Eskaig for very much longer.'

Startled, Mairi asked: 'You're not thinking of leaving?'

'I may have to.' He gave Mairi an outline of the dispute between Church and State, and the widening breach within the Church itself.

'What will happen to you? What will you do?'

'It all depends on the people here. If they agree with what I'm doing, I'll stay on as a Free Church minister. If they don't. . . .' Wyatt shrugged. 'If they don't, then I'll know I was a better soldier than I am a minister.'

Mairi was very upset, but before she could say anything more they both heard a sound from the ridge they had crossed a short time before. Moments later they were joined by Stewart Ross, the second-youngest of Mairi's brothers.

'Hello, you two. I thought you'd have reached the Fraser place by now. What's held you up?' He turned a cheeky grin upon Wyatt. 'Not interrupting anything, am I?'

Mairi did not respond to his cheerfulness. 'Wyatt was just telling me he might have to leave Eskaig. There's a dispute within the Church. But what are you doing here?'

Stewart Ross lifted Mairi's bundle with ease and tucked it beneath an arm. 'I thought Donnie might need a hand to get things together up at the Fraser place. There'll be more snow on the way in

240

a day or two, and old man Fraser won't be much help.'

'Does Pa know where you are?'

'No, but Ma thought it would be a good idea. Shall we go?'

Wyatt would have liked to speak at much greater length to Mairi, but neither of them could have anticipated the unexpected interruption. Lifting his own bundle, he set it on his shoulder and followed Stewart Ross. Along the way he had to repeat his story of the problems of the Church of Scotland for the benefit of Mairi's brother.

Stewart Ross was more philosophic than sympathetic.

'It sounds a bit like a family argument to me. You ministers should be ganging up against the English government, not quarrelling among yourselves.'

The young man spoke in the manner of many Highlanders, as though there had never been union with England.

'I agree,' said Wyatt. 'Although first we need to decide who's right and who's wrong. The trouble seems to be the more we talk the wider grows the rift between us.'

'I doubt if *not* talking will help, either. Take Pa and Hamish Fraser, for instance. They haven't spoken for nigh on thirty years, yet they hate each other as much as they ever did. . . .'

For the remainder of the journey to the Fraser cot Stewart Ross chatted on about the feud between Eneas Ross and Hamish Fraser, its causes and effects. If he noticed there was no response from Wyatt and Mairi, he did not let it silence him.

When the roof of the Fraser cot came into sight, protruding from the snow of the high moors, it was apparent something was wrong. There was no smoke coming from the chimney. The three travellers looked at each other in alarm, not daring to voice their thoughts. Then they began to run. Only when they topped a low rise immediately before the house did they slow their pace. Donnie and Hamish Fraser were hauling a wooden sled piled high with peat turfs towards the house.

When Donnie caught sight of the approaching visitors he released the sled-rope, let out a shout of joy and ran to meet them. After hugging Mairi and Stewart, he shook hands with Wyatt and beamed at all three.

'You don't know how good it is to see you. All of you. I've

longed to hear someone talk the way we always did during the winter months at home. What wouldn't I have given to hear Pa telling us about his army days, with Ma smiling knowingly when he stretched the truth a bit more than usual. Have you done that these last weeks?'

'Of course, but Mairi spent every spare minute of the day stuck in a corner with her learning-books ... and we missed you,' said Stewart Ross.

'We were worried because we couldn't see any smoke when we came in sight of the cot. Where's Seonaid?' asked Mairi.

'Lying abed. She's been ill. I don't know what it was. Something to do with the baby, I think. Belly cramps and a bit of a fever for a while. She's a lot better now. She was up for a while this morning.'

'What about the fire?'

Donnie looked embarrassed. 'I hadn't got around to everything before winter set in. There wasn't enough peat up by the house. The fire went out three days ago.'

'What have you eaten in those three days?' Mairi put the question.

'Same as we seem to have eaten for most of the winter. Cheese. I tried making bannocks before the fire went out, but they dropped in the ashes and burned while I was tending Seonaid.'

Hamish Fraser called out peevishly to know what was happening. Donnie grimaced and he suddenly looked very tired. 'He'd be a lot easier to get along with if he didn't moan all the time. I told him so once, and he sulked for a week.'

At that moment a figure appeared in the doorway of the Fraser cot. It was Seonaid – but a very different Seonaid from the girl who had married Donnie only a few months before. Her hair had not been washed during the long winter months and it straggled about a face totally devoid of any colour. She wore only a cotton night-dress, or it might have been a slip. The garment was stretched so tight about her distended stomach it had split apart at the seams.

Seonaid had not yet seen them and she called out: 'Where's Donnie, Pa? Where's he gone? Call him and tell him I need him. I want some water. . . .'

Mairi became suddenly brisk. 'Stewart, go and help Donnie with the peat. Wyatt, can you get a fire going? Leave Seonaid to me. When I've tended to her I'll start something cooking.'

Less than an hour later strips of salt beef were sizzling in a skillet, bannocks were heating on an iron girdle over the fire, and Seonaid was sitting up on her dry-heather bed, her hair washed and tied in a ribbon behind her head. She looked better already.

Meanwhile, Wyatt was stacking peat turfs while Donnie and Stewart were out searching for sheep lost in the snow among the surrounding crags.

Hamish Fraser sat in a corner of the cot saying little and doing nothing. He resented the intrusion into the privacy of his home, especially by the two extra Frasers, and made no attempt to hide his resentment.

Wyatt attempted to draw the blind man into conversation on a number of occasions, but eventually gave up. He felt he could be of more use to the small family group by helping with the chores.

In spite of his hatred of the Ross family, Hamish Fraser ate every scrap of the meal cooked by Mairi. However, when Donnie and Stewart came inside the cot laughing and joking together he suddenly snapped: 'I don't know what you two have to be so cheerful about.'

'Come now, Mr Fraser, you've every reason to be cheerful, too. We've just found all except one of your sheep; you've peat here at the house, a fire going, and good food in your belly. What more could you want? Something to drink, perhaps?' Stewart fished inside his shirt. 'Here, I've brought Pa's flask with me. It's full of good whisky.'

'I'll not drink Ross whisky. It's galling enough to have to eat your food. As for reason to be cheerful . . . there's a lot of winter to come yet. When it's over all we have to look forward to is a visit from the factor. The constables will be with him, too, I've no doubt.'

'Why should the factor come calling on you with constables?' Wyatt asked sharply.

'You'd better ask Seonaid's man. He's the one who's supposed to be running things now. Although how he's going to keep a wife and child without a roof over their heads I don't know.'

Wyatt looked to Donnie, and the young man shrugged his shoulders. 'It's not as bad as that. A sheriff's man served a paper on us a day or two before the snows began. It's nothing, really. The sheriff's man said it's probably no more than a means of increasing our rent, that's all. We'll manage.'

'If you believe *that*, you're a bigger fool than your father,' Hamish Fraser snorted derisively.

'What does this paper say?' Wyatt persisted.

Again Donnie Ross shrugged. 'I don't know. He can't see, and neither Seonaid nor I can read. The sheriff's man said—'

'Do you still have the document?'

The urgency in Wyatt's voice finally got through to Donnie, and he looked at Seonaid.

'It's on the top shelf – over there.'

Donnie found the document and handed it to Wyatt. Three days without heat in the cot had made everything damp. The paper lay limp in Wyatt's hand, but he knew what it was even before he looked at the bold heading that dominated the page:

WRIT OF REMOVAL
John Garrett representing Lord Kilmalie of Eskaig
versus
Hamish Fraser and Others

Wyatt looked up from the document in dismay. 'This is a writ of removal. A clearance order!'

'There!' exclaimed Hamish Fraser. 'What did I tell you? Didn't I say that's what it was? You didn't believe me. Called me an old fool behind my back. Now who's the fool, eh? Now who's the fool?'

While Hamish Fraser gloated over the accuracy of his gloomy warning, Donnie looked stunned.

'Garrett can't do this, can he? He can't just throw us out of the cot?'

'The factor can do whatever he wants – when he wants to do it. The minister in his comfortable kirk in Eskaig can pray as much as he likes to God. Up here in the mountains it's *Garrett* who's *our* God.'

'Blasphemy won't help anyone,' Wyatt snapped. 'I'll speak to Garrett when I return to Eskaig.'

Hamish Fraser snorted and turned his sightless eyes on Wyatt. 'Speak to who you like, Minister; it'll do us no good. Seonaid went to see Garrett once before when he ordered us out. She thought she'd succeeded in keeping us here. Now she knows better.'

Sitting on her bed, Seonaid's glance was fixed upon the bulge that stretched the fabric of her nightdress.

'Garrett wants us out, and there's nothing anyone can do about it. This is just a beginning. The Rosses will be next. Then it will be every other cottar in these mountains. Garrett wants sheep in our place. That's what he's always wanted. Sheep don't answer him back, or question his way of running things. He doesn't even have to leave his house to make money. He can just sit indoors and wait for the sheepmen to bring him their rent once a year. There was a time when a laird was proud of the number of clansmen who owed him their allegiance. Now the landowner's ashamed of his kinsmen and never comes near them.'

'I think I've heard the same sentiments from Eneas Ross,' said Wyatt quietly. 'You and he are not so different, Hamish.'

'We're both Highlanders. It's *all* we have in common – that and the fact we'll *both* be homeless come spring. You wait and see. Garrett has a free hand now, or so I hear. He'll make the most of it while he can.'

After spending a couple of hours at the Fraser cot, Mairi declared they would need to leave if they were to reach the Ross croft before dark. After holding a brief prayer meeting, Wyatt went outside before the others. He was joined by a worried Donnie Ross and his brother.

'Were all those things Seonaid's pa said the truth? Can Garrett really turn us out with nowhere to go?'

'I wish I could say it might be otherwise, Donnie. With the authorisation document Garrett has been given by the new Lord Kilmalie his power on the Eskaig estate is absolute.'

'What of Seonaid and the baby? It's due about March.'

'I'll do what I can, but don't build up any hopes. Prepare what you can for a move; and, if you have nowhere else to go, come to the manse.'

'Or come home,' put in Donnie's brother. 'I think Pa's already sorry for the quarrel between you. He wouldn't see you with nowhere to go, not with Seonaid due to produce a baby.'

'You're forgetting, we'll have Seonaid's father with us. He and Pa have sworn they'll never set foot in the other's home.'

'I'll try to discuss the matter with your father, Donnie,' said Wyatt. 'He's a good man. He'll not see anyone wandering homeless in the mountains – not even Hamish Fraser.'

Mairi came from the house and after giving her youngest brother an affectionate embrace she, Stewart and Wyatt set off for the Ross home.

Before they passed out of sight of the cot, Wyatt looked back. Donnie stood in the doorway with an arm about Seonaid's shoulders. Both were waving. There was no sign of Hamish Fraser.

CHAPTER THIRTY-THREE

ENEAS ROSS listened to news of the impending eviction of Donnie and the Frasers in a grave silence. When Mairi and Stewart had between them told their father all they knew, he looked to Wyatt for confirmation.

'Do you think Garrett means to do it, Preacher? Or is he just trying to bring the Fraser girl back to heel?'

'Pa! She's our Donnie's wife now. . . .'

The big red-bearded Highlander spat in the fire. 'I'm not talking of *marrying*.' He looked questioningly at Wyatt.

'Garrett means it, I'm sure. He'll have the constables in the mountains as soon as the snows have gone, unless I'm able to change his mind.'

'What will our Donnie do – and the baby? It must be due soon after the factor intends putting them from their home. Eneas, what can we do?' Magdalene Ross stood at the edge of the group about the fire in a state of deep distress.

'*We'll* do nothing. It's not our problem.'

'But our son's being turned out of his home. Our boy Donnie, and his wife. Soon there will be a child, too – our grandchild.'

'Don't talk so foolishly, woman.' Eneas Ross roared the words and stood up from his low stool. 'You don't believe the Fraser girl's baby's been sired by Donnie, any more than I do. If I had to put a name to its father, I'd say it was Garrett's bastard.'

Eneas Ross spat into the fire once more. 'A man like the factor probably wouldn't care about turning his own child out of doors.'

'I don't think Garrett's alone in that – even if it were true, Eneas.

Think about it.' Wyatt spoke quietly, almost gently, but his words went home.

'Donnie's no longer a child – isn't that what you all told me when you begged me to allow him to wed the Fraser girl? I said she would turn out to be nothing but trouble. I was right. Donnie's a married man now. He must look after his family, same as I do. Unless I'm mistaken, I'll be hard put to take care of my own this year. Garrett was only waiting for the right opportunity to start clearances on the Eskaig estate. My son . . . my *son* handed him that opportunity. Offered it to Garrett with both hands. I'm away outside for a while.'

Wyatt would have followed Eneas Ross from the house, but Magdalene restrained him with a hand on his arm. 'Let him go. He'll sit on the wall in the darkness, smoking and thinking.' Magdalene looked up at Wyatt apologetically. 'It's something he's done whenever he's had a problem since the children were small. He says he can think better when he's by himself in the dark. He's right. There were times when I felt my brain would burst with all the children in the house together.' She looked about her wistfully. 'Things haven't changed very much, have they? They're all still here . . . except for little Donnie.'

Magdalene Ross turned to her daughter. 'Was he all right? How did he manage through the snows?'

For a few minutes it seemed Magdalene Ross might dissolve in tears. She won the struggle to regain control of her feelings, but her voice came out as no more than a hoarse whisper. 'He's so young to have the responsibility of a wife and baby. I wish there was something I could do to help him.'

Mairi put an arm about her mother's shoulders. 'He's managing fine, Ma. Seonaid hasn't been too well, but she's on the mend now. Once this business with the factor is sorted out they'll both be as happy as any couple anywhere. You'll see.'

Magdalene Ross nodded her head vigorously. 'Yes. Yes, you're right.' She patted her daughter's hand absentmindedly. 'I'm his mother. I worry about him. I worry about *all* of you. Now, come and help me with supper. You too, Tibbie. I've never cooked for a minister before. It's a good thing we have that sheep.'

Ian Ross rose from his stool by the fire and snuffed out the spluttering wick in a hanging cruise lamp that had been filled with melted mutton fat. He handed it to Tibbie to be refilled, then spoke to Wyatt. 'You'll enjoy a good meal tonight, Preacher. Ma's the best cook in the mountains. Can I give you a wee dram now?'

'Later. I'd like to go outside and talk to your father first.'

'Do *you* think this trouble with our Donnie is the beginning of another clearance?'

'I wish I knew, Ian. I hope not. I might know more when I've spoken to the factor.'

'You tell him if he tries to turn the Rosses out of our home he'll not be dealing with blind men or boys, or sick old soldiers like Lachlan Munro. We'll fight to keep our home, just as generations of Ross men have fought to help the lords of Kilmalie keep their lands.'

'Fighting a man who has the law on his side will gain you only sorrow, Ian. Let's have no more talk of violence.'

Leaving Ian Ross murmuring rebellion against John Garrett and all those who stood with him, Wyatt left the cot.

It was dark outside. Clouds were beginning to build up from the north, obscuring moon and stars. Wyatt could not see Eneas Ross until the bearded patriarch's pipe revealed his position. He was seated on the low wall that protected the croft's vegetable garden from the stock animals.

Wyatt made his way cautiously to where the other man sat, the aroma of strong tobacco drifting to meet him. He stood in silence beside Eneas Ross for some minutes, until the cold of the night caused him to shiver.

'Ay, it's cold, Preacher. You'd best not waste too much time getting back to Eskaig in the morning. There's more bad weather on the way.'

'You can cope well enough with the weather, Eneas. I'm more concerned with what will happen up here when the spring comes.'

'If there's one thing that living in the Highlands has taught me, it's to take one problem at a time. How has young Donnie survived the bad weather?'

'He's managed. Only *just*, but he and the others have come through so far.' Wyatt thought that everyone in the Ross house, with the exception of Magdalene, would be surprised to hear Eneas Ross enquiring after the health of his youngest son.

'Will they get through another bad spell over there?'

'If they're not snowed in for as long again, they'll be all right. Stewart helped Donnie find the sheep and bring them in.'

Wyatt sensed that Eneas Ross was nodding his satisfaction. 'Those two boys always got on well together. Donnie will make out. He's a sensible lad. *Too* good for the Fraser girl.'

'Donnie and Seonaid *are* fond of each other, Eneas. Your son is also very fond – and proud – of you. If you were to accept the marriage, Donnie would be the happiest young man in the mountains.'

'I doubt if my blessing would make any difference. A curse was put upon any union of the families by a stronger man than I, almost a hundred years ago. No one's been able to break it since.'

'Surely you don't believe in some obscure curse, Eneas. Superstition is something for savages without religion to believe in.'

'This curse is more than superstition, Preacher. A Ross was left lying wounded on the field at Culloden by a Fraser who was to marry his daughter. When the English soldiers found the Ross they killed him. Before he died he put a curse on any marriage between a Ross and a Fraser. The curse worked. The dead man's daughter married the Fraser, but on their wedding night a candle was overturned and they both burned to death.'

'That was a hundred years ago. People don't believe in such "curses" any more.'

'Then, they should. Only a foolish man would go against it. Did you know Hamish Fraser's wife, Seonaid's mother, was a Ross?'

'No. No, I didn't.' It explained a great deal of the bitterness Hamish Fraser felt for the Ross family.

'She was a distant cousin. The daughter of my father's cousin. Not that she'd have been any happier with Hamish had she been a Cameron, a Mackenzie, or from any other clan. The man's a pig. If he hadn't been blind, someone would have killed him by now. Young Donnie's the most patient boy I've ever come across, but he'll fall out with Hamish if the marriage lasts long enough.'

'What will you do when Garrett puts them out in the spring?'

'As I said, Preacher, I take one problem at a time. I'll decide what to do when spring comes. I'm likely to have the same problem myself before too long. I should have seen it coming, I suppose. It's happened most everywhere else. It was bound to happen here, sooner or later. It shouldn't affect *you* too much. Might even save you a deal of walking. You'll still have the kirk and the folk of Eskaig to preach to.'

'My father lies in a grave in Eskaig because of a clearance, Eneas. I can't stand back and do nothing – although I, too, might have troubles of my own by then.'

Wyatt told his companion of the problems besetting the Church.

Eneas Ross knocked out his pipe carefully against the wall and began to refill it immediately. 'What's happening to this world of ours, Preacher? When I was a boy there were three things that were unchangeable: the weather, a man's home – and the Church. We've just had the worst snows anyone can remember, the factor's likely to clear us from our homes – and now the Church is tearing itself apart!'

'What do you think you *might* do if Garrett forces you to leave here?' Wyatt persisted. The Highland family's movements were important to him.

'Who knows? A man likes to feel he'll be buried alongside his father one day. Mine is in the graveyard in Eskaig, too, along with the boys Magdalene and I lost.'

Eneas Ross still carried a tinder-box. Striking a flint to it now, he lit a taper and applied it to his pipe. As he sucked it into life his blue eyes were fixed on Wyatt's face. When the tobacco was glowing and the taper extinguished he said: 'Why are you so interested in what I'm going to be doing?'

Wyatt took a deep breath. This was a matter he had wanted to discuss with Eneas Ross since before the snows came. Now the moment was here he wished there had been time to rehearse the words he wanted to say. To express his thoughts and feelings clearly.

'I want to marry Mairi.'

The ensuing silence lasted for so long that Wyatt wished he had brought the subject up in daylight, so he could see Eneas Ross's reaction.

'What does Mairi think of the idea?' Eneas Ross spoke slowly and evenly, his voice carrying no hint of his thoughts.

'She needs to be convinced she'll make a good wife for a minister. Perhaps it will be easier for her if I'm ousted from Eskaig.'

'Perhaps. I *do* know the girl's fond of you. I suspect you're the reason she's working at reading and writing at all hours of the day and night. She's done well, Preacher. She's able to read to us every night from the bible you gave her. Magdalene thinks it's wonderful.'

Wyatt was delighted with Eneas Ross's words. 'Can I take it you have no objections – if I can persuade Mairi to marry me?'

'If Mairi's decided she wants to marry you, then nothing I say or do will stop her. On the other hand, if she doesn't want you, then nothing *you* do or say will change her mind.'

'I think she'll say Yes . . . eventually.'

'Then, here's my hand, Preacher. I'll be proud to call you my son.'

'You've spoken to Pa about marrying me? You had no right to do that without discussing it with me first.'

Mairi was walking part of the way back to Eskaig with Wyatt. They were on an exposed mountain slope, and a strong wind blowing from the north-east made conversation difficult. Wyatt was beginning to wish he had delayed his revelation until they reached the shelter of a few trees just ahead of them, but a snowstorm was on the way. Mairi would soon need to turn back. He had not been able to put it off any longer.

'I *have* discussed it with you. Every time we've met.'

Mairi lengthened her stride as the wind howled in cold fury.

'What did I tell you then?'

With a sense of relief, Wyatt and Mairi stumbled over the last few yards of hardened snow to the trees. They had gained shelter from the physical force of the wind, but there was a note of ominous urgency in its voice.

'Mairi, you must return home now. There's a blizzard not far off. . . .'

Mairi looked up at the sky and then to the north, where thick low cloud was advancing towards them, swallowing the mountains in its path.

'We have a few minutes yet. What did I tell you when you last asked me to marry you?'

'You said something foolish about not having enough learning to be the wife of a minister of the Church.'

'That's right. And nothing has changed.'

'Hasn't it? Your father says you're sitting up all hours of the night learning to read and write. He says you read the Bible to the family most evenings.'

'He was trying to impress you, that's all.'

'I *am* impressed.' Wyatt thought he felt the first flake of snow on his face, herald of the approaching snowstorm. He wished there was more time.

'Mairi, I *love* you. I want you to be my wife. Say Yes. It's a very simple word.'

'I can't, Wyatt. Not yet.'

Her last two words gave him some hope – but she *had* to return home. He must hurry from the mountains, too, or the blizzard would overtake them both before they reached their respective homes.

'I'll be back in the spring to ask you again. You told me before that you are more than fond of me. It's given me comfort during the time we've spent apart. Can I still have that, at least?'

Mairi nodded, and Wyatt would never know how close she was to telling him all he wanted to hear. What she herself knew. That she loved him.

He kissed her then, and as he held her he could almost have taken his chances with the advancing blizzard, but he would not put Mairi at such risk.

'Run now, Mairi, or I shall *worry* about you until the spring.'

She went without another word, and as she left the shelter of the trees the wind snatched at her cloak. She began to run, her bare feet retracing the footsteps they had made on the way to the trees.

Wyatt watched her for as long as he dared. It was a picture he would carry with him through the remaining days and nights of winter. The image of the barefoot girl he would one day marry.

CHAPTER THIRTY-FOUR

WYATT REACHED the lochside before the full force of the blizzard struck. As he floundered through early-drifting snow he was content in the knowledge that Mairi would have reached home at least half an hour earlier. Long before the blizzard broke over the higher lands.

Wyatt crashed open the door of the manse, stamping snow from his shoes and beating it from his coat with cold hands.

To his surprise there was a cheerful fire in the grate. Alasdair Burns greeted him with a tumbler of whisky and the information that venison was cooking in the pot, the meat brought in by young Ewan Munro as a present. It seemed a deer, driven from the mountains by the weather, had 'given itself up' in the garden of the Munro croft.

When Wyatt expressed doubts about the truth of Ewan Munro's story, Alasdair Burns replied that it was lacking in generosity to question 'the Lord's bounteousness'.

'It's not the Lord's bounteousness I'm questioning, Alasdair, but Ewan Munro's explanation.' He sniffed the air. 'It does smell delicious, so we'll allow it to pass this time. It's very kind of you to cook it for me – but how did you know when to expect me?'

'I knew you'd see the storm coming, same as we could at lochside. You'd know to leave the mountains before it arrived.'

Alasdair Burns's face broke into a smile. 'I also knew you'd wait until the very last minute before leaving Mairi Ross.'

Wyatt did not reply to Alasdair Burns's explanation. Instead he said: 'Stay and eat with me, Alasdair – but we'll need to watch the weather. It was beginning to drift when I came off the mountains.'

'I hoped I'd be invited, so I've made enough for the two of us. I've news for you, too — about the Church and the threatened Disruption. Coll Kennedy sent word that Parliament in London has rejected all the demands made by Convocation. The Government insists that patronage must be retained, with all it entails. They're being dangerously short-sighted, Wyatt.'

The news took some of the pleasure from Wyatt's memories of the last minutes he had spent with Mairi. How could he ask her to share such an uncertain future with him? He consoled himself with the thought that Coll Kennedy's information might not be entirely accurate. After all, he had probably received it secondhand, possibly from a crew member in one of the boats passing through Loch Lochy.

Coll Kennedy's information was all too accurate. It *had* reached him from a ship taking passage through Loch Lochy, but it was taken from a Glasgow newspaper. Sir Robert Peel, Prime Minister of Great Britain, had dealt with the problems of the Church of Scotland with a firmness bordering on impatience. When his Tory colleagues expressed doubts about acting in such an arbitrary manner, Peel told them he was following the advice of senior members of the Scottish Church, moderate men who were in a position to know the thinking of their fellow-ministers. They had assured him it needed only a little firmness from the Government to bring the dissenting churchmen 'to heel'.

The Prime Minister assured his doubting colleagues he was aware of the numbers attracted to the Edinburgh Convocation. Nevertheless, he was confident most of the ministers had attended the meeting to *listen*. Indeed, it was the *duty* of ministers of the Church to hear what their fellow-ministers had to say. Unless they did, they would not know how best to counter the lies and misrepresentations which were all they had to offer.

The Prime Minister's information was that if a Disruption of the Church was attempted very few of those who attended the Edinburgh meeting would cast in their lot with a breakaway movement.

The House of Commons endorsed the views of the Prime Minister. The move to free the Church of Scotland from patronage and other ills was soundly defeated.

Meanwhile, as the Government in London congratulated itself on the manner with which it had dealt with the rumblings of the northern Church, Scotland shivered beneath an all-embracing mantle of snow and waited for the spring.

It was March before Wyatt was able to reach the factor's house to discuss the eviction of the Fraser family. Unfortunately, he discovered that John Garrett had also taken advantage of the improving weather and had gone to Edinburgh once again.

Charlotte Garrett was in London, staying in the home of her sister and receiving treatment from the finest physicians in the country. There were hopes that a few more months would see her return to something approaching normality. It was good news indeed for Evangeline, who was now free to return to the school in Eskaig. Alasdair had managed to keep the school open for the Eskaig boys, but no children from the mountains could attend until there was a more general thaw.

Evangeline and Alasdair Burns had not seen each other since the temporary thaw of January. So warm was their reunion that Wyatt suspected they would not be able to keep their romance from the factor for very much longer. When John Garrett *did* find out, Wyatt believed, it would cause the greatest argument that had ever been known in the already troubled Garrett household.

However, when trouble came, it was from another quarter.

Conditions on the mountains improved rapidly, and Wyatt cheered himself with the thought that he would soon be able to visit the Ross family – and the Frasers, of course. In the mean time the mail had reached Eskaig for the first time in some weeks, and Wyatt was busy bringing himself up to date with the happenings inside the Church of Scotland.

He was replying to one of his letters when he heard excited voices outside the manse. As he reached the door it was flung open, and Alasdair Burns and Evangeline helped Mairi inside.

Every bit as wet and bedraggled as when she had helped to rescue the Munro girls, Mairi was in a state of near-collapse.

'Wyatt . . . thank God!' Suddenly all her remaining strength left her and she sagged between the two teachers, as though in a faint. Wyatt caught her before she slid to the ground, and when he picked her up she was a wet lifeless mass in his arms, and alarmingly cold.

Wyatt carried Mairi closer to the fire and set her down on a wooden armchair. 'Alasdair, you know where the blankets are kept. Fetch as many as you can find. Evangeline . . . do you know what this is about?'

'No. I was teaching when Alasdair came in to tell me he could see Mairi coming down off the mountains. She was obviously close to exhaustion. The snow must still be deep up there. When we went to help her, all she would say was she had to reach you.'

Alasdair returned with the blankets and pulled the armchair closer to the fire. Mairi stirred and looked up at Wyatt.

'Evangeline will get you out of those wet things. Wrap yourself in these blankets. I'll borrow some clothes and bring them back—'

'No!' Mairi was trying hard to speak between chattering teeth. 'You must help. It's Donnie. . . . He's been arrested. Taken to Fort William. My brothers . . . all of them have gone to break him free.'

Everyone in the room stopped what they were doing and stood as though they, and not Mairi, were frozen.

'Why has he been arrested? What's happened?' As he spoke Wyatt wrapped one of the blankets about Mairi as she told her disjointed story.

'The sheriff's men. The constables. They came to the mountains as soon as they could find a path from Fort William. They've evicted the Frasers. Donnie tried to stop them. It was senseless of him. He couldn't do anything on his own. There was a fight. Donnie's been hurt. The constables took him off with them – after they'd put a torch to the cot.'

Wyatt was aghast. 'What of Seonaid? She must be expecting her child any day now. . . .' A sudden thought hit him. 'How did you learn about this? Who told you . . . Hamish Fraser?'

'Seonaid came to the house. I don't know how she did it; the snow's still thick up there. I think the constables were using the weather, hoping no one would learn what had happened until it was too late to do anything. Ian took Pa's gun and called for the boys to go with them. Pa tried to stop them, first off. When he saw they weren't going to listen he said he'd go with them. Ian said he was to stay home, and there was a fight. Ian hit Pa with the butt of the gun and laid him cold. Then the boys went off. Ma was tending Pa and crying. I said I'd come down for you. There's no one else can help.'

Wyatt's thoughts were in a turmoil. 'Where's Seonaid now? Is she staying at your place?'

'No. . . .' Mairi began shivering uncontrollably again, although whether it was the result of cold or shock was impossible to tell. 'She went back . . . to where the cot had been. She'd left her pa there. Ma told her she was to bring Hamish to our place . . . but you know what he's like. He'd rather die than accept Ross hospitality.'

'God! What an awful mess.'

'I'm sorry. . . .'

Wyatt turned to see Evangeline in tears.

'Why should *you* be sorry?'

'This is all my father's doing. He wants the mountains around Eskaig cleared. The Highlanders must *hate* us.' Alasdair tried to comfort her, but Evangeline moved away. 'I'll put on a hot drink for Mairi and get her out of those wet clothes. You two men go off and do what needs to be done. Don't come back in without knocking first.'

'Mairi's exhausted and chilled through,' said Wyatt. 'Build up the fire. When she's warmer put her to rest in my bed. Alasdair, you go to Eskaig and ask Mrs Gordon if she'll loan Mairi some clothes; they're about the same size.'

'What will you be doing?' asked Alasdair Burns.

'I'm going to Fort William to learn what's happening.'

'I'll come with you.' Mairi struggled to throw off the blankets.

'You'll do no such thing.' Wyatt leaned down and tucked the blankets firmly about her again. 'You'll remain here until I return. That will be one worry off my mind.'

Turning to Evangeline, he asked: 'Are you expecting your father home?'

'He returned last night – but he's not in a good mood.'

'Neither am I. I'll call in to see him on my way to Fort William.'

Wyatt was not optimistic about his mission. He did not know what he would learn at Fort William and he was going to see John Garrett with nothing to offer. He had no power to halt the evictions he feared had only just begun with the Fraser cot.

Wyatt pushed open the door of John Garrett's office, pursued by a protesting servant who had informed him the Kilmalie factor was 'busy'. John Garrett was not alone. There was a giant of a man in the room with him. Totally bald, but with a full bushy beard, it was as though the hair had slid down to strengthen the whiskers on his face.

Wyatt remembered seeing the man once before. Then he had been leader of a band of armed shepherds from the lowlands, driving a huge flock of sheep through Eskaig, heading north.

'What the devil do you think you're up to, Jamieson?' The factor jumped to his feet and glared at the frightened servant-girl in the doorway behind Wyatt. 'I thought I told you I wasn't to be disturbed?'

'Don't blame her. An army of servants wouldn't have kept me from you today. I want to talk to you – about clearances.'

'Make an appointment. It won't be this week. Anyway, I have nothing to say about any tenancies that have been terminated. They're estate business. Nothing to do with the Church. From what I hear, *you're* likely to be evicted soon, and with less notice than I give.'

'I'm here to talk of what's happened at the Fraser place. The eviction of a blind man and his daughter. You remember *Seonaid*? Oh, yes, I know you remember *her*, Garrett.'

John Garrett's glance went from Wyatt to the wide-eyed servant-girl and finally settled upon the giant shepherd who was taking a silent interest in the argument between minister and factor.

'My servant-girl will take you to the kitchen for a drink and a bite to eat, Polson. I'll send for you when I've dealt with Minister Jamieson.'

As the bearded shepherd followed the servant along the corridor, John Garrett walked to the door. Closing it, he turned back to the angry minister.

'Let's get one thing straight, Jamieson. I don't like you and I never have. You're soft – too soft to be in a living up here. The Highlands are changing. It needs men here who understand that. Not pious preachers who put their hands together and fall on their knees praying things will stay as they've been for a hundred – no, *two* hundred years. You'd see men living in hovels like animals, keeping themselves and their landowners poor. They need to move to where there's land to support them and allow the men they've been bleeding dry for years to put the mountain land to some proper use. Landowners want a return on their property. Time has run out for the cottars and crofters. Now it's time for men like me.'

'It will never be time for a man who'll burn a cot and turn a blind man and his heavily pregnant daughter out in the snow.'

Garrett's head jerked up in surprise. 'What do you mean, "heavily pregnant"? The girl hasn't been married more than a few months.'

'She's not the first girl to carry an unborn baby to her wedding – but most have a roof over their head when the baby's born.'

'I had nothing to do with burning them out. Fraser broke the terms of his tenancy by allowing the Ross boy to move in with him. The warrant was in the hands of the sheriff's men. . . . Where is the girl now?'

'Where the constables left her, out in the snow. Eneas Ross won't have her in the house because he doesn't believe the child has anything to do with his son.'

Once again Wyatt's words hit the factor hard. 'I . . . I'll see what can be done for her.'

'I'd say you've done enough already – unless you can rebuild her home. Where is this going to end, Garrett? How many more cottars are to be turned out before you're satisfied?'

'That's none of your business. I suggest you give some thought to your *own* future. If this "Disruption" that's being talked about occurs, you'll be out of church and manse, and I swear you'll not have a square foot of Kilmalie land on which to worship.'

'Right now I'm far more concerned for the Highlanders—'

'I've said all I have to say to you. Either you leave immediately, or I'll have my men put you out.'

For a moment Wyatt toyed with the idea of goading John Garrett into attempting physical violence against him. It would give Wyatt great personal satisfaction to 'defend' himself against this man. He rejected the idea quickly. It would achieve nothing, and there were far more important matters to be attended to.

'We'll talk again, Garrett. Until we do, I suggest you forget any ideas you have of clearing the mountains and putting Polson's sheep up there.'

'And I suggest *you* mind your own damned business. Now, get out. I've things to do.'

Wyatt left the house knowing he had failed to secure any respite for the unfortunate Highlanders. He also knew his mission had been doomed long before it began. John Garrett was determined to clear the Kilmalie estates.

Wyatt was witnessing the destruction of a people for whom he cared deeply.

CHAPTER THIRTY-FIVE

WHEN JOHN GARRETT rode his horse into the mountains there was still a great deal of snow about, but others had passed this way within the past twenty-four hours. By following their tracks he was able to avoid the deeper drifts. Not until he reached the high mountain moors where tracks divided and led to individual cots and holdings did he encounter virgin snow. Here the horse occasionally floundered into a deep drift, but there was no fear of the factor losing his way across the trackless snow. He could see smoke spiralling to the sky from the smouldering Fraser cot that was his destination.

As he drew near, Garrett looked for signs of life. When he saw none he began to think Wyatt had deliberately sent him all this way on a fruitless journey. Probably so he might see for himself the handiwork of the constables from Fort William.

As Garrett approached the smouldering shell that had been the Fraser home, his anger rising, he saw a movement downhill from the house. Close to the fast-moving stream, Hamish Fraser stood up. His keen ears had detected the sound of the approaching factor.

There was a shelter of sorts close to the blind man, in a furrow in the ground scratched hundreds of centuries before by the finger of a glacier. For most of its length the furrow was filled with snow, but at one spot the snow had been scooped out, almost to grass. Laid across this hollow were half a dozen lengths of charred wood, topped with scorched-heather thatch, rescued from the burned cot.

There were many tracks leading to and from the crude shelter. Far more ominous, the snow to one side of the shelter was dyed red in a trampled area about six feet in diameter.

'Who's that? What do you want with us now? Haven't you done enough? Leave us alone, do you hear?'

'Stop your whining, Fraser. You should have thought of the consequences before taking in a man from outside the family. You knew it contravened your tenancy agreement.'

'Factor! Donnie Ross married my daughter. He's my son-in-law!'

'I don't give a damn who he is. Where's your daughter now? Where's Seonaid?'

'If she's still alive, she'll be in the shelter. She stopped screaming more than an hour ago. I haven't heard a sound from her since. What are you going to do with us, Factor? What will you do with *me*? Will you leave a blind man to die in the snow without a roof over his head?'

'Here, hold my horse – and don't stand too close to him or he'll likely bolt.'

It was the end of a long spell of severe weather. Hamish Fraser had shared the cot with chickens and a cow, added to which was the pungent aroma of smoke from the burned cot.

John Garrett ducked inside the crude shelter and needed to remain stooping. The roof was no more than four feet high at its highest point. It was sheltered from wind in here, but the hard-packed snow on the ground provided proof it was no warmer than outside.

There was an untidy heap of damp thatch at the back of the shelter, piled against a wall of snow. When his eyes became accustomed to the gloom, John Garrett saw someone was lying on the primitive bed. It was Seonaid Fraser.

At first John Garrett thought she was dead, but as he moved closer she stirred.

'Seonaid! Are you all right, girl?'

The reply to John Garrett's question was a faint whimper. He leaned closer – and suddenly he realised the sound had not come from Seonaid. She lay on the thatch-bed, her bare breast being nuzzled by a tiny wrinkled baby. The newborn child was wrapped in a piece of cloth that looked as though it might be an old dress. It was the baby who had whimpered. It repeated the sound now, nuzzling the nipple of Seonaid's breast with an impatient strength and unpractised instinct.

Suddenly there was a movement from Seonaid, and she fingered the nipple into the baby's mouth. It immediately began to suck, noisily and inefficiently.

'What have you come here for? Do you have news of Donnie, or have you come to burn the shelter, too? If you have, you'll be adding murder to eviction. I'll not move.'

'I called for the eviction warrant months ago. The decision to enforce it now was made by the Sheriff.' John Garrett's voice sounded strangely hoarse, even to himself. 'The baby . . . is it young Ross's child?'

'Donnie *is* my husband, although I might well be a widow now if the constables didn't stop beating him before they reached Fort William.'

'That isn't what I asked.' Some of John Garrett's irritable arrogance returned to him. 'Nine months ago you were still visiting me at Corpach. I want to know about the child.'

'Why? Would you be able to marry me if I told you he was your son? Could you give him *your* name? God knows, he'd be ashamed of it after today's happenings. No. He'll grow up bearing the name of Ross and learn to hate John Garrett.' There was no mirth, only pain in Seonaid's short laugh. 'How will it feel, knowing your own son is growing up hating *you* more than anyone else does?'

'Then, it is my child . . . my *son*.'

Something akin to awe crept into John Garrett's voice. He moved closer and crouched over the makeshift bed to peer down at the noisily feeding infant.

'Seonaid . . . why didn't you *tell* me? I'd have taken care of you *and* the child. You can remember how we used to talk when we were together? I told you then how I've always longed for a son. I've wanted one more than anything else in my life. You didn't need to marry anyone, or be reduced . . . to this.'

John Garrett's gesture encompassed the primitive shelter and Seonaid's bed of scorched thatch. 'You and the baby can't stay here. I'll send someone up and have you moved. Where do you want to go? It can't be Eskaig. I wouldn't be able to visit you there. I'll give you a house in Fort William – or even Edinburgh, if that's what you want. I could come there and stay with you both—'

'Are you forgetting I'm a married woman, John Garrett? I'm Mrs Donnie Ross.'

'It's no more of a marriage than mine. You're suckling *my* baby.

My *son*.' There was a strange timbre in John Garrett's voice that might have been excitement or emotion. 'I'll take care of him – and of you. I've always said I would. You know I have.'

'Then, why am I lying here on stinking damp thatch, in a hole in the snow, with not so much as a stick of furniture, or even a fire to warm me?'

As Seonaid finished speaking she began to cough. Unexpectedly robbed of the teat from which it had been drawing sustenance, the baby first complained, then began a desperate sucking search.

John Garrett watched in awed fascination for a moment or two, then he ducked outside the flimsy shelter.

Hamish Fraser was still holding the reins of the factor's horse. The animal had found a patch of stunted grass where the heat of the burning cot had melted the snow. It was impossible to tell whether Seonaid's father had heard the conversation between his daughter and the Kilmalie factor. He was some way from the shelter but he had exceptionally good hearing.

'Fraser, leave the horse to graze. It won't go far. Get a fire going by the shelter for Seonaid and the baby.'

'Why should you care about either of them?' Hamish grumbled the question as he made his way towards the ruins of the cot. 'Would you care if *I* was up here alone, with nothing to warm me? And what of Seonaid's man? Will you be visiting Fort William tolbooth to see that they've made *him* comfortable?'

John Garrett was not listening. Striding to his horse, he removed the saddle and stripped the blanket that served as a saddle-cloth from the animal's back. Ducking inside the makeshift shelter once more, he laid the blanket over the lower half of Seonaid's body.

'It's not much, but with the fire it will keep you alive.' Reaching inside a deep coat-pocket, he pulled out a large pewter flask. 'Here, it's brandy. It'll warm you if the fire burns low. I'll come up here myself first thing in the morning to take you to Fort William.'

'What of Donnie? He was hurt when they took him away.'

'I can do nothing for young Ross. That's between him and the sheriff. I'm only concerned for you and the baby. The estate owns a number of houses in Fort William; you can move into one of them for a while. I'll have provisions bought ready for you.'

John Garrett leaned over the thatch-bed, and for a moment there was an expression on his face that only Evangeline Garrett would have recognised. He raised his hand as though to touch the tiny baby. Instead he lowered the hand again and backed away.

'Tell your father to build as big a fire as he can for tonight.' John Garrett hesitated before straightening up at the entrance to the primitive shelter. 'It might be better if you moved back inside the shell of the cot. It will be out of the wind—'

'No!' Seonaid's reply was emphatic. 'We'll not return to the cot. Neither will we take a Kilmalie house in Fort William unless you put it in writing that we can't be turned out whenever you've a mind. And we'll want payment for what was destroyed.'

Seonaid was in great discomfort. The birth had been uncomplicated and instinctive, but painful. Yet her mind was clearer than it had ever been. She had seen the fight between Donnie and the sheriff's men. It had been brief but vicious, and one of the men had been bleeding profusely when they dragged Donnie away.

He would be taken before the magistrate in Fort William and imprisoned for months, perhaps even a year or more. In the meantime Seonaid, her father and the baby would need to survive without him. Who better to look after them than John Garrett?

'When you've written it down you can give it to Minister Jamieson. If he says it's all right, I'll go to your house. If not. . . .' Seonaid shrugged. 'I'll stay up here with the baby.'

The suggestion that Wyatt should be made aware of the arrangement almost brought Seonaid's scheming to an abrupt end. John Garrett drew in his breath with the intention of telling her he would *never* agree to Wyatt becoming involved. Just then the baby made a diminutive protest as drowsiness coupled with lack of experience caused the food-source to escape him yet again.

'You'll have a secure tenancy, but don't push me too far, woman. I have only to walk away from here and forget you ever existed and you'll have no hope for the present, or a future. *Nothing.*'

'Nothing . . . except the baby.' Seonaid jerked the baby away from her breast roughly, and the unkind severance caused the surprised child to break into a thin uneven wailing.

'Be ready to move in the morning.'

John Garrett ducked clear of the shelter as Hamish Fraser came from the cot, the wind coaxing flames from a charred piece of wood held in his hand as he felt his way with his feet.

John Garrett made no move to help the blind man. Saddling the horse, he swung to its back.

'Be sure you're ready to leave in the morning, Fraser. I have other work to do and I'll not waste a full day on you.' Having issued this warning, the factor turned his horse and rode away.

When Hamish Fraser had peat blocks piled about and over the crackling beam and he was satisfied the fire would not die, he went inside the shelter where Seonaid lay with her baby.

'What was the factor talking about? Where are we going?'

'He's giving us a house in Fort William. It's rent-free, and no one will be able to throw us out or burn it about our ears.'

'I don't want to live in Fort William! It's a *town*. We don't know anyone there.'

'Donnie's in Fort William. The sheriff's men carried him off, remember? I've got to find out what's happened to him. Besides, we can't stay here. We'd freeze to death in a week.'

'What about your mother. . . ?'

'What about her? You never concerned yourself with her when she was alive. She's had more attention from you since she died than she ever got when she was with us – and if *you* don't stop complaining you'll not live long. . . .' Seonaid picked the baby up roughly and fed the nipple of a swollen breast into its mouth yet again.

Hamish Fraser stood silently outside the shelter for some minutes, his head bowed. When he straightened up, he asked: 'Why should Garrett suddenly be doing this for us? I don't understand what's going on. First he clears all our neighbours out but allows us to stay. Then he gives us notice to quit and because we're not fast enough sends the sheriff's men here to burn us out. Then he comes here to offer us a house in Fort William. . . .' The blind man shook his head in bewilderment. 'It's all beyond me.'

Seonaid swung her feet to the ground, ignoring the crying baby left lying on the bed beside her. 'Don't try to understand John Garrett. He doesn't understand himself. You've got to play him at his own game. Take everything you can and give nothing in return. Oh, *shut up*!'

Seonaid picked up the tiny baby and shook it. The baby's crying became even more distressed, and Seonaid dumped it roughly on the coarse heather-thatch bed.

'God! He's not four hours old and I've had enough of him already.'

Standing up unsteadily, Seonaid took a tentative step towards the entrance to the shelter.

'Out of the way, Father. If I don't do something with that fire, it'll go out. And Garrett was right about one thing: we're going to feel the cold tonight.'

Kneeling beside the fire, Seonaid rearranged the peat turfs, allowing the chill wind more access. 'Go and find more peat. As much as you can.'

Hamish Fraser grumbled until Seonaid began shouting abuse at him. Surprised into silence, Hamish Fraser stumbled away to carry out his daughter's shrill instructions.

Not until he was well upon his way did Seonaid lapse into silence. Huddled over the fire, head bowed, a tear rolled from her eye and was lost in the fire with hardly a sound.

'Donnie! Donnie . . . I *need* you. Hold on until I come to you, Donnie. Hold on. . . .'

CHAPTER THIRTY-SIX

WYATT ARRIVED in Fort William to find the town in a state of turmoil. Armed militiamen guarded the roads, challenging everyone who approached. Beyond the guards, inside Fort William itself, Wyatt could see scarlet-uniformed militiamen milling about in apparent confusion.

When he identified himself and was given permission to pass, Wyatt enquired what was happening.

'It's a rising of the Highlanders,' came the surprising reply. 'There are great hordes of 'em up in the mountains preparing to come down upon us. They attacked the constables who were up there on their lawful business. I'd hurry on if I were you, Minister. If those Highlanders attack, there'll be some hard fighting, and I wouldn't like to be responsible for your safety.'

The militiaman broke off to challenge a horseman approaching Fort William, leaving Wyatt to make his way into town. Had he not known something of the background to the story being told, the preparations being made to repel an 'imminent' attack might have alarmed him more.

Wyatt went straight to the tolbooth, the building that served both as gaol and administrative centre for Fort William. Here he found the sheriff-substitute busily organising militiamen, signing orders for the requisition of stores, and authorising the issue of arms and ammunition. In between he dictated letters to be sent to Edinburgh and Glasgow, acquainting the authorities there with the dangerous situation existing in the Highlands around Fort William.

Wyatt stood waiting patiently for ten minutes while orders were given or amended and people hurried in, or left in equal haste.

When the sheriff-substitute did acknowledge Wyatt's presence it was with a display of irritation.

'What d'you want, Minister? Be brief, if you please. I'm a busy man.'

'I've come from Eskaig. I'm the minister there. I would like to see Donnie Ross.'

A silence fell upon the room, and everyone looked in Wyatt's direction.

When the sheriff-substitute eventually replied, he said: 'We'd *all* like to see Mr Ross, Minister. The last one to see him was Constable Donald. One of the Highland ruffians who rescued Ross struck the constable on the knee with a broadsword. The blow appears to have severed a tendon. He's crippled, Minister. A young man in the prime of his life and with a family to support.'

Wyatt murmured that he was sorry to hear the news of the constable's injury, but the sheriff-substitute interrupted him. 'We're *all* sorry, but none of us is as sorry as those rogues are going to be when we catch up with them. It's a pity only one of the constables was armed. He's confident his musket-ball found its mark, but one gun wasn't enough to stand off a host of men intent upon criminal mischief. Have you any idea who they might be, Minister? It's said Ross has a great many brothers. It will likely be them, I'm thinking.'

Wyatt shook his head vigorously. 'There are many Highlanders from beyond my parish who might have carried out such an attack. They probably didn't even know young Donnie. It was enough to fight any constables with the gall to come into the mountains.'

The sheriff-substitute never once took his eyes from Wyatt. 'I wouldn't question what you're saying, Minister, but what makes you so certain it *wasn't* the Ross family who rescued the prisoner?'

'I married Donnie Ross not four months ago. His family were uncompromisingly opposed to him marrying a Fraser. So much so they've disowned him. They lay the blame for his arrest fairly and squarely on his marriage. They wouldn't lift a finger to help him.'

The sheriff-substitute's gaze remained on Wyatt's face for a few minutes more, and then he nodded, apparently satisfied, and proffered his hand.

'I'm obliged to you, Minister. You've saved us from a futile journey to the Ross home. I understand conditions are still far from ideal in the mountains. We'll wait for the Army to arrive and seek our men further north — though I doubt we'll have much success. I've sought men there before. The people are as wild as the mountains themselves.'

Wyatt left the tolbooth unrepentant at having lied to the sheriff-substitute. He had gained a reprieve for the Ross family. He looked towards the Highlands. Many of the ridges were shrouded in cloud. By the time anyone from Fort William marched up there the wind and snow would have obliterated all tracks that might lead the sheriff-substitute's men straight to the Ross croft.

He hoped none of the brothers had been badly wounded by the constable's musket-ball. He would take Mairi back to her home in the morning and tell Eneas Ross what was happening in Fort William. The sheriff-substitute seemed to have believed Wyatt, but it might be as well if the Ross brothers came down from the mountains to Eskaig while the Army was around. Donnie would certainly need to be hidden.

Eneas Ross and his sons came down from the mountains to Eskaig that same night. Mist and snow muffled the sound of their footsteps, and the darkness hid their sorrow, for with them they brought the bodies of Donnie Ross and his brother Malcolm.

It was the intention of Eneas Ross that only the menfolk of the family should be mourners at their burial. The weeping of women might be overheard — and it was imperative that no one else know what was happening in the Eskaig churchyard. If word ever reached the sheriff-substitute at Fort William, he would know immediately *how* the two Ross brothers had died. Wyatt would be arrested and the remainder of the Ross men hunted down and thrown into gaol.

Eneas Ross's plans had to be changed when Mairi opened the door of the manse in response to their knocking. When Wyatt had returned from his visit to Fort William it had been far too late for her to go home. She had remained at the manse while Wyatt spent the night with Alasdair Burns in the small house attached to the school.

Mairi shed her tears in the manse, while Eneas Ross explained to Wyatt what had happened. Meanwhile, the six remaining sons worked in relays to dig two graves in the hard Eskaig ground.

Donnie had been more severely hurt than Seonaid had realised when she carried the news of his arrest to the Ross home. In all probability his skull had been fractured by the baton of a Fort William constable. The constables were carrying Donnie between them when the brothers effected his rescue. He had regained consciousness only briefly before dying inside the home where his father had sworn he would never set foot again.

Malcolm had been shot in a cowardly manner by one of the constables. The man had thrown down his gun in the snow when Eneas Ross and his sons fell upon the party from Fort William. As the brothers were carrying Donnie away he had snatched up the gun and fired a single shot after them, before turning tail and running.

The musket-ball had passed through the small of Malcolm's back and lodged somewhere inside him. At first it had seemed he was not too badly hurt, but it had been impossible to staunch the bleeding and halfway home he had collapsed.

Malcolm was conscious until the very end, and he died holding his mother's hand, only a few minutes before his unconscious brother breathed his last.

'I would have buried the boys up on the mountain with no fuss, and no fear of anyone else ever knowing,' explained the grief-stricken father, broken-voiced, 'but Magdalene said we could trust you and she insisted they be buried here, with you to pray over them.'

Eneas Ross was silent for a long time, and when he looked at Wyatt again he was close to tears. 'I could understand Malcolm being killed. Of all my sons, he was the wildest. The most reckless. Of the others, Ian has a hot temper; so, too, have Dugald and Seoras. But Donnie had nothing but love and kindness for everyone.'

There was a long and uncomfortable silence, broken eventually by Wyatt. 'What of Seonaid now?'

'She's our Donnie's widow. Ian called on her to tell her of Donnie's death. He found the child had been born. Ian said there was no sense in the girl after he told her, but I'll send Magdalene and Tibbie to fetch her. We'll take care of her.'

'And her father?' This was not the moment to push Eneas Ross, but the question had to be asked.

'Hamish Fraser. . . ?' It was as though the question came as a surprise. Suddenly Eneas Ross inclined his head. 'He took Donnie in, and had his house burned because of it. Ay, Hamish, too, if he's a mind to come.'

'You're a good man, Eneas.' Wyatt grasped the other man by the shoulder. 'Now let's go and commit Donnie and Malcolm to the Lord.'

In the churchyard, the scene illuminated only by two candle-lanterns, the Ross brothers were laid to rest in graves less than the usual depth. The necessity to make no noise had curtailed the efforts of the gravediggers, but it was agreed the graves were 'a decent depth'.

Wrapped in plaids of the Ross tartan, brought from the Highland croft, the two young men were lowered into the ground. With a thick cold mist swirling about them, the small knot of mourners murmured a soft 'Amen' to each of Wyatt's prayers. Then Eneas Ross himself took up a spade and hid his sons for ever from the eyes of the world.

Afterwards, declining an offer to rest awhile in the manse, the Ross men returned in the darkness to the high land that was their home, and Mairi went with them.

CHAPTER THIRTY-SEVEN

JOHN GARRETT was feeling more kindly disposed towards his fellow-men than at any time since he had first come to the Highlands as Lord Kilmalie's factor. He had been that way since leaving Seonaid and the baby – his son – the day before.

In Fort William he had made all the necessary arrangements for the house that would be occupied by the family from the high-moor cot. He had arrived after all the excitement about the feared raid by Highlanders had died away and gone about his business quietly, speaking to no one in the town.

Garrett had toyed with the idea of making enquiries about the Ross boy, but dismissed the thought. The authorities would deal with him in their usual manner and he would not be a problem for many months to come. Until then it would not be wise to show an interest in the prisoner – and today there were more pleasant things to occupy his mind. Today he was removing his son from the wastes of the high mountains to a far more suitable home in Fort William.

Riding along and leading a second horse behind him, John Garrett allowed his thoughts to meander into realms of fanciful speculation.

Hamish Fraser had no place in his plans. The blind cottar would have to go – and soon. There must be someone prepared to look after him. If not, there was a poorhouse in Fort William.

John Garrett realised he could not keep Seonaid and the boy in Fort William for too long. Evangeline had told him during the course of a recent heated argument that his indiscretions were the subject of gossip. He did not want his son to grow up an object of scorn. *His son!* He needed a name. It would not be Scots. Albert, perhaps, after the man who had recently married Queen Victoria. Or William, the name of the late king. On the other hand, the boy could be named John, after his father. Seonaid might have her own thoughts on a name, but she would have to accept his decision. John Garrett intended to raise his son in *his* way.

Perhaps Seonaid and the boy should go to Glasgow. It was far enough from Highland gossip. But then he would not be able to see them often enough, and Seonaid was an attractive girl in an earthy primitive way. There would be too many temptations for her in such a place. He had no intention of allowing Seonaid to corrupt *his* son's morals.

There was *another* way John Garrett might see more of both mother and son. Something he had contemplated when he was having his affair with Seonaid. . . .

The Eskaig factor did some hard thinking as he rode into the mountains to collect his son and the woman who had given birth to him.

As he approached the crude makeshift shelter, John Garrett frowned. The only smoke visible was drifting up from the still-smouldering cot, and there was no movement he could immediately detect. Then he saw Hamish Fraser huddled beside the stream. He sat hunched on a rock, a still and dejected figure.

John Garrett reined in his horse and slid to the ground. The snow had melted on the well-trampled areas, and there was enough grass showing through here and there to keep the two horses occupied for a while.

After another glance at the still figure by the stream, the factor ducked beneath the low roof of the shelter and went inside.

Seonaid was lying on her side on the primitive bed, her face turned from him. The blanket was pulled up about her so that only the upper part of her head could be seen. He could not see the baby, but presumed it must be cradled to her beneath the blanket for warmth.

'Seonaid? I thought you'd be up and ready to leave. I've got a fine house for you, in Fort William.' John Garrett looked about him. The few possessions Seonaid and her father had saved from the fire were strewn haphazardly about the crude shelter. No attempt had been made to gather them together.

There was a total lack of response from the girl, and John Garrett became alarmed. Crossing to the blanket-covered figure, he reached out an arm towards her.

'Seonaid? Are you all right?'

'Go away and leave me alone.' Seonaid's voice was hoarse and strained, as though she had been crying for a long time.

'What is it? What's the matter with you?'

John Garrett's hand rested on her shoulder outside the blanket, but no sooner did he touch her than she came violently to life, throwing off his hand.

'Get away from me!' Seonaid sat up and put her feet to the ground in a swift movement. A knife was stabbed in the ground close to the snowdrift wall of the shelter. Snatching it up, Seonaid held it threateningly towards the factor.

'Get away . . . right away, or I swear I'll stick this right through you.'

The blade of the knife had been worn away by years of honing on the doorstep of the Fraser cot, but enough steel remained to enable Seonaid to carry out her threat.

As he backed away, John Garrett was looking not at the knife, but at the empty heather bed.

'Where's the baby? What have you done with my son?'

'Oh, so it's *your* son, is it? Not *our* son, but *yours*?' Seonaid was wild-eyed and unkempt. John Garrett backed away a little farther.

'Where is he, Seonaid? I have a right to know. . . .'

'Rights? You talk of *rights*? What are they, Factor Garrett? What are these *rights* you're talking about? Would it be the right to bed any girl who comes to you begging you not to evict her blind father? The right to turn folk from the homes where they and their fathers and grandfathers were born? Is it the right to beat a young man to death because he objects to your men firing a cot with his wife still inside?'

As Seonaid spat the final question at John Garrett she looked every bit as mad as his own wife, and he took a couple of involuntary paces backwards, ducking outside the shelter.

'What are you talking about? Young Ross has been taken to Fort William for resisting the sheriff's men. You told me so yourself.'

'Yes, and they were still beating him worse than a tinker beats his dog as they dragged him away. His body was brought back from

Fort William last night. *You* killed him. You killed him as surely as if it were by your own hand.'

The knife in Seonaid's hand waved wildly in front of his face, and Garrett added the length of another backward stride to the distance between them.

News of Donnie Ross's death had taken him by surprise, but he was not unduly distressed. There were far too many Rosses on Kilmalie land. They needed culling. Besides, it greatly simplified his relationship with Seonaid.

'I'm sorry about your husband, Seonaid. It was none of my doing, but it gives me an added responsibility for you and the boy now. I *will* look after you. You'll like the house in Fort William. I'll settle you in and give you money to buy clothes for yourself and . . . and my son.'

John Garrett's pride was tempered by concern. He could not think where the child might be. Unless they had placed him in the warmer shelter of the burned-out cot.

'Where is he, Seonaid? Where is the boy now?'

The point of the much-sharpened knife still pointed in John Garrett's direction, but the expression on Seonaid's face had changed. There was disbelief there – and something else as well. Something much uglier.

'You *do* care! Having a son really *means* something to you. I believe that for the first time in your life you've found someone who means more to you than your own miserable self.'

'Don't play foolish games with me, Seonaid. I've already said I'll take care of the boy. He'll never want for anything. He'll grow up to be a son I'll . . . we'll *both* be proud of. I'll look after you, too, and your father, until we can make other arrangements for him.'

Seonaid continued to stare at him with an expression he could not identify, and it alarmed him.

'Damn you! What else do you want from me? Yes, yes, yes! I am proud to have a son. I've always wanted a son. There, now I've said it. Where *is* he?'

'I'm *glad*. I'm glad you care.'

At last John Garrett thought he knew what her expression meant, and it put cold fear in his belly. There was triumph in Seonaid's voice. Fierce malignant triumph.

'Now you might understand something of the pain that's in me.

Pain at losing the only person in my life who's ever loved *me*. I've cursed you, John Garrett. I've cursed you for what you did to Donnie, and what you've made *me* do. Now I know I did the right thing and I'm *glad*.'

Seonaid's tortured expression belied the statement, but she repeated it over and over again.

'I'm glad. So help me, I'm glad. I'm *glad*. . . .'

'What are you saying? *Where is the boy?*'

John Garrett took a pace towards Seonaid, but a sudden thrust of the knife caused him to draw back again hurriedly.

'He's *dead*. He's dead, just like my Donnie.'

John Garrett stared at Seonaid in horrified disbelief, and when he spoke the words came out in a hoarse whisper. 'I don't believe you. You're lying, knowing it'll hurt me.'

'Oh, it's hurting you, John Garrett. I can see that all right. And now I'll hurt you some more. He was a fine healthy boy. He even looked like you, God help him. But I killed him. I killed your bastard son, just as you killed my Donnie. I put the blanket over his face and smothered him. I did it because of the Garrett blood he had in his veins, and the blood of Donnie that's on your hands. *I killed him, John Garrett.* Killed him and buried him up here in the mountains, without so much as a twig cross to mark his grave. You'll never find him. He's gone as though he's never breathed the air on this earth. Your son, John Garrett. *Your dear, bastard son!*'

The cry of anguish that escaped from John Garrett's throat sent a hungry eagle wheeling away in search of other hunting-grounds.

John Garrett rode away with the sound of Seonaid's laughter in his ears. Not until he had disappeared from view did she sink to her knees in the melting snow and the laughter change to bitter inconsolable weeping.

CHAPTER THIRTY-EIGHT

AN AIR OF UNEASY CALM hung over Eskaig for many weeks after the burning of the Fraser cot and the death of Donnie and Malcolm Ross. It was as though the Highland community was holding its breath, waiting for 'something' to happen. Seonaid had not moved into the Ross home. The decision had been forced upon her by Hamish Fraser's refusal to forget the feud between the two families. Instead, Seonaid and her father had moved from the mountains to Eskaig. Both were living at the inn, where Seonaid worked as chambermaid and serving-girl, while her father stood at a sink in the scullery, his blindness no more than an inconvenience in the unexacting chore of washing pans, pots and dishes. The people of the village knew Seonaid had lost her husband and child. They sympathised with her for the manner in which Donnie had died. No one asked after the fate of the child.

Then John Garrett left on a trip to Glasgow. He said nothing to anyone of his plans, and it was not known how long he would be away. The tenants of the Kilmalie estate breathed sighs of relief at his departure, but Wyatt could not relax. He believed Garrett was planning something, perhaps a final clearance of the Kilmalie estates.

Wyatt would have liked to pursue his suspicions, but the affairs of the Church of Scotland had reached a critical stage and he, too, had to leave for Edinburgh within the week. Fortunately, little was likely to happen with the factor absent.

There was to be a meeting of the General Assembly of the Church, in Edinburgh on Tuesday, 18 May 1843, when it was believed the Disruption of the Church of Scotland would be announced.

Wyatt and Coll Kennedy travelled to Edinburgh together to attend the Assembly. Although not members of the General Assembly itself, they were assured of seats in St Andrew's Church, where the Assembly was to meet.

They found Edinburgh in a ferment about the forthcoming meeting, and there appeared to be more sober-garbed ministers in the city than residents. Suddenly, the prospect of a Disruption within the Church which sometimes seemed so unreal when viewed from Wyatt's remote Highland parish was about to become a reality. It was at once both exhilarating and awesome in its enormity.

One of the first calls Wyatt made in Edinburgh was on Charles Graham, administrator of the estates of Lord Kilmalie. Graham had written to Wyatt during the winter, to inform him that money left to him by the late Lord Kilmalie was awaiting collection. He suggested Wyatt call in and see him when he was next in the city.

Charles Graham seemed genuinely pleased to see Wyatt. The promissory note was at his home, and he invited Wyatt to dinner that evening, in order that he might collect it. When Wyatt explained he was accompanied by the minister from Letterfinlay, the administrator promptly extended the invitation to include Coll Kennedy.

There were a number of guests for dinner, and Wyatt realised it was likely to be a lively evening when he discovered that seated opposite to him at dinner was the Reverend Hamilton Logan, a leading 'moderate', as those who accepted the State's jurisdiction over the Church were called.

Unaware that his two fellow-ministers did not share his views, the Reverend Hamilton Logan did his best to impress them with his importance, once he had established *they* were not members of the General Assembly. He had that day been to a reception given by the city in honour of the Marquis of Bute, Lord High Commissioner, who was to represent Her Majesty the Queen at the General Assembly.

'It was a *splendid* affair,' declared Hamilton Logan. 'One of those occasions we enjoy all too seldom in this somewhat staid city of ours.' Looking condescendingly at Wyatt and Coll Kennedy, he added: 'You really should have arrived in Edinburgh in time at least to observe the comings and goings of the Lord High Commissioner's guests. You'll have seen nothing like it in the Highlands, I'm certain.'

Both Highland ministers agreed they had seen nothing like it and concentrated their attention on the plates in front of them. The moderate minister began immediately to give a detailed and over-loud account of the happenings at the Lord High Commissioner's reception to the unfortunate guest seated beside him.

Of far more interest to the two Highland ministers were the observations of a guest seated beside Wyatt. When he realised the two men were in the city to attend the General Assembly, he told them of public opinion on the issue.

It seemed the attitude of moderates like Hamilton Logan had hardened in the past week. They believed that when it was put to the test no more than a handful of ministers would go through with the Disruption and leave the Church. Knowledgeable sources in Edinburgh put the number as low as forty.

Wyatt and Coll Kennedy looked at each other in dismay. If the rumours were true, it would have disastrous consequences for those ministers who were determined to stand by their convictions. With more than a hundred ministers, a 'free' church stood a chance of success. Forty would not be enough.

Immediate discussion of the important issue became impossible when the Reverend Hamilton Logan once more included them in his one-sided conversation.

'I trust you've been listening to my description of the reception held for Her Majesty's High Commissioner in Holyrood Palace. I am quite certain the members of your congregations would find it *fascinating* to hear of such an event. It would no doubt enliven a dull winter's evening. Although perhaps they might find it difficult to comprehend a gathering of dignitaries in such a place. You'll have no palaces in your Highlands, of course?'

'I suppose the mountain peaks raised by God's own hands would stand comparison with a palace,' mused Wyatt thoughtfully. 'Do you think that might provide my simple parishioners with a suitable analogy?

While the Reverend Hamilton Logan mulled Wyatt's words over in his mind, Coll Kennedy said: 'I think it would. And, in order that they might have an idea of the numbers attending, you might refer them to the gathering of sheep before the drovers bring them down to the lowlands.'

As those who heard the exchange tried not to smile, Coll turned his attention to the garrulous minister, whose face had taken on a decided flush. 'Was the Earl of Glenadon at this reception?'

'I. . . . Yes, I do believe he was.' The moderate minister looked at Coll Kennedy suspiciously, suspecting he was about to be subjected to more Highland 'humour'. 'Have you met him somewhere?'

'He's my brother.'

Nonchalantly knocking back his wine and holding the glass up to an advancing servant, Coll Kennedy added: 'No doubt another brother was there, too. Sir Robert Kennedy of Fraochburn? I believe the two are inseparable these days.'

Conversation swelled about him when Coll Kennedy stopped talking. It owed as much to real interest as to amusement at the manner in which the Letterfinlay minister had put down his city colleague. It was rare for a man with such a background to choose the Church of Scotland in which to make a career.

Later that evening, as the men gathered in the library, the Reverend Hamilton Logan singled out Coll Kennedy for his attention.

'I'm surprised a man of such good family should be languishing in an obscure Highland parish, Minister Kennedy. You ought to be a member of the General Assembly, at least. Would you like me to mention the matter at this year's Assembly?'

Coll Kennedy shook his head, but the Reverend Hamilton Logan persisted. 'There will never be a better opportunity for advancement. It's possible some of the Assembly will be resigning because of this present foolishness. There might be opportunities for both of you. I'm not talking merely of playing a part in the administration of your church. There will be good livings left vacant. Livings far more congenial than some remote Highland village. You could come to Edinburgh, where there are generous patrons – men like Charles Graham. Think about it.'

'I have thought about it. For many years I've prayed that preachers like you might forsake Mammon and find the path back to God.'

Coll Kennedy was a man who found it difficult to be serious for very long, but he was serious now.

'I'm a minister of God. A *servant* of God. I serve gladly and with humility where I can best do His will. I believe I better fulfil the needs of His people in the Highlands than I might here, beset by the temptations of wealth and false ambition. I'm a humble man, Minister Hamilton Logan, but I have great pride in my love of the Lord. That's why I'll never be a member of the General Assembly of the Church of Scotland. Indeed, after tomorrow I fear you and I will no longer belong to the same church.'

Turning away from the suddenly speechless Reverend Hamilton Logan, Coll Kennedy said: 'I think I'd like to leave now, Wyatt. My family always told me I habitually disgraced myself – and them – in polite company. I fear a Highland parish hasn't improved my manners. Anyway, this city whisky is for weaning babies. I've a bottle of the *real* stuff packed away in my things.'

'I'm sorely tempted to come with you, Minister Kennedy. It's a long time since I tasted whisky that put the smell of a peat fire in my nostrils. Come into my study for a moment. I want a word with Wyatt, and I've a bottle hidden there that I brought from the Isles a year or two ago.'

Neither minister had observed Charles Graham come up behind them. Now, with a hand on the shoulder of each of them, the host led them to a small oak-panelled room. When he closed the door behind them the sounds of talk and laughter in the library were abruptly cut off. From a cabinet he produced three glasses, filling them from a dumpy unlabelled bottle.

When Coll Kennedy raised the glass the aroma reached his nose and an expression of sheer joy touched his face. 'Ah! Now, this is *real* whisky.'

'It is indeed, Minister Kennedy, although it would no doubt be a little fierce for the palate of the Reverend Hamilton Logan. I fear he prefers both whisky and his religion well watered down. I'll leave the bottle beside you. I have something in my desk for Wyatt.'

Charles Graham sat down at his desk and opened the top drawer. Reaching inside, he withdrew a small sheet of thick paper, on which were a few lines of extremely neat handwriting. Handing the paper across the desk to Wyatt, he said: 'Here you are. I've had this for a couple of months. I didn't want to send it, and I guessed you'd be here for the meeting of the General Assembly.'

Wyatt read the writing on the paper, and gasped. It was a

promissory note made out in his favour, for *two thousand and four hundred pounds*! It was a fortune.

'I told you when we met in Eskaig that Lord Kilmalie had remembered you in his will. You'll find all the details in here. . . .' Charles Graham passed a thick brown envelope to Wyatt and smiled at his bemused expression. 'The late Lord Kilmalie was a generous man.'

'That's more than might be said for his successor.' Wyatt spoke as Coll Kennedy lolled back in an armchair savouring his drink. 'Using the power granted to him by the new Lord Kilmalie, John Garrett's made a start on clearing the mountains and bringing in sheep. It's gone quiet since two men died as a result, but he'll start again, I'm quite certain of it.'

'So that's Garrett's game.' Charles Graham frowned. 'I fear your factor may be acting a little hastily, Wyatt.'

Both ministers waited for Charles Graham to say more, but he hesitated, as though there was something he wanted to say but was not certain this was the right moment. 'I received some news only last week which may have a startling outcome for John Garrett. Unfortunately, it needs to be confirmed. I'm afraid I can't say more until I have additional information in my possession. Incidentally, there are rumours that John Garrett is in Edinburgh. Someone thought they saw him at the offices of the Prosecutor Fiscal a day or two ago.'

'Surely, if he were here, he'd have called to see you?'

'I would have hoped so, but John Garrett does many things I don't understand. Just accept my information as a warning. If I learn what he's doing here, I'll pass the knowledge on to you.'

May 18th was a fine day, bright but cold. The few clouds in view held off, as though, in common with the whole of the city, they, too, were waiting. Many of the shops had closed for the day. So, too, had most of the city's business centres. Their employees, presented with an unexpected holiday, took to the streets and gravitated to the vicinity of St Andrew's Church where the General Assembly was to meet.

As Wyatt and Coll Kennedy made their way through the streets they could sense the underlying excitement of the gathering crowds. There was a feeling of anticipation. Of waiting for something that few could have put into words.

The two Highland ministers did not immediately head for St Andrew's Church. Instead they made their way first to the church of St Giles, where Dr Welsh, the retiring Moderator of the Church of Scotland, was preaching.

The Moderator was a stalwart supporter of those who advocated a stand against the Government on the question of patronage. For his sermon, Dr Welsh chose the text 'Let every man be fully persuaded in his own mind'.

It was an analytical rather than a stirring sermon, but it left no man in the church in doubt of where the moderator stood – or why.

When Wyatt and Coll went out into the streets again the excitement had heightened and they hurried through crowds on their way to St Andrew's Church.

There were so many ministers and members of the public already cramming the hall that the two Highland ministers were forced to stand at one side of the vast assembly. As they struggled to maintain their places more people were admitted behind them and Coll Kennedy nudged Wyatt.

Seated near the front of the hall, on the same side, was the Reverend Hamilton Logan, the minister who had bored the party at the home of Charles Graham with his talk. He sat among the 'moderates', none of whom had attended the service conducted by Dr Welsh. The Edinburgh minister appeared pale-faced and drawn.

'He looks as though he stayed drinking indifferent whisky for too long last night,' whispered the Letterfinlay minister. 'I trust he has stomach enough left for what will happen today.'

Wyatt nodded, without voicing a reply. The excitement of the occasion held him in its grip. He felt as he had during his army days, when a battle was imminent against frightening odds. The moment when every thinking man envied those who had found excuses to avoid the fighting.

When it seemed that no more spectators could be allowed into the building without those inside being crushed to death, a sudden hush fell upon the church.

The silence advanced with almost discernible precision ahead of Dr Welsh, who would be Moderator for only a few more minutes.

As Dr Welsh took the chair, the sound of marching feet could be heard outside the building and a fanfare heralded the arrival of Her Majesty's representative, the Marquis of Bute.

When the High Commissioner had taken his seat on the throne, attention immediately shifted to the Moderator. Pale, but dignified, Dr Welsh offered up the opening prayer. When the 'Amen' died away, there was a brief moment of uncertainty before the Moderator addressed the General Assembly and Her Majesty's High Commissioner for the last time, in a voice that carried to every man in the church.

'Fathers and brethren. According to the usual form of procedure this is the time for making up the roll, but in consequence of certain proceedings affecting our rights and privileges – proceedings which have been sanctioned by Her Majesty's government, and by the legislature of the country – more especially in respect that there has been an infringement on the liberties of our Constitution, so that we could not now constitute this Court without a violation of the terms between Church and State in this land, as now authoritatively declared, I must protest against our proceeding further. The reasons that have led me to this conclusion are fully set forth in the document which I hold in my hand and which, with permission of this House, I shall now proceed to read.'

The hand that held the written protest shook slightly as Dr Welsh read out the principles the Church had tried unsuccessfully to uphold against the encroachment by the State.

When the Moderator reached the end of the protest, he declared that because of the State's interference all those who concurred would now withdraw from the Assembly. By this action they would sever all connection with the established church. They would go forth and seek to restore the original standards of the faith of the Church of Scotland in a free church.

A sigh escaped the lips of the assembled ministers. Every man there had been holding his breath, so as not to miss a single word of the Moderator's statement.

It was done! Now there could be no going back. No compromising. Those who followed the Moderator from the hall would raise the Lord's standard in a new and free church.

Dr Welsh laid the written protest on the table before him, bowed to the High Commissioner, then turned and walked to the door.

This was the moment for which the Assembly and most of Scotland had been waiting. How many of the ministers would follow Dr Welsh, thereby expelling themselves from the church they had served well for most of their long lives?

Two senior ministers fell in beside Dr Welsh, and as they passed from the building to the street others followed on behind. The waiting crowds cheered, then drew back to make a path for the ministers.

Inside the hall the moderates were smug at first as the two senior ministers stood up to follow the retiring Moderator. Their smugness changed to perplexity as more and more ministers and elders left their seats to join the growing procession of dissenters. As row after row left their seats, the dismay behind them grew.

Wyatt and Coll Kennedy waited respectfully for the members of the Assembly to pass before they joined with other ministers at the end of the long procession.

Before they did so, Wyatt gave Coll Kennedy a violent nudge and inclined his head towards the ministers who were passing. Among their number was the Reverend Hamilton Logan. Catching the eye of Wyatt, he appeared momentarily embarrassed. Then he inclined his head, and in that moment Wyatt knew the Disruption had succeeded.

Wyatt and Coll Kennedy followed their fellow-ministers to Tanfield. Here they would lay the foundation of the newborn Free Church of Scotland.

Watching them, unseen in the crowd, Factor John Garrett was well satisfied. At last he knew of a way to remove Wyatt from the living of Eskaig and prevent him from interfering in the plans he had laid for the Highland estates of the absent Lord Kilmalie.

CHAPTER THIRTY-NINE

ALTHOUGH RESTLESS TO RETURN to Eskaig, Wyatt was forced to remain in Edinburgh for nine days after the Disruption. There was much work to be done to ensure the success of the newly established Free Church of Scotland. Finance was of great importance. Much money was needed to build churches to serve the communities and bring them back to God.

Ironically, one of the first acts of the ministers of the Free Church was to sign the 'deed of demission'. By this act 474 ministers signed away a hundred thousand pounds in emoluments, granted to them by the church they had left. It was a solemn moment. A time for faith. Ageing and frail men gave up all they had in the world, putting their trust in the God they sought to serve with greater honesty.

When Coll Kennedy left Wyatt at Fort William the two friends shook hands gravely. Their futures were uncertain, each man's place in the community dependent upon the respect in which he was held.

'God go with you, Wyatt.'

'And with you. Don't forget to keep in touch.'

With a jaunty wave of his hand, the tall preacher stepped ashore. Swinging the bag he carried to a shoulder, he set off northwards, his long-legged stride taking him towards Loch Lochy and the mountainous parish of Letterfinlay.

Donald McKay steered his small vessel away from the Fort William quay and headed for the narrow channel to Loch Eil.

'You'll not be knowing what to expect in Eskaig, Minister?'

'The spiritual well-being of every man, woman and child in the district is in the balance, Donald, yet I'm not even certain they know of the Disruption yet.'

'Oh, they know, Minister. I brought the news from the General Assembly here myself. They've had a whole week to decide which path they'll be treading. They trust you. If *you* tell them what they should do, they'll follow.'

Donald McKay spun the wheel as the tricky current caught the under-powered little vessel and swept it towards the bank. When the boat was once more in the centre of the channel he said: 'Trouble is, the factor knows about the Disruption, too, and he's likely to have thought up something for you.'

'Perhaps he's not returned from Glasgow yet.'

'He's been home nigh on a week.' Donald McKay spat over the side. 'Travelled up in a ship with a colonel and a hundred or so soldiers – *Irish* soldiers. I just heard the news back at Fort William. The soldiers are in camp there.'

The news horrified Wyatt. Regular soldiers in the Highlands were bad news for everyone. The presence of *Irish* soldiers was alarming. There was little love lost between the two races. The only reason the Kilmalie factor could have for bringing them here would be to back up a major clearance.

John Garrett had played a crafty and patient game. He had anticipated a split in the Church and been equally confident Wyatt would side with the dissenters. Wyatt no longer had the support of the established church behind him, and the sympathies of the courts were with Garrett and all he stood for. It gave him a free hand to do as he wished on the Kilmalie estates, with no one to restrain him. Within a year there would be no need for a minister here – free church *or* established. John Garrett could clear every man, woman and child from the vast area that comprised the Eskaig parish.

Wyatt's long brooding silence was broken by the boatman. 'I'd say something's already happened, Minister. You've never drawn a larger crowd than are waiting today.'

Wyatt looked up to see many people standing beside the ramshackle jetty, with more hurrying along the road from Eskaig. It seemed the entire village had turned out to meet him. In the van were the church elders – but Wyatt saw immediately that one was missing. Angus Cameron had not come to greet him on his return.

When Wyatt stood on land, the elders came forward, one by one, and gravely shook his hand in a gesture of support. Many others expressed their approval of his actions as Wyatt moved through the crowd. He was greatly moved by their faith in him, especially when he learned what had happened in his absence.

Factor John Garrett had not wasted any time since his own return. Three days ago he had gone to the manse escorted by a platoon of Irish soldiers. Under his direction all Wyatt's personal property had been removed and dumped in an untidy heap in the churchyard. A number of elders had hurried to the scene to protest at what was being done, only to be told Wyatt was no longer a member of the Church of Scotland. Consequently, he had no right to live in the manse.

A number of women tried to gather up Wyatt's possessions, but Garrett warned them that anyone in the village who harboured either Wyatt or his property would be immediately evicted from their home and ordered from Kilmalie lands.

'I have a little surprise for Factor Garrett – but where's my property now?' Wyatt asked the question surrounded by Eskaig villagers, all anxious to add snippets of information or express opinions as they made slow progress towards the village.

'It's in the schoolhouse. Alasdair Burns took it in during that first night. The factor raged on at us when he learned it had gone, but no one told him where it was.'

'I'm grateful to you. To all of you. We have serious matters to discuss now I'm back in Eskaig. The spiritual well-being of our people. The support for a free church was much greater than expected. We'll soon be able to appoint ministers to as many parishes as the established church. For a while we'll likely be the only church here. . . .'

The sudden silence that greeted his words was broken by one of the elders. 'Garrett's already put up a new minister for the living. Angus Cameron and his wife moved into the manse yesterday evening.'

Wyatt was more hurt than surprised. It had always been a very badly kept secret that Angus Cameron nursed an ambition to occupy the Eskaig manse. The early rift between himself and Wyatt had been covered up rather than healed.

'What of his induction?'

'It's to be this Sunday. I think Garrett expected it to be an accomplished fact before you returned from Edinburgh.'

John Garrett had laid his plans well. With a new minister in the manse, and Kilmalie tenants threatened with dire consequences if they gave shelter to their disestablished minister, the factor must have thought he had won the day. One of Wyatt's first duties would be to disillusion him.

The elders suggested it might be better if Wyatt stayed at the Eskaig inn for a while. It was the only building in the village that did not belong to the Kilmalie estate, and Annie Hamilton would not be intimidated by John Garrett's threats.

Wyatt had other ideas. Accompanied by the anxious villagers, he made his way to the school, which was virtually on the doorstep of the manse. Here he said a short prayer and led them in singing a hymn which could not fail to have been heard in the manse. Then Wyatt left his supporters with a promise that he would remain to offer them a Free Church service next Sunday – the day of Angus Cameron's induction. He also arranged to meet the elders in the school building later that evening.

In the house attached to the school there was no suggestion that Wyatt's stay would be temporary. Wyatt had his own bedroom, and his clothes had been neatly folded, or hung in a large cupboard that also served as a wall divider.

Wyatt had wondered what Evangeline's reaction had been to her father's latest actions, but Alasdair Burns informed him she had travelled to London only days after Wyatt left for Edinburgh. The doctors looking after her mother felt she was almost ready to return home to Scotland but there was a need to discuss her future. In the absence of her father, Evangeline had gone to London to speak to them on his behalf.

While Wyatt was eating, Alasdair Burns asked: 'Do you want to discuss our future plans just yet? We'll no doubt both be turned out when the factor realises you're staying here.'

'We'll *neither* of us be turned out. I'll be seeing Garrett in the morning. I intend to ask him to allow me to use the kirk if the people decide they want a free church here in Eskaig.'

Alasdair Burns looked at Wyatt as though he had been stricken down by insanity. 'Garrett will never allow you anywhere near the kirk. He's far more likely to have the military run you and me clear across the border into England.'

'Garrett will have neither of us run out of Eskaig. I have documents here from the late Lord Kilmalie. They state that the school, this house and the land on which they stand belong to *me*. The Army will help him as far as it dares to go, but no commanding officer is going to break the law for a Highland factor.'

It was almost dark outside already. Donald McKay's steam-boat had been late reaching Eskaig. As Alasdair Burns went round the house lighting candles, Wyatt said: 'It's likely to be a long day tomorrow, and I must speak to the elders tonight. First, though, I want to visit the churchyard for a wee while. . . .' Wyatt hesitated before asking: 'Have you seen anything of Mairi while I've been away?'

Alasdair Burns shook his head. 'No one's seen hide nor hair of a Ross for weeks, although there are rumours galore of men from as far away as Glen Shiel coming to visit Eneas. I fear there's something afoot at the Ross croft. Perhaps someone should warn Eneas of the Irish soldiers stationed at Fort William. They'd light a fire beneath a Highlander just to watch him dance.'

Alasdair Burns might have been exaggerating the Irish soldiery's dislike of the Highlander, but not by much. Soldiers of the two countries were never sent overseas in the same troop-transport and, if at all possible, were rarely garrisoned within fighting distance of each other. The Irish 27th Regiment had seen service in Africa when Wyatt was there, and it was a well-known fact that the Irishmen would as soon fight a Highlander as a Zulu.

'I'll go on to have a word with Eneas tomorrow, after I've seen Garrett.'

'I thought you might. Here, take this lamp with you to the churchyard. There's no moon tonight, and it'll be dark by the time you return.'

Wyatt did not take the lamp outside the schoolhouse. It was still light enough to see, and Wyatt would have no difficulty finding his way back. He had visited his father's grave almost every day since coming to Eskaig. He could have found his way blindfold.

As Wyatt skirted the small familiar kirk, he saw that candles had been lit inside. Acting upon impulse, he opened the kirk door quietly and slipped inside.

It was a few moments before he saw Angus Cameron. The new

Eskaig minister kneeled in front of the altar, a still, shadowy figure, head bowed in prayer.

Wyatt had almost reached him before Angus Cameron became aware of his presence. Wyatt's foot brushed against a misplaced pew, and the praying figure straightened up and turned.

When he recognised his visitor, Angus Cameron rose to his feet. 'What are you doing here? You're no longer Eskaig's minister. Has no one told you. . . ?'

'I know all about it, Angus, but don't let me disturb you. Let's pray together . . . for our people. The people of Eskaig.'

'We no longer belong to the same church. *I'm* the minister now. You'd better leave.'

'We're both men of God, Angus, whichever church we belong to. Of far more importance is what's likely to happen to the people of Eskaig if Garrett has his way.'

'If you don't leave, I'll have the factor report you to the authorities in Fort William for attempting to stir up trouble. There's no longer a place for you in Eskaig.'

'There's more need than ever before. More need for *both* of us, can't you see? Garrett isn't working for the welfare of the people of Eskaig, and he certainly doesn't care about the Church. He's playing the age-old game of "divide and rule". He wants to clear the Kilmalie estates. While there's been one church with a single voice to oppose him, he's needed to restrain his ambitions. If he can effectively divide *us* against each other, he can do what he likes. I came to ask if we might share the kirk. . . .'

'It wasn't Garrett who split the Church. *You're* the "free church" man.'

Wyatt realised he was getting nowhere. Angus Cameron had achieved his lifetime's ambition. He was resident in the manse. He would not give it up easily.

In a final bid to gain the support of the new minister, Wyatt said: 'If we fight each other instead of fighting Garrett, we'll wake up one day to discover we have no parishioners left to fight *for*. Garrett will have cleared the mountains – and Eskaig, too.'

Angus Cameron appeared to ponder this, and for a moment Wyatt thought his words had finally made an impression on the new Eskaig preacher. Then the stubborn expression returned to the older man's face.

'You'll not get yourself back in the manse or this kirk with clever words. You chose to leave our church, now you must pay the price. Either you get out of my kirk now, or you'll be reported to the magistrates. Go away from Eskaig. You don't belong here. You never have and you've brought us nothing but trouble.'

As dusk closed in upon the peaceful churchyard, Wyatt thought of Angus Cameron's words. *Had* he brought trouble to the people of Eskaig? What would have happened had he not come here as their minister? Was he right to try to oppose Garrett's plans? Would it make any difference to the outcome?

On his knees beside his father's grave, Wyatt thought of the man who was buried beneath the almost indiscernible grassed mound. His father had wrecked his health in the battle to save the homes of his parishioners and the only way of life they had known. Yet the Islands had been cleared despite all his father had done. He had died a defeated and heartbroken old man. Had anything *he* did been worthwhile for either people or preacher?

Wyatt wondered whether he should have learned a lesson from his father's experience. Instead he was not only opposing the clearance policies of the landowners, he had also joined battle with the State-supported might of the established church. Wyatt stayed sunk in his thoughts beside the grave until he heard the elders of Eskaig making their way along the road to the school.

CHAPTER FORTY

WYATT'S CALL on John Garrett at the factor's Corpach home began in exactly the same way as an earlier visit. He was let into the house by the same dour, vaguely disapproving, middle-aged maid-servant. When she went upstairs to inform the factor of his visitor, Wyatt heard the same whisperings from the room when the servant returned downstairs to where Wyatt waited in the hall.

John Garrett had never been short on arrogance, but when he came down a few minutes later the arrogance was heavily tinged with disdain.

'I never expected to see you back in the Highlands, Jamieson. Common sense should have told you there was no place for you here. Eskaig has a new minister, one who knows on which side his bread's buttered. There's no room for you, or the trouble-making church you now represent. In case you haven't heard, I've not only taken back the manse on behalf of the *established* church, I've also warned the villagers against allowing you to stay with any one of them.'

'I haven't come here to quarrel with you, Garrett. I had hoped you'd raise no objection to me conducting a Sunday service in the kirk.'

John Garrett hooted with mirth. 'You're on the wrong side, Jamieson. It's the *devil's* cheek you have. The church is under Kilmalie patronage. As long as I'm factor here you'll never be allowed so much as a square *foot* of Kilmalie land on which to preach. That leaves you with *nowhere*. Go back to Glasgow, Jamieson – and take that one-legged schoolteacher with you. There's no place for him here, either.'

'I'm sorry you feel like this, Factor. Neither Alasdair Burns nor I will be leaving. We've both work to do, and since you've brought an Irish regiment to the district I suspect my presence in Eskaig will be needed more than ever before.'

John Garrett's anger flared up, but before he could speak Wyatt held up a hand to silence him. 'Before you repeat yourself, I'll not *need* to preach on Kilmalie property. The late Lord Kilmalie left me the land on which the school is built, to do with as I will. I've brought a copy of the deed with me. The original is in the safe hands of Charles Graham. I had hoped you and I might have been able to reach some form of agreement on the use of the kirk. I perhaps should have known better. I'll be holding services in the school building until we can build a new kirk on the land. Goodbye, Garrett. I see no reason why we should meet again.'

Wyatt turned to go, but then paused. 'By the way, Alasdair Burns has received a letter from Evangeline. She hopes to be bringing her mother home later this week. I don't think Mrs Garrett will take kindly to sharing your bedroom with anyone else.'

For once John Garrett did not come back at Wyatt with a ready reply, but Wyatt walked from the factor's house with a sense of failure. He knew he had been hoping for nothing short of a miracle in thinking he and the Kilmalie factor might have been able to talk matters over sensibly. Their mutual dislike created an insurmountable barrier between them. It had been a naïve and forlorn hope. Wyatt's concern now was for the welfare of the people in the mountains who barred the way to the extra profit Garrett hoped to make from the introduction of huge flocks of sheep.

The expression of welcome on Mairi's face when she walked from the Ross cot and saw Wyatt approaching helped dispel much of the uncertainty Wyatt felt about his present rôle in Eskaig affairs. Running to meet him, she hugged him close, and her kiss drove all other thoughts from his mind for a while.

News of the Disruption within the Church had somehow reached the remote Ross croft, and Mairi's first words were of its effect upon Wyatt.

'I never expected to see you up here so soon after the Disruption. What's happening in Eskaig? Are you still our minister?'

Wyatt told Mairi of his eviction from the manse and of Angus

Cameron's appointment in his place. By the time they reached the door of the croft Eneas Ross had appeared, and Wyatt was obliged to repeat his answers to the same questions.

'That's the gratitude of a Cameron for you,' nodded Eneas Ross sagely. 'They've always been men you'd be better stamping on when you have them down, not extending a hand to help them up again. There's never been any gratitude in Angus Cameron's soul.'

As Eneas Ross was speaking, a number of unsmiling men emerged from the croft behind him. Wyatt recognised a few of them as cottars. Among them were men he had last seen at the funeral of the Highland centenarian Archibald Mackinnon. Many more were strangers of about Eneas Ross's own age – and the majority carried muskets or rifles.

'Kinsmen of mine,' said Eneas Ross in the briefest of explanations. To the 'kinsmen', he said: 'This is Preacher Jamieson from Eskaig. He's a dissenter and has just been turned out of the manse by Factor Garrett.'

His introduction provoked a few grunts that might have expressed sympathy. They could equally have indicated lack of interest.

'The preacher's an ex-army man. A captain in the Seventy-Second Regiment.'

There was an immediate change in the attitude of Eneas Ross's 'kinsmen'. Smiles appeared on their faces for the first time, and each of them stepped forward politely to shake Wyatt's hand.

Eyeing the armed men, Wyatt asked: 'Is there any special reason for this family gathering?'

Expressionless, Eneas Ross shook his head. 'It's been a long time since we last met. Now seemed as good a time as any.'

'I disagree.'

Wyatt's unexpected comment took his listeners by surprise, and Wyatt explained. 'Factor Garrett returned from Glasgow a few days ago with at least a full company of an Irish regiment. They're garrisoned at Fort William.'

The concern shown by his listeners told Wyatt that, without exception, Eneas Ross's 'kinsmen' were military men. They realised the implications of having Irish regular soldiers garrisoned in the Highlands. Many Irishmen were brought up on tales of Highland savagery. Scots soldiers had been used to put down the sporadic uprisings in that tortured country, and Highland regiments had proved particularly effective.

Wyatt pressed home his point. 'If the Irish find a Highlander carrying a gun, they'll shoot him on sight. You'd be wise to break up the family gathering and send everyone home.'

When none of the men would meet his eyes, Wyatt knew they had been plotting something. Whatever it was, his news had not caused them to change their plans. Wyatt decided he must drop all pretence and appeal to them directly.

'Rumours are rife in Eskaig. Whatever it is you're plotting, I hope you'll see sense and forget it altogether now you know about the soldiers.'

Eneas Ross's face took on an expression of Highland stubbornness such as Wyatt had seen many times before, and his hopes plummeted.

'You've probably been too tied up with affairs of the Church to take notice of what's been happening about you, Preacher. The Army isn't here to support only Garrett. Landowners are clearing tenants from Glenelg to Morvern. Emigration has become such good business that shipowners are bringing vessels into Fort William and offering five-pound passages to Nova Scotia. My father witnessed the hunting down of the last wolf in the Highlands. *I've* no wish to live to see the passing of the last Highlander.'

'You can't fight the landowners, Eneas. At least, not *your* way.'

'It's too late for any other way, Preacher. They're evicting and burning. You can't fight force and fire with words.'

'Think about it very carefully, Eneas. You've already lost two sons. Let that be enough.'

'Is dying as a man more to be feared than living as a coward?' Eneas Ross answered his own question with a shake of his head. 'I'll take your advice kindly because it comes from a man who's faced death himself. You're still the same man, Preacher. If you weren't, you'd be living well in the manse in Eskaig now, taking Kilmalie money. Men like us can't change, either. It's what sets Highlanders apart from other men. Kings and generals have known it for hundreds of years.'

'Nonsense! It's *pride*, Eneas. The sort of pride the Bible tells us leads only to destruction. Your family deserves more. Magdalene and Mairi – *they* deserve more.'

Wyatt made the plea as Magdalene Ross appeared in the doorway of the croft looking anxious. She was far removed from the confident and contented woman he had first met here little more than a year ago.

'I was a soldier when Magdalene first met me. She understands. As for Mairi ... you've said you want to marry the girl. Take her for a walk to the ridge and ask her again. She's talked of no one else these past weeks.'

With a jerk of his head to his 'kinsmen', Eneas Ross led them back inside the croft. In the doorway he turned. 'Don't take her too far off, Preacher. We can teach the Irish to respect Highland *men*. I wouldn't trust them with our women.'

Eneas Ross ducked inside the low doorway of the croft and was followed by his 'kinsmen', leaving Wyatt staring after him.

'Would you like to take that walk? You don't have to....' Mairi was looking at him uncertainly.

'Of course I would. For weeks I've wanted to be with you again. Even when I should have had my mind on other matters. But I'm worried about what might happen if your father and the others clash with Garrett and the Army.'

'So am I. Tibbie is, too. It's more difficult to know what Ma's thinking. She believes she's being disloyal to Pa if she doesn't agree with him – when we're around anyway.' Mairi took his hand in an affectionate gesture as they walked together from the croft.

'She'll be even more disloyal if she doesn't try to stop him acting foolishly. She must know that.'

'Ma hasn't been seeing things too clearly since Donnie was killed. He was the baby of the family, a wee bit special for all of us....' There was a break in Mairi's voice, and Wyatt squeezed her hand sympathetically. 'One day Ma will be all weepie about Donnie; the next she'll be saying that if he'd been killed in Spain the family would have taken their revenge on the factor by now.'

They walked on in silence for some minutes before Mairi said: 'All we've spoken of so far are *Ross* troubles, but how about you? Ewan Munro was up here a day or two ago to bring us the Munros' first calf. It's payment for the cow Pa gave them when they were given the croft. But what's happening to the Church? How do you see your future?'

Wyatt told Mairi of all that had occurred in Edinburgh, and of the plans for an evangelical Free Church of Scotland, stronger than the church in which it had its beginnings.

'You *will* be staying in Eskaig?'

'I hope so.' They topped a small rise and could see a waterfall tumbling down towards Loch Arkaig, some miles away, with the high peaks of Glengarry beyond. Farther away the peaks appeared to have been painted in pastel shades of mauve by distance.

Mairi stood in an unself-conscious pose, the dress moulded to her body by the wind. 'It's a beautiful land, Wyatt, yet there's been so much blood spilled in these mountains. Why?'

Wyatt shook his head. 'The beauty is God's handiwork. It's men who do the fighting.'

Mairi looked at Wyatt as though seeking something in his face. Then she moved towards him and kissed him, and his arms went about her.

When a need for breath made Mairi turn her face away, she stayed close, her head against his chest. 'I'm frightened, Wyatt. Frightened of what will happen to us; to Pa and the boys – and to this land of ours. I feel as though I'm clinging on by my fingernails to everything I know and love.'

'That isn't so. Your hold on me grows stronger every time we're together.' He tried to think of words to reassure her. 'As for your father . . . I've deliberately exaggerated things to him, in the hope of stopping him from doing anything foolish.'

Again Mairi sought the truth in Wyatt's face. She found what she was seeking, but her kiss was briefer this time.

'You're a very nice man, Wyatt Jamieson.' She pushed herself from him and, ignoring his protests, kept an arm's length between them.

'Do you still want to marry me?'

Wyatt could hardly believe he had heard her aright.

'You know I do. Wanting to marry you gets in the way of every other thought that comes into my head. I wake in the night and reach out to see if you're lying beside me, not wanting to accept I've been dreaming. I love you so much, Mairi.'

Mairi was silent for so long that Wyatt was afraid his confession might have frightened her in some way. He was wondering whether he should apologise, when she spoke again.

'All right.'

That was all, just two words: 'All right.'

He waited for her to say more. When she remained silent, he said in confusion: 'What do you mean . . . "All right"?'

'I mean all right – I'll marry you.'

Wyatt's mouth spoke two or three sentences before any words came out.

'You mean it? You *really* mean it? You'll *marry* me?'

She nodded, his astonishment both delighting and amusing her. 'Yes. I've learned to read and write. I haven't got any shoes yet, but I will. I won't disgrace you. . . .'

Words were squeezed from her as Wyatt hugged her clear of the ground and swung her around in a circle. Then Wyatt kissed her and kissed her again.

Eventually she managed to push him from her. 'Wyatt . . . listen to me. When? When do you want me to marry you?'

'Soon. *Very* soon. As soon as I know what my future is to be.' Suddenly he sobered. 'I'll know this Sunday whether or not I'll be staying in Eskaig. If Angus Cameron gets overwhelming support from the people, I'll have to leave. I'll return to Edinburgh and seek somewhere else to work.' Wyatt hesitated. 'Would you leave the Highlands and come with me, if it's necessary?'

'I'll go wherever you go. But what if the people choose you, and not Angus Cameron?'

'Then I'll stay and build a kirk beside the school. A house, too. It won't be large, but there'll be enough room. . . . I've drawn a plan. . . .' Suddenly Wyatt's heart was too full for words. 'Mairi, I *love* you!'

'I love you, too, Wyatt Jamieson.'

Back at the croft, Magdalene and Eneas Ross greeted the news with affection, but without surprise.

Magdalene Ross kissed and hugged them both, while Mairi's brothers and their 'kinsmen' crowded around to congratulate the newly betrothed couple.

Finally, it was the turn of Eneas Ross to clasp the hand of his future son-in-law.

'I'll be pleased to have you in the family, Preacher,' he said. 'Though it's taken you so long to persuade her to say Yes I was beginning to worry lest you weren't the man I believed you to be.'

CHAPTER FORTY-ONE

NEWS OF WYATT'S INTENDED MARRIAGE came as no surprise to a delighted Alasdair Burns. He had been expecting it for many months.

The village elders were less enthusiastic. Mairi Ross was an unsophisticated mountain girl. She had no knowledge of what was expected of a minister's wife, and no useful family connections to help in the difficult times ahead. However, the matter of Wyatt's marriage was overshadowed by the question of his acceptance by the community in his new rôle as Free Church minister.

If the people wanted him, and with the full backing of the newly formed church, he felt confident he could withstand the malicious opposition of John Garrett. Without the support of the parishioners, his presence could cause them only humiliation.

The elders were every bit as concerned about the outcome as was Wyatt. They believed in the principles that had brought about the formation of the Free Church, but if it failed in Eskaig *they* could not move on.

Angus Cameron had not been slow in pressing home this point during Wyatt's absence in Edinburgh. Had he not returned when he did, Wyatt believed at least two of the elders might have returned to the established church.

New support arrived shortly before the allegiance of the villagers was put to the test. Evangeline Garrett and her mother returned to their Corpach home late on Friday. Charlotte Garrett would never be cured, but she was more stable now.

Evangeline rode up to the Eskaig schoolhouse mid-morning the next day, and her initial greeting was for Alasdair Burns. Watching the couple together, Wyatt thought it probable they, too, would soon be contemplating marriage.

Evangeline was no less enthusiastic than Alasdair Burns had been at the news that Wyatt was to marry Mairi, but she was also filled with indignation at her father's treatment of the Eskaig minister.

'I learned only this morning that Father has moved Angus Cameron into the manse. It's *disgraceful*, Wyatt. By the time a servant told me the news my father had already gone out, otherwise I'd have told *him* what I thought.'

'I'm grateful for your concern, but don't even mention the matter to him. It will only start a family argument without serving any useful purpose.'

'It won't *start* the argument. I've something else to put to him that will do that. It seems my father's been a very busy man while mother and I have been away – and I'm not talking of *Kilmalie* business. I believe he's seeing that Seonaid girl again.'

Wyatt found it difficult to believe Evangeline's accusation after all that had happened, but Seonaid and her father *had* left the Eskaig inn and moved to Fort William. Wyatt had seen Seonaid shortly before the move when she told him she was going because she had an offer of more remunerative employment.

Annie Hamilton told a different story. She said Seonaid was lazy, and given to spending too much time away from the inn, sometimes being away for whole nights.

Wyatt remembered the whispering he had heard coming from John Garrett's bedroom. Sadly, he was forced to admit that Evangeline was probably right.

Sunday was a cloudy and blustery day. Wyatt thought it would probably favour Angus Cameron. Wyatt's strongest support was in the mountains behind the village. Bad weather was likely to keep the crofters and cottars at home, while Cameron's supporters had only to hurry along the road to the kirk to lend him their support.

'Don't worry, Wyatt, you'll get the result you want.' Alasdair Burns repeated his prophecy for the umpteenth time that morning. 'Cameron's seen as throwing in his lot with Garrett and the land-owners. The people of Eskaig won't forgive him for that.'

Both men had worked well into the night preparing the school for its Sunday rôle as the district's free church. It was by no means ideal, but it was spacious enough to hold the size of congregation Wyatt hoped to have, with seats for the elderly.

'What's happening here is being repeated in more than four hundred churches throughout Scotland today. The outcome will decide the future of the Church in Scotland. . . .'

'Not to mention your marriage to Mairi!'

'Have you and Evangeline ever spoken of marriage?'

'Many times. At least, *she's* spoken of it. I tell her it's madness even to think of such a thing, but there's more than a touch of her father in Evangeline Garrett. She'll not listen to anyone who isn't saying what she wants to hear.'

'What's wrong with the idea? It's not like you to think you're not good enough for a factor's daughter.'

'I'm as good as any man or woman anywhere, whatever their station in life. But it's also true to say I can't offer Evangeline all the things she's used to having.'

'I'm sure Evangeline has taken that into consideration. If you both planned to stay in Eskaig and teach, the Free Church could afford to pay you a small joint salary. . . .' Wyatt was thinking of Lord Kilmalie's legacy. 'You wouldn't live in luxury, but you'd get by.'

'Then, it seems we *both* have a great deal to win or lose today, Wyatt.' Alasdair Burns knew where the money would come from to pay for schoolteachers. He rested a hand affectionately upon his friend's shoulder. 'I'd better get out on the streets of Eskaig now and start driving folk to your service.'

For a long while it seemed Alasdair Burns might be having difficulty persuading the Eskaig villagers to attend Wyatt's first Free Church service. Long after the time when the congregation normally attended church there was no movement on the road from the village, and Wyatt was as nervous as on the day of his induction.

Services in the school had been deliberately arranged to coincide with the induction in the nearby kirk. It would leave no doubt in anyone's mind which church the people of Eskaig had chosen to follow. Looking to where Angus Cameron waited at the gate of the small kirk, Wyatt knew the Eskaig elder must be having the same misgivings as himself. He almost felt sorry for him.

John Garrett stood with Angus Cameron. The Kilmalie factor had arrived a few minutes earlier. Only one of his household, a hostler, was with him. Wyatt wondered what had happened to prevent the remainder of his servants from attending.

The presbytery were standing nearby. Only two were ministers who had attended Wyatt's induction. The remainder had joined the breakaway movement in company with Coll Kennedy. For a moment Wyatt wondered how the easygoing Letterfinlay minister was making out. Whether he had found a place in which to preach. Wyatt decided he probably had. Coll Kennedy was not lacking in enterprise. Wyatt would soon find out; he intended to pay his friend a visit at the earliest opportunity.

Some minutes before the services were due to begin there came the sound of a pony and trap being driven hard from the direction of Corpach, and Evangeline came into view driving at a recklessly fast speed. Pony and trap slackened speed at the gate of the kirk, but Evangeline did not haul the pony to a halt until she reached the school.

Throwing the long reins carelessly inside the small vehicle, Evangeline leaped to the ground. Ignoring her father and his companions watching from outside the kirk, Evangeline called to Wyatt: 'I hope I'm not late. I had things to do at home before I came out.'

'You're the first to arrive and you're very welcome. Come inside.'

As Wyatt ushered Evangeline to the school, he glanced towards her father, standing with the representatives of the established church. John Garrett's face was livid.

'You've made your father very angry, Evangeline. You should have stayed away. There'll be trouble for you when you return home.'

'More than you know, Wyatt.' Evangeline seemed surprisingly unconcerned. 'I refused to allow the servants to attend church with him. I said he'd let them get into lazy ways while I was away. As a punishment they have to work today and clean the house from top to bottom. They minded far less than Father did. Are there many people in Angus Cameron's church?'

'One. Your father's hostler.'

'Where's Alasdair?' Evangeline had been looking about her for the one-legged teacher. 'Is he inside the school?'

'He's in the village, trying to raise a congregation. I hope that might be him now.'

While they were speaking he saw a number of people leave Eskaig and head along the road towards the school – or the kirk next door. He looked for Alasdair Burns, but the schoolteacher was not with them.

There were far more people than he had expected to see, and he was apprehensive until he recognised a pale and sickly Lachlan Munro among them. Hope leaped suddenly high. Lachlan would not be here on Angus Cameron's behalf. Then he recognised the Ross family, too. . . .

Wyatt threw open the school gate as the procession reached him and the leaders turned in, nodding to him as they passed – and still they filled the road from Eskaig. By the time Mairi came in through the gate Wyatt was beside himself with joy. Every man, woman and child had turned into the school. Not one had passed by to go to the kirk.

'Come here and stand with me.' Wyatt reached out and took Mairi's hand, and she took up a position beside him. Magdalene Ross looked startled for a moment, then she smiled her approval. Wyatt had made a gesture, the implications of which would not be lost on the community.

Wyatt and Mairi stood together as Wyatt extended a greeting to those he knew, as well as to many he did not. The improvised church was filled to overflowing long before the tail-end of the procession reached the school. People began crowding into the schoolyard, and they had to squeeze close together to make room for those yet to come.

Bringing up the rear was Alasdair Burns, and with him Annie Hamilton, landlady of the Eskaig inn.

'Alasdair! I didn't know there were so many people in these parts. Where did you find them all?'

Alasdair Burns grinned triumphantly. 'You'd better ask Annie. She sent word out through the mountains that there'd be free whisky for any man who came in to your service today.'

'Is this true, Annie?'

'True enough. I cried for days over the death of Mairi's brother. He and Seonaid had a rare chance of happiness. The only chance *she'll* ever have. I'll not see the man who took that away from them score a victory when I can do something about it.' Annie Hamilton looked at the vast congregation and groaned. 'I believe I could have saved myself a fortune. Most were coming anyway.'

That morning, standing on a table placed in the entrance of the school, Wyatt preached the sermon of his life. Halfway through he was forced to break off and silence the spontaneous cheer that went up when John Garrett left the nearby kirk and rode away.

Cheers were unnecessary. The singing of a Gaelic hymn from a thousand throats reached out to taunt the factor when he was more than a mile away from the man he had set out to remove from office.

CHAPTER FORTY-TWO

THREE DAYS AFTER his Eskaig parishioners had expressed their confidence in Wyatt and the church he now represented, Wyatt set off for Letterfinlay to find Coll Kennedy.

It was to be more than a social visit. Wyatt intended to ask Coll Kennedy to come to Eskaig to conduct his wedding to Mairi, set for two months' time. There was no need to wait any longer. Although many problems were still to be overcome, the main one was behind him. The people had made their choice of minister and of the church to which they would belong.

Wyatt had called a meeting of his elders the previous evening and he found them in a rare mood of optimism. The doubts they had entertained about the future of the newly formed Free Church forgotten, the elders were loud in voicing self-congratulation on their foresight and wisdom.

Wyatt took advantage of their euphoria to obtain agreement to plans he had drawn up for a new building on the land the late Lord Kilmalie had given to him. It would embrace both church and school, with a small manse. There would not be a lot of land to spare, but in their present mood the elders were prepared to turn their hands to miracles.

It was a fine warm early-summer day, and Wyatt strode along the road happily humming a Wesley hymn. His happiness faded somewhat when he recognised a horseman travelling towards him as John Garrett.

As horse and rider drew near, Wyatt braced himself to receive a torrent of abuse. Instead Garrett passed by staring straight ahead, the expression on his face as tight as a drumhead.

Garrett had gone some ten horse-lengths past, when Wyatt turned and called to him: 'Factor! I'd like a word with you.'

John Garrett reined in his horse, but refused to turn around. He sat stiff and upright in his saddle, looking towards Eskaig until Wyatt reached him.

'What happened on Sunday was a victory for the Free Church, Factor, not a defeat for you or Angus Cameron. It was tangible evidence of what thinking church leaders have been saying for years. State interference in worship is bitterly resented. It's this I want to talk to you about. You saw for yourself the strength of feeling for the Free Church. If you were to allow us to worship in the kirk, the gesture would be deeply appreciated by all of Lord Kilmalie's tenants.'

John Garrett looked at Wyatt with loathing. 'Are you suggesting I should pander to the wishes of a few ... *peasants*, after they've deliberately and publicly humiliated me?'

'I've already said there was nothing personal in what they did. They were exercising their duty to worship the Lord in the way they believe is right. I'm asking you only to make a gesture of goodwill. One that would cost nothing.'

'Their *duty* is to Lord Kilmalie. Without *his* goodwill they'd have no land, no work – and no homes. They've shown how little loyalty they have for his Lordship. You remind them of *that* when they're paid back in kind.'

'I had hoped we might talk this matter out sensibly and reasonably, Factor. *I* have the welfare of my parishioners at heart. *You* are employed to safeguard the interests of Lord Kilmalie's estate. The two are not incompatible.'

'They weren't before you came to Eskaig. Minister Gunn and I worked together for many years in full agreement. Since you arrived there's been more trouble than Eskaig has ever known. You've turned Kilmalie tenants against me, and against their church. I don't doubt that you and that scheming teacher of yours also had something to do with the attack on the sheriff's men from Fort William. I'll make certain Lord Kilmalie's tenants know who to blame when their ingratitude reaps its reward – and it *will*, I promise you. They'll rue the day they listened to you. *You'll* be left wondering what happened to all the converts you claim to have made.'

John Garrett kicked his heels sharply into his horse's flanks, and the animal was startled to instant movement, leaving Wyatt gazing after horse and rider.

Wyatt's happy state of mind had taken a battering. He should have known better than to appeal to Garrett's better nature. The factor was quick to take offence at a slight, imagined or otherwise, and he was slow to forgive. It had been a forlorn whim-of-the-moment attempt at a reconciliation between the Kilmalie tenants and the factor. Wyatt tried to shrug off the disappointment he felt. At least it had probably left Garrett feeling better for having won the brief verbal encounter.

It was twenty miles from Eskaig to Letterfinlay, through some of the Highlands' most spectacular countryside. For eight miles the track ran alongside the Caledonian Canal, a great feat of engineering skill linking the deep-water lochs of the Great Glen, providing a safe passage from east coast to west.

Wyatt kept pace with a small steam-powered tug along the narrower part of the canal before the tug's captain called out to ask where Wyatt was going. When he replied he was on his way to Letterfinlay, the captain brought his vessel in close to the bank and offered Wyatt passage to his destination.

The Eskaig preacher was spared a long walk. Even so, it was afternoon before the tugboat captain waved a cheery farewell to Wyatt, after putting him ashore at Letterfinlay.

Wyatt had no difficulty locating the church. Tiny as it was, the building dominated the cluster of houses sprinkled haphazardly along the water's edge. The men here were mostly fishermen, although there were a number of crofts to be seen nestling among trees along the steep slope of the mountains on this side of Loch Lochy.

There was nothing to say which of the buildings was the manse, none being in any way superior to its neighbour. Wyatt made his way to the church, only to find his way barred by a stout chain and padlock securing the door. It seemed Coll Kennedy had also been barred from his church.

Behind one of the houses Wyatt found an old man at work repairing a salmon-net. The man had a clay pipe clenched between his teeth and, for some reason best known to himself, the pipe was upside down.

When Wyatt enquired after Coll Kennedy, the old fisherman's eyes came up to give Wyatt a brief but thorough appraisal before continuing with his work.

'Would you be the new minister, maybe?' The answer was slow in coming.

'No, I have my own living in Eskaig. I'm a friend of Minister Kennedy.'

This prompted another blue-eyed look from the aged fisherman. 'Maybe you are; but then again, you're maybe not.'

While Wyatt was pondering on a reply to this enigmatic remark, the fisherman spoke again, smoke leaking from between yellowing teeth. 'Are you for the new kirk or the old one?'

'I've joined the Free Church, the same as Minister Kennedy. Do you know where I might find him?'

'I know where you *will* find him, but I needed to know your church before I directed you. If I sent you the *quickest* way, you'd pass the landlord's house. General Lindsay's strong for the old church, and quick with his sporting-gun. The way I'll send you will lead you through Mad Macquarrie's territory. I don't know how partial he is to the new church, but he could never stand the old one.'

The old man pointed north-eastwards, where the mountains ran alongside the loch in a seemingly unbroken chain. 'Go along there until you come to the third wee burn. Follow it up the mountain; it's steep, but when you near the top you'll see a saddle between two peaks. Go through, but stay on the ridge until you meet with Mad Macquarrie. Ask him where to find Minister Kennedy.'

'What if I miss this Macquarrie?'

'You'll not even need to look for him, Minister. Mad Macquarrie will find *you*. Leastways, his dogs will. It's said he has a cave in the hillside up there somewhere, but no one has ever got past his dogs to find out. A word of warning to you. When the dogs find you, just stay where you are until Mad Macquarrie reaches you. They'll not harm you if you do as I say.'

'And if I don't?'

'They'll tear you to pieces for certain.' The old man smiled, the upside-down pipe still held fast between his teeth. 'Wouldn't you prefer to belong to the *old* church for an hour or two and go past General Lindsay's house? After all, even Peter told a lie about

311

which side he was on. I don't recall the good Lord holding a grudge because of it.'

'I fancy Saint Peter might have been more valuable to the Lord than a poor Highland minister. Have those dogs really been known to tear anyone apart?'

'No. At least, no one's returned to brag of it. You'll be taking the mountain path, then, Minister?' When Wyatt nodded, the old fisherman said: 'You'll be all right. When you meet up with Mad Macquarrie, say you were sent by Old Joe the fisherman. Tell him I said you were to say there were deer seen on Beith Og only yesterday. If his dogs pull one down, I'll expect something for the pot. Good day to you now, Minister. It's a fine day to be going visiting.'

As Wyatt laboured up the mountainside he could not make up his mind whether the old fisherman had been having a joke at his expense with his talk of 'Mad Macquarrie'. He might be sitting at the lochside right now, chuckling at his success in sending a gullible preacher off on a long and fruitless journey. Wyatt took scant comfort from the knowledge that the old man had not lied about the steepness of the mountain slope.

The 'saddle' between the two peaks was not apparent until Wyatt had conquered the steep slope. Passing through to the far slope as directed by the old fisherman, Wyatt found himself gazing down into a steep-sided glen which had a river wending its way along the glen floor.

There was a croft in the valley, almost immediately below him, but the mountainside was far too steep to attempt to go straight down to it. Another, larger building could be seen farther along the valley. Wyatt decided to follow the ridge in this direction, as the old fisherman had suggested.

Wyatt was beginning to think Mad Macquarrie was, after all, a hoax when he heard the deep bark of a dog. It sounded alarmingly close! Then he saw the animal, and three or four more with it. The colour of weathered granite, the dogs must have been lying among the rocks of the peak ahead of him.

The animals were large. Frighteningly large. Each must have weighed as much as a small man and stood half as high. Wyatt's instinct was to run, but he remembered the old fisherman's warning. He had not been wrong so far. Wyatt hoped his accuracy extended to knowing the dogs' habits.

Watching the dogs bounding towards him, Wyatt realised it would have been useless to run. Bred to hunt down deer, the dogs would have caught him before he had gone a hundred paces.

The dogs behaved exactly as the net-repairing fisherman had predicted. Bounding right up to Wyatt, they bumped and jostled each other as they gambolled about him. One even came close enough to place a wet nose to his hand in apparent friendliness. However, when Wyatt raised his hand to pat the animal, the dog's ears went back and it showed formidable yellow teeth in a snarl that was echoed by the other dogs in the small pack.

Wyatt remained still as a strange figure advanced upon him along the ridge. Small and slight and accompanied by yet another of the great deerhounds, the man was dressed in a strange mixture of deerskin and sackcloth. He also wore an ancient and threadbare red tartan plaid slung over his left shoulder. It was difficult to observe his face. A shock of grey hair and an unkempt beard served to hide all but the man's eyes and nose.

In his hands the man carried a long-barrelled flintlock musket, of a pattern used by the British army on the battlefields of the world a hundred years before.

Wyatt knew he was about to meet Mad Macquarrie.

The man stopped six feet in front of Wyatt, cuffing away the dogs that crowded around him, tails wagging affectionately.

'A preacher! I might have guessed. There are more preachers than rabbits in the mountains these days. All are either running from the old kirk or looking for converts to the new one. Which are you?'

The strangely-attired mountain man's voice was not that of a vagabond. Eccentric Macquarrie might be, but Wyatt knew he was talking to an educated man.

'I'm a Free Church minister, but I'm neither running nor seeking converts. I came here from Eskaig to find an old friend: Minister Coll Kennedy. I met someone in Letterfinlay — Old Joe? He said you'd know the whereabouts of Minister Kennedy.'

'Did he now?' Mad Macquarrie put his head to one side, bird-like. 'Well, you could be telling me the truth. More likely it's a ruse to learn where Preacher Kennedy is holding his services now they've locked him out of kirk and manse.'

Mad Macquarrie shifted the position of the long-barrelled

musket, and Wyatt found himself staring into a barrel that would have satisfied the most finnicky army musketry sergeant.

'Old Joe also told me to tell you that deer were sighted on Beith Og yesterday. If you took one, he'd appreciate something for his cooking-pot.'

Mad Macquarrie chuckled and, much to Wyatt's relief, the barrel of the musket returned to the crook of the man's arm.

'Old Joe wouldn't have suggested I kill a deer if he'd thought you were a landowner's man. What's your business with Coll?'

'I'd like to see how things are faring with him. I also want to ask him to conduct a wedding in Eskaig.'

Some of the suspicion returned to Mad Macquarrie's eyes. 'I thought you said *you* were the preacher there?'

'So I am, but I can't officiate at my own wedding.'

'I suppose not. Too much "can" and "can't" attached to a church marriage. More than enough to frighten off a simple man like me. Pity, it means some woman's missing a rich experience.'

Mad Macquarrie turned away before Wyatt could determine whether or not he was joking.

'You know the way to the cave at Fintaig – *Upper* Fintaig?'

Wyatt shook his head.

Mad Macquarrie sniffed loudly. 'Then, you'll not be a drinking man. Tam Vass has a still there. His whisky would bring the angels down from heaven.'

Wyatt grinned. 'You need say no more. *That's* where I'll find Coll Kennedy.'

'I see you *do* know him. He has a service there two or three nights a week. Not on a Sunday, though. The landowner has his men checking the names of those who go to the old kirk every Sunday. He's threatened that anyone who's not there will be run clear out of the Highlands. So Coll has weekday services instead. He gets just as many as in the old kirk. Matter of fact, I might go there myself one of these days.'

'You're a Free Church man?' Wyatt tried to hide his surprise. He would not have looked upon Mad Macquarrie as being a religious man.

'No, but I get a terrible thirst talking to preachers who come here seeking out Coll Kennedy. He's had more visitors since he shifted his kirk to Tam Vass's cave than he ever did at Letterfinlay.'

Turning his attention to the dogs, Mad Macquarrie spoke to them as though they were children, detailing them to specific positions on the mountain ridge. Wyatt watched in amazement as each dog went to its allotted position. Once there it lay down and became indistinguishable from its surroundings.

'That's marvellous,' said Wyatt as he fell in step beside the man and the one dog that had never left his side. 'How long will they stay there?'

'As long as I'm away. If I left the mountains for a week, I'd come back and find them exactly where I'd put them.'

There was a pride in his voice when he said: 'If the landowner could find men or soldiers to obey him in that way, I'd be driven from the Highlands. Until he does, *I'm* the laird up here.'

CHAPTER FORTY-THREE

THE WHISKY-STILL owned by Tam Vass was in a cave high above the glen floor, although Coll Kennedy held his service close to the riverbank, far below.

Coll Kennedy had given Wyatt a warm welcome and declared he would be delighted to officiate at the Eskaig wedding. Furthermore, the Letterfinlay preacher declared it to be the first *good* thing to happen to him since the two ministers had returned from Edinbugh.

The patron of the Letterfinlay church felt it incumbent upon him to make things as difficult as possible for the only minister on his vast land-holding who dared to dissent. Barred from church and manse, Coll Kennedy had been harried from one preaching site to another before Tam Vass offered him sanctuary in his distillery. The site was an open secret to everyone except Revenue officers and landowners, but Vass assured the minister the patron would not seek him here.

Coll Kennedy could not have found a site better-suited to his personal tastes, although he would have wished for somewhere more accessible for those worshipping under the auspices of the Free Church.

However, the essential secrecy, coupled with the distances they had to cover, did not deter Minister Kennedy's congregation. Wyatt swore their long trek to the remote valley must have whetted their appetite for the teachings of the Lord.

Mad Macquarrie, who had been listening to the conversation, suggested it was more likely to be Tam Vass's whisky whetting their Highland thirsts.

Whatever it was brought the congregation to the spot, they took part in a service that few would ever forget. The grandeur of the Highland mountains would have made the mightiest man-made cathedral shrink into insignificance, while the music of the nearby mountain river could never be reproduced by an instrument.

During the service Coll Kennedy introduced Wyatt to the congregation. He said that Wyatt, too, had been evicted from home and kirk by a landowner who would not recognise the people's wish to have a 'free' church.

Wyatt felt a fraud standing with Coll Kennedy after the service while departing members of the congregation came to offer him their sympathy. The Eskaig school was an acceptable alternative to the kirk, while the schoolhouse provided him with accommodation that had to be superior to a cave!

Later, when the last worshipper had gone on his way warmed by religion and a 'wee dram' of Tam Vass whisky, Wyatt put his thoughts into words for the benefit of his fellow-preacher.

Coll Kennedy gave Wyatt a lop-sided grin. 'Oh, I'm not complaining. Matters could be far worse. Do you read Robbie Burns?'

When Wyatt nodded affirmation, Coll Kennedy said: 'Then, you may recall the grace he composed at the request of the Earl of Selkirk.

> "Some hae meat and canna eat,
> And some would eat that want it,
> But we have meat and we can eat,
> And so the Lord be thankit."

We have much to be thankful for, Wyatt. Many of our ministers are old men, and they've been cast out in the open with their families.'

The grin returned again. Coll Kennedy found it difficult to take the world seriously for long. 'Besides, what man in his right senses would complain about being accommodated in the finest distillery in the land?'

The cave was quite large and reeked of peat and whisky. Tam Vass was a small, bright, wrinkled man who looked and smelt as though he had been pickled in whisky and hung up to dry in the smoke of a peat fire.

Much of the apparatus for the still was hidden within the cave, smoke from the fires escaping as best it could. As a result much of the cave was hidden by thick acrid smoke. However, it was clearer close to the cave entrance, the smoke tending to hang close to the roof, awaiting an opportunity to flee on the wind that blew along the glen.

Within the cave, their activities hidden from view, two men could be heard talking as they worked. As Tam Vass disappeared into the smoke, Coll Kennedy explained that the unseen men were putting whisky in small barrels, ready for transportation. When darkness fell men would arrive with donkeys to carry the whisky over the mountains beyond Glen Gloy. On the other side was Loch Lochy. Here a rendezvous had been arranged with a boat traversing the Caledonian Canal. The whisky would ultimately find its way to discerning customers in the lowland towns and cities.

'What if the landowner were to have the cave raided? He'd make the most of your being here.'

'He'd also deprive a great many of his fellow-gentlemen of the finest whisky they're ever likely to taste. Oh, no! He and his men stay well away from Glen Fintaig. I'm safer here than I'd be anywhere else – and the accommodation suits my temperament. Ah! There you are, Tam.'

Tam Vass reappeared, apparently impervious to the thick acrid smoke. In his hand he held a large stoneware jug which he set on the floor in front of the preachers.

Coll Kennedy sat down cross-legged in front of the jug, and Wyatt followed his example.

'Where's Mad Macquarrie?' Wyatt could not see the strange dog-owning man, but he could easily be hidden by the smoke.

'He's gone.' Tam Vass handed each man a small wooden drinking-cup known as a *quaich*. Carved from a single block of wood, each cup was elaborately decorated and made with a solid 'ear' on opposite sides, in order that it might be held more easily. 'Macquarrie enjoys good whisky as much as any man, but he's not happy around people. He's returned to his dogs.'

'What's his story?' Wyatt held his *quaich* up for Tam Vass to fill from the jug.

'Macquarrie's story?' Tam Vass filled his own *quaich*, placed the jug on the floor of the cave between them, then sat on the floor facing his two guests. 'Nobody knows anything for certain about Mad Macquarrie. He's been up in these mountains for a great many years. There were stories of a strange being roaming the area surrounded by the devil's hounds for a long time before anyone caught a glimpse of Macquarrie. Where he came from no one knows. Some romantics say he's the bastard son of a duke, his mother a servant who ran away to escape the family's anger. Another rumour has it that he's from a good family, but was outlawed for killing his brother in a fight over a girl. There could be some truth in it, at that. He's an educated man and he has a terrible temper when he's roused. Yet I've never known him so much as raise his voice to those dogs — and he'd climb Ben Nevis rather than talk to a woman.'

'He's a strange man,' Wyatt agreed, accepting more of the truly excellent whisky from the jug, held this time by Coll Kennedy. 'I've heard tales of men living like Macquarrie, but have never met one before.'

'He's not the first in these parts,' said Tam Vass, settling back against the cave wall. 'There was a man lived over your way, Preacher Jamieson. Somewhere up around Beinn an Tuim. He'd lived there many years and was an old man when I was a boy. It was whispered he was a son of Charles Stuart, his mother the daughter of a family who hid the prince after Culloden. There was another. . . .'

Talk and whisky were passed around among the three men until long after darkness blanketed the mountains. It was good company, and the whisky was far more potent than any sold by the innkeepers of the land. Wyatt did not even remember retiring to a bed of heather, laid in a niche in the cave wall. At some time during the night he thought he heard men tramping to and fro along the length of the cave, but it might have been no more than the thumping inside his head that remained with him for much of the return journey to Eskaig.

Wyatt was halfway between Corpach and Eskaig when he saw a number of men on the slope of the lochside mountain. They were in a line from the loch to where the undergrowth ended some way up the slope, systematically working their way towards Corpach. They were probably searching for a lost animal, a calf, or even a sheep, but it was unusual to see so many men involved in such a hunt.

Then Wyatt noticed that each man carried some form of weapon. In most cases it was no more than a long stout stick, but a few wielded ancient claymores, while at least two carried muskets. It always alarmed Wyatt to see Highlanders carrying muskets in public view. There was a long history of discontent in the mountains, and the carrying of firearms was forbidden by the authorities unless a good reason could be given. The authorities often used the possession of firearms as an excuse to bring the power of the law to bear upon whole communities.

It was possible there was justification for the men to be armed. Foxes sometimes became troublesome and over-bold, raiding outlying cots and crofts and killing livestock. When this happened a hunt would be organised and carried out with high spirits and a great deal of noise. These men were going about their business unsmiling, and with a grim efficiency.

'What are you hunting?' Wyatt recognised one of the men closest to him and called his question.

When the man appeared puzzled, Wyatt shouted: 'I've been away since early yesterday morning. Visiting the minister at Letterfinlay. Is there a rogue fox around?'

'No, Minister, it's not a fox. It's men. . . . At least, that's what their own kind would call them. Up here we call them something else.'

Now Wyatt really *was* alarmed. A manhunt would not have been sanctioned by anyone in authority.

'*Who* are you hunting, and why? What's all this about?'

There was an exchange of glances between the nearest men before the one who had spoken before called: 'We're after two men, Minister. Two Irish soldiers by the sound of it. One of the crofters came down from the mountains to call us out. Every able-bodied man for miles around is out looking for them, too. They violently ill-used a girl who was rounding up cattle in the mountains.'

'Who is the girl?' Suddenly the looks that had passed between the men became meaningful. 'Is she all right?'

'We don't know how she is, Minister. All we know is it was the Ross girl.'

Wyatt headed straight into the mountains, all his other problems put aside, his thoughts in a turmoil. He *had* warned Eneas Ross and Mairi that the Irish soldiers were in the area. He should have made more of the hatred the Irish soldiers felt for the Scots. It was small consolation to tell himself he had never expected them to attack a lone woman — attack *Mairi*.

The incident had outraged the whole community. There were more men in the mountains than Wyatt had ever seen before. Long lines of them combed through the undergrowth of the lower slopes, while others searched the tumbled rock places about the mountain-tops. More than once the searching men changed direction to inter-cept and identify the lone preacher hurrying towards the Ross home. Each greeting upon recognition was followed by the same question: 'Have you seen anything of the Irishmen?' And each band of searchers included at least one armed man.

Wyatt was thinking more clearly now, and he warned the men against confronting any large bodies of soldiers or of taking the law into their own hands if the attackers were found. Both warnings undoubtedly fell upon deaf ears, but they needed to be said, and repeated. The incident involving Mairi was serious enough in itself. Its repercussions could spell disaster to the whole of the Highlands.

When Wyatt came in sight of the Ross croft, he slowed for a moment. He had not thought of what Mairi's reaction might be at seeing him — or even whether she would be well enough for him to see her. He was still undecided when Magdalene Ross came into the garden of the croft with a bowl of vegetable waste which she threw out for the chickens.

When she saw Wyatt she put a hand to her brow, squinting against the light of the sun until she identified him. She did not wave but placed the bowl on the ground and stood waiting for him to reach her.

Magdalene Ross had been crying. Her face was blotched and puffy, her eyes red-rimmed and bloodshot.

Taking hold of the woman's hands in a gesture of sympathy, Wyatt said: 'I came as soon as I heard. How is she?'

As Magdalene shook her head, her eyes filled with tears. 'She's been badly beaten. Her face. . . . But it's in *here* where she has the worst pain. . . .' Magdalene Ross put a hand to her breast, then clutched at Wyatt. 'I've seen this happen many times in my own country. First with the French and then . . . yes, with English and Scots soldiers, too. But that was *war*. Such things happen. But *here*! She went out to find the cows, a happy beautiful girl. She came home *crawling* and badly beaten. Why? Why did it happen?'

Magdalene Ross's words might have been a knife plunged deep into Wyatt's stomach and twisted. In that moment there was no Christian compassion in his heart. Had the two Irish soldiers suddenly appeared before him, he would have killed them where they stood.

There was a sound in the doorway, and Wyatt turned. He saw Mairi standing there. She appeared tired and drawn, but a brief expression of pleasure crossed her face when she saw him – and there was not a trace of bruising there.

'Wyatt! Oh, my dear. It's good to see you.' Mairi ran to him and hugged him. 'I can't think of anyone I'd rather see just now. Come inside and talk to Tibbie. Tell her that what's happened doesn't matter. That everything will be all right. Tell her no one blames her for what happened. . . .'

'Tibbie. . . ?' Wyatt stood in stupid confusion and repeated: 'Tibbie. . . ?'

'You *have* heard what happened to her? The Irish soldiers you warned Father and me about? They're animals. No, *worse* than animals for what they did to Tibbie. I hope the men catch up with them and kill them both. . . .'

CHAPTER FORTY-FOUR

THE SEARCH by the Highlanders spread in the manner of a disturbance on a still pond. When word of the rape of Tibbie Ross reached other communities their menfolk turned out to join in the search and pass on the message: 'Find the Irishmen.' Within twelve hours mountains, glens and lochsides were being combed by grim-faced men as far as thirty miles from Eskaig.

As swiftly as it had begun, the search was called off. No reason was given, and men returning to their homes said nothing. Wives did not ask. A deep secret silence settled over the mountains.

For a week the Highlands waited. Then the bodies of two deserters from the Irish regiment were pulled from the water at the southern end of Loch Lochy. Both men had been stabbed to death.

Official reaction to the death of the two Irish soldiers was exactly what Wyatt had feared. Their desertion was forgotten, and the two men were given a funeral with full military honours, as though they had fallen in battle. The eulogy recited at the graveside even hinted that the men might have been abducted before being brutally murdered.

The result was an immediate increase in tension between the resentful local population and vengeful Irish soldiers. The soldiers needed little encouragement to recall the wrongs, imagined or otherwise, their people had suffered at the hands of Highland 'occupation' troops in the past.

Incidents between soldiers and Scotsmen increased, and fights were frequent in the taverns and drinking-houses of Fort William. Far more serious was the manner in which the Irish regiment was used to support the authorities in the new wave of clearances being carried out in the Highlands about Fort William.

High in the mountains south-west of Loch Lochy the cottars gathered together in a confused and pathetic group and refused to accept the clearance notices being brought to them by a timid sheriff's officer. Making no attempt to call attention to the office he held, the official scurried back to Fort William, greatly exaggerating the resistance of the cottars in order to justify his lack of success.

Within hours the old bogy of a Highland insurrection had been resurrected yet again and wild rumours circulated in the town. At dawn the next day, sheriff's officers headed for the mountains once again. This time they were accompanied by a magistrate, the sheriff-substitute and the factor. As an escort they took with them forty Irish soldiers, who marched out of Fort William to the steady beat of a drum.

High in the mountains the sound of the drum drew the cottars. At a narrow and shallow ford they gathered to plead their case, women well to the fore.

A woman walked to the centre of the ford and begged the sheriff-substitute to return to Fort William and leave them to live their lives in peace. The plea was made in Gaelic and understood by only two of the assembled officials. It was certainly not a language that had been studied by the mounted factor. Encouraged by the presence of the troops, he rode into the stream, heading towards the cottars' self-designated spokeswoman. When he reached the middle of the shallow but swift-flowing stream, the woman made another appeal in her unintelligible language.

The factor's horse, made nervous by the fast-running stream, would not stand still. When its hoof turned a pebble beneath the water the animal stumbled, fell against the woman and knocked her off balance.

Not all the cottars gathered on the far bank saw the manner in which the incident occurred. As the woman floundered to the bank Gaelic abuse was hurled at the horseman and suddenly a stone sailed through the air from the assembled Highlanders. It hit the horse on the face. Startled, the animal backed, slipped and fell, ducking its rider in the icy water.

The factor surfaced to a howl of delighted derision from the cottar women. The sight of the wet and bedraggled factor caused almost as much amusement in the ranks of the Irish soldiers, and this might have been the end of the incident. Unfortunately, another volley of stones sailed through the air, hurled by half a dozen children of no more than twelve or thirteen years of age, standing behind their parents.

As the missiles landed in the water about the bedraggled factor and his threshing horse, the angry man shouted at the amused soldiery: 'What the hell are you standing there doing nothing for? Can't you see what they're doing? Or are you waiting for me to be killed before you take any action?' Another hail of missiles sailed through the air, and this time one struck the factor on the shoulder.

The officer in charge of the Irish soldiers immediately ordered them 'into line, at the double'. The men obeyed swiftly, and when they had formed a single long line they were ordered to take aim over the heads of the cottars.

Moments later the order 'Fire!' was given. A volley of shots rang out, echoed from the surrounding mountains.

As the smoke cleared and the last echo rolled away two of the cottars could be seen lying up on the ground. One was a woman who had been standing in the forefront of the crowd. Her death might have been the result of a deliberate disregard of orders, or due to a faulty charge in a soldier's gun.

The second death was almost certainly an accident, but no less of a tragedy. A young girl standing well back from the crossing had been struck by an almost-spent musket-ball, fired above the heads of the cottars.

As the cottars stood their ground in stunned disbelief, a shout went up for the soldiers to cross the river and disperse them. The Irish soldiers needed no urging. They splashed across the shallow ford, spurred on by the sight of cottars fleeing before them.

The stronger and more able-bodied of the cottars were able to reach the safety of the surrounding rocky heights. Others, not so fortunate, were clubbed down by musket-butts. If resistance was offered, be it by man, woman or child, the offender was beaten to the ground before being dragged back to the river and placed in the charge of the sheriff's officers.

At the end of half an hour, the last of the hot and triumphant soldiers returned to the riverbank. The still-wet factor looked about him at the two bodies and eight injured prisoners, three with broken limbs. Well satisfied with the morning's work, he offered his congratulations to the soldiers' commanding officer.

'It's exactly what was needed to show them we'll stand no more nonsense. I'll have little trouble with this lot after today.'

'I trust you're wrong, Factor. Our men haven't been brought all this way to do no more than fight a handful of women. Your own militia could have attended to that. I trust you'll be able to offer us something rather more worthwhile before we have to return.'

'Yes. . . . Yes, I think I might. There's a family I want to evict who should put up enough of a fight to keep both you and your men happy.'

The factor was John Garrett, and the family he had in mind belonged to Eneas Ross.

The factor for the Kilmalie estate had instituted the most wide-reaching clearances this part of Scotland had known. With the aid of the military he was emptying vast areas of the mountains north of Eskaig. The evicted Highlanders shouldered their few salvaged possessions and set off in search of another place to stay, leaving their homes burning behind them. While the ashes were still smouldering, sheep were moved in by the hundred; by the thousand – and in tens of thousands. They cropped hard-won gardens to the ground, their cloven hoofs trampling on the pride and aspirations of a whole people.

Few of the dispossessed Highlanders were able to find a permanent refuge. Some wandered aimlessly about the mountains for days until they disappeared, no one knowing where. Others made their way to Eskaig. Here they sought the sanctuary of the school, or camped above mouldering ancestors in the churchyard.

Wyatt tried to speak to John Garrett, to plead with him to halt the clearances, but John Garrett was rarely at home. Mostly he was out with the Army, supervising the clearance of Kilmalie lands. Many of his nights, too, were spent away from home, John Garrett choosing to remain in Fort William whenever he could.

The scale of the clearances was far worse than anything Wyatt had anticipated, and feeding the victims became a major problem. The homeless families were kept alive mainly by the generosity of local fishermen. It was fortunate, too, that the weather was kind. When it changed it would be impossible to put everyone under cover unless Angus Cameron opened his church to the refugees, and this seemed highly unlikely.

Eventually, in sheer desperation, Wyatt wrote to the Kilmalie estate office in Edinburgh. He described the plight of the Highlanders and begged Charles Graham to use any influence he possessed to bring the clearances to an end.

Wyatt doubted whether his letter would serve any useful purpose. The new Lord Kilmalie had given John Garrett unlimited powers to run the Eskaig estate, and the factor was using them to the full.

John Garrett was also using far harsher tactics in his clearances than ever. Until recently it had been the practice to issue clearance warnings, giving tenants time to rid themselves of livestock and reap their crops. This had been discontinued. Most tenants were receiving no warning at all. The clearance note was served with immediate effect. Those who were slow to obey found their homes and possessions burning about them.

With so much happening about Eskaig, Wyatt had not seen Mairi for many days. He could not justify leaving the crowded school for the time it would take to go into the mountains on a visit. There were persistent rumours that the Highlanders were preparing to fight back against the authorities. Wyatt wanted to be on hand in order to quash such foolishness before it involved the Army.

One day, as Wyatt was trying to make room in the school for three more homeless families, Mairi came down from the mountains to find him.

Surrounded by the bewildered crying children of the latest arrivals, Wyatt was crouching beside an elderly cottar woman, trying to explain why she had to give up some of the tiny floor-space previously allotted to her. His combination of firmness and cajoling achieved only partial success, but he gained enough floor-space for the mother and her smallest children to sit down.

Straightening up, Wyatt found Mairi standing before him, cradling one of the youngest new arrivals in her arms. The families had spent the night in the open, on the mountains. The baby's face still bore smudges from the smoke of its burning home and mud from the earth of the mountains, mixed together by tears and rubbed in with grubby fists.

'I seem to have chosen a bad time to come and see you.' Mairi's smile was thin, and Wyatt thought she looked tired and pale.

'There are no good times right now.' Wyatt could not conceal his delight at seeing her. It was an unexpected bright spot in the increasing burden of misery descending upon him from the Highlands. 'But any day when I can look at you has to be a good one.' There were only three weeks to go before their planned wedding. This Sunday he would read out the first of their banns.

Relieving Mairi of the child and passing it to its mother, Wyatt gripped Mairi's arm and led her out through the back door of the schoolhouse. The kitchen garden was here, carefully and lovingly cultivated by Alasdair Burns. No one had been allotted camping-space here – yet. Overlooked by many cottar families all around, it lacked privacy, but at least it was possible to talk quietly without being overheard.

'Is all well with you, Mairi? And the family . . . Tibbie?'

'Tibbie's recovered from the beating she took. For the rest of it . . . I don't think she'll ever forget.' She hesitated a moment. 'I don't think Ian or Father is able to forget it, either. They both look upon it as a personal humiliation. An attack on their manhood. It doesn't make it any easier for Tibbie.'

'They've avenged any insult to the family honour. The whole of the Highlands is aware of it. We must hope the commanding officer of the Irish soldiers never learns what really happened, or regimental honour will become involved, too. We can do without that. Our only hope is that the clearances will end soon and the soldiers leave. Then perhaps people will be able to start piecing their lives together.'

Mairi studied the ground at her feet intently. 'Pa says the only way to get rid of the soldiers is to drive them out. To fight and beat them.'

'That's nonsense, Mairi. *Dangerous* nonsense. The days are long gone when the clans could rise and drive an English army from the Highlands. We have no clans any more. The old chiefs are gone – and the old clan loyalties. Most of the landowners are living in London, and half are English. We've grown weaker over the years, while the English hold has grown a thousand times stronger.'

'Ma tried to tell Pa the same thing, but he won't listen. He told her that if Wellington had accepted the odds against him the French would still be occupying Spain.'

'What will he do? I've been hearing alarming rumours for days, but no one can tell me anything.'

Mairi shook her head. 'I don't know. There are armed men coming and going at all hours of the day and night. *I'm* worried, Wyatt.' Mairi suddenly looked desperately unhappy. 'I want to marry you, Wyatt, but I *can't* – not until things are more settled.'

Her words filled Wyatt with alarm. 'You mustn't say that, Mairi. I *need* you. I need you far more than a man of God should ever need anyone. Things will be better soon, you'll see.'

Wyatt had never seen Mairi looking so upset, and he put an arm about her. 'Come in the kitchen and have a hot drink. Evangeline's in there trying to make a few fishes and a little bread go far enough to cure the hunger pangs of a whole multitude. Alasdair should be back soon. He's gone off to the head of the loch to beg some salmon from the fishermen there. . . .'

Inside the kitchen Evangeline took one look at Mairi's taut tired face and produced a cup of tea so quickly it might have been awaiting the Highland girl's arrival.

'I've just this minute made this. Have you come down to settle your wedding arrangements with Wyatt? The whole village is looking forward to the great day. . . .' The old animosity between the two women had long since disappeared.

Mairi shook her head. 'There can be no wedding. Not just yet.'

'What you mean is until my father brings the clearances to an end?' Evangeline spoke with great bitterness. 'I wish I could tell you there would be no more, but he refuses to discuss it with me. I've tried ranting, reason and weeping. I've begged him to come here and see for himself what his clearances are doing, in the hope it might change his ways. He won't listen to me, or to anyone else. Clearing the Kilmalie lands has become an obsession with him.'

'Then, there's little hope of our croft being left alone?' Mairi asked the question in a flat resigned voice that Wyatt found distressing.

'If I could give you some hope. . . .' Evangeline left the sentence unfinished.

'The soldiers are killing livestock, too, wherever they find them, so the cottars will have no excuse for returning to the mountains. I've said I'll take the cattle to the shielings; they should be safe there.'

'You'll not go to the shielings – even if you take all your brothers along to guard you. Not after what happened to Tibbie.' Wyatt was aghast at the thought of Mairi taking cattle to the lonely Highland glens. There would have been safety in the numbers to be found at the shielings in previous seasons. This year there were few tenants left, and Irish soldiers were roaming the hills.

'The soldiers who attacked Tibbie were deserters . . . renegades. You said so yourself, and *they'll* attack no one again.'

'There are others. The shielings are no place for a young girl.'

'Wyatt's right—' Whatever else Evangeline was going to say was lost as those in the kitchen heard a commotion outside and a young voice calling for 'the minister'.

Wyatt had almost reached the door when it crashed open. Young Ewan Munro stumbled on the doorstep and fell headlong inside the kitchen.

The dishevelled boy scrambled to his feet and clutched at Wyatt's coat. 'Minister, Mr Burns says to tell you to come . . . come *quickly*! The soldiers are on their way to our place.'

Ewan Munro was gasping for breath. He had been running as fast as his legs would carry him, but there was more to be said.

'Pa's sick again, but he's got his knife.' Ewan's voice broke. 'He . . . he says he'll die before the factor puts us out again.'

CHAPTER FORTY-FIVE

THE FISHERMEN at the north-west end of Loch Eil lived on the opposite bank of the loch from Kilmalie lands. They were not affected by John Garrett's clearance plans. All the same, their sympathies lay with the dispossessed Highlanders. When Alasdair Burns asked them to sell some of their catch to help feed the many homeless families occupying the Eskaig school and churchyard, they offered him as much of their catch as he could carry, and would not accept payment. Salmon was food for servants and fisherfolk. There was no money to be made from such fish, and they had netted more than they would use.

The fishermen provided Alasdair Burns with an old piece of fishing-net in which to carry the salmon, but while they were tying it together one of the fishermen suddenly said: 'You'd better be taking an extra fish, Teacher. It looks as though the Army is on its way to burn out another poor soul.'

Alasdair Burns looked to where the fisherman was pointing and saw a single file of scarlet-uniformed men making their way down a mountain slope towards the comparatively flat ground at the head of Loch Eil. They had come from Fort William through the glens that cut deep into the mountains, north of Eskaig.

At first, Alasdair Burns thought the soldiers might be making for the road, in order to return to Fort William through Eskaig. However, before they reached level ground the soldiers changed direction. They were still descending, but were now heading *away* from Eskaig and Loch Eil. They were still about their despicable business – and the only croft in the direction they were taking belonged to Lachlan Munro.

'Damn them for the villains they are. They're on their way to dispossess a sick man. I'll be back for the fish later. I'm going to see if I can stop them.'

Alasdair Burns set off at speed, hopping in an ungainly manner on his one good leg and the wooden stump. Behind him there was a brief flurry of conversation between the half-dozen or so fishermen. Hastily covering the fish to prevent wheeling gulls from stealing them, they hurried after Alasdair Burns.

The home of Lachlan Munro was no more than a mile away. Alasdair Burns reached it while the soldiers were still making their way from the mountains. His first action was to send Ewan Munro to Eskaig to inform Wyatt of what was about to happen.

Next Alasdair Burns urged Elsa Munro to remove as many of her belongings as possible from the house and hide them in the bushes. The evicted tenants who had found their way to the schoolhouse in Eskaig had reported that the soldiers were no longer giving the Highlanders time to remove their possessions. An armful of clothes and hastily snatched-up pots and pans were all most had been able to bring out before lighted torches were thrown inside the cot and greedy flames swallowed up everything a Highland woman held dear.

Lachlan Munro was helped outside from his sick bed, protesting he would not be dispossessed by a bunch of 'Irish thugs'.

The ex-soldier was a very sick man. Laid low so often with the fever he had contracted in Africa, Lachlan Munro had fallen victim to a wasting lung disease. Never a large man, he was now little more than skin and bone, and acutely aware of his lack of strength.

'Just come and sit over here, and keep out of trouble.' Alasdair Burns was a bluff direct man, but he spoke as soothingly as he knew how to Lachlan Munro. 'We can always find a new home for you, but these pretty little girls of yours have only one father.'

The Kilmalie factor was not with the men coming to evict the Munro family. The clearance order was in the hands of a constable from Fort William, and he had an escort of twenty soldiers from the Irish infantry regiment.

While the party was still on high ground they could see the activity about the Munro cot, and the constable correctly guessed the reason. Serving clearance orders on hapless Highlanders was not to the law officer's liking. He suggested the soldiers rest as soon as they reached level ground. It would give the Munro family extra time to clear their belongings.

It also meant that Wyatt, Evangeline and Mairi, accompanied by a number of dispossessed cottars from the school, had time to reach the scene.

They arrived soon after the constable had served the clearance order on Lachlan Munro, but before the lighted torches held by two of the soldiers had been applied to the cot.

Alasdair Burns was haranguing the constable and his escort with some success, and the sergeant in charge of the party had not yet given the order to fire the building.

With the arrival of a hostile and vociferous crowd of Highlanders, the uncertainty of the Fort William constable grew. The Irish sergeant had more experience in dealing with hostile crowds and he ordered his soldiers to fix bayonets and face towards the newcomers.

Alasdair Burns was not pleased to see Evangeline among the new arrivals, but he did not allow it to halt his rhetoric. He pointed to her companions as an example of the numbers of ordinary people made homeless by the Army and the authorities they were supporting.

The teacher's argument began to excite the homeless cottars, and the constable from Fort William became increasingly concerned. In sharp contrast, the Irish sergeant viewed the Highlanders with a calm disdain. He would be the man to make a decision, and it was to him that Wyatt directed his appeal.

'You've carried out your duty, Sergeant. The constable has served the clearance notice. Why don't you take your men on now, before there's trouble?'

The sergeant was aware from Wyatt's mode of dress that he was a minister, but the soldier had little time for representatives of any church.

'I don't need a preacher telling me how to carry out my duties. If there's going to be trouble, it will come as a result of the one-legged man. He's making your people excited with his talk. When he fastens his lip I'll put a torch to the cot and we'll be on our way — unless you have something else planned?'

'My concern is for Lachlan Munro and his young family. He's a sick man, Sergeant. He was an army man, too, with the Seventy-

Second Regiment until he was struck down with fever in Natal – a sergeant, like yourself.'

The Irish sergeant cast a quick glance to where Lachlan Munro sat propped against a low wall, head back, talking softly to his son.

'He has my sympathy. A brave man deserves something better than a lingering death. But he'll be the first to understand I'm merely doing my duty. No more, and no less.'

'You've *done* your duty. The constable has served the notice. Won't you just leave now, *without* firing the cot?'

'My colonel's orders are to burn every cot as soon as a clearance order is served. There's to be no reoccupation. These people are lucky to have had so long to clear their belongings. Had the colonel been here today, everything would have gone up in flames within a minute of the order being served. As it is, I think it's high time I took my men back to barracks.'

Without any further warning, the sergeant signalled to the two men who held the flaming torches. Acknowledging his command, the two men turned towards the cot. One man threw his torch high on the thatched roof. For a moment it seemed the burning brand would roll back down to earth, but it caught in a piece of protruding twig, and flames began to eat into the thick thatch.

The second man went to the open door and threw his torch into a corner where the three youngest Munro girls had shared a dry-heather bed. There was a momentary lull, and then the heather ignited with a great roar. Seconds later flames were licking up through the roof.

As the crowd watched in momentary awe, a distraction came from an unexpected direction. The soldiers were keeping the crowd well clear of the house, but Lachlan's position was to the side and slightly behind their line. He suddenly emerged out of the smoke billowing downwards from the roof. He was weaving an erratic course, and it was not immediately certain where he was heading.

The Irish sergeant did not wait to find out. Pushing two of his soldiers aside, he darted between them and held out an arm to bar Lachlan Munro's path.

'Come on, old soldier. There's nothing for you in there now. Take your family off somewhere and make a new life—'

He never finished the sentence. Lachlan Munro closed with the Irish sergeant, there was a flash of bright steel and the sergeant reeled back, one hand clutching his stomach. It was a cut, not a stab wound, but there was sufficient blood in evidence to make it appear far worse than it really was.

Pandemonium broke out beside the burning cot. One of the Irish soldiers leaped at Lachlan Munro. Even as Wyatt shouted at him, he lunged forward with his musket and the long spike-like bayonet passed right through the sick man's frail body.

Lachlan Munro sat down heavily, still spitted on the soldier's bayonet. The soldier pulled it free with some difficulty, and as Lachlan Munro slipped sideways to the ground the soldier raised his musket to bayonet him again. Wyatt ran to his aid, but Ewan Munro was quicker. Darting beneath the threatening bayonets of the other soldiers, Lachlan Munro's young son cannoned into his father's attacker and knocked him off balance.

Another soldier went to the aid of his colleague, but suddenly the line of soldiers broke before the combined weight of the dispossessed Kilmalie cottars and the Loch Eil fishermen. As Wyatt knocked down the soldier who was about to strike Ewan Munro, a shot was fired from near at hand. Wyatt heard the booming voice of the Irish sergeant calling for his men to rally around him – and then he heard nothing more as a rifle-butt slammed against the side of his head. Wyatt slumped to the ground where he was trampled by the feet of soldiers and Highlanders.

A number of those in the crowd saw Wyatt knocked to the ground, and two of them fought their way towards him. Mairi reached him first and she crouched above him, doing her best to protect him from the feet of the brawling, shouting men all about them.

Alasdair Burns was less successful. Throwing soldiers clear as he met with them, he had almost gained his fallen friend when he was confronted by a soldier as large as himself. The soldier's bayonet-thrust was avoided easily enough, but the backward swing of the musket knocked the schoolteacher off balance.

Self-preservation was now uppermost in Alasdair Burns's mind, and he grasped the soldier about the waist, pulling him to the ground. As the two men rolled over, wrestling, the sergeant shouted for his men to 'arrest the one-legged troublemaker'.

His order was obeyed by a soldier who set about subduing Alasdair Burns with the butt of his musket.

Until this happened Evangeline had remained a horrified onlooker, but as the soldier continued to rain blows upon Alasdair Burns she leaped to his rescue.

Evangeline prevented further injury to Alasdair Burns, but the sergeant who was skilfully withdrawing his party from the affray shouted at his men to bring her and Alasdair Burns with them.

CHAPTER FORTY-SIX

WHEN WYATT regained consciousness he was unable immediately to distinguish between the roaring inside his own head and the sound of the wind-fed flames noisily consuming the thatch of the cot. As he sat up he winced with pain, and Mairi's arm went about him.

'Thank the Lord you're all right. You've been unconscious for so long I thought they might have broken your head.'

Wyatt only just stopped himself in time from shaking his head — and then he remembered how he had acquired the pain. He looked about him. He could see many people in the swirling smoke, but none wore a uniform.

'Where are the soldiers . . . and Lachlan?' Wyatt struggled to rise, although his head felt as heavy as a mortar-shell.

'The soldier's bayonet must have pierced his lung. He's a dying man. They've laid him over there, away from the smoke.' Mairi pointed to where a group of Highlanders were gathered on the lee side of the cot.

Wyatt made his way shakily towards them, and they stood back respectfully to allow him through. Lachlan lay on the bare trampled earth. Elsa Munro was on her knees beside him, weeping silently as she held one of her husband's hands in her own, patting it abstractedly. The Munro girls stood in a pathetic line nearby, also crying. Ewan Munro was the only tear-free face in the family, although there was enough anguish in his expression for all of them.

Wyatt dropped to one knee beside the ex-soldier, and the man who had endured so much pain managed the semblance of a weak smile. Lachlan Munro also tried to speak, but Wyatt needed to put his ear within an inch of the other man's lips in order to hear what he had to say.

'This is a better way to go . . . Captain. A man's way.'

'It's a *good* man's way, Lachlan. A courageous man. You've never been short of courage. The Lord has a special place in heaven for brave men.'

Lachlan Munro wanted to speak again, and Wyatt's ear brushed the dying man's lips.

'It's been a good life, Captain. . . .'

Without moving his head, Wyatt's eyes took in the ex-soldier's ragged children and the house that had been derelict before Lachlan Munro was given the tenancy for his last, pain-filled year. Yet he could speak of 'a *good* life.'

'Ewan . . . I must speak to Ewan.' The blood was bubbling in Lachlan Munro's throat now, and Wyatt signalled urgently for Ewan to come and take his place.

The boy kneeled at his father's side for perhaps two minutes, his ear close enough to catch the dying man's last words. Then a great shudder ran through Lachlan Munro's body and all pain left him.

Else Munro let out a great wail of anguish, and Mairi went to her. Ewan Munro stood up, still looking down at his father, and for a moment it seemed he, too, must break down and cry. Wyatt held out his arms to the boy, and for a while Ewan clung to him. Then he pushed himself away and squared his shoulders with a conscious effort.

'I'll go to the girls now. They'll need comforting. As Pa told me, I'm the man in the Munro family now.'

Wyatt watched as the young boy went to his five young sisters and encompassed them in his arms. Then he realised one of the cottars was speaking to him, and he turned to face the man.

'What will you be doing about the teacher and the Garrett girl? She's not a bad lass, for all she has the factor's blood in her veins.'

Wyatt looked about him, and for the first time realised Alasdair Burns and Evangeline were nowhere to be seen.

Elsa Munro had gone to her children, and Mairi guessed for whom Wyatt was looking.

'They've been taken by the Army. Alasdair tried to help you when you were knocked down. Then Evangeline became involved, and the soldiers took them both away.'

'Took them where?' Suddenly Wyatt's head was hurting more than ever.

'I don't know. Fort William, I suppose.'

'I must go and arrange their release.' Wyatt felt confused. 'How long ago did all this happen?'

'Half an hour, perhaps longer. So much has happened.' Mairi looked at his face, and she was concerned by what she saw. Wyatt was like a man in a dream. 'You'd better sit down. You look *awful*.'

'Was anyone else arrested?'

'No, but at least four were hurt. One of the fishermen was shot through an ear. He bled a lot, but it's not serious.'

'The others. . . ?' The two words cost Wyatt considerable effort. The world seemed to be see-sawing away from him.

'Bruises in the main. But you're not all right, are you? You'd better sit down. Here . . . quickly!'

Mairi shouted the last word as Wyatt swayed and would have fallen had she not held on to him, helped by one of the Loch Eil fishermen who had been standing nearby.

'Sit him down here.' With the fisherman supporting him, Mairi struggled to guide Wyatt to a rough-stone seat set against the garden wall. She was very concerned, believing the blows he had taken might have seriously harmed him. As she released her hold, a Highland woman came across to offer help. Without waiting for an answer she slapped Wyatt's face repeatedly.

Failing to achieve any response, the woman grasped Wyatt's wrist, feeling for a pulse. It was not clear whether or not she found it, but after about half a minute she dropped the hand carelessly, then lifted each of Wyatt's eyelids in turn.

'He'll be all right, hen,' she said to Mairi. 'The blow from the Irishman's gun must have bruised his brain, and it's swelled up in his head. When it's gone down again he'll be as right as rain.'

Mairi wished she felt as confident, but a few minutes later Wyatt recovered consciousness once more. He seemed a little vague, but declared nothing was wrong with him. As if to prove his point, he made arrangements for the Munro family to be brought to Eskaig, together with the body of Lachlan Munro.

Clouds were building up in the west. All the signs were that when the wind dropped the rain would come. He had to go to Fort William first, and then he needed to make Eneas Ross see sense. It was a task that had been made very much more difficult by the killing of Lachlan Munro.

By the time the small procession reached Eskaig it had formed itself into a funeral cortège. Wyatt learned that things had been happening here, too. The dispossed tenants and cottars occupying schoolhouse and churchyard were in a state of turmoil. Many of the temporary shelters had been broken up. In the schoolhouse there was now space, where only that morning men, women and children had jostled for elbow room. Even more puzzling to Wyatt was the small stream of Highlanders heading along the road that led to Corpach and Fort William. They carried with them the few meagre possessions they had brought from the mountains.

'What's happening?' Wyatt confronted a family of man, wife and five young children, none of the children more than seven years of age. They had come to Eskaig from a lonely cot, deep in the mountains, one of the first families to be evicted in this latest series of clearances.

'The factor's been here while you were away. He told us there'll never again be a place for us in the Highlands. He's arranged for two ships to be at Fort William to take us to Canada. The first is boarding now and leaves in a day or two. The other is due in a few weeks. There's a free passage and five pounds in cash for every family who accepts his offer. We're taking it.'

'What will you and the others do in Canada? Think about it, man. You've seven mouths to feed. Five pounds will last you no time at all. What will you do when it's gone?'

'Factor Garrett says there's free land for the asking in Canada.' The man shrugged. 'What have we to lose, Minister Jamieson? You've worked hard to give us food and warmth here, but there are three times as many Highlanders still in the mountains. You can't support us all. And what will happen when we're drummed off Eskaig land? You're right, five pounds won't last long – but until it's gone we'll have hope. There's precious little of that here.'

'Have you inspected the ships? How large are they? What condition are they in?' There was desperation in Wyatt's voice. 'I've *seen* emigrant-ships. I wouldn't travel in one as far as the Islands, yet you're trusting them with your life and the lives of your family on a voyage that will take weeks – *months* even. Think about it. For the sake of your family, *think about it.*'

Wyatt's plea went unheeded, 'I've done all the thinking that's necessary, Minister. There's nothing for us here any more. Look, *there* are your clansmen of the future.'

As though it had been arranged to mock the Highlanders, a huge flock of sheep was being driven from Corpach, forcing the departing refugees off the road, some to higher ground, others to the rock-strewn shore of the loch.

Another man, one of the family of the centenarian Wyatt had buried in the Eskaig churchyard, came to stand beside Wyatt as the sheep approached. 'He's right, Minister. They're the new laird's clansmen. They'll serve him as well as we ever did. He'll drive them where he wants. They'll bleed for him, die for him – and he'll end up with money in his pocket earned by their suffering. There's no difference between us at all.'

Wyatt had hoped to bury Lachlan Munro that same day, but Elsa Munro was deeply distressed at such haste. She declared tearfully that Lachlan had been stripped of all pride and dignity in the latter years of his life. She wanted her courageous husband laid in his grave with all the rights due to him. She wanted him to 'lie in', so that all those who had known him could come and pay their last respects to the former Highland soldier. She also wanted him buried in a wooden coffin, although she was less certain where the money would come from.

Wyatt said he would pay for the coffin, and when one of the Free Church elders offered his house for the 'lying in' Wyatt agreed to put off the ceremony for a day or two. It made a lot of sense. Far more important at the moment were the problems of the living – Alasdair Burns and Evangeline Garrett in particular. He also wanted to inspect the emigrant-ship and distribute some of the money left to him by Lord Kilmalie to the emigrating Highlanders. He must also make yet another attempt to speak to John Garrett.

Mairi had been watching Wyatt as he spoke to Elsa Munro and the elder. His pale face and abstracted manner concerned her. When Wyatt went inside the schoolhouse prior to setting off to learn what had happened to the two schoolteachers, she followed him.

'Are you certain you're well enough to go to Fort William? At least leave it until morning. . . .'

'Too much can happen overnight in a prison. I'll be all right.'

'Then, I'll come with you.'

'No!' It sounded too abrupt, too sharp, and Mairi showed her hurt. 'I'm grateful to you, Mairi. Had you not been with me, I, too, might be in the Fort William tolbooth now.' Putting his hands on her shoulders, he said: 'I want you to go home. Tell your father the Irish have tasted Scots blood and they'll be out for more. *He and his friends must do nothing to give them an excuse to attack Highlanders again.* Tell him I'm speaking now as a former army captain, not as a minister of the Church. We must do everything we can to cool things down.'

Wyatt gripped Mairi's shoulders more tightly. 'Meanwhile, you stay close to your home, you understand? There's to be no thought of going to the shielings. If you're still living in the mountains when this trouble is over, there'll be no shortage of grazing. If not . . . well, the sheep will have eaten all the grass in the shielings anyway. Do you promise me you'll do nothing foolish?'

Mairi nodded her agreement.

There were people about them, and Wyatt was able to give her only the briefest of kisses. 'Take care, Mairi. I want us to be married – and soon.'

'You take care too, Wyatt. And don't trust the Factor.'

Wyatt remembered Mairi's words as he neared the Garrett house on the Corpach and Fort William road. Nevertheless he turned into the long tree-lined drive and went to the house to speak to John Garrett.

The Kilmalie factor was not at home. Charlotte Garrett took him to the sitting-room and insisted he take tea with her before continuing his journey to Fort William.

Charlotte Garrett looked better than he had ever seen her, but Wyatt told her nothing of Evangeline's arrest; her sanity was far too precariously balanced. John Garrett was expected home that evening, and Wyatt left word he was on his way to Fort William on a most urgent matter. He suggested the factor should join him there without delay.

Charlotte Garrett was intrigued by Wyatt's secrecy, but when her questions were evaded she made no attempt to press him. She promised to pass on his message to her husband as soon as he returned home.

CHAPTER FORTY-SEVEN

JOHN GARRETT caught up with Wyatt in Fort William, only a few hundred yards from the tolbooth, the town's formidable stone-built administrative centre and gaol.

The factor's horse was hot and lathered. John Garrett had ridden up to his Corpach home and left again immediately upon receiving Wyatt's message. It was not because the factor believed the Eskaig minister had anything of importance to tell him. Garrett welcomed any excuse that would take him to Fort William.

'I've been told you need to see me "urgently", Jamieson. What is it – are *you* wanting to emigrate, too? Or have you decided to return to the *real* church? Whatever it is had better be important, or I'll have you charged for the weight I've run off my horse.'

'What do *you* call important, Garrett? A sick man killed by the soldiers who served your clearance order? His wife and six young children left without a father? Or news that your daughter's been arrested because she couldn't stand by and do nothing while Irish soldiers broke Scots heads?'

'What are you talking about? Evangeline isn't mixed up in any of this – unless it's your doing. Where is she?'

'That's what I'm here to find out.' Wyatt nodded towards the great grim tolbooth. 'My guess is she's in there.'

John Garrett's face registered horror as his gaze went from Wyatt to the tolbooth, and back again.

'You'd better be wrong, Jamieson. If Evangeline's been arrested, it will be due to *your* influence. You and that Glasgow rabble-rouser you've got in to teach school. I told her she should never have involved herself with Eskaig. Perhaps she'll be ready to listen to me now.'

'Will *you* listen to me and end the misery, heartbreak – yes, and *murder* resulting from your clearances? Bring them to a halt, Garrett. If you continue, there's going to be bloodshed in these mountains on a scale not seen since Cumberland's men set out to exterminate the Highlander.'

'Had Cumberland carried out his duties properly, I wouldn't have to be clearing Kilmalie land today. I've made the tenants a generous offer. Free passage to a new life and five pounds in their pockets when they get there. If you're so damned concerned about them, you'll make certain they go – *and* travel with them yourself.'

'Five pounds to compensate for all you and the soldiers have burned? That's generous? Even at the height of the Sutherland clearances the tenants were being given twenty-five pounds for new roof-timbers – and time to remove possessions and livestock.'

A peculiar expression crossed John Garrett's face, and in that moment Wyatt knew the truth. 'You've *been* given money to compensate dispossessed tenants – probably by the late Lord Kilmalie. It's the sort of thing he'd do; he was a generous man. How much did he give you, Garrett? What *should* the Highlanders be getting?'

'Go to hell, Jamieson! Better still, sail away to Canada with your own kind. You've no church, no status – and by the time winter comes there will be no one left to hear you preach. Get out before you lose everything and have *nowhere* to go.'

John Garrett swung his horse away and rode on to the tolbooth. He had to tether his horse some way from the entrance to the tolbooth building, and both men entered together, neither speaking to the other.

In answer to the clerk on duty inside the tolbooth office, John Garrett declared loudly that he had come to make enquiries about his daughter. Wyatt explained he was there on behalf of Alasdair Burns.

Both men were asked to remain in the office while the clerk went off to report their presence to his superior.

They waited in silence for perhaps ten minutes before the clerk returned, preceded by a rotund bald-headed little man whose forehead glistened with small beads of perspiration. He addressed himself immediately to the factor.

'Mr Garrett! I am Jeremiah Buchanan, sheriff's clerk. A delight to meet you, sir. I trust our little, ah ... *error* hasn't caused you to make a special journey here.'

The sheriff's clerk faltered, and his expression became that of a desperately worried man. 'I can assure you, sir, I had your daughter released from custody the *moment* I learned she was here. I have also protested in the strongest possible terms to the commanding officer of the Irish regiment. I have demanded that the man who ordered the arrests be *severely* punished and an apology tendered to your good self. I don't doubt—'

'Where's my daughter now?' John Garrett's brusque question brought to an end the protestations of the perspiring sheriff's clerk.

'At the inn. She and Mr Burns went there after ... a short while ago.'

'*Burns*? You had that rogue in prison and released him?'

The beads of perspiration joined together and found twin paths on either side of the bald temples to the clerk's plump cheeks.

'I had no alternative, Mr Garrett. Not after Mr Graham came in and ordered the sheriff-substitute to call in the clearance orders.'

'Mr Graham ... the Kilmalie estate administrator? He ... *called in the clearance orders*? He has no authority to interfere with my orders. What was he doing here? Where is he now?' John Garrett was beside himself with rage.

'Staying at the coaching inn, a few hundred paces along the road. Your daughter and Mr Burns are there, too.'

'We'll soon see about *that*! It's time I put a stop to that girl's nonsense once and for all. I should never have allowed her to teach at that damned school.'

Scowling deeply, John Garrett headed for the door. He had reached the doorway when the sheriff's clerk called to him, with desperation in his voice: 'Your daughter and Mr Burns ... they're married, sir.'

John Garrett spun around, and his expression caused the sheriff's clerk to back away, speaking rapidly in a bid to impart his news as hastily as possible. 'They were married by declaration, with the magistrate and Mr Graham as witnesses—'

'*Married by declaration?*' The veins stood out on the temples of the factor's blood-diffused face. 'That's a form of marriage used by cottars ... *peasants*! It can't be legal for the daughter of a *gentleman*. I'll see the magistrate and have it annulled.'

'Your daughter was very determined, Mr Garrett. She insisted. . . .'

'If what the clerk has said is true, there's nothing you or anyone else can do, Garrett. The marriage is as legal as if she'd been married by me – or by your archbishop in his cathedral of Canterbury. That's why so many English couples cross the border to be married. I believe the village of Gretna is becoming quite renowned for its "marriages by declaration".'

Wyatt was only marginally less surprised than the factor, although he was well aware of the way Alasdair and Evangeline felt about each other. But to get married in such a manner. . . . He tried hard not to take delight in the factor's discomfiture.

'We'll see about this! I'll not have my only daughter married to a political agitator . . . a gaolbird. I've some strong words to say to Charles Graham. *Very* strong words.'

John Garrett stamped from the office, and Jeremiah Buchanan sought a chair and dropped into it gratefully.

Wyatt hurried from the tolbooth to the inn and was close on John Garrett's heels when he came face to face with the Kilmalie estate administrator just inside the inn entrance.

Charles Graham was taken by surprise, but he recovered quickly, although there was no pleasure in his greeting. He extended his hand towards the factor. 'I was on my way to find a carriage and pay you a visit—'

'What's the meaning of putting yourself forward as a witness to this so-called marriage? *And* having the sheriff-substitute call in my clearance orders? You're the administrator of the Kilmalie estates, but I'm the factor in Eskaig. In *sole* control. *I* give the orders.'

A number of passers-by had stopped, attracted by the loud voice of the factor. Charles Graham said: 'I suggest we go inside and discuss this privately. Or would you prefer to see your daughter and her new husband first?'

'I'll deal with her later. Let's get *this* business straightened out first.'

John Garrett pushed past the Edinburgh-based administrator and entered the inn. Charles Graham saw Wyatt for the first time. 'You'd better come in, too, Minister Jamieson. What I have to say affects you and your people.'

The inn door was open, and John Garrett heard the lawyer's

words. Turning, he pointed a quivering finger at Wyatt. 'The business of the Kilmalie estate doesn't concern him. If you have something to say about Kilmalie lands, you can tell me in private. Jamieson doesn't even have a church in Eskaig now.'

'Nevertheless, he is the man chosen by the parishioners to be their pastor. *I* want him to hear what I have to tell you.' Charles Graham waved Wyatt inside the inn. 'After you, Minister Jamieson.'

Charles Graham paused to have a brief conversation with the innkeeper, which led to the three men being shown to a small private room.

'Please take a seat, gentlemen. I have ordered refreshments.' Charles Graham waved the others to seats as he placed his pince-nez on his nose. Unfastening an oilskin-wrapped bundle, he extracted a number of papers and proceeded to arrange them neatly on the table in front of him.

John Garrett's impatience would not allow him to sit still in the chair he occupied. He changed position frequently, his scowl deepening with the passing of time.

'Come on, man. You don't need a whole bundle of papers to explain why you countermanded my orders. Get on with it.'

'True, John. I don't need any papers to explain *why* I countermanded your instructions. However, I will probably require them in order to prove I have the authority to do so.'

When the papers were arranged to Charles Graham's satisfaction, the landlord appeared, holding open the door for a serving-girl carrying a laden try to enter. John Garrett fumed impotently as the Edinburgh administrator fussed about, ensuring that food and drink were placed within reach of his two guests.

Almost as though he was enjoying the irascibility of the Eskaig factor, Charles Graham maintained his silence on the subject of the meeting until the door had closed behind the innkeeper and his servant.

'Now, gentlemen, you are no doubt anxious to know what it is I have to say to you. . . .' Only the slightest pause acknowledged John Garrett's sarcastic derision. 'I can assure you it has an important bearing not only on the lives of each of us here, but also on very many more people connected with Kilmalie lands here and elsewhere.'

Charles Graham took a sip from a large brandy-glass and looked over the rim of his pince-nez at each of the two men in turn.

'You will recall that the three of us last met together in Eskaig when I came to inform you of the death of the late Lord Kilmalie . . . Lord *Cloudesley* Kilmalie.'

'Of course we remember. That's when *I* showed *you* the new Lord Kilmalie's letter giving me full authority to run the Eskaig estate in whatever manner *I* thought best. *Without interference* was what that meant.'

'You showed me a letter *purporting* to invest you with a great deal of authority, certainly.'

'Purporting? *Purporting?*' John Garrett was on his feet in an instant. Fists resting on the table, he glared menacingly at Charles Graham. 'Are you suggesting I *forged* that letter? By God, sir. I'll take you to the courts for such infamous slander.'

'*Slander*, John? Dear me, I've said nothing *slanderous*, surely? No, no. I accept that you presented the letter to me in all good faith. You believed *implicitly* in the authority contained therein – as indeed *I* did, at the time. Unfortunately, I fear the letter is absolutely worthless. You may as well use it as a taper to light your pipe.'

John Garrett was rarely lost for words, but for some moments he was speechless. When his voice finally returned he poured scorn on the Edinburgh administrator's statement.

'Are you trying to tell me Major Jock is an impostor? I don't believe you. This is a trick thought up by you and Jamieson to prevent me clearing the Highlanders from Eskaig.'

'It's no trick, John, and Major Jock was no imposter – at least, he *was* the genuine heir to the Kilmalie lands.'

'You're talking in riddles, man. If he's the genuine heir, then the authority in the letter in my possession is genuine, too.'

'Unfortunately not. You see, Major Jock never inherited the titles and estates of Lord Kilmalie. The ship in which he was returning to Australia foundered off the South African coast *three days before the late Lord Kilmalie died.*'

John Garrett stared at Charles Graham as the implication of his words sank in. 'You're lying. All right, Major Jock *may* be dead, but how do you know it happened *before* Lord Kilmalie died, eh? How can you prove *that?*'

Charles Graham sighed. 'I said I would need to supply you with proof of what I had to say. I have here statements from two of the ship's officers who survived the disaster. I also have statements from three surviving passengers. All witnessed the sad death of Major Jock. Needless to say, it has taken me some time to obtain these statements.'

John Garrett was shaken to the core, but he tried to pull himself together and exert the authority he believed he still possessed. 'If what you say is true, my letter *may* be worthless, but I *am* still factor of the Kilmalie Eskaig estate. I can still run it in the manner I think is best.'

'Not quite, John. Yes, you *are* the factor, although no doubt *my* recommendations to the new Lord Kilmalie will be considered very carefully — especially after I complete my investigations into the whereabouts of large sums of money paid by owners of sheep to obtain sheep-walks on Kilmalie land. Money that has failed to reach my office. In the mean time, as executor for the late Lord Kilmalie I, too, possess wide powers. I have exercised those powers today, by having your remaining clearance orders called in. Will you kindly ensure that any still in your possession and not yet executed is returned to the sheriff's office at the earliest opportunity?'

Charles Graham leaned back in his chair, the palms of his hands flat on the table before him. 'I would like you to continue as factor for the Eskaig estate — at least, for the time being. I expect you to do so with the good of the estate at heart. Are there any questions you wish to put to me, John?'

John Garrett stood up abruptly, the muscles of his face twitching. 'Go to hell, Graham — and don't gloat, *Minister Jamieson*. I'm not done yet. Not by a long way.'

The factor stalked from the room, very nearly knocking over the serving-girl as she returned to the room.

'Oh dear.' Charles Graham looked at Wyatt in mock surprise. 'I seem to have upset John — and I never told him of his daughter's marriage to Alasdair Burns!'

'He knows.' Wyatt stood up and shook the hand of the Edinburgh man warmly. 'Coming as it does on top of your news, he won't want to face his new son-in-law just yet. Returning to *your* news, who *is* the new Lord Kilmalie?'

'Ah! Now, there's something that's kept a great many people busy. Major Jock was Lord Kilmalie's only close relative, and it's been necessary to make extensive enquiries to find an heir to the Kilmalie estates. It *has* been settled, at last, although there is still doubt about the inheritance of the title. Fortunately, the title has very little significance for the man who now possesses the Kilmalie lands. He already has a somewhat superior peerage of his own. Indeed, it must be one of the oldest titles in the land.'

'Who *is* the man with this ancient title?' Wyatt prompted.

'I'm sorry, didn't I say? It's the Earl of Glenadon – the *sixteenth* Earl. Isn't he some relation to the minister you brought to one of my parties in Edinburgh?'

Wyatt nodded, his thoughts ranging too far ahead for speech. This could prove to be the best news Eskaig would ever have. The Kilmalie estates had been inherited by the brother of Minister Coll Kennedy!

That evening was spent in a strange mixture of celebration and sadness for Wyatt. Celebration because Alasdair and Evangeline were wed and the tenants of the Kilmalie Eskaig estate were to enjoy at least a temporary reprieve from the clearances. Sadness as he remembered the death of Lachlan Munro and the fact that the Eskaig Highlanders might have only a temporary reprieve. It would certainly not affect the extensive clearances being carried out elsewhere. Wyatt accepted he was witnessing the passing of a way of life. One that had been doomed since the Highland forces of the young Prince Charles Stuart suffered a crushing defeat on the battlefield of Culloden, almost a hundred years before. Yet, after Culloden, the surviving clan chiefs and their followers had shared a fierce pride in retaining their joint heritage. Now it was the successors of Scotland's hereditary chiefs, the 'lairds', the landowners, who were clearing the Highlands to make way for sheep.

Wyatt had taken a room at the inn, it proving impossible to return to Eskaig that evening. There was no moon that night to guide him along the indifferent roads. Besides, in the morning he intended travelling north to Letterfinlay, to speak to Coll Kennedy.

Wyatt had warned Evangeline and Alasdair to expect John

Garrett to interrupt their celebrations, but the evening passed without incident. Either Garrett had verified the legality of the Scots form of marriage and decided against confronting his daughter and newly acquired son-in-law, or he was still trying to come to terms with the shattering news he had received from Charles Graham.

CHAPTER FORTY-EIGHT

IT WAS UNDOUBTEDLY Wyatt's feeling of well-being that pro-mpted him to take the shorter and easier route to the cave at Glenfintaig. It took him closer to the home of General Lindsay, the Letterfinlay landowner, but today Wyatt was willing to chance a meeting with the Free Church-hating landowner. He wanted to discuss the new turn of events with Coll Kennedy, and return to Fort William before the emigrant-ship sailed for Canada. By then he hoped to be able to persuade the Highlanders to return to their old homes.

He had asked Alasdair Burns to arrange the funeral of Lachlan Munro for his return, and to despatch someone from Eskaig to inform Eneas Ross of what was happening. By doing this Wyatt hoped to forestall any trouble from the Ross family and their friends.

Wyatt was less than two miles from his destination when he was stopped by a gamekeeper. The man carried a sporting gun and stood among broken rocks to await the arrival of the Eskaig preacher. Wyatt had seen the man when he was still far back along the trail. He had contemplated leaving the trail and scrambling down the slope to the river-fed glen a thousand feet below, but decided against such a move. It would serve no useful purpose. The gamekeeper could do the same and still confront Wyatt if this was what he intended to do.

It was. Stepping on to the path in front of Wyatt, the gamekeeper held his sporting gun pointed at the Eskaig minister as he asked: 'Well, now, what do we have here? And what might a preacher be doing on General Lindsay's land?'

'Good day to you, Keeper. I'm passing through, on my way to see a friend.'

'The general wouldn't be at all pleased with me if he heard I'd allowed a man of the cloth to "pass through" his lands. You see, if you're a minister of the established church, he'll likely offer you refreshment and send you on your way with a donation towards your stipend. If you're not ... well, I'd rather not talk of unhappy things on such a fine day. If you'll just go back the way you've come, you'll see a path leading down towards the bridge. General Lindsay's house is the large one among the trees. I'll be walking right behind you every step of the way.'

They walked without talking all the way to the house, although the gamekeeper occasionally whistled a snatch of a tune.

The house by the bridge was surrounded by a high garden wall, and Wyatt paused at the large wooden gate.

'Go on through. We'll no doubt find the general up at the house. I hope for your sake he's in one of his rare good moods.'

General Alexander Lindsay was not in the house, and he was not in one of his rare good moods. He was in the garden berating a gardener for some minor indiscretion. The gardener was on his knees beside a flowerbed, and the red-faced landowner frequently belaboured his employee about the shoulders with a walking-stick to emphasise a particular criticism.

The footsteps of Wyatt and the gamekeeper crunching on the river-gravel of the path caused the irate landowner to turn to meet the new arrivals. The gardener threw a relieved glance in Wyatt's direction before crouching to his task once more. Then General Lindsay confronted Wyatt.

'I caught a preacher trespassing along the glen towards Upper Glenfintaig, General. I thought you'd want to speak to him.'

'Trespassing, eh? And a minister, my gamekeeper says. *Are* you a minister, or are you one of those turncoats who want to change everything and move another step closer to anarchy – like that scoundrel Kennedy?'

Wyatt's heart sank at the general's disparaging reference to the ejected Letterfinlay minister, but he did not allow it to show.

'I'm a minister of God, General. Accepted by the people of my parish to serve them. But, yes, I *am* looking for Minister Kennedy – that's if it's the same Kennedy you're talking about. Minister *Coll*

Kennedy? Brother of the Earl of Glenadon?'

General Lindsay had spent a lifetime in the Army. He had retired to Scotland and purchased the lands at Letterfinlay. Wyatt knew of Coll Kennedy's reticence in talking of his family and had taken a gamble that the fiery old army man knew nothing of Coll Kennedy's family connections.

The gamble paid off.

'Eh? What are you talking about? I'm speaking of Minister Kennedy who was preacher at my church in Letterfinlay – until he threw in his lot with this new-fangled "free church" nonsense.'

'We're talking of the same man, General. Coll Kennedy is brother to the sixteenth Earl of Glenadon. He's also a man of great principle, prepared to lose a comfortable home and living when there was a clash between material and spiritual considerations.'

While the Letterfinlay landowner mulled over Wyatt's revelation, Wyatt played what he hoped might prove to be his trump card.

'By the way, General. You wouldn't be the officer who fought with the Ninety-Second Regiment through the Peninsular campaigns and as a major held the position on La Haye Sainte at Waterloo?'

'Eh?' General Lindsay was startled. 'That's right, I was at Waterloo – and held the knoll at La Haye Sainte. That's why I have to use this damned stick. But what do you know of it, eh? You're far too young to have been there yourself – and you're a minister, aren't you?'

Wyatt had no intention of reopening *that* discussion, 'I haven't always been a minister. I was in the Army before I studied for the Church. I was a captain in the Seventy-Second. We formed part of Colonel Harry Smith's army in the wars against the kaffirs in Natal. I've often heard him speak of you.'

'Old Harry . . . of the Ninety-Fifth? Now, there was a man with the luck of the devil – if you'll pardon the expression, Minister. At Badajos it was, in Spain. We had to fight damned hard for the town. When the battle was won the troops got out of hand and sacked the place. Someone brought a fourteen-year-old Spanish girl to Harry seeking his protection. Pretty little thing she was, with a trim figure. Damned if Old Harry didn't fall head over heels for the girl and marry her! Most of us thought he was mad, but do you know that girl followed him through the whole campaign. Thought the world of him! Not only that, she turned out to be the finest army wife any soldier could have wished for. She was the making of old Harry Smith.'

The general beamed happily at Wyatt. 'So you fought alongside old Harry Smith, eh? Come on inside the house and share a bottle of something special with me. Not every day I have the opportunity of chatting to another army man. . . .'

With a hand resting affectionately on Wyatt's shoulder, General Lindsay led him to the house and in through the door. Behind him the forgotten gamekeeper watched in disbelief as the two men passed from view.

That afternoon, in the cave high on the mountainside above the river, Wyatt told an incredulous Coll Kennedy that the Letterfinlay minister had been invited to return to his church and the manse from which he had been so forcefully evicted only a few weeks before. What was more, General Lindsay wanted Coll Kennedy to explain to him the reasons why so many ministers had broken away from the Establishment and formed their own church. Of course, if Coll Kennedy also felt able to arrange for the general to be introduced to the sixteenth Earl of Glenadon at some later date. . . .

Coll Kennedy poured another drink for himself when Wyatt shook his head to decline a refill. 'I don't know how you did it, Wyatt. Most of the teachers I've had were inclined to say that modern-day miracles are restricted to the Catholic Church. Now I'm not so certain.'

'The Lord works in devious ways right enough, Coll. I don't doubt He had a hand in sending an ex-army pastor along the short-cut to Tam Vass's distillery today. He probably also had a hand in setting the gamekeeper on sentry duty at the right time. I wouldn't like to analyse His motives, though it could be to return you to your flock. On the other hand, it might be that He wants to remove you from so much temptation.'

'It might also be the power of Tam Vass's prayers. He swears I'm drinking away his profits.' Coll Kennedy took another drink of whisky and looked about him at the smoke-filled cave. 'I'll miss this place, Wyatt. It's been an experience I'll never forget. But being exiled here makes me feel like a one-legged man representing the Lord in a race. I can't do Him the service He deserves. I'm grateful to you, Wyatt, and very much in your debt.'

'You owe me nothing, Coll. We're both working towards the same end. But I'll be forever in *your* debt if you can arrange a meeting for me with your brother – the new laird of Kilmalie.' Wyatt had already told the Letterfinlay minister of the startling news brought to Fort William by Charles Graham.

Throwing back his head, Coll Kennedy emptied his glass and rose to his feet.

'There's no time like the present. It's been a long time since I last visited the ancestral home. As congratulations would seem to be in order, let's go and pay a call on brother Seoras.'

Glenadon had been the seat of the earls of Glenadon since the fifteenth century, and the family had lived on the site for as many years before. The two men reached the fortified house in Glen Moriston at dusk that same day after travelling deep into the Highlands north of Loch Lochy.

Coll Kennedy had borrowed a donkey from Tam Vass for Wyatt, but it was even more vicious than the Letterfinlay minister's own mount. Wyatt completed the journey leading his donkey and with a painful bite on his thigh.

From the somewhat shabby state of the house and many of the buildings in the grounds, it was evident that the lords of Glenadon were not among the wealthiest of Scotland's many peers. Coll Kennedy explained that this was due to the custom in the Kennedy family of producing as many sons as was humanly possible. This, said Coll, was a result of the Kennedy habit over the years of becoming involved in the wars of their neighbours and forfeiting the lives of many of their sons in the process.

From the conversations Wyatt had previously held with his fellow-preacher, he had formed the opinion that Coll Kennedy was the 'black sheep' of the Kennedy family, his relatives all deeply relieved when he left home. That this was not the case was made quite evident during the course of the evening.

Seoras Kennedy, sixteenth Earl of Glenadon, was delighted to have a visit from his younger brother, and the Earl's charming and aristocratic wife echoed her husband's delight. Their only regret seemed to be that none of the other Kennedy brothers lived close enough to be invited to share in the reunion that night.

Wyatt quickly realised that Seoras Kennedy belonged to the true Scottish aristocracy, in spite of his quiet, unassuming and rather 'bookish' manner. Yet the sixteenth Earl treated Wyatt as an equal and with great warmth. It made it easy for Wyatt to tell him the reason for the visit when Coll Kennedy brought up the subject of his brother's latest inheritance.

Wyatt spoke of the Highlanders who lived in the mountains; of the Rosses; of Lachlan Munro; of Seonaid and her blind father; and of the latest clearances.

When Wyatt ran out of words, the Earl of Glenadon said: 'What is it you would like me to do?'

'I'd like you to tell the Highlanders they might remain in the mountains, where they belong.'

Seoras Kennedy looked thoughtful. 'I know very little about Kilmalie lands. They are making a profit, so I'm told, but I believe it to be a marginal one.'

Looking at Wyatt in silence for a while, he said: 'It's a regrettable economic fact of life that landowners need to bring sheep into the hills in order to make a profit. I am no exception. You say great tracts of land have already been cleared of tenants? Would they *all* want to return to their old homes?'

Wyatt remembered his conversations with the dispossessed tenants and cottars in the school and in the churchyard. The words of those on the road to Fort William who intended to take a boat to a new life.

'A few would. I suspect many others have had enough. They've made the break and wouldn't go back now.'

Seoras Kennedy nodded. 'It's much the same elsewhere in the Highlands. Very well, I'll tell you what I'll do. There will be no more clearances, you have my word for this; but those who have been dispossessed will not be returned to their old tenancies. Those lands have been cleared for sheep; and if this factor is like others of his ilk there will already be sheep there. However, they *will* be given an equal amount of land within areas already tenanted. As far as is possible, they may choose their lands. In the event of any disputes *I* will be the final arbiter. They can have two rent-free years as compensation for what they've lost. For the following two years they will pay the same rent as they were paying before. If they've lost stock in the clearances, I'll do my best to make it up from what I have on Glenadon lands. In other words, Minister Jamieson, I'll do all I can for them short of giving them money – that is rather hard to come by at the moment. How does such an arrangement sound to you?'

It was more – far more – than Wyatt had dared hope to achieve when he set forth from Fort William that morning. It was an honest and generous settlement by the new landowner of the Kilmalie estates. When Wyatt tried to express his gratitude, the Earl cut short his thanks.

'*I'm* a Highlander, too, Minister Jamieson. I belong to a family which prides itself on honouring the duties life has imposed upon it. However, the root of the problem would seem to be Factor Garrett. Charles Graham has already expressed *his* thoughts on the man to me. I'll get rid of him, of course, but I shall need a replacement. Is there anyone you could recommend?'

When Wyatt hesitated, Coll Kennedy spoke the name of the man Wyatt had in mind.

'There's a very good man, and he's living in Eskaig right now. Alasdair Burns – or Alasdair Burns Anderson, to give him the name he was born with.'

The Earl of Glenadon frowned. 'I seem to have heard that name. . . .'

'He was imprisoned some years ago. I believe he was convicted of "sedition". What it really means is he was arguing for a fair deal for men like the Highlanders, but he said it in the wrong places. He's a good man, an honest man. I'd stake my life on him.'

To Wyatt's surprise, the Earl of Glenadon smiled at Coll Kennedy. 'It sounds just like our Malcolm.'

To Wyatt, the Earl said: 'Has Coll told you of our brother Malcolm, who spent a spell in an English gaol for espousing the Chartist cause?'

Wyatt shook his head. Nothing would ever surprise him again.

'Malcolm went to prison because of his honesty, not for any form of deception. I understand a great many good men suffered far more, for the same reasons. Very well, Minister Jamieson. Send your friend to see me as soon as possible. If I think your opinion of him is sound, he'll be the new factor of the Kilmalie estate at

Eskaig. Now, before we see what we've been able to find for dinner, there's one thing more to be cleared up. I believe you've been ousted from your kirk in Eskaig? As your new patron I feel I should do something about it, right away....'

CHAPTER FORTY-NINE

WYATT RETURNED to Fort William well satisfied with all he had achieved during the past few days. It was far more than he would have believed possible when he left Eskaig on the day of Lachlan Munro's death. Now he intended to find the would-be emigrants and tell them about the new landlord of the Kilmalie estates. Hopefully some would remain in Scotland – and Wyatt was convinced this would be in their best interests.

He was returning from Glenadon alone. Coll Kennedy had been persuaded to remain for another twenty-four hours by the promise that two more of the Kennedy brothers could be 'gathered in' by evening for a small reunion. Wyatt was invited to stay and take part in the family's celebrations, but he felt much was happening elsewhere that required his attention.

Before going on board the emigrant-ship, Wyatt paid a visit to the bank in Fort William and drew out some of the money left to him by Lord Kilmalie. Paid to him in gold sovereigns, it was more cash than he had ever carried before.

He took it to the quay accompanied by two of the stoutest clerks from the bank, detailed by a concerned bank manager to escort him. Fort William was a Highland town, its citizens among the most honest in the land; but not all the would-be emigrants were honest local men. On board would also be criminal fugitives from the cities of the south, fleeing from justice. An emigrant-ship provided such men with a secure sanctuary from pursuit.

After a brief tour of the ship to locate his late parishioners, Wyatt stood on the deck and waited for them to gather around him. He sincerely hoped the emigrant-vessel was not indicative of the great new life these people hoped to find in Canada. The ship was old, and smaller than Wyatt had expected. Probably of no more than four hundred tons. The main timbers seemed alarmingly sponge-like, and Wyatt wished he knew enough about ships to form an expert opinion of the seaworthiness of this particular vessel.

Accommodation for the emigrant families would be extremely cramped and uncomfortable. Wyatt estimated there were at least five hundred emigrants on board, accommodated in two holds. Each hold was about forty feet long, twenty feet wide, and had seven feet of headroom. Bunks for the passengers were merely wooden slatted shelves, three tiers high. On these the emigrants were expected to arrange themselves as best they could, irrespective of sex and with no pretence of privacy.

The Eskaig emigrants had already learned that the five pounds given to each family would be gone long before they began a brave new life in the new land. Their passage to Canada was inclusive only of accommodation and water. They were required to take with them sufficient provisions to feed themselves for six weeks. It had not been pointed out to them that some bad voyages had been known to last as long as eleven or even twelve weeks during exceptionally adverse weather.

There were more than sixty emigrants from the Eskaig district. Wyatt told them of the new landlord and his terms for allowing them to remain on Kilmalie land. They raised a cheer when he informed them John Garrett was not to remain as the factor.

When Wyatt had finished talking, no more than seventeen Highlanders decided to return – nine from the same family. Wyatt pressed the others to reconsider their decision, but their determination to find a new life in Canada would not be shaken. All their lives they had been totally dependent upon the whim of factor and landowner. For much of the time they had lived with the constant threat of eviction. Now the threat had been fulfilled. They had been forced to watch helplessly as flames devoured their homes and possessions.

They accepted what Wyatt said about the new landowner. They were ready to believe he might even keep his word to them. But what would happen if he were struck dead in a week – a month – a year? They were likely to have to make this same decision again.

No, they would go to Canada and carve a new way of life from the wilderness. Free from the greed of landowners, tyrannical factors and the ever-present threat of 'clearances'.

It was useless for Wyatt to tell them they would take most of their own problems with them to the new land. Poverty, cold and sheer desperation would drive many to sell their future to any man who could afford to keep their families alive. They would commit themselves to a life of servitude as binding as the duty owed by a clansman to his chief in the Middle Ages.

When Wyatt had exhausted all his arguments without changing their minds, he gave up. The crew of the emigrant-ship were preparing for sea. They cursed the Eskaig minister for gathering so many people on the deck where they were working, but he ignored them and spoke to his people once more.

'How many of you will still have money left when you're put ashore in Canada?'

The Highlanders looked at each other but they did not reply. Each was reluctant to let the others know the extent of his poverty.

Wyatt sighed. 'It doesn't matter. I want all those who are still determined to go to line up in front of me. I intend giving every man, woman and child ten sovereigns and I want you to keep them until you land in Canada. The money should see you through the first few weeks, at least. One day, when you've all made your fortunes, you can donate the same amount, plus interest, to the Eskaig kirk. Perhaps I'll have the richest kirk in the whole of Scotland then. Now, take your money. We'll have a short service, and I'll wish you God speed – and may fortune favour you in Canada.'

Wyatt handed out four hundred and seventy sovereigns before conducting a service that was attended by most of the emigrants and a great many of the crew. It was said afterwards the voices from the emigrant-ship, raised in praise of God, moved more than one resident of Fort William to tears.

It moved Wyatt greatly, too. He walked away from the ship not daring to look back at the departing Highlanders lest they see the tears he shed for them.

Wyatt called a meeting of evicted tenants and Eskaig villagers in the school that evening and passed on the promises made to him by the

Earl of Glenadon. Evangeline was at the meeting, too, but Alasdair was not. He had unexpectedly gone into the mountains that morning and had not yet returned.

Wyatt told Evangeline of the Earl's plans and left her with very mixed feelings about the changes. Of one thing she was certain, though. She would move her mother to Eskaig before the news of his dismissal reached her father.

Long before Wyatt had finished talking there was so much hubbub in the room it became useless to try to say more for the moment. At the height of the excited commotion Alasdair Burns slipped into the room, having come straight from the mountains. As he made his way towards Wyatt, one of the cottars called to ask how the factor had taken the news that his clearance plans had been brought to an end.

Wyatt had not told the meeting who their new factor was to be, but he would never have a better opportunity than now.

When he broke the news there was a brief moment of astonished silence, then the room erupted with a mighty roar of approval that might have been heard all the way to Corpach. The delighted crowd surged about Alasdair Burns, and before he guessed their intentions two men lifted him to their shoulders. As they paraded him around the room others reached up to shake him by the hand or pummel his back.

Alasdair Burns allowed the jubilant men to make a couple of turns about the room before struggling free from their grasp and slipping to the ground when he neared Wyatt.

'It's great news,' agreed Alasdair Burns when Wyatt reached him with his own congratulations, but the prospective factor's solemn expression belied the words and as quickly as he could he drew Wyatt to one side, saying quietly: 'I need to talk to you, Wyatt. Away from here.'

There had to be something seriously wrong for a man to remain unsmiling and serious at a time like this, and Wyatt led Alasdair Burns clear of the happy crowd as swiftly as he could. Having any form of conversation inside the schoolroom was out of the question. Everyone there wanted to tell Alasdair Burns how happy they were for him – and for themselves.

It had begun to rain outside, but at least there were no villagers about.

'You've no need to tell me something's wrong,' said Wyatt when they reached the road. 'Has it to do with Garrett?'

'Yes ... but Eneas Ross hasn't made things any easier for himself.' Alasdair Burns cuffed rain from around his mouth. 'Garrett took a small party of soldiers up to the Ross place, apparently to serve a clearance order on Eneas. Ross and his friends beat the soldiers off, and now they're claiming a great victory. Eneas has sent a call out for all Highlanders to join him and chase the Irish soldiers out of the mountains – and then drive the sheep out after them.'

'When did Garrett take the soldiers up there? He was told by Charles Graham there were to be no more clearances.'

'It seems Garrett didn't agree. He tried to serve the clearance notice the day you set off to see Coll Kennedy again. I think this was one he was determined to serve, Wyatt. It's his way of getting back at you.'

'Was anyone hurt in this skirmish?' Wyatt was deeply concerned. It was such an incident as this he had been trying so hard to prevent. Now, just when it seemed the Highlanders' cause had been recognised – on the Kilmalie estate, at least – John Garrett and Eneas Ross had between them managed to undo much of the good that had been achieved.

'I don't know.' Alasdair Burns shrugged his shoulders apologetically. 'Eneas Ross has been celebrating the Highlanders' "victory" ever since it happened. He'd give a man the story of Killicrankie and swear it happened the day the soldiers came calling on him. The Highlanders have come off best in a skirmish with a handful of soldiers and they're convinced they've defeated the whole army. They are in a dangerous state of mind – and the danger is to Ross and his family.'

'You'll make a wise factor, Alasdair. Get some rest now. I'll send a letter to Eneas – Mairi can read it to him. First thing in the morning I'll go to Fort William. In the mean time pray I'm not too late to stop the Irish colonel teaching Eneas Ross just how wrong he is.'

CHAPTER FIFTY

FOR LIEUTENANT WILLIAM CONNOR this was his first 'overseas' posting. He had joined the Irish regiment only eighteen months before. The son of a sound landowning family, he was following in the footsteps of his father who had been a major in the Irish 27th Regiment during the Peninsular campaign.

William Connor was by nature a studious young man, his thirst being for knowledge rather than for the blood of an enemy. Indeed, he *had* no enemies – and few friends. He was also an only child, so the mantle of his father's hopes and ambitions could not be draped about the shoulders of a brother. Destiny – and Major Connor – had chosen a military career for William.

Army life meant that William Connor was mixing with men of a *coarser* nature than he would have otherwise have chosen to be his companions. This was not too bothersome while the regiment was in barracks in Dublin, where there was a full social life to be enjoyed. Young men of 'good' families were welcome in most of the fashionable salons in the city.

Then part of the Irish regiment was suddenly uprooted and sent to Glasgow. The good life came to an end overnight. For generations the soldiers of Ireland and Scotland had been used to put down troubles in each other's land. The methods they used would outrage and alienate the population of both lands for many years to come. Lieutenant Connor and his brother officers were no longer welcome guests at civic and private functions. Instead they were shunned by society and derided by the populace whenever they marched out of the barracks where they were billeted.

It came as almost a relief when the Irish soldiers were ordered to

Fort William. They were to deal with what was officially described as 'dangerous restlessness' in Highland areas where legitimate clearances were being carried out.

The Irish soldiers camped on land just outside the Highland town and were kept busy escorting factors and sheriff's men engaged in serving clearance orders on Highland tenants.

It was not work that particularly appealed to William Connor. He had too sensitive a nature to remain unaffected by the plight of women and children turned out of homes which were then destroyed behind them. Nevertheless, he enjoyed the awesome vast-ness of the Highlands and the breathtaking beauty of the moun-tains. He particularly enjoyed taking a small party on patrol with no fixed orders and only a loosely defined route to follow.

William Connor was on such a patrol in the mountains between Loch Eil and Loch Arkaig, following the course of a fast-running mountain river. There was a strong hint of rain in the air, but it had held off so far and the youthful lieutenant was enjoying the morn-ing – until he saw John Garrett riding towards him.

Of all the clearances he had been obliged to witness, William Connor disliked those ordered by Garrett most of all. The High-landers in the mountains lived in abject poverty. Perhaps they *should* be grateful to be evicted and given the opportunity to make a new life somewhere else. This did not excuse Garrett's methods. He seemed determined to cause maximum distress and humility to the unfortunate cottars.

'I'd expected to meet up with you much earlier than this. I was led to believe you'd be at Loch Arkaig by now.' John Garrett's greeting bordered on rudeness.

'I didn't realise I was marching to the clock, Mr Garrett. Now you *have* found me, is there something you want?'

'Yes. I've a clearance order to serve on a Kilmalie tenant. He's likely to cause trouble. I want your assistance.'

'It seems a great many Kilmalie tenants are "likely to cause trouble". Could it have anything to do with your manner towards them?'

'That remark smacks of impertinence, Lieutenant Connor. Are you going to help me serve this clearance order, or do I return to your colonel and tell him you refused?'

It was a bluff. Colonel Fitzpatrick, the officer commanding the

Irish soldiers, had been told by the sheriff-substitute that Garrett no longer had the authority to order clearances and was likely to be replaced in the near future. With his removal the need for the Army would be gone. The Irish soldiers were at this very moment preparing to leave Fort William, but the young lieutenant knew nothing of this. When he and his platoon had set off on patrol John Garrett was still one of the most important men in the district.

'Have you brought no constables with you?' The young Irish officer was uncertain of the law governing these clearances, but always before there had been constables or sheriff's officers present.

'No. I expect *real* trouble from this man. If some of his friends are present, they're likely to be armed. This is a task for the Army, not for unarmed officials.'

The Irish soldiers were listening, and their expressions showed the excitement they felt. They had joined the Army to fight. *Who* they fought was of no great importance.

'Very well. Where does this tenant live?'

'Over there.' John Garrett pointed to where the mountains rose high to the south. 'There's a useful pass no more than half a mile ahead.'

John Garrett was jubilant. He knew he was unlikely to be factor of the Kilmalie estate for very much longer. Before he left he was determined to clear Eneas Ross from the estate. He had been given details of proposed army patrols more than a week before. It was fortunate for him that this patrol was led by the regiment's most inexperienced and junior officer. A more senior man might have asked some awkward question, or even refused to take action without the written authority of his commanding officer.

Some of the eagerness felt by the soldiers waned when the Kilmalie factor led them on a steep climb to the high lands where the Ross family had its home and it began to rain. However, half an hour's rest at the top restored at least some of their enthusiasm. The short delay did not suit the mood of the impatient factor, but he curbed his irritation. He wanted nothing to go wrong with his plans now.

The twenty soldiers marched towards the Ross croft in single file. The holding had been in view for some time, but they had seen no movement of any kind. It was so quiet that their leader, a corporal of many years' service, began to get an uneasy feeling. Quickening his pace, he joined the officer leading the party and suggested the men should halt to load their muskets before approaching any closer to the Highland croft.

'No.' Lieutenant Connor spoke after some hesitation. 'If we stop now and load our guns in full view of the house, it would be unduly provocative. In spite of what Factor Garrett has said, I do not anticipate trouble. We've never had any before; I doubt if today will be any different.'

Corporal Allen was not reassured. 'There's something here I don't like, sir. It's too quiet by far. At least halt the men and let me go up to the house alone first.'

Again Lieutenant Connor declined to accept the corporal's advice. 'We'll march up to the house together, Corporal. A show of strength. There's no Highland cottar would dare attack twenty of Her Majesty's soldiers going about their lawful business. Fall back with the men, if you please.'

Lieutenant William Connor's words were no more than half a minute old when he was proved tragically and dramatically wrong.

The soldiers were less than fifty paces from the low wall surrounding Eneas Ross's croft when there came a loud shout. The word was in Gaelic — and its effect immediate. A number of men, possibly as many as seventy or eighty, suddenly rose from behind the wall, yelling war-cries that had once been sufficient in themselves to carry the field of battle. Some of the men brandished ancient claymores, others held cudgels. A few, no more than eight, peered at the Irish soldiers along the barrels of a wide variety of firearms.

The soldiers came to a halt, and Corporal Allen looked to the young lieutenant, awaiting an order. It never came. Lieutenant William Connor stood as though turned to stone. The sudden appearance of the Highlanders had released a paralysing fear that gripped his mind and body. He remained rigid as another shout rose above the taunting 'war-cries'. William Connor saw powder-smoke erupt from pan and barrel — and it was the last thing he ever saw. A musket-ball ricocheted from the bridge of his nose and entered his head, lodging just beneath his brain. On its way it severed the optic nerve. The young lieutenant dropped to his knees, still conscious but totally blinded.

Behind him three of the Irish soldiers had also been felled by

Highland musket-balls. One rose to a knee immediately, but the other two stayed down.

Corporal Allen waited no longer. He shouted for the infantrymen to load their weapons. It was not an operation that could be hurried, and it was almost a full minute before the percussion muskets were ready to be fired. The Highlanders were speedier and had already fired a second ragged volley. This time they had loaded their ancient flintlocks hurriedly and their only success was an almost-spent musket-ball which struck John Garrett's horse, causing it to rear dangerously close to the soldiers.

William Connor had begun to scream now. A one-note hymn to pain that was unnerving.

'You ready?' Corporal Allen called to his men and received nods of confirmation.

'Right. Take aim – and choose your targets carefully.' The corporal set an example and spoke with his cheek resting against the stock of his musket. Raising his face, he called: 'Factor! Get that bloody horse out of the way before my men shoot him!'

John Garrett brought his horse under a form of control and drove him in a wide arc to the rear of the soldiers.

'Take aim . . . fire!' The order was marginally softer than the sound of the shots. Only three of the muskets fired, the corporal's and two others. Percussion weapons were notoriously unreliable in wet weather.

None of the Highlanders was hit, but the musket-balls passed close enough to make the Scotsmen duck from view quickly.

Corporal Allen was experienced enough to know that in these conditions his men could not hope to rout the Highlanders. He ordered the men to pick up their fallen comrades and quit the scene of the one-sided battle. He himself took the arm of the lieutenant. Although bleeding profusely from his wound, William Connor was miraculously still capable of walking.

His horse now under control, John Garrett's anger spilled over. 'What are you doing? You're not going to let a handful of ragged Highlanders chase you off? You came here to help me serve a clearance notice. You can't quit before it's done.'

'You want it served, you get on and do it yourself, Factor. If I get back to camp with the men I've got left, I'll have succeeded in *my* duty.'

'What sort of soldiers are you? I thought you could fight! A few shots and you're running home with your tail between your legs. . . .'

'If you've a complaint, make it in person to the colonel.' The corporal pulled William Connor roughly to his feet as he tried to sink to his knees, blood flicking from his face as his head jerked back.

'You see this?' There was scarcely controlled anger in the corporal's voice. 'Lieutenant Connor's not yet twenty and he's got a musket-ball in his brain. For what? To save the country from some invader? Or to free some poor suffering people who can't help themselves? No. He's been shot because you want to make a few extra shillings for some overweight landlord who's probably never known more than a moment's want or discomfort in his life. On your way, Factor. My musket's not loaded, but I've still got a sharp bayonet to find out the colour of *your* blood.'

At that moment there was a roar of triumph from the Highlanders as they rose from behind the wall and saw the Irish soldiers in retreat. They swarmed over the wall, brandishing their weapons and yelling wildly.

'Fix bayonets!' Corporal Allen shouted the order as he dropped Lieutenant Connor unceremoniously to the ground and set an example.

The other Irish soldiers followed suit, and as John Garrett kneed his horse clear Corporal Allen called: 'Form twos facing the enemy. Front rank kneeling, rear rank standing.'

It was a pitifully small force, eight men in each rank, with Corporal Allen standing two paces in the van, yet the quiet discipline of the soldiers who waited for them, bayonets at the ready, caused the Highlanders' charge to falter and come to a halt before they had covered half the distance from the cot.

One of the Highlanders threw up his musket and aimed at the soldiers. Two others followed his example; but the weather had taken its toll on Scots guns, too. The sound of three clicks carried to the ears of the soldiers.

After a few minutes of noisy uncertainty, one of the Highlanders said, in Gaelic: 'There's no sense running on to the soldiers' bayonets. We've won the day. Let them go.'

There were one or two dissenters, but the Highlanders began to back away towards the croft, some of them shouting obscenities at the soldiers as they went.

Slinging the now unconscious lieutenant across his shoulders, Corporal Allen ordered the men to pick up the wounded men and march off, towards Fort William.

CHAPTER FIFTY-ONE

COLONEL FITZPATRICK listened patiently and politely to Wyatt's plea on behalf of the Highlanders. All the while he spoke officers were coming in to report men ready to march and ammunition issued. Once a messenger arrived from 'the advanced party' with a note for the commanding officer.

Despairingly, Wyatt gave up in mid-sentence. It was apparent that nothing he said was making any difference. He had arrived at the camp of the Irish soldiers as they were moving out against the Highlanders. The messages reaching the colonel's tent made it apparent that other men had left Fort William very much earlier.

Seated at a table in his tent, the commanding officer looked up from the note he was scribbling. 'I *am* listening, Jamieson. Do go on.'

Wyatt shook his head. 'I'm wasting my breath. We both know it. I'm pleading with you to call off your action against the Highlanders, yet even as I speak you're sending more troops into the mountains. I had hoped you might show some compassion. The clearance orders should never have been issued. Garrett's the man you should be after, not a poor Highlander trying to cling on to the pitiful little he has.'

'Your Factor Garrett seems to have made himself scarce, Jamieson, though I *do* have men out looking for him. Nevertheless, I have just had the most unhappy task of composing a letter of sympathy to a very close friend. His nineteen-year-old son is dead after being blinded by a musket-ball from a Highlander's gun. Am I to tell *him* I allowed his killers to go free because the man who pulled the trigger had been unfairly treated by some factor?'

Colonel Fitzpatrick shook his head sadly. 'I can't tell him that – and I won't allow my soldiers to feel *their* lives are worth nothing. I hope one day to lead my men into battle – *real* battle. Every man behind me will be carrying a loaded musket. If I'm killed in action, I'd rather the musket-ball came from the enemy lines and not my own.'

The officer sighed and laid the pen down upon the paper. 'There are other, rather more serious implications to be considered. The corporal who brought the men back after this unfortunate skirmish reported there were approximately eighty attackers, each of whom was armed in some way or another. This might well be described as an "uprising", Jamieson. I have no wish to exaggerate the seriousness of the incident at all; I, *too*, sympathise with your people. However, if the authorities in London deem it to *be* an uprising, you'll have more soldiers than sheep in these hills. It will not be safe for a Highlander to show his head above a bush anywhere in the country.'

Colonel Fitzpatrick stood up and reached for his hat. 'While we're on the subject of sheep . . . I've had a report that your Highlanders are rounding up thousands of sheep and driving them towards us, along Glen Loy. From complaints I've been receiving during the past twenty-four hours it would seem your people have vowed to drive every beast from the mountains.' The colonel buckled on his sword-belt. 'I regret I cannot allow them to succeed.' He gave Wyatt an understanding smile. 'I think it will be better if you come with me, Minister Jamieson.'

'I have other matters to attend to, Colonel.'

'Then, I regret I must put it another way. I *insist* you accompany me.'

'You're *arresting* me?' Wyatt's indignation grew from dismay.

'That's certainly not a word I would use, Jamieson, but I know something of your background. You're a resourceful man, and admirably loyal to your people. I would prefer to have you where I can see what you're doing.'

The colonel hesitated before adding: 'I would also like you to see for yourself the events of today. I am not a vindictive man, Jamieson. I am not going into the mountains seeking revenge, but I fear history may try to distort my actions. You'll be able to set it right.'

Colonel Fitzpatrick was an infantry officer, but he was sufficiently senior to *ride* at the head of his men. Wyatt was well to the rear with a young officer as company and four soldiers who were never farther than a few paces away. Two of them had been present at the skirmish with Eneas Ross and his friends. Although Wyatt was not officially a prisoner, it would be impossible for him to slip away unnoticed.

There was an Irish soldier waiting on the bridge spanning the river at the entrance to the glen. The marching column came to a halt while he spoke at some length to Colonel Fitzpatrick. Then the colonel turned in his saddle and waved the men across the bridge. They were halted again while the commanding officer talked to his officers, Wyatt being kept well out of hearing.

When the meeting broke up, the officers hurried back to their men and small parties began moving into the wooded glen.

Wyatt was led farther away and made to sit down, the four soldiers making it very clear they resented being left out of the action in order to guard a Scots minister.

They were seated on a grassy bank for almost half an hour before a sound began to make itself heard. At first Wyatt was unable to identify it. Then he realised it was the bleating of sheep. Thousands of sheep.

The Highlanders were walking into a well-planned trap. Wyatt stood up, hoping to see something or someone, but the officer ordered him to sit down. When he made no move to obey, one of the soldiers spoke eagerly to the officer: 'Let me run him through with my bayonet, sir. He'll make no noise, I promise you. We can say he tried to run away....'

'Try anything like that and you'll be standing in front of a firing party tomorrow morning.'

The soldier scowled sullenly, and Wyatt knew the Irishman would need only the slightest excuse to disobey the warning given him by the officer.

Minutes later a vast sea of sheep spilled from the shadow of the trees and poured out across the wide glen entrance. Suddenly a single shot rang out from somewhere out of sight beyond the trees. It was immediately followed by a whole fusillade. Colonel Fitzpatrick's trap was sprung.

Disregarding the shouts of the officer and the soldiers guarding him, Wyatt sprinted to where sporadic firing could still be heard. There was a shot from behind him but it must have gone well wide – and then Wyatt was in among the sheep. Spurred on by the shots behind them, the creatures were running in all directions, like water down a mountainside. Great streams curving in all directions, some joining up again, others taking their own course.

The ambuscade had been well executed. The bodies of Highlanders lay crumpled upon the ground. Wyatt ran towards them – and the first body he saw was that of Stewart Ross, one of Mairi's brothers.

Wyatt kneeled by the body and checked for life. There was none. Single shots were still being fired from widely dispersed spots up and down the glen, but a bugler was playing a recall now. The brief one-sided battle was over.

Wyatt was saying a brief prayer over the body of Stewart when a sergeant came to him and said: 'There's one of yours asking for you. You'd better be quick. He'll be dead soon.' Having delivered his abrupt and callous message, the sergeant walked away and shouted at some stragglers, ordering them to hurry towards the sound of the bugle.

Wyatt looked about him and saw a Highlander propped against a tree. It was Ian Ross, and he was very badly wounded. Wyatt could tell even before he pulled aside the bloody plaid and uncovered the blue-edged hole in his chest that Eneas Ross's eldest son had received a mortal wound.

Wyatt looked up from the wound and saw the accusation in Ian Ross's face.

'I came to plead with the colonel not to seek revenge. They wouldn't let me return for fear I'd warn you,' Wyatt said shortly. 'Why, Ian? Why this foolishness?'

'We beat them in the mountains.' The pride in the statement overrode the pain, but Ian Ross's breathing was ragged. He was losing a great deal of blood, and Wyatt could do nothing to staunch the bleeding.

Wyatt resisted an urge to tell the dying man the so-called victory in the mountains had resulted in this savage reprisal in which many other Highland men had been shot down.

'Have you seen any of the others?' Ian Ross tensed and gripped Wyatt's wrist. 'We were all here. All my brothers.'

Wyatt fought hard to contain the horror that filled him. The trap had been very well planned. How many more of Mairi's brothers would he find lying dead in Glen Loy? To Ian Ross he managed to say: 'No, I haven't seen any of the others.'

Ian Ross relaxed, and his hand fell away from Wyatt's arm. 'Thank God. They must have got away.'

Wyatt tried not to think of the scattered shots farther along the glen. He doubted whether many Highlanders had managed to escape.

'I'll go and find a surgeon—'

'No!' Ian Ross leaned his head back against the rough bark of the tree. 'He'll be able to do nothing. I haven't long. . . .'

When Eneas Ross's eldest son looked at Wyatt again, his eyes were those of a dying man. 'Tell Ma I'm sorry. Tibbie. . . .' An expression of pain crossed Ian's face, but it had nothing to do with his wound. 'Tell her . . . what happened doesn't matter any more. I couldn't have wished for a better wife.'

Ian Ross fell silent for a full minute, although blood was making his increasingly shallow breathing noisy now. Wyatt thought he had said all he had to say, but with a conscious effort Ian Ross found some more words.

'Make Pa listen to you, Preacher. Old days . . . are gone. Tell him.'

Ian Ross said no more. Two minutes later he stopped breathing, and Wyatt said a prayer over the second of the Ross brothers to die that day. There were seven other Highlanders lying dead in the glen, and Wyatt breathed a bitter sigh of relief when he checked the last and learned it was not a Ross. His relief was premature. Irish soldiers returning from their pursuit carried in two more bodies. One was Mungo Ross.

There were tears in Wyatt's eyes as he rose from the body of the third Ross to die. He turned to find Colonel Fitzpatrick standing watching him.

'You know these men?'

'They were my parishioners.' Wyatt spoke guardedly through his grief. The commanding officer might be planning retribution against their families, too.

'They'll have brought sorrow to many homes by their foolishness,' said the colonel with what seemed to be genuine regret. 'A father can find pride in the manner of his son's death, but a mother's grief is fed by memories of the child he once was. The bodies will be taken to Fort William. Their next of kin may claim them without any questions being asked.'

'It's all over now, then? You'll be returning to Fort William?'

'Not quite. This whole sorry business began when my men were fired on from a croft only a few miles from here. When the croft has been destroyed justice will be satisfied.'

Wyatt was alarmed. Colonel Fitzpatrick was talking of the Ross home. Mairi's home!

'Colonel, three of the dead men here are from that croft. *Three brothers*. Isn't that justice enough for you?'

'The officer who was shot from the croft was an *only* son. To his father and mother he was the *whole* of their family.'

'And will they lose their home, too – and a lifetime's possessions? The boys' father is an ex-soldier, Colonel. He fought through the Peninsular campaigns and at Waterloo. Is this how it's all to end for him?'

Colonel Fitzpatrick appeared to be digesting Wyatt's words for a long time. Then he said: 'I'm sorry, Jamieson. This must be seen to be done. No one can be allowed to use arms against the Army to prevent eviction – lawful or otherwise. I intend resting my men here for an hour. You can use that time to remove what you can from the croft. My men will burn the house and everything remaining inside. Nothing more.'

CHAPTER FIFTY-TWO

ENEAS ROSS looked back only once at the ragged plume of smoke rising from the burning croft. It was all over. The life he had known. His family.... Five sons dead within a twelvemonth, among them his firstborn. The boy he had watched with such pride as he grew to manhood.

He had learned of the disaster of Glen Loy long before Wyatt arrived. The three surviving brothers had fled the scene of the ambush and not stopped running until they fell in through the doorway of their mountain croft. Even so, the bearded patriarch had not known the full extent of the tragedy until Wyatt broke the news of the death of his other three sons.

Eneas Ross had walked away from the croft refusing to remove a thing from the building. It would be a funeral pyre for his sons, a primitive tribute.

The three women, too, were bitterly grief-stricken, but they and the surviving sons salvaged what could be carried off. They left when the drum-beat setting the pace for the Irish soldiers could be heard approaching.

Eneas Ross felt numb and old. Very, very old. He could hear the women sobbing and wailing. It was the natural thing for them to do. Mairi had lost three brothers today and Tibbie a fine husband. While Magdalene had lost three children ... three of her 'babies'. But their noisy sorrow did not impinge upon his own deep-rooted grief. To anyone who did not know him well Eneas Ross would appear to have taken the news of the tragedy calmly and without emotion. Such an assumption was a very long way from the truth. With the death of his sons – of Ian in particular – Eneas Ross had died inside. Wyatt had told him of Ian's last words, and the head of the Ross family reflected upon them. How much had *he* as their father contributed to their deaths by his talk of past glories? It would never be known, but nothing could prevent Eneas Ross torturing himself for the remainder of his life in search of an answer.

Lachlan Munro was buried with those who fell at Glen Loy in a ceremony that emptied every house and cot for many miles around Loch Eil. Men, women and children packed the small kirk, and a hopeful sign for the future of the area was the presence of the Earl of Glenadon's steward, sent by the Earl to represent him at the funeral service.

Both kirk and manse had been returned to Wyatt, Angus Cameron having vacated them before the Earl's notice was served on him. The Eskaig elder had lost the respect of the parishioners and when he learned John Garrett was being replaced he knew his last bastion of support had fallen.

After the funeral service a brief funeral tea was held in the grounds of the manse, where the Ross family was staying. Alasdair and Evangeline Burns were here. So, too, was Charlotte Garrett.

John Garrett had not been seen since the day when he accompanied the Irish soldiery to the Ross home. He had returned to the house at Corpach, gathered up clothes and personal belongings and left. Charlotte Garrett was staying with her daughter and new son-in-law at the schoolhouse for the time being.

When the time came for Alasdair to take up his post as factor of the Kilmalie estate they would all move back to the Corpach house. Until then they were comfortable enough. There seemed little doubt that the post of factor would go to Alasdair. The Earl of Glenadon's steward had interviewed him at some length, and the two men got on well together. The steward told Alasdair that the final decision rested with the Earl, but *he* was going back to Glenadon with a recommendation that Alasdair be appointed factor immediately.

There were still a number of victims of the clearances camped in the churchyard. When Wyatt carried the daily pot of hot soup out to them that evening, Mairi came with him, trying not to look at the mounds of earth where five of her brothers now lay buried.

Afterwards, as darkness moved in upon them, they walked

together at the edge of the loch and Wyatt asked Mairi if she had thought any more of the future.

Mairi shook her head. 'I can't make plans just yet, Wyatt. Not until I know what Pa intends to do.'

'He can have the old croft back if he wants it; or build a new one if that's what he would prefer.'

'He won't talk about it, Wyatt. Not yet. It's too soon for him to think of the future. I'll have a word with him in a day or two, when I think he's ready.'

Mairi found Wyatt's hand. 'It's been a bad time for all of us, but nothing that's happened has changed the way I feel about you. I still love you.'

'Then, everything will work out, Mairi. You'll see.'

Wyatt's words had a hollow ring to them the next day when Eneas Ross announced his intention to emigrate to Canada.

He broke the news at the table, when the family and Wyatt were sitting down to dinner. Eneas Ross had spoken so little since his sons died that it came as a surprise when he suddenly said: 'I have something to say to you all.'

Spoons and knives were lowered as everyone looked to Eneas Ross.

'I've decided to leave Scotland. Make a new life somewhere else, in Canada maybe.'

The stunned silence was broken by Wyatt. 'Have you thought about this, Eneas? I mean *really* thought about it?'

'I've thought about it well enough. All that's left for me in Scotland – for any of us – are sad memories of what was, and thoughts of what might have been. But there's no going back and I've become a stranger in the land of my birth. The land that's robbed me of five grown-up sons.'

'There are the others to think of: Magdalene and Tibbie and the other boys.'

'True, I still have three sons. They're fine boys, but no one can take the place of a firstborn son. If I stay here, they'll reap the bitterness that's been sown within me. They deserve better. Tibbie is as much a daughter to me as my own, but she can come with me or stay, same as Mairi. As for Magdalene. . . .' Eneas Ross looked to his wife to provide an answer to Wyatt's question.

Magdalene Ross had been torn apart by grief, but she said: 'You've no need to ask me, Eneas. You know my answer. I have buried ten children in your country. Part of my heart will always be here with them, but I followed you for many hundreds of miles in Spain, sharing your victories and your defeats. Accepting them because I was *your* woman. I am *still* your woman and you need me more than ever now.'

The look Magdalene Ross gave her husband was a mixture of haughty Spanish pride and uncertainty. Suddenly a wail of anguish escaped from her, and she turned and ran from the room. Mairi was only moments behind her. After a few seconds' hesitation Tibbie went, too.

Wyatt tried to talk Eneas Ross out of his decision, convinced it had been taken for the wrong reasons, but the Highlander had made up his mind – and his three surviving sons were firmly on his side. They had suffered a tragic and humiliating defeat. By going to Canada they could put the past behind them and start anew. The more they talked, the more enthusiastic they became. As far as the male members of the Ross family were concerned, Wyatt's arguments were wasted.

The Ross women remained together all evening in the room set aside by Wyatt for the two girls. Eventually he asked Evangeline to go in and tell Mairi he wished to speak to her.

They walked together in the garden and passed meaningless comments about the weather until Wyatt said: 'I don't seem able to change your father's mind about going to Canada.'

Mairi shook her head. 'He sees it as the only way to regain his pride. If he stays here, he'll always be haunted by the ghosts of Ian and the others.'

There was one more question that had to be asked.

'When the others go . . . *you'll* stay here and marry me?'

Wyatt knew what her answer was going to be when she would not look at him, but it was a long time before she spoke.

'I can't, Wyatt. I can't leave Ma and Pa, not the way they are now. They need me . . . Ma especially.'

'*I* need you, Mairi. I need you more now than ever before.'

Mairi dared not let him see how close she was to tears.

'Things are going well for you now, Wyatt. You have all you want. Your church, a factor who's a friend, and a landowner who respects you. Pa has lost almost everything he's lived his life for. He's very close to total defeat, and Ma is broken-hearted at the death of the boys. If she lost me now, it would be the end for her, I know it would.'

Wyatt tried to choose his next words very carefully. They were among the most important he would ever speak.

'Mairi, all the things you say I have now are not really *mine*. They're to help me carry out the Lord's work, here in Eskaig. I'm grateful for them, but you mustn't confuse them with *my* needs. I'm just an ordinary man. A man who's sometimes frightened, often lonely – and always weak. I share the needs and emotions of my fellow-men. I've already told you I love you, and need you. Will it help you change your mind if I also tell you that without you there will be a huge gap in my life that other things, however important, can only be a substitute for?'

'I'm sorry, Wyatt. I *do* love you. I always will. But you're strong. Ma and Pa are not. They need me. . . .'

Suddenly, Mairi turned and ran back inside the house – and Wyatt knew he had lost her.

CHAPTER FIFTY-THREE

THE EMIGRANT-SHIP *Maid of Gloucester* sailed along Loch
Linnhe to Fort William three days later. She was a much larger craft
than the previous emigrant-ship and altogether newer. She would
not be remaining at Fort William for long, because it was not
believed there were many emigrants to be embarked here. The
majority would be taken on board at Oban, just outside the loch.

During the three days the Ross family remained at the manse,
Wyatt tried his utmost to persuade Mairi to change her mind and
stay with him – but to no avail. She admitted she did not *want* to
go. That she wanted nothing more from life than to marry Wyatt
and be with him wherever he went. Nevertheless, she felt it her duty
to go to Canada and help her parents recover from the tragedy that
had overtaken them.

On the last evening, as the sun sank beneath the lofty bulk of Ben
Nevis, Wyatt and Mairi stood together on the bank of the loch,
gazing out across water that mirrored the sunset colours of the sky.

'It's not too late to change your mind.' The words were spoken
more in desperation than in any hope that Mairi might act upon
them.

'Don't, Wyatt.' Mairi touched his arm and kept her hand there.
'Don't ask me any more.'

'There's an awful lot of water between here and Canada for our
love to bridge. . . .'

Mairi put a finger to his lips. 'Hush now! Perhaps one day you'll
come to Canada.'

The suggestion was not entirely new, but it took Wyatt by surprise. There had been talk when he was last in Edinburgh of the

Free Church financing overseas missions. Canada had not been mentioned, and it would be some time before any plan came to fruition, but. . . . Then he thought of Eskaig. There was so much work to be done to build new lives for the many victims of the clearances.

'Well?'

'I can't, Mairi.'

'Why not?'

'I've a duty to perform here, in Eskaig. A duty to my church and to people like these. . . .' He pointed to the homeless cottars still living in the churchyard. 'People like your ma and pa.'

'I have a duty towards them, too, Wyatt. Would you respect me if *I* did what you've said you can't do?'

Wyatt shook his head miserably. 'No.'

'Then, let's look out at the loch and the mountains and try to pretend it isn't the last time I'll ever see them.'

There was a break in her voice, and Wyatt put his arms about her and held her to him.

From the garden of the manse, Magdalene Ross looked down at the embracing couple standing at the loch-edge. She watched them until the shadows of the night hid them from view, then she went slowly inside.

Later that same evening Ewan Munro came to see Wyatt. In a fair imitation of a man, he told Wyatt that after discussing the future with his mother he, *too*, had decided to take the family to Canada. There were, he said seriously, 'better prospects for the girls to make good marriages in the New World'.

Resisting an impulse to ruffle the boy's hair in a gesture of affection, Wyatt replied in the same serious vein, weighing the pitfalls and the advantages of such a move. He ended by agreeing that Ewan had reached a sound conclusion.

'You're a sensible lad, Ewan. When you reach Canada discuss things with your ma before making a move and you'll do well there, I'm sure.'

'Thank you. It's been rumoured that the new landowner's giving twenty-five pounds to every man who emigrates with his family. Will I get that, too?'

'You will. And, what's more, I'll be doing the same as I did for the emigrants who left in the last ship. There will be ten sovereigns for every member of an Eskaig family who takes passage to Canada. That will be seventy sovereigns for your family. I'll give it to you tonight. Your ma can stitch it away safely in your clothing before you go on board – and, remember, don't tell a soul about it. Not everyone on board is as honest as those you've known here.'

'I'll remember.' Ewan Munro's excitement, at least, was that of a young boy. 'It's a *fortune*. I only wish Pa was here to see how much money we'll all have. . . .'

Wyatt had to pay out rather more than he had anticipated. Fifty-three victims of the clearances, including the Rosses, followed Ewan Munro's example and decided their futures lay in Canada and not in Scotland. The whole village turned out to wish them well, and Wyatt accompanied them to Fort William. Eneas Ross in particular had been a man of some stature in the mountain community.

On board *Maid of Gloucester*, Wyatt received a surprise; it was one that did not delight Eneas Ross. Among the emigrants were Seonaid Ross and her blind father!

While the members of the Ross family were stowing their few possessions below decks, Wyatt found himself alone with Seonaid.

'You're the last person I expected to find on board an emigrant-ship – and with your father, too. I trust he won't be a liability to you there.'

'He's my *father*,' said Seonaid in a tone of voice that reminded him of Mairi. 'Anyway, I'll be able to take care of him. He'll not want for anything – in the ship *or* when we get there.'

'Oh!' Wyatt raised an eyebrow. 'I've been hearing rumours about you, Seonaid, but none of them mentioned you were rich now.'

'It never pays to listen to rumours.' Seonaid spoke stiffly. 'Were any of them about Garrett and me?'

Wyatt nodded.

'Then, they weren't rumours; they were true.' Seonaid looked for censure from Wyatt, but his expression told her nothing. 'It doesn't matter *what* they say now. I've got the last laugh on them – and on Garrett.'

'What do you mean, Seonaid? What have you done?'

'I've *done* nothing – certainly not what John Garrett's expecting me to do. He'll be waiting in Glasgow. Expecting me to come and live with him there. He's in for a big disappointment, I can tell you.'

There was something more than triumph in her voice.

'Seonaid, did John Garrett give you money to make your way to Glasgow to be with him?'

'He did more than that. He gave me money *to look after* for him, in case he was stopped before he left Fort William.'

'That's stealing, Seonaid.'

'Is it? I'd call it payment for what Garrett has done to me and to many others. Are *you* going to tell him?'

Wyatt changed his reply twice without speaking. Then he shrugged in resignation. 'You're beyond my redemption, Seonaid. . . .' He could see Mairi coming towards them. 'Take care of yourself in Canada and try not to forget the girl you once were.'

'Thank you, Minister. I wish you were coming, too.' Before Wyatt could guess her intention she kissed him, then ran off, almost knocking Mairi over along the way.

'What was that about?' Mairi asked Wyatt.

'Nothing. I merely wished her well in Canada.'

'Seonaid will survive, wherever she is,' said Mairi. 'But she's not a bad girl, for all the rumours about her.'

'I haven't come on board to talk of Seonaid.' Wyatt took Mairi's arm and led her to the rail. Here they engaged in a disjointed and meaningless conversation until one of the ship's crew began walking about the deck, blowing a whistle and calling for non-emigrants to leave the ship. It was the moment Wyatt had been dreading. He and Mairi looked at one another, each frightened to say what needed to be said.

Suddenly, abruptly, Wyatt pulled her to him. 'Goodbye, Mairi.'

'Goodbye. . . .' It was so final. 'I love you, Wyatt.'

'I love you, too.' He pushed her away and left the ship, not saying goodbye to anyone along the way and hardly seeing where he was going.

As he walked down the sloping gangway, a lone piper began playing a Gaelic tune, its translated title being 'We Shall Return No More'. Wyatt kept on walking, not daring to stop or look around.

Behind him on the deck of the ship, Mairi watched the dark-clad dejected man going away from her.

'If I had a man like Minister Wyatt, I wouldn't let him walk away from me.' Mairi had not been aware that Seonaid was standing beside her. 'I wish he was *my* man. . . .'

For four days after *Maid of Gloucester* sailed from Fort William, Wyatt threw himself into his work with a zeal that the villagers swore would burn him out in a week. He tramped the mountains with cottars and crofters evicted by John Garrett, helping them choose new sites for their holdings. He obtained materials to raise roofs and he worked to clear ground. His day began at dawn and ended when the sun went down. Then he went to work and pray in the church, the candles burning until long after the villagers had gone to their beds.

Evangeline had a long talk to him when he returned one evening, hardly able to stand because he was so weary after a long day in the mountains. She understood *why* he was working himself so hard, as did the villagers. She told him they would all rather he left them and went to Canada. It would be better than watching him kill himself on their behalf here in Eskaig.

Weary and irritable though he was, Wyatt knew she was right. His self-pity was selfish. He had told Mairi he could not go to Canada because he had a duty to the people of his Highland parish. He had to face that duty and perform it to their best advantage, as his father had once done.

His thoughts reminded him that he had not visited his father's grave for far too long. Thanking Evangeline for her concern, he went to the churchyard. There were still a few families living here, but they would not disturb him.

He spent a while weeding the grave before dropping to his knees to pray. His prayers took the form of a talk he might have had with his father had he still lived.

As he prayed, Wyatt was aware of the children of the evicted cottars playing in the churchyard. It was a pleasant sound, a reminder that happiness did not end with loss of possessions.

Some of the children came close, out of curiosity, but he did not look up. Then footsteps came closer, and he sensed that someone was standing near. Still he continued his prayers – until something landed on the ground beside him. Something that jingled with the dull sound of gold coins in a small bag.

He opened his eyes and saw a small linen drawstring bag from which a number of sovereigns had spilled. Startled, he looked up – and saw Mairi. Barefoot and travel-weary, she could still smile.

Wyatt scrambled to his feet, too astonished to speak.

'I've brought your ten sovereigns back. I didn't feel I should keep them as I'm not emigrating.'

He held out his arms, and they clung to each other, both laughing, yet close to tears.

'How. . . ? Why. . . ?'

'I left the ship at Oban early this morning.'

'That's fifty miles away! You've walked all that distance?'

'Ma walked much farther for Pa, as she told me soon after we left Fort William.'

'She and your father. . . . What will they do without you?'

'Ma said she'd be more content knowing I was with you than having to spend every day seeing the unhappiness in me – and Tibbie's promised to take care of her. She will, too. She's always been like a true daughter to Ma.'

'What of your father?'

'There were a lot of families came on board at Oban. Among them were two old soldiers who'd been with Pa in Spain. With a crowd of old friends and three sons . . . he's going to be all right.'

Wyatt hugged her again. 'You'd better come inside the manse. . . .'

'Don't forget your money.'

Wyatt stooped to pick up the coins, and stood weighing them in his hand. 'I'll accept this as a dowry. You can have it back when our first child is born. What's more, I'll *double* it for every child that comes after!'

'Steady now, Minister Jamieson. Shouldn't you make an honest woman of me before your thoughts turn to making me a rich one?'

Whether or not this is your first or latest E. V. Thompson read, you might be interested to hear that a new club has been formed.

For just £7.50 a year you will receive a quarterly newsletter containing:

- information on E. V. Thompson – his past and his present
- previously unpublished short stories by the author
- free service for specially inscribed books by E. V. Thompson
- news on forthcoming books
- week-end breaks in E. V. Thompson country, with a chance to meet the author in person!

  And much, much more!

If you would like more information on the club, please write to the address below. Alternatively, send off your £7.50 now and join the growing list of members.

Subscription form

Name _____

Address _____

_____ post code _____

Method of payment *cheque/postal order/Access/Visa/
(*delete)

☐☐☐☐☐☐☐☐☐☐☐☐☐☐☐☐☐☐☐ Credit card no.

Signature _____ Date _____

Send to: The World of Writers, Gwynnalt House, Cliff Street, Mevagissey, Cornwall, PL26 6QW

E. V. Thompson
The Music Makers £3.99

The moving story of a land in torment

In the troubled countryside of Ireland, the 1840s are harrowing years, the seasons when potato crops fail and the gaunt spectre of hunger stalks the green landscape.

Against this stark world stands Liam McCabe, one-time fisherman of Kilmar, who has turned his hand to the trade of politics, offering his fellow countrymen the thing they need most: a glimmer of hope.

Never far away are the women in Liam's life: Kathie, the winsome fiddler's daughter and Caroline, a dazzling lady of aristocracy. But Liam will need more than just their support as he confronts a host of enemies amidst a web of corruption that marks the breeding ground of a nation's torment.

E. V. Thompson
Becky £3.99

A moving, memorable story of obsessive love and destructive passions

A good artist is accepted *wherever* he chooses to work, but in a nineteenth-century slum he must observe the rules of the people who live there. *Their* code. Break it and he might as well pack up and leave.

Fergus Vincent had left a career in the Navy to seek out his lifelong friend and mentor, Henry Gordon. But Gordon lies dead in the notorious Lewin's Mead slum, victim of the scourge of the poor: alcoholism.

Grieving for the loss of his friend, Fergus decides to fulfil Gordon's self-appointed mission to record the lives of the poor on canvas. A mission that will lead him to Becky, the wayward ragamuffin orphan destined to capture his heart and have an irrevocable effect on his life, his love and beliefs.

Becky is a poignant and involving love story that vividly portrays the Bristol of the mid-nineteenth century. But it is also an enthralling tale of many contrasts, creating an unforgettable tapestry of human passion and sacrifice.

All Pan books are available at your local bookshop or newsagent, or can be ordered direct from the publisher. Indicate the number of copies required and fill in the form below.

Send to: **CS Department, Pan Books Ltd., P.O. Box 40, Basingstoke, Hants. RG21 2YT.**

or phone: 0256 469551 (Ansaphone), quoting title, author and Credit Card number.

Please enclose a remittance* to the value of the cover price plus: 60p for the first book plus 30p per copy for each additional book ordered to a maximum charge of £2.40 to cover postage and packing.

*Payment may be made in sterling by UK personal cheque, postal order, sterling draft or international money order, made payable to Pan Books Ltd.

Alternatively by Barclaycard/Access:

Card No.

Signature:

Applicable only in the UK and Republic of Ireland.

While every effort is made to keep prices low, it is sometimes necessary to increase prices at short notice. Pan Books reserve the right to show on covers and charge new retail prices which may differ from those advertised in the text or elsewhere.

NAME AND ADDRESS IN BLOCK LETTERS PLEASE:

....

Name ——————————————————————————

Address ——————————————————————————

——————————————————————————

——————————————————————————

——————————————————————————

3/87